The Eddie Devlin Compendium

The Bloody Wet

T.R. St. George

Copyright © 2002 by T.R. St. George.

Library of Congress Number: 2001118481

ISBN #:   Softcover   1-4010-2804-7

All rights reserved. No part of this book may be reproduced or transmitted in any form or by any means, electronic or mechanical, including photocopying, recording, or by any information storage and retrieval system, without permission in writing from the copyright owner.

This is a work of fiction. Names, characters, places and incidents either are the product of the author's imagination or are used fictitiously, and any resemblance to any actual persons, living or dead, events, or locales is entirely coincidental.

This book was printed in the United States of America.

To order additional copies of this book, contact:
Xlibris Corporation
1-888-7-XLIBRIS
www.Xlibris.com
Orders@Xlibris.com

War is a thirsty business. Wise commanders will bear this in mind and, insofar as operational conditions permit, supply their troops with strong drink, for otherwise the common soldiers will waste much time in efforts to obtain such drink.

–Ghenghis Khan

IN MEMORY OF MIMI (1920-1994)

The Bloody Wet | 9

Base Section. A U.S. Army subsidiary headquarters, usually located in a port city, commanding a varying number of sundry Service Force units (Quartermaster, Engineer, Truck, Dock, Post Exchange, Fuel, Finance, Laundry, Signals, Bakery, Military Police and Medical battalions, companies and detachments) all in theory devoted to supplying and supporting the combat units much farther forward.

From left, Sgt. Harry Parker, Cpl. Arnold Saljeski, First Lt. William K. (Billy) Gote and Pfc. Edward T. Devlin.

Papua New Guinea etc.

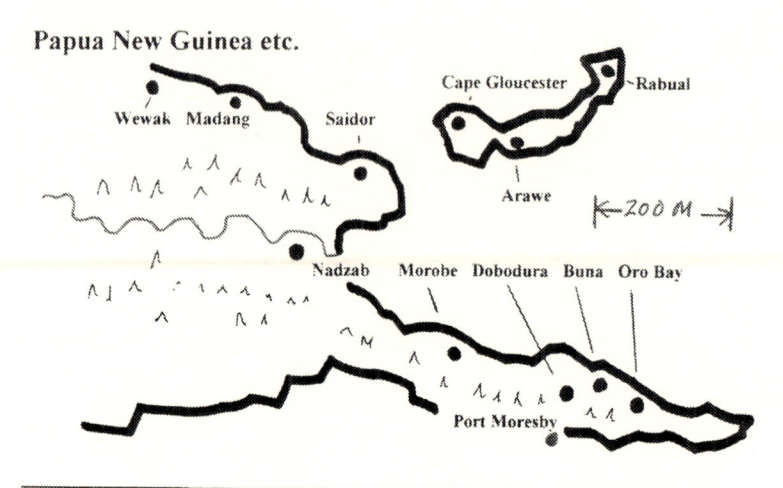

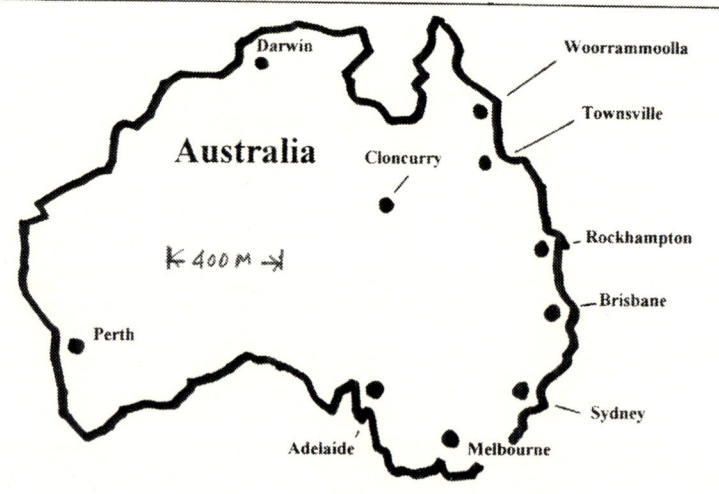

Wewak · Madang · Saidor · Nadzab · Morobe · Dobodura · Buna · Oro Bay · Port Moresby · Cape Gloucester · Rabual · Arawe

⊢ 200 M ⊣

Australia

Darwin · Woorrammoolla · Townsville · Cloncurry · Rockhampton · Brisbane · Perth · Sydney · Adelaide · Melbourne

⊢ 400 M ⊣

The Bloody Wet | 11

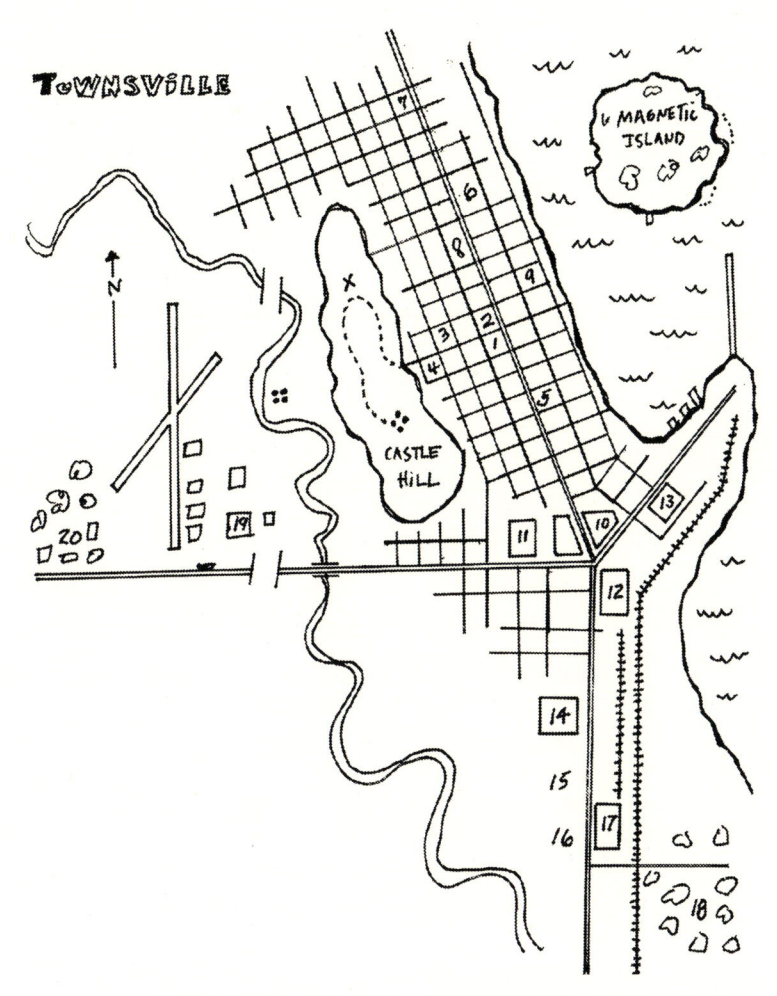

TOWNSVILLE, AUSTRALIA: DECEMBER 1943. (1) Base Section HQ. (2) Burns-Phelps Pty. Ltd. (3) Manic Manor. (4) Col Allen's billet. (5) Flinders Street EM Club. (6) George Hotel. (7) Officers Club and Mrs. Rooney's. (8) 301st MP Co. (9) Townsville Constabulary. (10) Pro Station. (11) Barrier Arms. (12) Q&NR depot. (13) Goose & Feathers. (14) 12th Station Hospital. (15) Happy Valley. (16) 3rd Replacement Depot. (17) Charters Downs horse track. (18) 404th QM Truck Battalion (C).

This is the third in a series of works that follow a dozen characters, Eddie Devlin chief among them, from the Stock Market crash of 1929 to the Millenium and beyond. The previous titles, also published by Xlibris, are "Old Tim's Estate" (1929-35) and "Wildcat Strike" (1939).

1

25 NOVEMBER 1943
GENERAL HEADQUARTERS, SOUTHWEST PACIFIC AREA
DAILY COMMUNIQUE

Allied Ground Forces under the command of Gen. Douglas MacArthur continued their advance westward from Nadzab in the Markham River valley, overcoming scattered enemy resistance and liberating Ebola Village, and continued mopping-up operations in the Finschafen area. Allied Air Forces under Gen. MacAthur's command flew 98 sorties despite inclement weather, inflicting heavy damage to enemy positions and personnel at Wewak and Madang. Light Naval Forces under Gen. MacArthur's command shelled enemy positions ashore and sank two enemy barges off Arawe on the south coast of New Britain.

* * *

In Townsville, high up on the eastern Australian littoral at the edge of the Coral Sea, the sun at 1630 hours is beginning its descent down a cloudless northwestern sky and the outside temperature has dropped to 96 degrees F. It's still, however, summer coming on in the Southern Hemisphere, close to 100 F. inside the U.S. Army Base Section HQ in a former two-story sugar warehouse with thick stone walls and a corrugated tin roof at the foot of Hill Street. Those stone walls soak up the heat and retain it. Or so thinks Col. Webster R. (Web) Allen, the Base Section commander since late October, a thin bone-weary National Guard officer just turned forty-four, temporary in grade, a permanent captain, a country lawyer in those distant days Before The War, once an Infantry officer but reclassified, dumped in the Quartermaster Corps, consequently disenchanted, beset also by malaria, damped down with a daily Atabrine tablet, the new malaria suppressant, but lurking, ready to spring, a partially slipped disc, some bad memories and a raging case of prickly heat lodged in his crotch.

But he won't think about the prickly heat: thinking about it makes it itch. Instead, slumped at a gray metal Government Issue desk with a field phone in a leather case hung at its side in his second-floor office overlooking Hill Street, his tropical khaki uniform, crisp at 0700 hours, soggy with sweat, Col. Web Allen stares through his GI reading spectacles at the V-mail form on his desk, blank but for the date and salutation, "Dear Mert." And awaits an inspiration. None comes. V-mail is a revolutionary new way to communicate. Its page-size forms are microfilmed at the GHQ Postal Unit in Brisbane, this microfilm sped to (and also from) the United States by air, reconstituted at half-size on shiny film and delivered—in less than two weeks, sometimes. The GIs call it dehydrated mail. But it's no good without an inspiration. And it's been twenty months since last he saw Mert, twenty years since they took each other to have and to hold, forsaking all others. Mert expects a weekly V-mail. Otherwise she worries. But what is there to say? "I am safe and well and hope this finds you and our dear daughters the same."

There is of course some truly exciting news. "I met a fascinating American Red Cross girl a couple of weeks ago, her name is Jill Tucker, I'm in love with her and we've been screwing ourselves silly ever since." But that's not for home consumption. Not hardly. Col. Web Allen, awash in guilt, sighs, removes his spectacles and slides the blank V-mail into his desk. He'll try again tomorrow. "Sergeant Abbott."

M/Sgt. George Abbott, Col. Web Allen's chief clerk, a skinny Old Regular in his mid-forties with ill-fitting GI dentures, pops out of the small adjoining office he shares with Sgt. Brendan Costello, another Old Regular. "Sir!" He does not salute. Web Allen dispensed with those in his office a month ago. Salutes often drew sniper fire in the fighting at Buna Government Station.

"Is my car here, Sergeant? Is Colonel Fogerty still here? Did he draft the new Uniform Regulations?"

"Parked outside, Sir. Think the driver's across the street. I don't know, Sir. I believe Colonel Fogerty uh just left, Sir."

Across the street means the American Red Cross Enlisted Men's Canteen on the ground floor of the local Masonic Lodge. GIs on leave and Base Section GIs loaf there. Lt. Col. Parnell (Cob) Fogerty is the Base Section chief-of-staff Web Allen inherited. Another Old Regular with five enlistment stripes, a CWO (Chief Warrant Officer) when The War began in Europe, rapidly promoted thereafter when the U.S. Army exploded, Fogerty's a permanent first lieutenant with an Old Regular's occupational disease: a little drinking problem. Or more accurately a big drinking problem. He nips throughout the day from a bottle stashed in his desk and often leaves work early for a snort or two at the Base Section Officers Club he pretty much personally administers before the club opens, a local custom the Australians call "Befores."

"Damn it, Sergean! Go get my driver! Tell him he's supposed to stay with the vehicle. Tell him again. I'll see Colonel Fogerty in the morning."

"Sir!" M/Sgt. Abbott returns to his office: it also opens into Fogerty's adjoining office. No doubt he'll pull rank and send Sgt. Costello, a tubby little man at 5-7 and 200 pounds, to raise the driver. The fact that these two resemble two comedians whose hilarious antics in a film called "Buck Privates" are now on display at some of the half-dozen outdoor GI movies in and around Townsville has not escaped Col. Web Allen.

The Base Section HQ work day, officially 0800 to 1700 hours, is over or close enough. Web Allen plucks his officer's cap from the rack behind his desk, puts it on, leaves his office and goes down rickety stairs into the former warehouse's main storage area, a large two-story space jammed with GI desks awash in paperwork. There are barred windows high in its stone walls and small offices partitioned off with the plywood at the rear. Napoleon got it wrong, Web Allen thinks. An Army, or the U.S. Army at any rate, marches on paper. Half the desks are empty. Many HQ personnel, like Lt. Col. Fogerty, leave work early. Most of those left appear to be staring into space, dreaming of home or sexual conquests past and future. A few are pecking at typewriters, seeing to the speedy prosecution of The War. A dammed comfortable war in their case, Web Allen thinks, recollecting his long years in an Infantry rifle company. They're safe and dry, fed three times daily, the only threats to their lives and limbs infrequent exposures to social diseases if precautions are not taken and occasional punch-ups with their Allies, the Australian troops in Townsville. A pasty-faced lot, most of them. Many, Web Allen suspects, skip the half-hearted morning calisthenics at the HQ Enlisted Men's tent camp in South Townsville they call Happy Valley. Three days in a rifle company, Web Allen also thinks, would kill most of them. He may make those half-hearted morning calisthenics mandatory.

"Tenshun!" M/Sgt. Walter Tschida, another Old Regular, rising from his desk at the foot of the stairs like a jack-in-the box, interrupting the speedy prosecution of, bellows. All present rise, spilling coffee and paperwork, and snap, more or less, to attention.

"At ease," Col. Web Allen says. All present sit and he leaves his HQ, saluted by and saluting the beefy MP in sweaty khakis on door duty. His car, an olive drab '41 Dodge four-door with a white star painted on its roof, is parked at the curb. His driver,

Cpl. Bruno Fazoli, a stocky Italian with curly black hair, is loping across Hill Street.

"Sorry, Sir," Fazoli, he needs a haircut, producing a sloppy salute, says. "I had a go pee." He opens the near rear door on the Dodge for Web Allen, slams it shut, gets behind the wheel and, the Dodge laboring, missing on a two cylinders, drives up Hill Street, a steep street that climbs half-way up the flank of Castle Hill, the massive hogback, four-hundred feet at its summit, that looms over Townsville.

There are on both sides of Hill Street desiccated palm trees, houses, yards with grass the color of sand. The long months without rain the Australians call The Bloody Dry is still going strong. The last house on the right is a large two-story frame monstrosity with lots of gimcrack and a brick patio under a sagging canvas awning on its downhill side. The American Red Cross female personnel in Townsville, there are about a dozen, billet there. The last house on the left, fifty yards along, a bungalow called Jasmine Cottage, is Web Allen's billet. Both billets are leased to the Australian War Authority, sublet to the ARC and the U.S. Army. Reverse Lend Lease, this is: the accounting will be worked out After The War. Hill Street's battered pavement ends at Jasmine Cottage but a dirt track winds the rest of the way up Castle Hill. The summit's a Restricted Military Area. There's a tall ACS (Allied Communications Service) radio mast up there and an AMF (Australian Military Forces) anti-aircraft battery, quick-firing Bofors never fired in anger, sometimes fired for practice, its crew near bonkers with boredom.

There are, Web Allen notes, four U.S. servicemen sprawled on deck chairs on the ARC billet's patio. He takes them to be Americans anyway: they're wearing pants. The AMF in Townville wear shorts. Four red-blooded American lads then, enjoying some R & R. Are they, Web Allen wonders, Base Section personnel, men he in theory commands, or transients?

Whatever, Web Allen, suppressing a nagging conscience, Mert's blank V-mail, has better things to think about. A lukewarm shower with gravity-fed water from the corrugated tin tank atop Jasmine Cottage his orderly, Pvt. Jesus Cerna, is supposed to pump full each morning. Some crisp clean tropical khakis, assuming Pvt. Cerna remembered to send his uniforms to the 114th Portable Laundry Detachment and the 114th remembered to send them back. And at 1800 hours, more or less, Jill Tucker will be along, on foot perhaps, it's a short walk from the ARC billet, or sometimes another ARC girl named Davis brings her in the ARC jeep. Jill will shower too, the shower at the ARC billet seldom free, wrap herself in the terrycloth robe she leaves in Jasmine Cottage and prepare their dinner. An omelet most likely accompanied by a fierce local red wine in a bottle with no label provided by Cpl. Fazoli, who has some kind of trade agreement with the Italian community in nearby Charters Towers. No doubt this agreement involves the illegal transfer of U.S. Army comestibles, American tobacco products or even gasoline, any of which is a court-martial offense, but Web Allen's not going to make that an issue. Jill Tucker, she's got a great sense of humor, calls this wine "a full-bodied Plonk '43." Plonk is Australian for cheap wine and by extension any intoxicating beverage. And once they finish their full-bodied Plonk. He has, Web Allen finds, half an erection.

The Dodge pulls up at Jasmine Cottage and stalls. Fazoli hops out, opens the rear door and snaps off another sloppy salute.
"Oh-seven-thirty in the morning," Col. Web Allen says, "Be on time and get another vehicle. Take this one back to the Motor Pool. Red Line it." List it inoperable and take it out of service, that means. "Tell them to send it out to the 330th Ordnance. It needs a tune-up. And get a haircut."
"Yessir!" Fazoli says.
He hops in the Dodge, turns it around and drives down Hill Street. He'll take the Dodge back to the Base Section Motor Pool on North Flinders Street and Red Line it but not right away. First, this pre-arranged, once it's dark and the night falls swiftly in

The Bloody Wet | 19

Townsville at 19 Degrees South Latitude, he'll pick up little Susie Buncom, just turned eighteen, a pert cupcake, at her old man's fish-and-chips shop (Buncom's Famous Fish & Chips) in South Townsville, where she works days, hide her in the rear seat in the Dodge because transporting civilians in a military vehicle or use of same for personal purposes is forbidden, regale her for a time with tales of his hometown, Hoboken, N.J., where the streets are paved with chocolate, then park on one of the abandoned roads to abandoned military campsites in the scrub south of Townsville, join little Susie in the rear seat and, taking precautions, screw little Susie. Cpl. Fazoli has a standing arrangement sealed in plonk with the night duty sergeant at the Motor Pool as to what time (1700 hours) he turned the Dodge in.

Fazoli, though technically at war, serving his nation in a faraway land, never as the saying goes had it so good. Rolling down Hill Street, he waves to the four U.S. servicemen on the ARC patio. He more or less knows two of them.

* * *

The two Fazoli more or less knows are Sgt. Harry Parker, the ranking non-com, there are only two, in the 301st Military Police Co's. Criminal Investigation Detachment (CID), and Cpl. Arnold Saljeski, the movie non-com in the Base Section Special Services Office. The other two are First Lt. William K. (Billy) Gote, a C47 Skytrain pilot in the 34th Troop Carrier Squadron based at Seven-Mile Strip (between Five-Mile and Twelve-Mile) outside Port Moresby in New Guinea, and Pfc. Edward T. (Eddie) Devlin, the clerk and half the present strength of the 4th Army Historical Detachment, likewise located at Seven-Mile.

Four red-blooded American lads then, these are, tossed up by The War in Townsville, enjoying some R & R, Rest & Rehabilitation, smoking real Camel cigarettes instead of the previously unknown brands (Chelseas, Regents, Fleetwoods) the PX stocks, drinking Swappa slings from jelly glasses, Swappa the way everybody pronounces SWPA, the War Department abbreviation for the Southwest Pacific Area. The slings are gin, no ice, cut with bitter GI canned grapefruit juice. Gin is easier (though by no means easy) to get in Townsville than other liquor. There's a Gilbey's distillery, the biggest building in town, four stories, six counting the water tank on spindly legs on its roof, hard by the Queensland & Northern Railway yards.

They are not buddies, these four, in the usual military sense. In fact, they now consider buddies a dirty word. They only all met last night at a party at the ARC billet. Their ranks and military units differ and they have not, or not yet anyway, shared any memorable wartime experiences. But for The War it's highly unlikely they'd have met or found themselves in Townsville. If asked they would say they are friends. The War produces a lot of instant if short-lived friendships.

The reason they think buddies a dirty word is the Camels. Alison Culpepper (Boots) Davis, a Red Cross female personnel, gave Billy Gote a whole carton this morning. "For services rendered," Billy's said several time, leering, though he may be lying. Or maybe not. Billy Gote, never mind there's war bride, Mrs. William K. (Beverly) Gote, back in Onamee, Kansas, has taken quite a shine to Boots Davis and vice versa over the past forty-eight hours. And he's sharing the Camels but there was a note in the carton.

"Hi, Buddies! Please accept these smokes from all of us here on the Swing Shift at Douglas Aircraft, Long Beach, who contributed to their purchase."

Cpl. Arnold Saljeski, a man enamored of the Army's all-time favorite all-purpose word, summed up their reaction. "They no fuckin buddies a mine! Fuckin de-fense workers! Pullin' in the fuckin dough! Hunnert fuckin bucks a week! My fuckin brother-in-law, he's one those fuckers. Camden Ship. Fucker hopes the fuckin War lasts ten fuckin years!"

They're smoking the Camels though while sipping their slings and discussing such interesting subjects as is anybody likely to get into Betty Jo Fricker's knickers before dawn, knickers a funny

Australian word for a female undergarment they've adopted, Betty Jo a medium-built American Red Cross female personnel just arrived in Townsville, the consensus worth a try: a rumor the Base Section may amend the local Uniform Regulations to no longer require the wearing of neckties, olive drab, tucked in between the third and fourth shirt buttons, with the Class A (tropical khaki) uniform: and is there any way they can get more booze so as not to run short at the big Thanksgiving Day party that will racket through the ARC billet tonight, climaxing at midnight, this the plan anyway, with the ritual carving of a 20-pound previously frozen genuine Stateside tom turkey even now roasting in the old bottle-gas stove in the billet kitchen.

It's still Wednesday, 24 November, in that dim distant world, Back in the States, but Thanksgiving Day in Swappa, well west of the International Date Line.

This party will be hard on the old house but it's survived numerous parties in the past eighteen months. It belongs to a retired sugar broker and his wife, now living with their daughter in Adelaide, South Australia. Like a good many other inhabitants of Townsville (ten-thousand is one guess, a third of the population), the broker and his wife buried the family silver, leased their house to the War Authority and vamoosed in the fall of '42 (fall in the Southern Hemisphere) when it looked as if the bloody Japs were going to invade Australia somewhere along the undefended coast north of Townsville, butcher all the men and rape all the women.

This did not come to pass however. Gen. Douglas MacArthur, ordered out of the Philippines, where U.S. and Filipino forces were slowly losing the battle for the Bataan peninsula, reached Australia in a battered B17 bomber with his wife and son and the boy's Chinese amah, told the world, "I shall return," refused to concede Townsville to the Japs, scrapped an imaginary defensive position called the Brisbane Line and launched what he termed "offensive operations." These did not amount to much but two U.S. fighter squadrons flying P40s were for a time based at Garbutt Field, then a grass strip a half-mile west of Townsville. The pilots were quartered in the sugar broker's house, four to a room on army cots draped with mosquito nets. Later on, when the fighter squadrons moved to Port Moresby in New Guinea, the big 1500-mile long island between Australia and the Equator, and the Base Section was established in Townsville, junior officers were quartered there. They were moved out a year ago, joining other Base Section officers (but for the C.O.) in the George Hotel on North Flinders Street, leased along with its private beach to the U.S. Army, and the broker's house sublet to the ARC, then (fourteen months after the invasion threat evaporated) establishing a beachhead in Townsville. Visiting fireman if important enough (politicians, generals, stars of stage screen and radio on USO tours) also lodge at the George.

The early tenants, red-blooded American lads far from home, inflicted heavy damage to the old house. Half the furniture and most of the china the broker's wife did not store are broken. Many names (Sheila, Pat, Bunny, Sybil, Cat, Geronimo) and phone numbers adorn the wall beside the phone in the living room. There are cigarette burns like black dormant caterpillars everywhere and a persistent plugging-up problem with the Winston Churchill, which is what the Australians call the water closet, meaning john or head, when they don't call it the loo. Nevertheless, the old house is a home away from home now for a dozen ARC female personnel and, now and then, a few lucky male service personnel. Two among the former, Agnes Moore, the local ARC Director, and Hannah Hardy, the Staff Leader, are tough old birds in their forties, Red Cross Lifers, veterans of numerous previous disasters natural and man-made. The rest, called Staff Assistants, are mainly adventuresome Liberal Arts graduates in their twenties. They call the old house Manic Manor. Boots Davis, a lithe Southern belle (Old Miss '39) with Camels to give away came up with that. Most of these personnel are absent now, doing whatever it is they do at various Red Cross outposts, though two called Flotsam and Jetsam (Flots and Jets) who worked the 0600 to 1500 hours shift at the Garbutt Field Canteen are asleep in the upstairs bedroom they share. Asleep or doing whatever it is lesbians do: that's the rumor.

There is a yard and there used to be a garden and a trimmed hedge behind the house, the garden the former sugar broker's pride and joy, but military traffic, mostly illegal since not authorized for personal use, has churned up the yard and pretty well wrecked the hedge and the garden. Beyond the wrecked hedge Castle Hill rises steeply, bare but for a few scraggly trees and thin grass burned brown.

The sun by now is low in the sky and the shadow cast by Castle Hill is creeping across Townsville, most of which is on the flat quarter-mile between the hill and the harbor, a thin slice of civilization, mostly frame houses with corrugated tin roofs and a block off the waterfront on Flinders Street, the main drag, a dozen blocks of two-and three-story brick commercial buildings. The harbor still lies glittering in the sunlight, dark blue water splashed with silver. Thirty-odd vessels, Liberty ships, Victories, rusty old tramps, two tankers and a lean gray U.S. Navy cruiser, the USS Little Rock, lie at anchor in its reaches. A supply convoy came in in the night. A dozen Libs and Vics, two LSTs (the new Landing Ships, Tank) and a few smaller craft, nondescript island traders, are tied up at the docks along Cape Cleveland, the harbor's southern arm, discharging and loading the sinews of war. A long stone breakwater angles off the end of the Cape. An ammunition ship low in the water flying a huge red DANGER pennant, ostracized in view of its potential for disaster, is anchored at its tip. Beyond the breakwater the Coral Sea, more dark blue water splashed with silver, stretches away to the horizon. The Great Barrier Reef is out there somewhere.

Townsville though its significance is declining is the busiest port of entry in Swappa, the chief supply base for the Allied Forces under Gen. Douglas MacArthur's command.

To the north the harbor is protected by Magnetic Island, an

island shaped like a sombrero, covered with scrub, that rises steeply up out of the sea. There are two narrow beaches, one for Officers Only, both protected by shark nets, on its seaward shore where the surf rolls in and a U.S. Navy seaplane base and a USAAC (U.S. Army Air Corps) crash boat detachment in one of its shoreside coves. An ancient ferry the U.S. Armed Forces call the Poontang Special chugs to and from Magnetic Island twice daily. There are a few primitive weekend cabins over there, some for rent, and a weekend in one of them with a primitive female is one of the major war aims embraced by the U.S. Armed Forces in Townsville. The other is finding booze.

"I might get a couple jugs off our Squadron p.o.," First Lt. Billy Gote says, "But I had a belt the asshole once, he thought he was a copilot. So I hate to ask him."

Billy Gote's a lanky fellow in his mid-twenties with a yellow Atabrine tan, straw-colored hair cut short and eyes of an unknown color behind the dark pilot's sunglasses he wears at all times. His tropical khakis are faded white and bear no insignia. His silver wings and first john bar are pinned to his rakish Fifty-Mission cap, a garrison cap with the grommet removed. He also is out of uniform in that he's wearing RAAF (Royal Australian Air Force) flying boots: swashbuckling black boots, kangaroo hide, fleece-lined, wear forever. U.S. air crews are not supposed to wear them however, because, should these crews have to bail out of an aircraft in the event of some emergency, those boots are likely to fall off, leaving the bailees to land in their socks or bare feet as the case may be. But Billy Gote decided early on in his time in Swappa that if ever he faces such an emergency he'll damn well ride his C47 down into the sea or jungle. He can't as he sees it very well bail out anyway like a rat departing a sinking ship if he has passengers aboard unless they're paratroops and also have 'chutes. Ordinary C47 passengers except generals are not issued 'chutes, the cost considered prohibitive. And he sure as hell won't bail out anyway into a tropical sea full of sharks, poisonous sea snakes, deadly sea wasps, etc. Or the goddamn jungle either, risking a slow death hung up in a tree, starving to death while eaten alive by God knows what. Hairy red spiders big as saucers for one thing. Anywhere that's not sea or jungle, Billy Gote is confident, he can crash land his 47, a war-worn craft called the Lucky Lil, and walk away from it. He no longer knows where his 'chute or self-inflating life-jacket called a Mae West are. The 'chute may be somewhere in the airplane but more likely by now, its nylon suitable for intimate female garments, his flight engineer, Sgt. Clive (Porky) Wallace, has bartered it for sexual favors.

Billy Gote is in Townsville on a ham-and-egg flight, a vaguely illicit mission though all the USAAC units with aircraft fly them. He plans to load the Lucky Lil first thing in the morning and fly back to Seven-Mile Strip with the ham, eggs, other fresh meat, fresh fruit and vegetables, milk, good Australian beer and booze (if any) Second Lt. Leonard (Asshole) Nadler, the procurement officer the 34th Troop Carrier Squadron maintains in Townsville, has procured with the Squadron mess fund. Billy Gote would like to stay longer, spend more time in bed with Boots Davis, but reckons he's stretched his stay as long as he dares on the usual grounds, a mysterious mechanical problem unexpectedly (or more accurately, expectedly) developed by the Lucky Lil. And he ought not to be drinking, fraternizing, with three Enlisted Men. That's contrary to Army Regulations. But the Army Air Corps is or is thought to be pretty democratic and Billy Gote, a civilian in uniform, is not much bothered by the ARs.

"How about you guys' NCO Club," Pfc. Eddie Devlin, still on the subject of more booze, says. "Don't you guys get a ration?"

Eddie Devlin's a skinny young fellow with an Atabrine tan and a GI haircut, coming up on twenty-three, wearing fairly clean khakis a size too large. The chief usher at the best theater in Winatchee Falls, Minnesota, when drafted, he's in Townsville for the third time with travel orders he typed, forged, himself in the absence of his C.O., Capt. Clapham Panmander, the other half of the 4th AHD, a crazy old coot, forty if a day, a cow college professor in civil life, who, stuck in a Stateside camp, feels he "missed" the first Big War and is dammed if he'll miss this one. The old coot's somewhere in the Markham Valley with the Allied Ground Forces, the Australian 9th Division and a U.S. parachute company, advancing westward from Nadzab.

Eddie came to Townsville with Billy Gote and will fly back with him the morning. They met in October at another Manic Manor party. Eddie was in Townsville on legitimate orders then with a requisition for a typewriter for the 4th AHD. His requisition proving worthless, he looked up Saljeski, they'd met in June at Townsville's infamous 3rd Repple Depple (Replacement Depot), and with Saljeski's help liberated a typewriter from the Base Section Special Services Office before heading for the party. In June, after graduating twice from an Army Administration School, his papers lost the first time, Eddie was a private off the SS Mariposa, a Matson Line liner turned troopship. He subsequently spent three miserable weeks in the 3rd Repple Depple before to his horror and dismay, there being no crying need for more clerks in Swappa, he was made an Infantry replacement and promptly shipped out on a C47, his first flight, to Seven-Mile Strip, then over the Owen Stanley Mountains to Dobodura, thence by truck to the beach at Buna Government Station and onward aboard an LCT (Landing Craft, Tank) to Morobe, where the 41st Infantry Division was digging Japs out of the razorback ridges south of the Markham Valley.

An Infantry replacement, God help him!

And God in the person of another replacement, a clumsy kid whose name he never knew (or maybe it was just dumb luck) did help him when the replacements were detailed to unload the LCT before going up to join a rifle company in the razorback ridges. The clumsy kid dropped the base plate of an 80mm mortar on Eddie's left foot, breaking three bones, which Eddie sometimes calls "my wound." Evacced back to Dobodura and by air to the 7th Station Hospital at Seven-Mile Strip, his foot was still in a cast when Capt. Panmander, just arrived in Swappa, came through the wards looking for a clerk and finding one who'd been to Administration School twice got Eddie a ds tdy (detached service, temporary duty) transfer to the 4th AHD and a month later a promotion to Private First Class.

"Yeah, they be a NCO Club ration," Sgt. Harry Parker, a native of Maine who talks without opening his mouth, says. "But we git it awready and drank it and all we gittin' now anyway is bee-uh."

Harry's thirty, a big man like most Military Policeman, 6-1, 210 pounds, with a square weathered face, heavy shoulders, big hands and a battered nose. His khakis are clean and crisp and a tight fit. He has a dozen uniforms altered by a former tailor in the 202nd Bakery Co. and changes two or three times a day. Ostensibly, Harry is on duty at the CID, investigating pilfering on the docks, but he wants to get the roasting turkey "started right" before returning to duty. Harry liberated the turkey, trading the chief steward aboard one of the Libs in the supply convoy a "genuine" Japanese Samurai sword for it: a genuine Samurai practically guaranteed to have lopped off a few American heads (the Japs quick to behead people) turned out by a craftsman in the 330th Ordnance (Vehicle Maintenance & Repair) Co. who now and then lops a leaf spring off a vehicle the 330th is maintaining or repairing for the purpose and owed Harry twenty quid lost at blackjack. Once upon a time in civil life Harry was a chef, well, fry cook, or so he claims. He also claims to have been a Golden Gloves heavyweight champion, at what level is unclear, and at other times a lobsterman, bartender and dancehall bouncer before becoming a peace officer, a deputy sheriff in Hancock County, where his Uncle Wilbur is the sheriff. That was essential employment and might have kept Harry out of the service, out of The War, but he was single (well, divorced, one minor son) and had never been to a war. He enlisted or so he claims the day after the Japs bombed Pearl Harbor. All of which may be true. The claims made by newfound friends in the service are generally impossible to prove or disprove.

"You know why all we gettin' for a fuckin ration now is fuckin beer?" Saljeski, a rhetorical question, says. "Fuckin Base Officers Club is gettin' all the fuckin booze."

Saljeski's a short slovenly soldier in his late twenties with thin red hair and freckles (half Irish, he claims, his mother a Mahaffey) who wears at all times a grimy cardboard issue pith helmet tipped low on his forehead. His khakis and the necktie tucked in his shirt are stained and wrinkled and he's not very clean either. Nevertheless, he claims to have been before he was drafted a hotshot door-to-door vacuum cleaner salesman who enjoyed many a merry "demonstration" with lonely homemakers in his territory, West Philadelphia above 52nd Street, where he also was the back-up projectionist at a neighborhood theater.

A low number drafted early, Saljeski wound up in the 32nd Infantry Division Signal Co. and alone among these four can truthfully claim to have crossed the Army's Great Divide and been, if briefly, "in combat." Ten days, counting five in the Division Aid Station with raging malaria and a 106 degree temperature. No matter. Saljeski was shot at in earnest and personally in the fighting at Buna Government Station a year ago and while he no longer dwells on that (bloody bits of Pvt. Roy Hopper, hanging in his climbing belt, turned into hamburger by a Nambu light machine-gun while up in a tree stringing wire beside the corduroy road they called Highway 1, they took turns in the trees and it was Hopper's turn, raining down on him where he lay on his belly in the swamp beside Highway 1, the Nambu banging away but firing over his head, shit in his pants and twenty black leeches on his body, he pulled them off at the Aid Station while still mildly hysterical), he can dredge it all up if he wants to, seizing the floor at bullshit sessions with the Base Section commandos with the telling phrase, "When I was in combat."

Saljeski has chronic malaria impervious to Atabrine, a legacy of the Buna swamps, chills and fevers and a general malaise at unexpected times, but he can live with that. It's why along with 2200 other former Division officers and men he's Limited Service and a rare square peg in a square Army hole, the movie non-com in the Base Section Special Services Office in charge of film distribution to the outdoor GI movies. He has a '39 Ford panel truck, a monster perk, permanently assigned to him for this purpose. He also repairs projectors though not very adept at that and he has more to say.

"You know how much fuckin booze the fuckin Base Officers Club gettin' for the fuckin holidays, Christmas and New Year's?"

Another rhetorical question? Not exactly. Harry and Saljeski have discussed this previously, many times, and several times since meeting Billy Gote and Eddie Devlin at last night's Manic Manor party. But further proof though little is required that the chief war aim of Base Section officers everywhere is to enjoy a life style few could afford in civil life is always welcome.

"How much?" Eddie Devlin says.

"Eighty fuckin cases!"

"Jeezuzz!" Billy Gote and Eddie, amazed by this figure, say.

"Gal you pokin' works the Base QM tell you that, Sal?" Harry says.

"Roger. Mickey Rooney. Fact, she type the fuckin req and purchase order. And run off some exter copies. Not for nuthin' though or love. I had a give her a fuckin carton Fleetwoods."

"Jeezuzz," Eddie Devlin, who can do simple sums in his head, says. "You know how much that much booze be worth in Moresby? Lemme see. Eighty cases times twelve jugs in a case times fifteen quid."

"More'n that in Nadzab," Billy Gote says. "I was up Nadzab last week. There's a fighter group up there now. Thirty-Eights. And a A-Twenty squadron. Lots a flight pay and some jump pay, the Parachutes. Jug'll fetch twenty quid in Nadzab. Thirty, it's scotch."

"They gettin' some fuckin scotch," Saljeski says. "Ten fuckin cases."

"Okay, lemme figure," Eddie says. "Eighty times twelve times twenty and ten times twelve times thirty times a quid's worth, three-bucks-twenty. Jeezuzz! In Nadzab that booze be worth sixty-five-thousand-two-hundred-and-eighty bucks! In real money!"

A stunned silence greets this revelation. All products of The Great Depression, they find $65,280 a sum difficult to imagine. Take a Pfc. paid $54 a month, Eddie calculates, more than a hundred years to match that.

"Lieutenant," Harry Parker says. "Lemme ask you something. How much booze can that airyplane you flying haul?"

"Booze?" Billy Gote says. "Hell, I don't know. Forty-Sevens are rated at fourteen-thousand pounds cargo. But they'll carry more. How much does booze weigh?"

"Thirty-five, forty pounds a case about. On a average," Harry, former bartender, says.

"Three thousand pounds then, more less, eighty cases," Eddie, math whiz, says.

"No sweat then," Billy Gote says. "But what the hell are we talkin' about anyway? You got some kind of wild crazy idea in your head, Mister Military Policeman?"

"Yeah, I have," Harry says. "I mean we have. Sal and me. But we don't jedge it to be so wild. Or crazy either. We give this matter a lot of thought and study, Lieutenant, and we figger there's a way we can liberate that booze the Base Section Officers Club figger it be gittin' for the holidays. I believe Sal mention we already got the paperrwork. So we can liberate it. Hijack it. Like they used to, it was Prohibition. Then you fly it up to Nadzab there in your airyplane, Lieutenant, and sell it there and by golly, I got no argyment with Eddie's figgers, we all be rich! Rich rich sons-uh-guns! Lemme jist baste the turkey and I'll tell you how we calculate we can do it. That's if you be game for it, I mean. Anybody want another sling?"

They all want another sling under the circumstances and Harry goes into the house to baste the turkey and build more slings.

Thirty minutes later, having heard all the details and considered the fact that "if something goes wrong" and they get caught they'll no doubt spend the rest of their lives in the Leavenworth Federal Prison (unless the Base Section succeeds in getting them hung or shot or drawn-and-quartered), Billy Gote declares the plan Harry and Saljeski have concocted probably feasible and agrees to "what the hell, give it a shot," and Eddie agrees to his part in it. Considerable trust is involved. Billy Gote will have all the money when he sells the booze and there's no way he can mail it. "Squadron censor sees that kind a dough he'll shit!" But Harry and Sal and Eddie will get their shares, never fear. "I can always find Eddie and you guys, I'll fly on down here with your shares. I give my Squadron C.O. a case of scotch he'll clear me for Tville any time I want. I prolly have to give him a case anyway, set things up. Hell, Lieutenant Colonel Hampstead, he's a scotch man. I give him a case scotch he'll fly your shares down here himself. Without an airplane. Just flappin' his goddamn arms!"

They drink to that. It's not just the money. Any opportunity to as Saljeski puts it "really fuck a bunch a Base Section officers" is a wonderful thing. The money looms large though. The way Eddie sees it, $64,128, subtracting the scotch Billy Gote will give his C.O., split four ways, he'll be set for life with $16,000 and change! Once The War is over. With just a little luck, Eddie figures, he'll survive The War punching a typewriter in the 4th AHD while Capt. Panmander, the bloodthirsty the old coot, undertakes the "field work." Harry also is pretty sure he'll survive The War and so is Saljeski. So is Billy Gote though he sometimes has moments of doubt.

16 DECEMBER 1943
GENERAL HEADQUARTERS, SOUTHWEST PACIFIC AREA
DAILY COMMUNIQUE

Allied Ground Forces under the command of Gen. Douglas MacArthur landed early today at Arawe on the south coast of New Britain. Scattered enemy resistance was overcome and a perimeter established and reinforcements are going ashore. Allied Air and Naval Forces under Gen. MacArthur's command supporting the landing destroyed or damaged 10 enemy aircraft and sank two light naval craft. Elsewhere, Allied Air Forces under Gen. MacArthur's command flew 102 sorties inflicting heavy damage to enemy positions and personnel at Wewak and Madang and Allied Ground Forces under Gen. MacArthur's command continued their advance westwards in the Markham River Valley, liberating Sowela Village, and continued mopping-up operations in the Finschafen area.

* * *

The communique is released to the press at 0600 hours: read, then mimeographed copies distributed to the correspondents assembled at what the GHQ PIO (Public Information Officer) calls the "daily briefing" in a conference room on the top floor of the four-story Bank of Queensland on High Street in downtown Brisbane. The bank's still in business on the ground floor. GHQ occupies the rest.

Capt. Harvey Milch drafts the communique each evening following receipt of the day's Operations Reports. He's another square peg in a square Army hole. A New York advertising man in civil life, he wrote the label copy for a canned soup line. Col. Dupont Swiller, the PIO, edits this draft, making minor changes, and clears it with Lt. Gen. Richard Sutherland, the GHQ chief-of-staff, and G2 (Intelligence chief), lest the Japs learn something they already know. Maj. Morgan Pierpont reads the communique. He used to do some Shakespeare in another life, mostly summer stock, and sounds a little like the Lord God Almighty (off camera) in films dealing with Biblical themes. Swiller, a World War I retread, a permanent captain in the Army Reserve and the public relations director for the Maryland Poultry Association in civil life, thinks this fitting: Douglas MacArthur and the Lord God Almighty are known to be very close. Sometimes, if the communique is breaking a Big Story as on this morning, Swiller himself is present though silent: he stutters.

The reading over, a flunky captain distributes the copies and, sometimes, maps. Then Pierpont takes questions. If he doesn't want to answer one or doesn't know the answer, often the case, he declines to answer on security grounds. He regularly declines to answer on those grounds a question put regularly by the Australian Press Association correspondent, Jack (Bluey) Mahaffey, a insolent specimen with red hair and an artificial left leg, wounded at Tobruk in the Western Desert, who thinks and often says he thinks the bloody Yanks though Allies are johnnies-come-lately to the Bloody War. Swiller and Pierpont think Bluey subversive. Some Ally! His question, unanswered, is: "His hit true wot we 'ear, Ginrill M'harther's hadwance 'eadquarters in Moresby is bloody hair-conditioned now?"

There generally are three or four other Australian and eight or ten U.S. correspondents at the briefing. Swappa doesn't draw correspondents like the ETO (European Theater of Operations) does. Who wants to liberate Sowela Village when Paris is waiting? Most of the correspondents are nursing hangovers of fairly high voltage but 0600 hours in Brisbane is 3 p.m. the day before in the eastern United States. Allowing an hour for cable transmission, the communique and any Big Stories it discloses will reach The New York Times and other major East Coast newspapers in time for the afternoon news conferences at which those newspapers determine how they'll play the day's news.

There is, Swiller and the rest of GHQ are convinced, a foul conspiracy Back in The States engineered by the Joint Chiefs and that bastard in the White House to deprive Gen. Douglas MacArthur and the Southwest Pacific Area of the coverage he and it so richly deserve. Not to mention troops, supplies, new weapons, aircraft, landing craft, USO tours, etc. Swiller is doing his best to combat this foul plot. That's why the flunky captain slyly takes attendance at the briefing and why most of the correspondents though cursing the hour and their hangovers get out of bed for it. Correspondents who (unless on assignment in what's called "the field") regularly miss the briefing do not get the little favors Swiller sometimes bestows: a prized 5A Travel Priority, a decent bottle of scotch, an "exclusive" interview with a terminally inarticulate air ace. "Exclusive" means exclusive within a given circulation area.

The briefing over, the wire service correspondents but for Bluey Mahaffey, who files later, race down two flights of stairs, the elevators too poky, to the ITT cable office, where they file, first come first filed, short ledes, 100 words max, then in the order of their arrival one or more largely imaginary 200-word ads. These limits are imposed because the military cable traffic is picking up as the day gets underway in Swappa. Longer stories, features, are transmitted during the night.

INS (Hearst's International News Service) usually wins this race, beating The Associated Press, United Press and Reuters handily. INS, his name is Lester Lowell, is twenty-three. A beginning reporter in the INS Honolulu Bureau when the Japs bombed Peal Harbor, he helped cover that, a hell of a Big Story, then volunteered to join a U.S. troop convoy bound for the Philippines but diverted to Australia. He also has the best imagination or one at any rate not yet stultified by too many briefings and fell victim a year ago during a brief "exclusive" interview to MacArthur's undoubted (when he wishes to turn it on) charm. INS subscribes to Swiller's conspiracy theory and is doing his best to combat it. The other correspondents call him "Swiller's whore" though not to his face, he's a husky young fellow, but that's mostly jealousy. Lester Lowell has a permanent 5A Travel Priority and just was invited to fly to Port Moresby today with a visiting VIP (Very Important Person) in MacArthur's very own personal B17, the one called The Spirit of Bataan, ETD (Estimated Time of Departure) 0830 hours.

"I heard Swiller setting that up before the briefing," the Milwaukee Herald, chewing on a tough sausage the Australians call a banger in the National Hotel coffee shop a block up High Street, says. "Doing his whore another big favor."

Most of the correspondents quarter at the National. Those employed by individual newspapers meet in the coffee shop after the briefing for breakfast, at which they compare notes on Australian women and bitch about Swiller, the GHQ censors, the on-going shortage of decent liquor, etc. The National is the second best hotel in Brisbane. MacArthur and his family (wife, son, Chinese amah) and the GHQ staff if colonels or some kind of general have taken over the best one, the Lennon, though leading members of the Australian government, VIPs if important enough and rare top stars of stage screen and radio on USO tours also put up there.

"Who's the VIP this time?" the Kansas City Star says.

"I don't know," the Milwaukee Herald says. "I didn't hear Swiller say."

"U.S. Rep. Festus Lee Claypool of the Great State of Mississippi, Number Two Democrat on the House Armed Services Committee, that's who," the San Francisco Chronicle says. He has a reliable source, a sergeant from Daly City who sees the passenger manifests at ATC (Air Transport Command) HQ at Brisbane's airport. "He blew in yesterday. But it's embargoed until Festus' ass is safe Back in the States. Swiller's giving him the A Tour. Moresby and back on a short leash."

"Yew bloody Yienks," Bluey Mahaffey says. "Yew don't know as 'ow to 'andle a bloody boffin comes out for a look-see at the bloody war. Bloody boffin come out for a look-see in the Western Desert, we tike 'im up the bloody front and drop a mortar round near enough 'is arse 'e dirties 'is bloody britches. We gave the bloody bahstid a tiste of the bloody war!" Like many correspondents, Bluey adopts the editorial "we" when describing exploits he witnessed while with troops.

No one responds to Bluey's suggestion, if it is a suggestion. They're all pretty tired of Bluey and his eternal bloody war stories, mainly because but for the Chronicle they are unable to match them. The Chronicle might. He was eighteen and a U.S. Marine gassed in the Meuse Argonne in the other Big War. But nobody in this war, he's learned, gives a diddly shit about his war: nobody much gives a diddly shit about anybody else's war.

"Is MacArthur going?" the Portland Oregonian says.

"No," the Milwaukee Herald says. "Not that I heard anyway. Hell, you know Dugout Doug's dug in for the Duration at the Lennon."

Dugout Doug. A Navy label originally, it refers to Douglas MacArthur's perceived preference for the big tunnel on Corrigedor during the battle for the Bataan peninsula, before he was ordered to Australia. Yet he also is said to be personally fearless or was anyway in the other Big War. Walked around on the trench parapets armed with a swagger stick, splendidly uniformed, oblivious to enemy fire, so the stories go.

The Chronicle, an old-fashioned patriot for all his journalist's ritual cynicism, believes those stories, he first heard them in France, and he doesn't much like the Milwaukee Herald. "Mac's not the only one," he says. "Dug in here for the Duration."

"Aye, yer bloody roight!" Bluey Mahaffey says, and laughs. He has a harsh irritating laugh that sounds like a dog barking.

The Milwaukee Herald blushes but let's that pass. The other correspondents consider him, a label he detests, a "hometown correspondent." His first questions on encountering an American in uniform who smells like a story are: "Are you from Milwaukee? Or somewhere in Wisconsin?" If the answer is No, he has no story.

The Herald's name now is David Dudley Hull. It was Davey Hull when he was a copyboy at the Herald launching a career in journalism, Dave when he became a sportswriter, David when after he often got the scores wrong he was shifted to general assignments and David D. when, following a minor palace revolution at the Herald, he was sent off to Madison to cover the capitol and the state Legislature.

A short balding pasty-faced man with a weight problem, thirty-four years of age, married but childless, David D. Hull began to fear when the draft age was raised to thirty-five that he'd be drafted. Like most Americans at the time he knew next to nothing about the military and also began to fear through many sleepless nights that if he was drafted the Army would simply give him a little Basic Training, he'd heard about that, then ship him right off to some front. To get killed. He knows better now. There are all kinds of military jobs that are pretty safe. Safer probably than his old Milwaukee neighborhood what with all the coons streaming up from the South to grab jobs in the defense plants. The fifteen or twenty thousand U.S. troops in Brisbane (the exact number a Military Secret) certainly are safe enough. Or safe anyway from the enemy, the Japs. Allies are another matter. The Australian troops in Brisbane, mainly hardbitten AIF (Australian Imperial Forces) veterans back from the Western

Desert, like to beat up any bloody Yanks they can catch. But they don't shoot at Yanks. Well, there is a rumor, a GHQ colonel was shot at but missed by an AIF lance jack with reason to believe his wife and the colonel etc. But that's never been confirmed.

David Dudley Hull often thinks he might have wangled a commission and become a PIO, his experience. But it's too late for that now and he's safe from the draft with an on-going deferment so long as he's a correspondent overseas. Fearing the draft, he put in for the Swappa assignment the Herald was reluctantly establishing, mainly because the 32nd Infantry Division, a Wisconsin-Michigan National Guard outfit, was over there, had been for more than a year and badly bloodied to boot in the fighting at Buna Government Station. But the awful expense of maintaining a correspondent in Swappa (salary, lodging, meals, cable charges) wasn't something the Herald was going to undertake lightly. Hull got the assignment, knocking around the Legislature he'd met some of the Division's peacetime brass, and a uniform allowance he spent on tailored khakis with large green-and-gold War Correspondent shoulder patches. He also talked Jake Jasper, the Herald's executive editor, into his new byline: David Dudley Hull. That has a ring to it, Hull feels, rather like the byline of that other famous correspondent, Richard Harding Davis.

Then, kissing his wife Gertrude goodbye, David Dudley Hull caught a train to San Francisco, where his 1A Travel Priority did not entitle him to air transport. He didn't much want to fly over all that water anyway. He was put aboard a troop convoy with a thin two-destroyer escort that went first to Panama to pick up the 112th (Bushmasters) Regimental Combat team. Nineteen long scary days and sweaty mostly sleepless nights later, in the course of which he was often seasick and said many prayers he'd not said in twenty years that the vessel he was on would not be torpedoed, he reached Brisbane, safe though eighteen pounds lighter.

By then most of the Division's peacetime brass, found wanting at Buna Government Station, were reassigned to training duties and Service Force units. No matter. The Division less one infantry regiment already back in New Guinea was in camp thirty miles south of Brisbane, still licking its wounds and absorbing replacements. Which he might have been one of if drafted, David Dudley Hull often thinks, with a shudder. He visits the Division two or three times a week (Swiller lays on a staff car and a driver) and has regained the weight he lost crossing the Pacific, eating free in the Division HQ Officers Mess though charging the Herald for those meals on his expense account. He's also tracked down a number of Wisconsin GIs who survived the fighting at Buna Government Station and have hairy tales to tell, which David Dudley Hull embellishes with the military jargon he's picked up. He regularly apprises the folks back home that these "boys" are all fat and sassy, in good health and high spirits, itching for "another whack at the Japs," news that certainly would surprise these GIs. He's also committed adultery twice with a barmaid at the National who thinks all correspondents dinkum lads.

David Dudley Hull's not stirred from Brisbane except to visit the Division. Jake Jasper's suggested several times in letters and even cables, noting it's costing the Herald "a pile of money" to maintain a correspondent in Swappa, that David Dudley Hull get himself "frontwards" and "file soonest eyewitness combat flavor." But Jake Jasper's 10,000 miles away. There's an ugly rumor though that the rest of the Division soon will ship out for New Guinea and an upcoming "show." David Dudley Hull, again beset by sleepless nights, doesn't know what he'll do if that happens. Tag along with Division HQ most likely, which he surmises will be reasonably safe. Having dodged the draft he has no desire to witness any combat, whatever its flavor.

"Mister 'ull," Elwood, the National's octogenarian bell captain, shuffling up to the correspondents' table, says. "Cable for you."

David Dudley Hull reluctantly tips Elwood a shilling, sixteen cents in real money and opens the cable: ten words exactly, the maximum count for the minimum charge. Upgo frontwards instanter file bang bang or homecome likewise Jasper.

"Bloody 'ell!" Bluey Mahaffey, quick to perceive fear having seen a lot of it, says. "Mister 'ull 'as got some bloody bad news. Wife run off with a bloody blackfellow, did she?" And laughs his barking laugh.

"Oh shut up!" David Dudley Hull says. "I have to. Well, my editor has an assignment for me. I have to go to New Guinea. Soon as I can. But gosh, I don't have any kind of Travel Priority."

"See Swiller," the Chronicle says. "Ask him he'll put you on the goddamn Bataan."

"Gosh, you think he'd do that? This is a pretty well uh pressing assignment. But I have to pack."

"Ask him. Call him. You got time. Bataan's ETD is oh-eight-thirty."

"By golly, I will," David Dudley Hull says, and departs, hastily.

"Bahstid dint pie fer 'is bloody breakfast," Bluey says.

"I'll take care of it," the Chronicle says. "Worth it, get his fat ass out of here."

Meanwhile, back at GHQ, the flunky captain paddles down the hall to the Message Center and puts the Daily Communique on the Allied Forces teletype network. Laced with creative spelling by the weary GIs on the 0000-to-0800 shift in the Message Center, several of whom were printers in civil life, the communique rattles off to Swappa's other major commands: Australian Field Marshal Sir Thomas Blamey's Ground Forces, Fifth Air Force, Seventh Fleet, the Royal Australian Air Force, U.S. Service Force HQ in Sydney and its Base Sections in Sydney, Melbourne, Brisbane and Townsville.

* * *

In Townsville this teletype is the first thing Col. Web Allen sees on reaching his office in the former sugar warehouse at 0800 hours, ready or not ready for another miserable blistering day in the middle of The War. M/Sgt. Abbott is under the delusion the Daily Communique is important and after reading it himself with moving lips leaves it on the paperwork already piled high on Web Allen's desk.

The Daily Communique seldom inspires Col. Web Allen. Nevertheless, hooking his GI spectacles over his ears, he scans it. It does not inspire him but he can interpret it. "Today" means yesterday in Swappa: the Communique is written for domestic U.S. consumption. So it's H-hour-plus-26 or so for the poor bastards in the "alleid grund froces" at Arawe. They are not identified. Units never are in Swappa, not by GHQ anyway, though Tokyo Rose in her radio broadcasts often names them. Neither are officers but for an occasional air ace. Military Security, GHQ claims, but Web Allen has his own theory. Nobody is going to steal Douglas MacArthur's thunder. And "under the command of Gen. Douglas MacArthur" does not mean the great man is actually present at Arawe, directing fire and deploying troops, though some idiots Back in The States may think so. MacArthur may be at his Advance Headquarters in Port Moresby, 250 miles from Arawe, rumored to be air-conditioned now, but more likely he's in Brisbane, 1500 miles from Arawe. Douglas MacArthur may be personally fearless, so the stories go, but he also, Web Allen believes, is a man who likes his comfort. MacArthur at any rate (like the British General Staff, which stayed well clear of the mud along the Somme) never once crossed the Owen Stanley Mountains, The Hump, twenty minutes from Moresby in his B17, for a firsthand look a year ago at the bloody fighting in the mud and swamps and jungle and tidal creeks and kunai grass full of ticks vectoring scrub typhus or the Japanese bunkers defending Buna Government Station. Web Allen knows that to be a fact. He was there, a rifle company commander then for three days the Battalion S2, intelligence officer. But all that and the bad thing that happened there to the late Sgt. Barney Clark is an unhappy chapter in his life Web Allen does not wish to dwell on, so he doesn't.

Tomorrow's Communique no doubt will declare the Arawe beachhead "secure but for scattered enemy resistance" with "mopping-up operations in progress." That'll be a laugh though a bitter one. The mopping-up will go on and on, the goddamn Japs never surrender, producing each day some KIA (Killed in Action) and WIA (Wounded in Action) among the Infantry doing the dirty work. The Infantry has a little joke about that: Yeah, you and me and Dugout Doug know this fuckin place is secure, but the fuckin Japs don't know it.

Web Allen drops the teletype. Too much Communique is bad for his blood pressure, which isn't all that hot anyway, 150 over 88 according to the sawbones at the 12th Station Hospital. H-plus-26 though, the grapevine should have a sitrep (situation report) on Arawe. "Sergeant Abbot!" Abbott pops into the office. "Have you heard what outfit made that landing at, what is it, Arawe?"

"Hunnert-and-Twelfth RCT, Sir. That's the grapevine says."

Col. Web Allen and M/Sgt. George Abbott

Good news then, though not for the 112th Regimental Combat Team. It might have been, Web Allen was thinking, his old outfit, the 128th Infantry Regiment, said to be back in New Guinea. "Is Colonel Fogerty here?"

"Uh no, Sir. Not yet, Sir."

This news is not unexpected. Lt. Col. Parnell Fogerty seldom turns up before 0830 hours. By 0900 though, braced with the lethal coffee laced with medicinal gin Sgt. Costello brews on a hot plate, he's functional and through the rest of the day a wily, reasonably efficient chief-of-staff with useful Old Regular pals all over Swappa.

"Well, when he gets here go through this stuff on my desk. Give Colonel Fogerty anything needs immediate attention. I've got to be on my way. Is my car here? Did you get hold of Colonel Ives personally yesterday, remind him I was coming?"

"Yessir. Personally, Sir. Car's here, Sir. I think the uh driver, he's across the street."

"Damn it! Go get him. Chew his ass! Tell him he's supposed to stay with the vehicle! Tell him again! We have to swing by the George, pick up the JTC XO. And what are you doing wearing a necktie, Sergeant? You're out of uniform. Take it off."

"Sir!" Reluctantly, M/Sgt. Abbott removes his olive drab necktie and rolls it around his fist. The new Base Section Uniform Regulations Fogerty finally got around to drafting, no neckties with the Class A khakis, went into effect Monday, but Abbott apparently feels naked without one.

And the 112th RCT, a further report from the grapevine has it, is taking twenty percent casualties at Arawe. But who gives a diddly shit about that in Townsville, 900 miles from Arawe? Nobody, Web Allen surmises, while his Dodge, tuned-up but riding rough, it feels like it's missing a leaf spring, crawls along Flinders Street, Townville's main drag. Already, at 0830 hours, the sun is a white hot smear in the northeastern sky, it's 95 degrees F. and climbing outside and more like 115 F. inside the Dodge. Fazoli left it parked in the sun with the windows rolled up while he dawdled over coffee with other loafers in the Red Cross Canteen.

Col. Web Allen dwells for a time on the pleasure it would be, though he is not normally he believes a vicious or vindictive person, to have Fazoli taken out and shot. And others too: these are not normal times. Maj. Gen. Ernst (Butcher) Schultz, for instance. Brig. Gen. Sedgewick O. Bargle by all means. The entire 114th Portable Laundry Detachment, which somehow managed to lose all his tropical khakis, which is why he's wearing his dress gaberdines, the kind called pinks, scratchy gaberdines hell on his prickly. But he won't think about his prickly heat. If he does it will itch as even now.

Suppressing itchy thoughts, Col. Web Allen surveys the passing scene. It does not inspire him. To his right are air raid shelters, raw concrete structures sixty feet long chalked with the U.S. Armed Forces' universal battle cry, "Kilroy was here!" They were built down the middle of Flinders Street in 1942 when, the way local historians put it, the bloody Japs were "bombing" Townsville. In fact, Web Allen's learned, a single Jap aircraft once circled over the city on a moonlit May night then dropped two 250-pounders on the mudflats a mile down the coast. The shelters are boarded up following several rapes or alleged rapes in their dark interiors, the rapists alleged to be bloody Yanks, but still reduce traffic on Flinders Street to two narrow lanes, which is why the Dodge is crawling along behind a U.S. Army tank truck with Danger Aviation Fuel on its rear.

Castle Hill looms up beyond the shelters and the buildings along Flinders Street. There's a ragged black smear on one of its rocky outcrops, all that's left of a U.S. B25 bomber and its crew, flying into Townsville in a dense fog with a faulty altimeter during the previous rainy season the Australians call The Bloody Wet. The blazing wreckage, everybody in it dead, spilling down the hill, killed a pet goat subsequently valued at 100 quid by its bereaved owner and set fire to an empty chicken coops. Which is more than you can say for the bloody Jap.

Web Allen had never heard of Townsville until the Division landed at Adelaide in mid-May 1942, just about the time the U.S. Navy was claiming victory in the Battle of the Coral Sea, carrier vs. carrier, claiming also to have halted the Japs' drive south and lifted the threat of invasion. Most of the citizens who hastily left Townsville just prior to all that are back now there's money to be made off the bloody Yanks, but the current population, much of it is military, is a Military Secret.

Some military, Web Allen think, eyeing the specimen sharing the Dodge's rear seat: a big man in his early thirties, thirty pounds overweight, with a red meaty face, wearing crisp green fatigues with a Service Force shoulder patch, paratrooper boots, sunglasses, a helmet liner and a pistol belt with an empty holster since only guards and MPs are authorized weapons in Townsville.

An empty holster all right, Web Allen thinks. Maj. Clarence Borgan. They met last night in the bar at the George hotel, Jill Tucker stuck with a hospital shift at the 12th Station until 2100 hours. Borgan's the acting excutive officer at the Service Force Jungle Training Center (JTC) near Woorammoolla, a dot on the littoral 200 miles up the coast. He was in Townsville, he said, to "check on some supplies," then voiced complaints about the air transport situation. "Two goddamn days I hadda wait, that airstrip there in Woory, get a seat on a goddamn airplane, and now I got to get back."

Web Allen in a weak moment offered Borgan a ride back to Woory. "I'll be flying up there myself tomorrow to inspect the Center." Borgan promptly panicked, stuttered nobody told him, stuck at the airstrip, there was an inspection. Web Allen quelled his panic. "Don't worry, Major. Colonel Ives knows I'm coming." Protocol that, simple decency, there being no sneakier trick in the Army than to spring an inspection without first warning the commanding officer concerned, in this case Col. Jefferson Davis Ives. Borgan, his panic subsiding, then snapped at the ride offer and, Web Allen surmises, went about the real purpose of his trip, which was to sample what passes for fleshpots in Townsville. With some success apparently. He appears to be nursing a terrible hangover at any rate, evincing few signs of life though he seems to be breathing.

Some military and there's another one. Capt. Forrest (Fats) Forney, the Base Section Special Services chief, a paunchy Reservist in tailored khakis (two ax handles across the ass, Web Allen's grandfather would have said), a Toledo, Ohio, dry-cleaning mogul in civil life, headed thirty minutes late for his office half a block along in, fittingly enough, a former peacetime dry-cleaning establishment.

Special Services. Those words, Web Allen surmises, may conjure up in some minds British Commandos with blackened faces in a rubber boat silently approaching a hostile shore. Capt. Forney's mission, however, is to maintain morale among the Base Section EM. He and his men distribute athletic equipment, comicbooks, Armed Forces paperbacks, chess and checker sets, movie films, Yank The Army Weekly and other magazines, etc. They also organize athletic contests between units and at rare intervals entertainments featuring touring USO performers. Capt. Forney commands a second lieutenant and nine EM and what they all do all day is a mystery to Col. Web Allen. Well, he knows what one, Sgt. Wilbur (Slugger) Radke, does: virtually nothing. Radke, a utility infielder with the Toledo Mud Hens in civil life, was except he was drafted thought to be headed for the Major Leagues. Drafted, he wound up in the 3rd Repple Depple, an Infantry replacement. Capt. Forney, a longtime wild-eyed Mud Hens fan, somehow got wind of that and got Radke a ds tdy to Special Services and, presently, a promotion to sergeant. Radke's at second base and the clean-up hitter now, batting .672, on the Base Section softball team, undefeated (6-0) since he joined it. Forney, the team manager, seems to think this a major contribution to the War Effort. Often says that anyway at the George Hotel bar and cites a precedent. Sgt. Joe Dimaggio, former New York Yankee MVP, there was a story in Yank Magazine, is serving his country on an Army baseball team in Hawaii.

The Bloody Wet | 47

Well, Mom, apple pie and baseball. That in a nutshell (or a pie pan) is The American Way of Life often cited at the War Bond rallies Web Allen's seen on the Movietone Newsreels that sometimes accompany the outdoor GI movies.

Beyond Forney's office, forty-odd soldiers, Australians and a few GIs, Caucasians all, stand waiting in a line snaking along the sidewalk to the Rose & Crown, the pub at the end of the block that will open at 1000 hours. There are perhaps 8,000 American Negro troops in Townsville (port battalions, truck battalions, miscellaneous Quartermaster outfits, their unit designations followed by a (C) for Colored) but the races do not mix. That also is The American Way of Life, the way God and the War Department want it, though God's preference is a guess. The War Department clearly stated its view in a 1941 Directive. "Department policy is not to intermingle Colored and white troops. This policy has been proved satisfactory over a long period of years and to make changes would produce situations destructive to morale and detrimental to the preparations for national defense."

Following the attack on Pearl Harbor, the nation at war, the Draft in full cry, the War Department gave this matter further serious thought and issued a Memorandum, the thrust of which was and is: "Every effort should be made to maintain in the Army the social and racial conditions which exist in civil life in order that the normal customs of the white and Colored personnel may not be suddenly disrupted."

The Colored troops (their colors range between coal black and several shades of tan somewhat lighter than Fazoli's swarthy complexion) toil day and night on the docks and in the massive supply dumps in the scrub south of Townsville and bang all over the area in their trucks but off-duty it's as if they live in another country. The normal customs have not been disrupted. The Colored have their own Booker T. Washington Red Cross Club in a Quonset hut in South Townsville, capacity 400, two Red Cross men (C) run it and billet in it, but mostly now when off-duty (C) units are confined to their campsites out in the scrub. In early '42, when the first (C) units arrived and the invasion threat, never mind the Navy's claims, still lingered, this was not the case. A number of local lasses truly believed these troops to be "American night-fighters," which was what these troops said they were. There are a number of half-caste babies in Townsville now. But the invasion threat evaporated, Australia revived its long-standing White Only Policy and there's a rumor GHQ has acceded to an Australian request to ship all the (C) units to New Guinea no later than 31 January.

In fact, Web Allen recollects, he saw an MO (Movement Order) yesterday. The 404th QM Truck Battalion (C) will be loading a Forward HQ and two companies less a platoon on an LST bound for Oro Bay at midnight.

The Rose & Crown will open at 1000 hours, close at noon, reopen between 1400 and 1600 and 1800 and 2000 hours. This is a system devised and imposed by The Bloody Austerity, which is what the Australians call their omnipresent War Authority and its wartime rationing. The theory is this system reduces the consumption of alcohol vital to the War Effort. In practice it simply increases the speed with which alcohol is consumed then looses upon the streets sloshed soldiers prone to, as angry Letters to the Editor of the daily Coast Times often put it, "relieve themselves in public and accost respectable women with indecent proposals."

Oh war is hell all right, Web Allen thinks, the troops outside the Rose & Crown bringing to mind similar letters in an earlier time in another place: 1941, peacetime still Back in the States, when he was a first john and the Division, ordered into federal service, equipped with World War I leftovers, was floundering around in the mud in a World War I Louisiana training camp. Youthful sloshed damn Yankee National Guardsmen were sometimes loose upon the streets in nearby towns then, "relieving themselves in public etc." Or so said angry Letters to nearby Editors from citizens often claiming to be Good Christians. Web Allen hopes those Good Christians are happy now, raking in the dough with their defense jobs. Some hundreds of those youthful once sloshed damn Yankees are dead or missing or missing some of their parts. And more no doubt soon will be if the 128th Infantry is back in New Guinea, and there's a rumor the rest of the Division will be too, shortly. Damn the Good Christians.

But thoughts of this nature ("Essentially untargeted anger insufficiently suppressed," the goddamn shrink at the 5th General Hospital in Brisbane called it, but what did the goddamn shrink know about anger?) also are bad for Web Allen's blood pressure. He suppresses them and the Dodge crawls by the Rose & Crown and slams to a halt inches short of Danger Aviation Fuel at Townsville's busiest intersection.

"Fuckin coon!" Fazoli, assuming the tank driver to be Colored, says. "They never signal or nuthin'. They just fuckin stop!"

They sit waiting while a sweaty 301st MP directs traffic, most of it military, through the intersection. To the left, Dock Street runs down to the docks on Point Cleveland. There's a pub along there, the Goose & Feathers, that serves Colored, and two whorehouses riddled with VD. They're Off Limits to U.S. troops but a Pro Station (Pro as in prophylactic, dispensing post-coital preventive medicine) remains operational at the corner of Dock and Flinders Streets, the green identifying light bulb over its door dim in the sunlight. The Q&NR depot, said to be a replica of London's Paddington Station though much smaller, is on the other corner. The Gilbey's distillery looms up behind it. Two 301st MPs, big men in crisp khakis, belted and buckled and armed, are strolling outside the depot like gunboats showing the flag, trolling for AWOLs.

Beyond the intersection, this a quaint Empire custom, Flinders Street becomes Charters Road, which slices through South Townsville past Buncom's Famous Fish & Chips, some greasy restaurants, other small businesses, mostly modest homes, some on pilings because the nearby Ross River often goes over its banks during The Bloody Wet, and farther along on the river's formerly vacant flood plain the 12th Station Hospital, Happy Valley EM camp and 3rd Repple Depple. There's a horse track opposite the Rep Dep, Charters Downs, closed now by The Bloody Austerity. The 330th Ordnance Co. and the 14th K9 (Dog) Detachment are installed there, their shops and kennels under the grandstand, their personnel in dark green pyramidal tents in the infield.

The MP blows his whistle and the Flinders Street traffic moves. Fazoli turns right onto Garbutt Road (Dock Street like Flinders changing its name) by the Tivoli Cinema and the Barrier Arms, a ramshackle two-story hotel, its old red brick black with soot. The rocky south face of Castle Hill rises behind it. The Tivoli's still showing Desert Victory, the violent British war film documenting the breakout at El Alamein in the Western Desert more than a year ago, starring in part the AIF troops now advancing westward in the Markham Valley. The AMF in Townville say bloody Yanks who see Desert Victory all the way through "get another bloody medal."

The Barrier Arms is an authorized EM billet. Half a dozen EM are perched like crows on a fence on the railing on its second-floor porch overlooking Garbutt Road. The second-floor rooms open off this porch. The EM are mostly air crews, Web Allen surmises. Aircraft bound for New Guinea often RON (Remain Over Night) in Townsville for a last fling. Scheduled turn-around flights from New Guinea often do too. All the distances in Swappa are appalling (650 miles to Brisbane, 1100 to Sydney, 1200 to Darwin, 1000 to Nadzab) but a C47 can fly the 650 miles between the Port Moresby airstrips and Townsville and return between dawn and dusk. Few do, however. Their crews find some excuse, some imaginary mechanical malfunction, and stall around until 1500 hours, by which time it's too late to clear for Moresby, where the airstrips, still subject to occasional air raids or at any rate Yellow Alerts, have no lights and shut down at 1830, when the tropic night falls swiftly.

Beyond the Barrier Arms there are a few small houses at the

base of Castle Hill, then the Dodge is out of Townsville and on both sides of Garbutt Road the land stretches away, flat and brown, baking under the sun, bare but for thin stands of salt grass and a few scraggly trees beside the Ross River. Garbutt Road crosses the Ross halfway to Garbutt Field. The Ross loops around the north end of the airfield and South Townsville in a giant S on its way to the sea through a tangle of mangrove swamps. Dust devils dance in the distance. Dust fine as chalk sifts into the Dodge. There's been no rain in Townsville or elsewhere along the littoral for going on nine months. But the Bloody Dry will soon be over, the Australian say. The huge stratocumulus clouds looming up daily out where the Coral Sea meets the horizon, they say, will roll in over the coast one of these days or nights and "spill bloody buckets, rine bloody cats and dogs then, it will."

The Dodge hits a pothole, Garbutt Road is mostly potholes. Web Allen's slipped disc slips, producing sharp pain. "Damn it, Corporal! Watch out of those potholes!"

"Yessir!" Fazoli says, and promptly hits another pothole.

"Owth! Thunofabidth!" Maj. Borgan says. He bit his tongue. Sucking his injured tongue, showing further signs of life, he says, "Thith road's uh bidhth!"

Indeed it is. The main route west from Townsville, Garbutt Road is blacktopped as far as the Second Air Depot (SAD), a sprawling USAAC aircraft repair and modification facility in a eucalyptus grove beyond Garbutt Field, but the blacktop takes an awful beating. Trucks pound over it all day and half the night. Most are U.S. Army 2.5-ton GMCs and Studebakers, the kind called a deuce-and-half, though the RAAF airport squadron that runs and rules Garbutt Field has a few snub-nosed Italian Fiats captured in the Western Desert.

Beyond SAD, Garbutt Road becomes the Bruce Highway, a narrow gravel track that goes over some low hills and on and on across the bleak empty endless miles the Australians call The Outback (or sometimes "miles and miles of fook all") for 475 miles to Cloncurry, pop. 800, where it pretty much peters out. The only sign of civilization along this track are the weathered poles hung with sagging telephone lines, one civilian, one strung by the U.S. Army, that more or less connect Cloncurry and two nearby U.S. Army outposts with the rest of the world. Since, what with The Bloody Austerity, the average Australian has no petrol unless an American flogs him some (their vehicles run badly on some kind of gas produced by burning charcoal in a tank like a 50-gallon water heater bolted to the rear bumper) almost the only traffic on the Bruce Highway is an occasional U.S. Army supply column serving the two outposts: a POW camp holding two dozen Japs (all but two wounded when captured) and a mile away on a low hill called Flat Mountain the main Swappa stockade, Flat Mountain Stockade. Some hundred GIs court-martialed for and, that being the purpose of a court-martial, convicted of various serious crimes (desertion, murder, rape, striking a superior officer, blatant homosexuality, flogging gasoline) are doing duration-to-life in the Stockade or, a half dozen, deserters and murderers and rapists, waiting to hang if their sentences are not commuted (all have been to date) by Gen. Douglas MacArthur or, their last chance, the commander-in-chief in the White House.

Col. Web Allen saw the POW camp and the Stockade once in early November, flying out and back the same day in a borrowed airplane to inspect them shortly after taking command of the Townsville Base Section. Both are GHQ operations but the Base Section supplies them and provides the MP camp complements that run them, rotated out of the 301st MP Co. for thirty-day tours. The noon temperature in the shade at the Stockade was 102 F. but it was still spring in the Southern Hemisphere. "Bloody cool," an ancient sun-dried Australian at the Cloncurry airstrip said, compared to summer's average 118 F. and the all-time Australian record, 128 F. Worse than the heat were the flies, millions of tiny black flies that tried to crawl into Web Allen's ears, eyes, nose and mouth. The ancient Australian ignored them.

The Dodge hits another pothole and slams to a stop inches short of Danger Aviation Fuel. "Shit!" Fazoli says. "They still fixin' the fuckin bridge!"

The bridge over the Ross. It was, Web Allen's heard, under water for a month when the Ross went over its banks during The Bloody Wet a year ago. Which was why or part of the why the stuff the 54th Troop Carrier Wing then based at Garbutt Field was supposed to deliver to the Division at Buna Government Station (ammunition, weapons, rations, wound packs, medicines, morphine) was slow to arrive or more often did not arrive at all. Web Allen knows all about that too and mainly still blames the incompetents in the Townsville Base Section supposed to forward those items. Incompetents too lazy to build a Bailey bridge, too dumb to organize a ferry. Incompetents he now commands but he sees no poetic justice in that. No poetry certainly and no justice either. Most of those incompetents are still in Townsville, mainly concerned in Web Allen's view with their own safety and comfort and the sexual opportunities offered healthy young men (and some not so young or healthy) 10,000 miles from home with money and American cigarettes and chocolate in their pockets and a war on. A smidgen of guilt jars Web Allen. Who is he, he's a fair man, to begrudge other red-blooded American lads a little sexual opportunity?

Now, at any rate, a year later, a year late, Maj. Luce Boldt, the Base Section engineer, and the 118th Engineer Bridge Co. are building a new raised bridge over the Ross. One span's been completed but until the other one is traffic at the bridge is reduced to one lane alternately eastbound and westbound.

They sit waiting while eastbound traffic hammers over the bridge. Fazoli lights a cigarette and so with shaky hands does Borgan. Web Allen smokes cigars but not often. Cigars are hard to get in Swappa unless you're a PX clerk. He licks dust from his teeth. Sweat trickles down his ribs. Fazoli, he observes, needs a haircut. He also observes through a gap in the traffic one of the anti-aircraft batteries still guarding Townsville, four sand-bagged

Bofors under a torn camouflage net on a slight rise beside the Ross. Its AMF crew, stripped to shorts, shoes and bush hats, are brewing tea. AMF troops also walk guard behind the rusty barbwire still strung along the local beaches. The privates are paid two bob a day, thirty-two cents in real money. For fun they beat up any bloody Yanks paid seven bob a day and more they can catch.

"Uh, Colonel, Sir?" Borgan, removing his sunglasses and shifting his big bottom to face Web Allen, says. "Something I want to ask you."

"Yes?" What now?

"I uh understand, Sir. I mean I heard. The Base Section officers here in Tville, they get like a liquor ration. I mean their O Club does. What I was wunnering was since we're attached the Base for rations and like that up the Training Center and we're the hell out in the boonies and there ain't any booze in Woory anyway, that's a fact, the goddamn Parachutes, 503rd, their goddamn jump pay, they grab it all. I was wunnering is there some way us officers up the Center there could get in on that? Get some kind of regular liquor ration, I mean. We sure would appreciate it, Sir."

Winded, Maj. Borgan subsides and sits staring at Web Allen like a large debauched servile sheep dog. Smelling like one too, smelling of sweat, stale beer, armpits, after shave.

Web Allen frowns as if giving this request serious thought. In fact he's recalling from their muddled conversation in the George Hotel bar that Borgan is new to Swappa, green as his fatigues, plucked from the officer pool at the 3rd Repple Depple three weeks ago and shipped off to the Jungle Training Center. Where, the Army is full of surprises, he's now the acting XO. Well, he was in ROTC in college, he said, and in civil life the football coach and civics teacher at an Indiana high school. The Rep Dep conceivably thought him a leader of men, or boys anyway. More likely though his name simply came up early in the alphabet when the Rep Dep got an order: ship one warm breathing major to the JTC. And new and green he may be but he's swiftly latched onto one of the principle war aims embraced by the U.S. Armed Forces in Swappa.

"Well, yes," Web Allen says. "The Base Officers Club gets some kind of liquor ration. Once a month, I think. But that was set up before I took command. I don't know much about it. My chief-of-staff, Lieutenant Colonel Fogerty, handles it. What you should do is put a request through to him. Put it through channels."

Borgan's red meaty face collapses. He's not that green. He knows the kiss of death, Put It Through Channels, when he hears it. "Yessir, I'll do that," he mumbles, then slumps on the hot leather seat, no doubt harboring homicidal thoughts.

Let the bastard sulk, Web Allen thinks, or learn distilling. Jungle Training Center: that's another laugh. An idiotic idea spawned by that bastion of idiocy, Service Force HQ in Sydney. Web Allen knows all about that too. Discharged from the 5th General Hospital with a somewhat cloudy medical record and reclassified, he spent nine miserable months at Service Force HQ. Was there in fact when the JTC was conceived by Brig. Gen. Sedgewick O. Bargle, the Service Force deputy commander, a rail-thin West Pointer often identified by his initials who had nothing much else to do and thinks he should get a Legion of Merit for his brilliance.

The JTC occupies 200 leased acres, sand dunes and scrub, behind a gap in the mangrove swamps ten miles south of Woorammoolla. A tent camp, though the Permanent Party (Borgan, a captain, two lieutenants and a dozen sergeant-instructors of various grades) have plywood huts, it overlooks a stinking gray-green mudflat half-a-mile wide at low tide. The sea there is full of sea snakes and sea wasps, a deadly jellyfish. The dunes are full of sand fleas. The scrub is full of ticks and a vine like poison ivy and large meat-eating ants and the mangrove swamps breed mosquitoes by the billions. All of which Web Allen discovered on his first and only previous visit to the JTC for a change-of-command ceremony a month ago. Another miserable day, hotter than blazes and he was bitten by several ants, but for meeting the new JTC commander, Col. Jefferson Davis Ives.

Col. Ives may be an old reprobate. Hell, he is an old reprobate, first to admit it, a huge old reprobate, 6-4 in his socks, 250 pounds, with a big hard belly, fifty-plus, overage in grade, West Point '12, a Cavalryman by trade and proud of it, who, regulations be dammed, still wears tailored jodhpurs, riding boots, spurs and a battered campaign hat and now he's a long way from GHQ, where he was a censor and facial hair was prohibited, a flowing Cavalryman's mustache. Web Allen, though pretty straight-laced himself (well, used to be, raised that way) has always rather liked reprobates. He has a "weakness" for them, his wife Mert says. Reprobates with style anyway and Col. Jefferson Davis Ives has style to burn. So in his way did the late Sgt. Barney Clark.

More guilt, a monstrous whack, jars Web Allen. He shoves Mert and the late Sgt. Clark from his thoughts. "How's Colonel Ives these days?"

"Awright, I guess," Borgan, still sulking, says. "We don't see whole lot of him."

Col. Ives, though he commands the JTC, does not billet there. He took a quick look at its wildlife when taking command and decided to bivouac at the King Edward Hotel in Woorammoolla. He is after all, he told Web Allen, "Dependently wealthy. Ma waff, Miz Sally, her family, they own 'bout half a Jawja." Then in short order Col. Ives somehow acquired a large green Packard staff car and a WENL driver, whatever a WENL is, one of the Australian women's auxiliary services. Col. Ives' WENL is Mrs. Patricia Forbes-Fowler, said by him to be a "good-lookin' uppa class lady" in her thirties with a husband, a captain in the Australian 8th Division, missing at Singapore. Mrs. Forbes-Fowler drives Col. Ives to and from the JTC two or three times a week for a quick look at its operations. Like Web Allen, he considers the

JTC ludicrous. The old reprobate spends the rest of his time laying siege to Mrs. Forbes-Fowler's virtue, matching pints with the locals at the King Edward and playing poker with paratroop officers and the ensign commanding the U.S. Navy detachment based, nobody knows why or what for, in Woorammoolla. He's found the Navy easy picking at seven-car stud.

Ostensibly, the JTC's mission is to train Service Force GIs, two weeks at a time in batches of 200, for life in the jungle, where it's assumed they'll one day find themselves. Whip them into shape too. There's a world-class obstacle course winding through the stuff like poison ivy and the wildlife in the scrub. And teach them to disembark from troop transports, struggle down cargo nets into bobbing landing craft. The JTC does not have a transport of course or landing craft. The first is impractical and landing craft, though the mysterious Navy detachment in Woorammoolla has two, are in short supply in Swappa. The ETO is getting most of them, for the Second Front. The JTC makes do with a wooden mockup of a ship's hull twenty feet high draped with a genuine cargo net. The mutinous trainees who survive the obstacle course are hustled up a ladder behind this mockup and down the net in full gear into a simulated landing craft, a saw-edged stand of salt grass at the base of the mockup. Casualties at the JTC are running about thirty percent: cuts, bruises, sprains, ant bites, low-grade malaria, sunstroke, an occasional fracture. The JTC's permanent XO is in traction in the 12th Station Hospital after snapping a femur in a fall from the cargo net while demonstrating technique.

None of which bothers Col. Web Allen. The JTC belongs to Service Force Training Command in Sydney. He only has to inspect it once a month, this on orders from Brig. Gen. S.O. Bargle, because he's in the neighborhood so to speak, nobody in Training Command wants to pry their fat ass out of Sydney to do it and somebody has to do it, the Army convinced, not without cause, that units and personnel unless inspected at frequent intervals are likely to fall upon slovenly ways.

So Col. Web Allen will inspect the JTC. No doubt (Col. Ives knows the drill) he'll find all its pyramidal tents properly pitched, taut and in line, the trainees' cots properly made, taut and in line, their toothpaste, razors, extra blades and the socks they save for inspections properly displayed in the manner prescribed by the Field Manual, the messhall scrubbed, ovens scoured, pots and pans burnished bright enough to reflect a soldier shaving, largely fictitious menus properly posted, all the cooks in the whites they save for inspections, their fingernails pared, and the rest of the personnel, Permanent Party and trainees, clean and neat, in proper uniforms, all their buttons buttoned, clean-shaven, no facial hair, all the weapons they will never fire clean and oiled, no speck of dust on them or in them, and all the unit vehicles, four jeeps and a weapons-carrier, washed and polished, the mudguards lightly oiled, parked hub-to-hub, all training canceled (Col. Ives knows the drill) for forty-eight hours to achieve this perfection, and all the little white stones bordering the JTC walks and roadways, the uniform size of a softball, spaced as if laid down with a surveyor's transit, which they may have been, freshly painted.

The U.S. Army sets great store by these little white stones and so by all accounts does Brig. Gen. S.O. Bargle, who does not have a fat ass and sometimes pries it out of Sydney for sneaky (no advance warning) inspections. The last time the s.o.b. blazed through Townsville, the story goes, he did not find the little white stones in the Base Motor Pool white enough and made the Motor Pool GIs dig them up and paint them and plant them again while he stood by, watching them work.

No doubt, Web Allen surmises, the JTC trainees are even now painting little white stones whiter. No doubt too the JTC is making life somewhat more miserable than it has to be for these trainees. Well, what the hell, they're Service Force troops. Base Section commandos, the Infantry call them with scorn and envy. Little misery will do them good. Web Allen may wear Quartermaster Corps insignia (a golden wheel with an eagle on its rim said to signify an outfit going around in circles quick to shit on people) but he still thinks like the Infantry. Compared to Infantry or Infantry in combat anyway the JTC trainees live in utter luxury. They're dry. They're fed mostly hot meals regularly. They're not "sleeping" in wet holes in the ground they had to dig. They can sleep and change uniforms and wash and they have latrines and do not have to carry their own toilet paper. Or do without. No toilet paper. Now that's a little horror of war, Web Allen thinks, you never hear much about, never see mentioned in dispatches, but a little horror all the same.

And, the ultimate luxury, the JTC trainees barring an occasional fall or a few bites are perfectly safe. No one is shooting at them or ever has or probably ever will. No, strike that, a lawyer's phrase. Col. Jefferson D. Ives was shot at but missed while out for a morning canter on a borrowed horse in Victoria Park in Brisbane. An AIF lance-jack back from the Western Desert whose wife Col. Ives admits he was humping now and then (but they were just friends, he says, it wasn't anything serious) was the logical suspect. He was heard to say in barracks, "I'll get the bloody big bahstid next time!" He was not charged, however. There were no witnesses and relations between the AIF and the U.S. Army were already pretty touchy. Col. Ives was relieved of his censor's job at GHQ and ordered to Woorammoolla to command the JTC. "In the interests of Allied Relations," he says. Col. Ives has friends in high places, other old Pointers. The former JTC commander is a GHQ censor now.

"Hey, 'bout time," Fazoli, tossing his cigarette, slapping the Dodge into gear, says. The MP at the bridge is waving the westbound forward. Fazoli changes lanes and bumps over the new bridge, sixty feet of heavy planking with no railing. Below it the Ross River is a thin trickle of brown water winding through the rocks in its shallow bed. A dozen engineers in dirty fatigues, most stripped to the waist, are toiling there, erecting bracing for the other span, directed by a second lieutenant in khakis and a cardboard pith helmet. The bridge construction began a month ago but is proceeding at a pace, Web Allen calculates, akin to that practiced by the Work Progress Administration during The Great Depression.

The Dodge bounces off the end of the completed span, hits a pothole, bumps by the waiting eastbound traffic and, Fazoli bluffing an oncoming deuce-and-a-half, turns through the Main Gate into Garbutt Field, alien though allied territory. USAAC personnel man the Control Tower, Operations Office and Air Freight sheds, but a RAAF airdrome squadron maintains and polices the field. The RAAF sentry in baggy blue coveralls at the gate, armed with a slung Lee-Enfield rifle, does not salute the Dodge despite the eagle on its license plate denoting the presence of a live U.S. bird colonel. Australian troops will only salute their own officers and not all of them.

The Dodge crawls by three large quonset huts (the Air Freight sheds), the field speed limit 10 mph, and the ATOP (Air Transport Office, Personnel)), a smaller quonset with a permanent frieze of gear-laden servicemen of two nations slumped in its sparse shade doggedly awaiting air transport. There's another small quonset beyond the ATOP with a long sign on its roof, American Red Cross Garbutt Field Canteen Transients Only. Opposite these quonsets are half a dozen aging two-story RAAF barracks, their camouflage paint faded. The traces remaining look like a fungus infection. The RAAF officer who runs the field, Wing Comdr. Haines Hewlitt-Packard, has a second-floor office in one of them. The walks between the barracks are surfaced with crushed shells. A plump AWAAF (Australian Women's Auxiliary Air Force) is trotting down one of them, kicking up puffs of dust. Borgan observes her jiggling buttocks. Beyond the barracks on low ground sloping down to the Ross River is the USAAC Transient Area, a dozen sagging pyramidal tents once the scene of high-stakes poker games fueled by flight pay but mostly empty now.

The Dodge angles across blacktop going soggy in the heat to the Control Tower, three cinderblock stories and a fourth, mostly green-tinted glass, built by the Americans. Stairs like a fire escape climb its side. The Ops Office is on the ground floor. In that distant era Before the War, Web Allen's heard, Garbutt Field didn't amount to much, just a short grass runway, a terminal in a tin hut and a windsock on a pole, but the Americans soon fixed that. An Aviation Engineer Battalion arriving in March '42 stretched the runway to 5,000 feet and covered it with all-weather steel matting, built another crossing runway, blacktopped that, built blacktopped taxiways and hardstands beside them on which to park aircraft and earthern revetments like great gray jello molds, bomb splinter protection, around the hardstands, erected the quonsets and blacktopped the area around them and Garbutt Road, all this blacktop churned out by the 10th Engineer Asphalt Co. at its portable plant still going strong in the scrub south of Townsville.

Some of the steel matting was replaced a month ago and any day now, the rumor is, the first ATC C54 Direct From The States (via Honolulu, Johnson Island, Pago Pago and New Caledonia) will land at Garbutt Field!

The steel matting glitters in the sun under a shimmer of heat waves. There's a big-bellied slab-sided B24 Liberator bomber, Macon Mabel on its nose, warming up on the concrete apron in front of the Control Tower. The thunder of its engines rolls across the field. Its twin vertical rudders, big as barn doors, bear the skull-and-crossbones insignia of the 90th Heavy Bomb Group, also known as the Jolly Rogers, Col. Kelly (Killer) Rogers commanding, which claims to be, the unit slogan, "The Best Damn Heavy Bomb Group in the World." Well, the best anyway, Web Allen recollects, at dropping to the goddamn Japs at Buna Government Station the ammunition, rations etc. the Division so desperately needed.

Fazoli brakes the Dodge to a jolting stop at a rudimentary pole fence outside the Ops Office, where three jeeps stripped of their canvas tops are parked like horses in a Western movie. A GI in khaki cutoffs, GI shoes, dogtags on a leather thong and a cardboard pith helmet, a popular USAAC uniform, comes out of Ops and stands blinking in the blazing sunlight, scratching his crotch.

Scratching his crotch!

Sudden as a panther springing, Web Allen's prickly heat erupts. A thousand tiny devils wielding red-hot pitchforks prance across his crotch. He grits his teeth and stifles a groan. His private parts are shaved bare and slathered with gentian violet, the treatment of choice for prickly heat at the 12th Station Hospital. "The old Navy treatment," the medic who shaved and slathered him said. "Scrape and paint fore and aft." This treatment is largely worthless but for the hilarity it provides. Jill Tucker, satisfied the g.v. will not rub off on her private parts, thinks his blue balls a scream. She heard about blue balls, she says, but never actually saw any. They're no joke though with his prickly heat raging. Web Allen would give a month's pay, $352 with his longevity and overseas bounce, to claw at his crotch. Scratch! But that's a disgusting habit and the relief it provides is short-lived. In the long run it just makes the prickly heat worse. Spreads it, they say. He grits his teeth and thinks about the treat it would be to sit naked on a slab of ice, which he was made to do many years ago at a fraternity initiation. His prickly heat wanes, waxes fierce again, fades.

Fazoli opens the rear door. Web Allen tells Borgan wait, gets out of the Dodge, glares at the GI who triggered his prickly heart and goes into Ops. The Macon Mabel is waddling onto the main runway. A counter divides Ops. Behind it a GI in khaki cutoffs is updating the Flight Information blackboard, everywhere CLR (Clear) but for DBO (Dobodura) and NZB (Nadzab), which have SC2 (Scattered Cloud at 2,000 feet). Another GI in cutoffs is pecking at a typewriter like a chicken pecking gravel. The Ops officer, a captain, fully-clothed, with his feet on his desk, is reading an Armed Force paperback edition of "The Origin of Species." In the other half of Ops, two pilots sporting silver wings who look to Web Allen to be about seventeen, wearing grubby khakis and

Fifty-Mission caps, are slouched on an old sofa belching stuffing and a salvaged aircraft bucket seat, reading comicbooks.

The captain takes his feet off his desk, marks his place among the species and comes to the counter. "Yessir, Colonel, what." Then waits, conversation on hold while the Macon Mabel roars down the main runway. "Can we do for you?" Web Allen produces six copies of his precious Authorization for Use of Military Aircraft. The captain takes three. "Yo, Sikorsky! You flyin' the colonel here to Woory? Look alive."

The seventeen year-olds rise languidly, stuff the comicbooks in their pockets and come forward. "Roger," the one wearing blue cowboy boots says. "Yawl got wheels, Cuhnel? Less git rot ott the airyplane then."

The airyplane is a C60, a small silver craft with two engines, on a hardstand halfway down the taxiway. Sikorsky pops the cabin door. Fazoli digs Borgan's valpak out of the Dodge. Borgan grabs it. "Got to handle with care," he says. "There some medicine in there the Lieutenant runs the O Club uh uh gave me."

Web Allen instructs Fazoli. "I should be back by nineteen-hundred but you check with Ops and be here. And get a haircut."

"Yessir!" Fazoli, showing the Air Corps a snappy salute, says, then jumps in the Dodge and tears down the taxiway at 40 mph. Fazoli's a speed freak but the Base Section speed limit is 25 mph.

Web Allen and Borgan climb into the C60. The cabin, nine seats divided by a narrow aisle, is somewhat warmer than a crematorium. "Yawl sit fohwud so's we git us a bettuh trim and buckle up now," Sikorsky says and goes into the cockpit with his copilot and closes the cockpit door.

They sit forward, Web Allen to starboard as befits his rank, and buckle up. Borgan tucks his valpak between his legs and leans across the aisle, over his sulks, leering, his old fawning self again. "This a purty nice airplane you got, Colonel. Purty nice for the Mile-High Club, huh?"

"Oh hell," Web Allen says. "This isn't my airplane. Second

Air Depot just lets me use it once in awhile. And if you ask me, the Mile-High Club is a lot of baloney!"

Rebuffed, Borgan sulks again, staring out the plexiglass window at his elbow. The Mile-High Club. Its members or alleged members claim to have enjoyed heterosexual congress in a USAAC aircraft at an altitude of 5,280 feet or more. Which is possible, Web Allen supposes. There are no doubt some sluts among the Army, Navy and Air Evac nurses and Red Cross female personnel likely to find themselves a mile up in a USAAC aircraft. Pilots are all quick to offer females, civilians too though that's a court-martial offense, rides in "their"aircraft, never mind those aircraft are the property of the Government of the United States. More likely though, Web Allen thinks, the Mile-High Club is an adolescent pilots' fantasy.

And the C60, for all practical purposes, never mind the Government of the United States, belongs to USAAC Col. Robert (Big Bob) Betrandus, the Second Air Depot commander, who always makes it out to be a great big favor when on rare occasions he lets Col. Web Allen use it. Three rare occasions counting this one. And Web Allen must first go through a lot of red tape. Get an Authorization for Use of Military Aircraft approved by Service Force HQ, endorsed by Fifth Air Force and Fifth Air Force Service Command, which takes about three weeks, longer if his original request is lost or pigeon-holed. And then, sometimes, the C60 is "not available" because Col. Betrandus is up up and away in it on one of his frequent forays to Sydney.

Before The War, Web Allen's heard, Big Bob was an airline vice-president. He got a captain's direct commission and was rapidly promoted. No years and years of weekly drills and two-week summer camps and three-plus years of active service, some of it dammed active, for him. And his promotion to bird colonel (temporary) pre-dates Web Allen's by three days. Which makes Big Bob if push comes to shove U.S. Armed Forces SOPOD (Senior Office Present on Duty) in Townsville. He has the time-in-grade. Three damn days.

The Bloody Wet | 65

The C60's starters whine. The engines cough, sputter, belch blue smoke and settle into a reassuring roar. Sikorsky runs them up, throttles back and the C60 trundles out of the hardstand and along the taxiway and onto the main runway, where Sikorsky runs the engines up again and exchanges garbled conversation with the Control Tower. Then they're rolling, gaining speed. The Control Tower flashes by and Web Allen, bracing his feet, sucking up his gut, never quite sure any aircraft with him in it will get safely off the ground, concentrates on getting the C60 safely off the ground.

He gets it off, safely. The wheels thunk into their wells, the C60 begins its climb and Web Allen peers down through the plexiglass at his elbow at Townsville. His fiefdom, so to speak. There's not much to see. Castle Hill's long hogback, lots of corrugated tin roofs, the harbor, Magnetic Island. The C60 crosses the coast, Magnetic Island slides away and there's nothing to see but sea and the massed clouds piling up on the horizon. The C60, Web Allen knows, will fly north over the sea parallel to the coast because the air there is smoother. The thermals rising from the parched littoral make the air there bumpy.

It is remarkable, Web Allen thinks, here he is a man who Before The War was up in but one aircraft, that over Mert's protests, an old Ford tri-motor the year (1936) they were giving ten-minute rides for $5 at the Pierce County Fair, and now he's an expert. Truth be told, he had some qualms about the tri-motor. While a lawyer for the Milwaukee St. Paul & Pacific Railroad in the late 1920s, settling claims for errant livestock killed by trains, he saw an airplane crash. It was a homemade contraption that "flew" barely twenty feet and the lone pilot wasn't killed or even injured, only bruised. Still.

But he's been up in a dozen aircraft counting this one, he still can tick them off, in the last fourteen months and, but for takeoffs and landings, so long as the weather is good and he can see the ground (or sea), he enjoys flying. Suspended in space, he seems also to be suspended in time, all his earthly cares on hold. On the ground a hundred things bedevil him, the incompetents he commands high on the list, all that suppressed anger, regrets both vague and specific, the late Sgt. Clark one of them, what he's doing to Mert another, though Mert doesn't know it he knows it. On the ground he worries. Guilt and worry chip at his sanity, which sometimes seems to be unraveling like an old torn sweater. Flying, up up and away in the wild blue yonder, the guilt and worries fade away, left far behind. Some literate pilots of course, that Frenchman for one, St. Somebody, have been saying this for years, touting the "peace" they find high in the sky. The "aloneness," some call it.

Alone in the sky (but for Sikorsky and the copilot, out of sight, and Borgan and Borgan's asleep, his mouth open, his sunglasses blank as bug's eyes, his red meaty face oddly vulnerable), Web Allen puts Mert and the late Sgt. Clark aside and dwells for a time on the wonderful surprising ridiculous troublesome fact he's in love! With Jill Tucker. He doesn't know what else to call it. And it is, patently, ridiculous. There's Mert and their daughters, Barbara, 17, Betsy, 13. And he as the damn saying goes is old enough to be Jill Tucker's father. She's twenty-four. A wonderful girl. Well, woman. Far more experienced in bed than he, it's clear. My god, the things she does and is teaching him to do! But it's not just the sex. Jill has a quick mind, great sense of humor. When with her, even when thinking about her, he feels young again, all things still possible, the future though fraught with dilemmas exciting. Love has him by the heels.

The C60's engines drone away, steady as a rock. The sunshine pouring through the plexiglass is warm at 5300 feet. A mile high. Web Allen dozes. Then wakes with a start when the C60 performs a slight rolling motion and squashes his nose against the plexiglass. There's another aircraft, a C47, approaching, waggling its wings in greeting. In an instant it flashes by.

* * *

The C47 is the Lucky Lil, three hours out of Seven-Mile Strip, bound for Townsville. Billy Gote doesn't know who Lucky Lil is or was but her voluptuous figure in a G-string with bare boobs big as basketballs reclines beneath his cockpit window. The Lucky Lil was First Lt. Archie Hunker's aircraft before Hunker, a senior 34th Troop Carrier pilot, got a sweet assignment flying some general around. He also got a spanking new 47 in which to fly this general around and Billy Gote got the Lucky Lil.

Billy puts the Lil back on George, the automatic pilot, taps his copilot's wrist and points at the coast drawing close to starboard: dark green mangrove swamps and, the tide at ebb, wide gray-green mudflats.

"You ever get in trouble along here, Lieutenant," Billy, shouting in view of the engine noise, says. "You mayday, hope the tide's out, pick one of them mudflats without any goddamn stumps sticking up in it and belly-in wheels-up. Same the tide's in but you can't see the goddamn stumps then. You'll slide a mile but live and talk about it. Sit tight then. Sooner later somebody with a boat come along."

Second Lt. Ronald Donald, a heavyset young man with a sunburned face, a spanking new replacement pilot with silver wings still sparkly as the Coral Sea, nods, just as if he understands this good advice. Lt. Gote is "checking him out" on this flight though reluctant to do so. The 34th Troop Ops officer insisted on grounds the squadron needs qualified pilots. Lt. Donald wishes Lt. Gote would let him fly the aircraft but he's not going to make a federal case out of it. He wants to make a good impression and Lt. Gote's a hard-bitten veteran, sixteen months in Swappa.

"Roger," Billy Gote, concluding a static-laced conversation with the Garbutt Field Control Tower, says. They're cleared to land. Roger is USAAC lingo for "I read you loud and clear, Message copied, Orders received and understood, Will proceed as instructed, I agree one-hundred percent, Okay, Gotcha, End of communication."

Billy Gote's conversation with the Control Tower does not though he's wearing his headset disturb the Lil's radioman, Cpl. Ernest Johnson, a skinny kid in green fatigue coveralls in the tiny compartment full of radio gear behind Lt. Donald off the narrow passageway leading back to the cargo compartment. Johnson's got his nose in a Flash Gordon comicbook full of nubile female Space Cadets in scanty uniforms. Sgt. Clive (Porky) Wallace, the Lil's flight engineer, is asleep in the tiny compartment across the passageway. A stocky Georgia cracker with a dark tan, Porky's hacked the arms off his coveralls to display his impressive biceps and tattoos. The left one's a heart with "Mother" on its surface. The right says "The South Will Rise Again!"

There also are two passengers aboard the Lucky Lil, Pfc. Eddie Devlin and Siggie Ferk, the World's Greatest Juggling Accordionist. They're sitting scrunched up wrapped in smelly o.d. blankets on the hard green plastic bench-seats in the cargo compartment, also the passenger cabin. Eddie's half asleep. Siggie Ferk, a fat little man with a bald head and weary eyes, is awake and in pain. A molar with a missing filling is giving him throbbing hell. He massages the hole in the molar, roughly the size of the old bomb craters he saw around Seven-Mile Strip and in Port Moresby, with his tongue, but the goddamn hole goes right on throbbing.

Siggie Ferk's beginning to wish he'd let the blacksmith disguised as a dentist in the 7th Station Hospital at Seven-Mile pull the goddamn tooth. But when he lost the filling biting on a bone chip in a godawful mutton stew in the Fifth Air Force HQ Officers Mess it looked like a good excuse to get the hell out of New Guinea and back to Australia with his 2A FAMOCA (First Available Military or Commercial Aircraft) Travel Priority. Three weeks in Guinea was enough, man his age, forty-eight. Well, fifty-five. Somewhere along the line his agent, Manny Mannstein, took seven years off his age. Whatever, the New Guinea weather was a bitch, fry eggs on the goddamn airstrips except there weren't any eggs, real eggs, just that powdered shit. Or a goddamn thing fit to drink, not for a man once a headliner in the nation's top Burly-Qs with a fifth-a-day Canadian Club habit. Jungle juice the GIs cook up in 55-gallon oil drums full of rotten fruit and old tires would kill a man. Goddamn GIs, raised on the goddamn movies, don't know a terrific act when they see one either, three Indian clubs in the air, the left-hand part of "Lady of Spain" and a few blue jokes.

But, prodded by Manny ("Great press, Sig, and your career could use a boost, which you better boost it or get used to the County Fair circuit"), he agreed to three months on the Swappa circuit, which the B-films producer turned major booking USO tours practically went off in his pants over because one-man shows, he could send them anywhere, no logistics problems, right up to the goddamn front. Or damn near. Technically, Siggie Ferk supposes, the goddamn front or fronts, where the shooting is, are two or three-hundred miles from the airstrips outside Port Moresby. But that was close enough. Still a Combat Area. Christ, there were two air raids. Well, Yellow Alerts, no actual enemy planes overhead or bombs dropping. The old slit trench in which he lay curled in a fetal position awaiting a violent death reeked of urine, goddamn GIs piss anywhere, and the only prayer he could dredge up, "Now I lay me down to sleep," was singularly inappropriate.

He's done his bit, Siggie Ferk figures, a month in Australia and three weeks in New Guinea. He'll get the goddamn tooth fixed in Townsville, find an Aussie dentist, Army dentists are all butchers. Look up Jill Tucker too. The Red Cross honcho in Moresby said she was in Townsville. Hell of a lay as he remembers it though he was pretty drunk at the time and lucky. J.T. prefers rank. That was her reputation anyway in Sydney. But the general she was shacking-up with was off somewhere seeing to The War and they hit it off pretty good, him and J.T., over drinks at the Service Force HQ Officers Club. He has a lot of stories of course, some true, about folks in Show Biz and their sexual shenanigans, which J.T. found interesting. Gave great head too. Made him reciprocate but no harm in that. If there's any C.C. in Townsville, J.T. will know how to get it. Or he'll look up the colonel at that Air Corps outfit, Second Air Depot, colonel loved the show and had some C.C. Then on to Sydney on good old FAMOCA. No doubt the Service Force HQ Special Services officer (a second-run theater manager in civil life) will make him do six more weeks, finish his tour, which he will in half-civilized places in Australia or if he can swing it entertain the Navy on a big ship bound for The States. Where Manny will bill him Direct from the Fighting Front, keep him off the goddamn County Fair Circuit. Hayseeds don't know a terrific act when they see one either.

The World's Greatest Juggling Accordionist pulls his smelly blanket tighter and tongues the hole in his molar. The goddamn airplane seems to be going down.

The Lucky Lil's slow descent wakes Eddie Devlin. He lights a cigarette and peers through a grimy plexiglass window, pleased to find the coast close at hand. This is Eddie's sixth flight, sixth time up in a C47, and while he pretends to be as nonchalant about air travel as he guesses Billy Gote really is he really doesn't like flying, especially over water. But this flight will soon be over and by sunset they'll be back at Seven-Mile Srip, another long flight over the Coral Sea history, the greatest ham-and-egg flight ever in Swappa, maybe the whole world. And soon then he'll be rich.

The Lucky Lil's descent also wakes Sgt. Porky Wallace. Yawning, he cocks a trained ear to the engines and is pleased to detect the port Pratt & Whitney R-1830-92 running a smidgen rough. Nothing to worry about but a good excuse to RON in Townsville and with a little luck (well, a lot of luck) get laid. Not at a cathouse either, they're Off Limits now anyway. But there's some amateur gash in Tville and while the odds on getting any of that are pretty high, around 3,000-to-1, Porky's confident that if anybody can get some, he can. If he says so himself (and he often does) he does pretty well in the gash department. He has some, not much, Southern charm, a lot of simple animal lust and, though no Boy Scout, he's prepared. There's a practically clean khaki uniform with his stripes, gaudy Fifth Air Force shoulder patch and medal ribbons attached, and a tie, you have to wear a goddamn tie in Tville, and a carton of Fleetwoods in his musette bag, and four issue condoms in his wallet.

Billy Gote disengages George. The Lucky Lil banks gently to port, out over the sea, then to starboard over the harbor, full of ships, and the scrub south of Townsville. Lt. Donald, peering down through his tilted window, is surprised to see a blacktop plant belching black smoke. His daddy has a blacktop plant in Des Moines and is doing pretty well blacktopping Army camps. The Lil begins to bounce and sway in the thermals. There's another C47 below them settling on Garbutt Field's main runway.

"Put her down, Lieutenant," Billy Gote says: an error in judgment perhaps, but the Squadron Ops officer will demand a report on Lt. Donald's skills.

Lt. Donald, startled, grabs his yoke and squeaks, "Full flaps and wheels!" Billy Gote, acting copilot, complies and reports: flaps full and locked, wheels down and locked. Porky Wallace plucks a ten-inch Stillson wrench from the rack in his compartment and eases up behind Lt. Donald. The Lucky Lil banks clumsily to starboard, levels off, sways, slides over Garbutt Road, sways, drops, lands hard well along the main runway, bounces, lands again, bounces, settles and rolls swiftly by the Control Tower.

"I'll take her!" Billy Gote, grabbing his yoke and chopping the throttles, says. The Lucky Lil, rolling along the main runway, slows. Lt. Donald blushes. Lindbergh he's not.

Porky Wallace relaxes. You never know though. Spanking new copilots sometimes do dangerous things. Asshole Nadler panicked going into Silli Silli, a scary little fighter strip at 4,000 feet in the mountains south of the Markham Valley, grabbed the controls and would've killed them all except Lt. Gote backhanded him across the chops and got the controls back. And there ain't no justice either: Asshole Nadler, grounded, is the Squadron p.o. in Tville, a soft life. It looked like this Donald was going to do something dangerous, Porky would have cold-cocked him with the Stillson.

Billy Gote swings the Lucky Lil off the runway onto the parallel taxiway and onto a hardstand in a revetment a quarter-mile from the Control Tower and kills the engines. Porky Wallace replaces the Stillson, goes aft, pops the door on the left side of the fuselage at the rear of the cargo/passenger compartment and swings it open. Cpl. Johnson removes his headset and stuffs his comicbook in a rack labeled Flares Only, empty of flares but full of comicbooks. Lt. Donald, proving he knows his stuff, fishes the post-landing checklist from under his bucketseat.

"Screw that" Billy Gote says. "Let's get outta here before we fry."

They drop from the open door onto the hardstand where the full force of the heat smites them. A jeep is rolling down the taxiway to pick them up. There's a 47 with a white star on its nose, some brigadier general's airplane, in the next revetment.

"Say, Lootenant," Porky, he's lugging his musette bag, says. "You notice that port engine runnin' a little bit rough? Maybe we should RON. Check the goddamn plugs."

"Forget it," Billy Gote says. "This one them quick turnarounds. I got to run into Tville, get the Base Section Ordnance Office okay a requisition. Then Air Freight is gonna load us with ammunition, high priority cargo, and we are gonna haul ass back to Seven-Mile. ETD prolly fourteen-hundred. You all wait in the canteen. Drink some coffee. Don't run off. That engine ain't got but a eighty hours on it."

Lt. Donald, who doesn't know much, guesses this is S.O.P. (Standard Operating Procedure). Cpl. Johnson doesn't care one way or the other: he leaves the running of the airplane to Lt. Gote. Porky Wallace finds it somewhat mysterious but accepts defeat. The port engine's not running that rough. Usually though, Lt. Gote, a pretty good guy for an officer, will RON as quick as anybody. Not always though, the cargo's high priority. Sometimes ammo is. They flew a quick turn-around in October with some high priority. A flush toilet for some goddamn general, nothing in the airplane but the toilet, some plumbing stuff and a hundred feet of pipe.

The jeep pulls up and they climb in, no mean trick, six of them and Siggie Ferk's bulging valpak, accordion in a battered case and a barracks bag full of souvenirs. The jeep drops them at the Red Cross Canteen. The driver tells Siggie there's a GI bus stops at the Canteen that will take him to the George Hotel. The 47 that landed ahead of the Lil is parked on the apron. Four GIs are unloading it, tossing mailbags into a waiting deuce-and-a-half while two second johns with holstered .45s stand watching them.

"That's the courier plane," Billy Gote, continuing Lt. Donald's education, says. "Good duty. Fly the safe-in-hand mail, Sydney to Nadzab and back, month at a time. RON in Sydney or Brisbane couple times a week. Get laid if you're lucky."

The Canteen's still Closed. Billy Gote leads them around behind it, a Ford panel truck parked there, and pounds on a door labeled Staff Only. A chubby blonde in the Red Cross tropical uniform (white blouse, seersucker skirt, loafers, minimal undergarments) opens it eventually and squeals, "Bill-ee!"

"Hi, Flots."

"Hey, long time no! Come on in."

They follow Flots' wiggly seersucker bottom through a storeroom into the Canteen. The storeroom's full of flour and sugar in fifty-pound sacks, lard in five-gallon tins, a broken doughnut machine and U.S. Army tires. There's a cluttered desk with a phone in one corner. Pops, a skinny old Australian who works for the Red Cross and flogs tires on the side, is fiddling with the doughnut machine. The Canteen proper has a long counter with stools, a dozen tables crawling with flies and numerous posters on its curved walls. Loose Lips Sink Ships, Support Your American Red Cross, Axe the Axis, Buy War Bonds, etc. A dozen GIs, airport personnel in cutoffs and greasy fatigues, are seated at the counter gassing with Jetsam, a skinny brunette in Red Cross tropicals. Cpl. Arnold Saljeski is straddling a stool but says nothing.

"How come the Canteen's closed?" Porky Wallace says.

"Doughnut machine broke," Jets says.

"Okay, crew," Billy Gote says. "Drink some coffee and wait for me."

"Hey!" Flots says. "There's a big party tonight at the Manor. You should come, Billy. It's a farewell party for Boots and Rose Pearl Stevens."

"Farewell? Where they going?"

"New Guinea. Port Moresby."

"Moresby! You tellin' me the Red Cross is sending women to Moresby! Moresby ain't been secure but about a year."

"Oh, don't be a smart ass," Jets says. "They would've gone, we all would've gone, a year ago. The Army wouldn't let us."

"When they going?"

"FAMOCA," Flots says. "Come to the party. You and the lieutenant here. I don't believe I know."

"Wish we could," Billy Gote. "Hell, I was gonna RON they could fly Moresby with me. Or Seven-Mile. That prolly where they going. There ain't much anything left in Moresby. Well, I guess there's a Red Cross guy there. But this one of them quick turn-arounds. Tell Boots I'll see her in Guinea."

"Are you going to introduce me to the lieutenant here?"

"Oh sure. Uh Flots uh this." Billy Gote flounders. Flots' true name and Lt. Donald's escape him.

"Gwen Miller," Flots says, and thinks: the things I did for you and you can't remember my name!

"Ronald Donald," Lt. Donald says and essays a little humor. "Gwen Miller the band leader, huh?"

"Okay," Billy Gote says, "You two get acquainted. C'mon,

Eddie."

Saljeski slides from his stool and the GI in cutoffs who triggered Col. Web Allen's prickly heat bursts from the storeroom with a sizzling news flash. "MacArthur's plane just landed!"

This event takes precedence over everything else. The troops Gen. Douglas MacArthur commands rarely see him or he them. He only sees other generals, admirals, Field Marshal Sir Thomas Blamey, Australia's prime minister, junketing U.S. Congressmen and war correspondents from Life Magazine, The New York Times and Chicago Tribune. He does nor review troops or pin medals on people. Well, he did pin one, a Silver Star, on a Texas congressman named Johnson who, out on a junket, flew one aborted mission in a B26 bomber without wetting his pants, but that was politics. GIs in Brisbane sometimes glimpse MacArthur in the Brit limousine on loan from the Commonwealth in which he travels the eight blocks between the Lennon Hotel and GHQ four times daily, he lunches with his family, but that's about it. Any opportunity to see the great man in the flesh is not to be missed. Flots unlocks the front door and Billy Gote, Eddie and Saljeski, who says they have plenty of time, join the pell-mell rush from the Canteen.

A big silver B17 with The Spirit of Bataan on its nose, all take-offs temporarily halted in view of its presence, is rolling down the main runway. It reaches the apron, performs a stately 180-degree turn on the apron and parks behind the courier plane. Its propellers wind down. Curious personnel, American and Australian, held back by RAAF sentries, gawk at it. More citizens of both nations, The War on hold, stream from the Air Freight sheds and the RAAF barracks. The Garbutt Field commander, RAAF Wing Cmdr. Haines Hewlitt-Packard, who doesn't particularly admire Gen. Douglas MacArthur or any bloody Yank, observes all this from his second-floor barracks office. He'd be down there to greet MacArthur of course, that's protocol, but his communications sergeant, who often monitors the bloody Yanks' radio transmissions, told him MacArthur's not aboard The Bataan. Ops also know that and this information spreads quickly among the gawkers. Shit! Mac ain't on the fuckin airplane!

Nevertheless those watching linger. Four GIs emerge from a hangar with a portable stairway on wheels and roll it to the door midway along The Bataan's fuselage. The door opens and several people emerge: a short fat old man in a seersucker suit and panama hat assisted by a tall young man in a dark civilian suit, an American captain and first john in natty uniforms and three men in wrinkled suntans with green-and-gold shoulder patches. This party straggles into Ops and additional information ripples through the crowd. Shit, it just some fuckin congressman and fuckin war correspondents. The crowd breaks up. The courier plane winds up its engines and trundles onto the main runway.

"Show's over," Billy Gote says. "Let's get our show on the road. Everthing all set, Sal?"

"Just about," Saljeski says and leads the way to his Ford truck parked behind the Canteen. They climb in and follow the deuce-and-a-half with the safe-in-hand mail out the Main Gate onto Garbutt Road, Eddie in the back with a jumble of movies in round film cans and a broken projector. "There is one fuckin little hitch. Motor Pool sergeant was gonna give us a deuce-and-a-half, they caught him floggin' gas. He's in the fuckin Flat Mountain Stockade. So we got to liberate a fuckin deuce. No sweat though. I can do that. Oh shit, the fuckin bridge."

"No sweat!" Billy Gote says, while they sit waiting and westbound traffic rumbles across the new span over the Ross River. "Jeezuzz! We got to liberate a truck! Like we ain't got our butts on the line awready! Tell us more, Sal."

* * *

Aboard the The Spirit of Bataan, a master-sergeant, two techs, a staff and a corporal, there's lots of rank on The Bataan, survey the green vomit splattered on the royal-blue carpet in the main cabin. The Bataan's a pretty fancy aircraft. The main cabin used to be the bomb-bay and some additional space aft. It's paneled, has six leather easy chairs bolted to the floor and large windows that used to be the waist-gun ports. The Bataan's not armed but is accompanied by two P38 fighters in Australia, they're landing now, and an even dozen in forward areas though it seldom ventures there. There's another cabin aft fitted with a dozen seats like those found on airliners and aft of that a john with a real commode and a holding tank.

"All right," the master-sergeant says. "Let's get this goddamn mess cleaned up."

"Why the hell," one tech says. "Dint the old fart hit the john he was gonna barf?"

"Prolly dint know we got a john," the other tech says.

"Fuckin PIOs know we got one," the staff says.

"Fuckin PIOs don't know shit!" the first tech says. "What are we gonna do, Sarge? Wait the old fart recovers then continue Moresby?"

"I don't know yet," the master-sergeant says. "Colonel's raising Brisbane on the ACS, find out. But let's get this goddamn mess cleaned up."

This order passes down through the ranks to Cpl. Batista Gomez, who figured all along he would get the clean-up detail. The other non-coms go forward, where they have cramped space in which to loaf and Gomez goes to the john to get water and his mop.

A somewhat similar operation is underway in Ops. U.S. Rep. Festus Lee Claypool, the Number Two Democrat on the House Armed Services Committee, a portly figure at 5-7 and 240 pounds, is sitting on the sofa with the burst stuffing, fanning himself with his panama hat while his aide, Calvin (Ace) Winsome, a former Old Miss basketball star, heir to the third largest cotton brokerage in Dixie, draft-proof in view of his essential employment, dabs at the vomit on Rep. Claypool's floral tie with a wet handkerchief. The Ops staff and several pilots standing around after giving up their seats watch this with interest. Rep. Claypool's the first VIP they've seen since John Wayne the movie star passed through Tville on a USO tour in July.

The PIOs, the flunky captain who takes attendance at the GHQ briefings and a flunky first lieutenant, offer Rep. Claypool water and an aspirin from the Ops first aid kit but he waves them off.

"Ah cain't drank that chlorumated wotta," he says in the cornpone voice Mississippi voters love. "Lawdy me! Ah am nevuh sick in ma tommy! It muss been some thang Ah et. Them Straylin mussels prolly. Mah pore tommy ain't ust that 'xotic fayuh."

Or some thang you drank, you old hypocrite, thinks James Enders, the Stateside pool reporter covering this junket, like a dozen belts of godawful Australian whiskey during their dinner at the National Hotel after Rep. Claypool was granted a brief audience with Gen. Douglas MacArthur. The good bourbon accompanying the junket ran out in Noumea. Enders is an old UP hand, normally the Washington Bureau assignments editor. He assigned himself, UP's turn to staff the pool, to Rep. Claypool's Southwest Pacific fact-finding mission because it looked like a good, i.e., quick and comfortable way, to get a look at the Real War. A reporter at heart, Enders wants a look at the Real War like everybody "stuck in Washington" says they want. But all he's seen so far are sundry brass and PIOs sucking up to old Claypool and now the old fart, he is after all seventy-seven, has taken sick well short of the Real War. He seems to be recovering though. His color's returned, bright pink laced with tiny blue veins. Up close he looks like a map of the Mississippi Delta. And the flunky captain is saying something.

Congressman Claypool, the flunky captain says, though confident his "distress" will soon pass, has decided to RON, "that's Remain Over Night," in Townsville, then fly to Port Moresby in the morning. Arrangements are being made to put the Congressman's party up at the George Hotel. The Bataan will be returning to Brisbane. "General MacArthur has to fly to Canberra tomorrow." But other air transport will be provided and a bus will be along shortly to take the Congressman's party to the George Hotel. "Lieutenant, tell the stewards on The Bataan to bring our baggage in here."

David Dudley Hull breathes a discreet sigh of relief. He's on his way frontwards, Swiller reluctantly put him aboard The Bataan, but in no hurry to reach New Guinea. Jake Jasper can't blame him for this delay. He'll get some self-serving quotes from old Claypool and file something. It'll be embargoed and the Milwaukee Herald won't waste much space on a Dixie Democrat anyway, but that will cover his ass. He asks INS, "Is there a cable office here?"

"Dammed if I know," INS says. "But you can't file from here. You have to safe-in-hand your copy to Brisbane, GHQ censors."

"Oh, sure. Right," Hull says. He's embarrassed to be getting instructions form a little squirt (well, a big squirt) he considers a kid reporter.

"Whar it be," Rep. Claypool says. "Yawl say we be, Cap'n? Townville?" The flunky captain says, That's right, Sir, Townsville. "Well, lawdy me! Ah do bulieve mah litull sistuh Scolett's litull gurl, Bootie Davis, be heeuh. Servin' her cunree inna Murkin Red Cross. Yawl check on that, Calvin. Mebbe Bootie lock and have dinnuh wi' us t'night. And fonn me some whuskey. Not that Straylin whuskey. Suthin' Ah can drank, seddle mah tommy."

* * *

"There's a fuckin pub on Dock Street serves coons," Saljeski says, while westbound traffic rumbles over the new bridge. "The Goose and Feathers. Coons park their fuckin truck behind it. Somebody allas liberatin' one. Guy the Motor Pool give me a universal key and a distributor arm. I'll liberate a fuckin truck. Don't you fuckin worry. But first we're gonna go my girlfriend's house and fix oursells up. I got to put on fatigues like the fuckin coons wear. Harry got shirts with Base Section patches for you guys and a MP armband for you, Eddie, and a fuckin tommy-gun. It ain't loaded. You're gonna be the fuckin MP rides shotgun when we pick up the booze."

"I'm kind of small for an MP," Eddie says.

"So what," Saljeski says. "You ain't gonna arrest nobody. I'm kind a white for a fuckin coon. I'm gonna put some burnt cork on me. What the fuckin Red Cross honcho in Moresby say, he give you my telegram?"

"He said, 'Soldier, that's a mighty big baby! Sixteen pounds!' I said my wife's a big girl."

"That's what Boots said when I asked her use her fuckin Red Cross clout and put a personal message on the ACS. So you guys'd know the day the fuckin booze gonna be picked up."

"Does Boots," Billy Gote says. "Know what that was all about?"

"No," Saljeski says. "I said it was just a joke I was playin' on Eddie. Boots is okay. She said the Red Cross allas sendin' guys been overseas two fuckin years telegrams they is proud poppas. Hey, let's roll!"

They bump across the new bridge behind the deuce-and-a-half with the safe-in-hand mail. The Red Cross is the conduit for urgent messages (births, deaths, etc.) from folks Back in The States to husbands, sons and siblings in Swappa. These come via cable to Brisbane, military cable traffic permitting, and are forwarded by various means to the appropriate Red Cross outpost for delivery.

"When do we get the booze?" Billy Gote says.

"Fourteen-hundred about," Saljeski says.

"Jeezuzz! That's cuttin' in pretty goddamn thin, Sal! It's gonna take us awhile, load it on the airplane, and Garbutt won't clear us for Seven-Mile much after fourteen-thirty."

"Yeah, I know," Saljeski says. "But Burns-Phelps, place we get the fuckin booze, sets the fuckin time. We'll make it though, we don't get held up at the fuckin bridge."

"Which we might," Billy Gote says. "Shit! Lemme think a

minute." He thinks a minute. "Okay. I can't clear for Seven-Mile, I'll clear for Woorammoolla and fly the airplane flat out. I can land Seven-Mile with my lights. Claim I had some kind of malfunction. Squadron C.O. will buy that, he sees some scotch. But no, that ain't such a good idea! Flak all around Moresby prolly think I'm a goddamn Jap and start shootin'! But I can land Woory, fly Seven-Mile in the morning. No, that prolly ain't feasible either! How long, you think, Sal, before the Base Section finds out their booze been liberated?"

"Not very fuckin long. Twenty thirty minutes prolly."

"So RON Woory ain't feasible," Billy Gote says. "USAAC runs the Woory strip. Time we get there the shit be flying. Base Section will figure right away it was flyboys liberate their booze and alert everbody and there's MPs in Woory might want to be heroes. No sweat though. There's a old fighter strip out in the boonies outside Woory. I can land there. We'll sleep in the airplane. Fly Seven-Mile in the morning. Might be listed missing but I'll say we had some kind malfunction then our radio went out. Squadron C.O., he'll buy that he sees some scotch. Fighter strip's beat-up some but I can land there. Guy in the Squadron did last week."

Eddie Devlin doesn't much like this plan but has no say in it. His part in The Great Heist, besides playing the MP riding shotgun when they liberate the booze, was to get Saljeski's message with the pick-up date because he was certain to be at Seven-Mile Strip and Billy Gote might be anywhere, flying some mission. As it happened, he had only two days after the Red Cross honcho in Moresby phoned him with the news about the sixteen-pound baby in which to and find and alert Billy Gote, so Billy could set up their mission to Townsville with his Squadron C.O. Then Eddie forged himself some travel orders. Capt. Panmander is at Arawe. The old coot joined the 112th RCT when it was staging at Oro Bay and made the landing.

"Okay," Saljeski says. "That's settle then. But I figger we'll get the fuckin booze and load it on your airplane in plenty time you can take off today." He halts the Ford for cross-traffic at Townsville's busiest intersection. "What we're gonna do now like I said is fix you guys up at my girlfriend's house. Then kill some fuckin time. Thirteen-hundred, we'll go down the Goose and Feathers. You drop me off and take my truck and go park behind the Special Services Office. There's a slot there says Movie Non-Com. I'll liberate a fuckin coon truck and pick you up and we'll liberate the fuckin booze! That only take about fifteen minutes. Burns-Phelps buggers help load it. Then we haul ass out the field and load it in on your airplane and you're on your fuckin way! I'll dump the fuckin truck out the field and catch the GI bus inna town."

It sounds simple enough but Eddie has a question. "What about the other truck? The one really supposed to pick up the booze? Won't that be this Burns-Phelps place?"

"Harry's gonna take care of that," Saljeski says, trailing the safe-in-hand mail truck through the busy intersection and along Flinders Street. "And my girlfriend, she lives nextdoor the O Club, her chickens allas gettin' out and drivin' the fuckin lieutenant runs the club crazy. We're gonna let them loose." They reach Hill Street. The safe-in-hand mail truck turns left and halts in front of Base Section HQ. There's a two-story stone building across Hill Street with a sign on it. Burns-Phelps Island Traders Pty. Ltd. "There it is," Saljeski says, slowing, then driving on. "The fuckin booze! The loadin' dock is around back in the fuckin alley."

"Jeezuzz!" Eddie says. "It's right across the street from Base Headquarters!"

"No sweat," Saljeski says. "Harry says that's the last place the fuckin Base Section commandos ever think we liberate their fuckin booze."

* * *

The Base Section Officers Club is a small bungalow set on

pilings (nearby Kaloola Creek often goes over its banks during the Bloody Wet) on North Flinders Street beyond the George Hotel. The elderly couple who own it, Ambrose and Mary McNab, are living with their son in Melbourne. Their furniture is stored, their bungalow leased to the War Authority, sub-let it to the Townsville Base Section. The pilings are enclosed now with unpainted lathe lattice-work and this space beneath the bungalow is the Club. It has a new cement floor, wet bar, new loo (female guests use the upstairs loo), dim electric lighting and a walled-off storeroom at one end. This construction was performed by the 202nd Engineer Co. A portable generator bound for the 7th Station Hospital at Seven-Mile Strip but waylaid provides the electricity. The local electric was cut off when the McNabs departed. The upstairs is furnished with army cots. Lucky transient officers sometimes billet overnight there and a few, luckier still, occasionally get laid in one of the bedrooms. The Club manager, Second Lt. Bernard B. (Bernie) Witters, sleeps in the other one.

All the Base Section officers are members but the Club's mainly frequented by warrants, lieutenants, captains, a few majors and Lt. Col Fogerty. Most higher ranks prefer the George Hotel bar. Transient officers except flyboys are granted temporary memberships for a quid, $3.20 in real money. Transient flyboys are not admitted. They and their goddamn ham-and-egg flights are blamed for the perceived shortage of liquor in Townsville. Transient flyboys join the Second Air Depot O Club, which gets its booze in Sydney. There's also a Base Section NCO Club in a ramshackle bungalow in South Townsville, no amenities added, the loo there in the backyard, where card games are played for money and flyboy non-coms with flight pay are welcome, but it's chief function is to distribute the monthly beer ration, two Imperial quarts per member. There's also an Australian officers club, the Australia Club, in an imposing house near the George Hotel, and an Australian Sergeants Mess, reputed to be the best of the lot, somewhere in South Townsville, but nonmembers get into those by invitation only. Few Americans have seen either.

Lt. Bernie Witters is twenty-six. He was an infantry replacement in the 3rd Repple Depple with a life expectancy, he truly believed, of less than the ninety days it took to turn him into a second john when the O Club opened as year ago and a guardian angel disguised as Lt. Col. Fogerty put a clerk at the Rep Dep to work searching 201 (Personnel) Files. This search turned up Witters, in civil life the assistant food-and-beverage manager at the Big Sky Golf & Country Club in Helena, Montana. Fogerty offered him ds tdy to run the club on two conditions: he won't get a promotion while manager and he'll slip Fogerty a jug from the club inventory every now and then. Both conditions were and are fine with Lt. Bernie Witters. He'd rather be a live second john than a dead first with posthumous medals and truly believes Lt. Col. Fogerty saved his life.

Oh God, if only he'd been satisfied with that!

But habit and greed proved too strong for Lt. Witters, a fat little fellow with prickly heat in his armpits, staring at a year's worth of purchase orders, requisitions, War Authority endorsements and largely fictitious inventories scattered across the table in his office, once the bungalow's kitchen. He often filched food and alcoholic beverages at the Big Sky. The O Club serves no food except stuff catered at occasional parties, but alcoholic beverages are like gold, better than gold, in Swappa. Transient officers bound for New Guinea will pay thirty, even forty, dollars for a jug. That big asshole from the Jungle Training Center went fifty for Australian whiskey! Over the months, Bernie Witters has filched from the Club inventory and peddled to transients (no Base Section officers, word would get around) quite a few alcoholic beverages. He has nearly a thousand quid, $3,000 in real money, in a cookie tin, his mother sends him cookies, buried under a jasmine in the bungalow's scraggly yard. But his fat little ass may be on the line. Maj. Warden Nitpicker, the Base Section Finance Officer, thinks it's time he inventoried the Club's liquor.

And Nitpicker once he gets an idea in his head hangs onto it like a goddamn bulldog.

Lt. Witters scratches his prickly heat and stares out the open window at his elbow at the dead brown grass in the yard and his jeep, another perk, parked there. He can lose a few reqs and purchase orders but the Base QM has copies, Nitpicker knows that, and if there is an inventory and the jokers who take it, god forbid, sample some of the bottles in the storeroom. That will be his ass! He's been replacing the beverages he sold with the Club's empties, filling those that contained gin with water, those that contained brandy or whiskey with tea, and placing discreet marks on their labels. He stocks the bar himself each afternoon then locks the storeroom so his bartender, Pfc. Vinnie Dugan, on duty from 1900 to 2200 hours, when the Club closes, doesn't grab one of those. But the jugs he bestowed on Lt. Col. Fogerty were irreplaceable and Dugan. An awful thought smites Lt. Witters. Has Dugan been swiping booze! He's a tough Irish kid from Hell's Kitchen, a clerk days in the 114th Portable Laundry Detachment, claims he was a Blarney Stone bartender Before The War. Dugan nips steadily while on duty, Witters knows that. But if Dugan's been swiping booze!

His only hope, Lt. Witters decides, and it may be a slim one, is somehow to fiddle the figures and jugs after picking up the Club's holiday consignment this afternoon. It's a big consignment, eighty cases. The deuce-and-a-half the 404th QM Truck (C) provides for this mission should be along soon. And he better have a look in the storeroom, goddamn Dugan probably picks locks.

"Cluck!" a White Leghorn hen with insolent beady little eyes, perched on the windowsill at his elbow, says.

"Shoo!" Witters, threatening the Leghorn with a purchase order, squeals. The Leghorn looks him in the eye and shits on the windowsill. "Shoo!" Witters, whacking at the Leghorn with the p.o., squeals. The hen flaps off the windowsill and Witters sees four more shitting on his jeep. "Goddamn chickens!" he squeals, leaps from his chair, races down the stairs, grabs a leftover lathe and charges from the Club, scattering another dozen Leghorns in the Club's driveway, whacking at them with the lathe. The Aussie broad who lives next door and owns the goddamn chickens must let them out on purpose, shit on his jeep, drive him crazy!

A 404th QM Truck (C) deuce-and-a-half pulls into the driveway and the driver sticks his head out of the cab. "Ah s'pose pick you up, Loo'tent, Sir?"

Lt. Witters, winded, pauses in his battle with the Leghorns. He's managed to kill two other times they got out, caught them and wrung their necks, and he'd like to kill more. "In a minute, soldier. I got to get these goddamn chickens out of here. Help me!" The driver considers this. "Come on! Goddamn it, that's an order!"

"Yassuh," the driver says and gets out of his truck. He's a very large man in no shape to chase chickens but an order is an order.

* * *

Pvt. Douglas NMI (No Middle Initial) MacArthur, a thin very black Negro in greasy fatigues, just turned nineteen, with a belly full of good Australian beer, comes out of the rear door of the Goose & Feathers and stands blinking in the blazing sunlight, peering at the half dozen trucks parked across the alley beside the Q&NR spur track that serves the docks.

His surname was handed down by his late great-granddaddy, once the property of an Alabama cotton king of that name. Douglas was selected by his daddy, who while attached to the 42nd (Rainbow) Division supply train in the Other Big War developed a severe case of hero worship for then Col. Douglas MacArthur. A mindless machine in a Fifth Army MRU (Machine Records Unit) dumped Pvt. Douglas MacArthur, just out of Basic Training, into the 404th QM Truck Battalion (C), then preparing for embarkation, and he's been the butt ever since of a lot of low-grade humor generated by those members of the 404th (C) who knew (or later learned) a honky general named Douglas MacArthur is the absolute head honky in this strange place, Swappa. Which is fine with Pvt. Douglas MacArthur. This attention almost sort of makes him "somebody" for the first time in his young life and he laughs right along with everybody else when they call him Dugout.

He's not laughing now though. There's a gap like a missing tooth or an open wound in the row of trucks parked beside the spur, an awful gap where he's pretty sure he parked the deuce-and-a-half he was practice driving, Bumper No. 40444, when Sgt. Washington said, "Stop the Goose, we'll have a beer."

Pvt. MacArthur really didn't want a beer but Sgt. Washington, a Baker Co. HQ non-com, a massive presence at 6-2 and 230 pounds, is checking him out for driver and if he makes driver he'll get out of the Baker Co. Motor Pool, where he now spends his days up to his elbows in gasoline, washing parts, and in time perhaps, his ultimate ambition, make Pfc.! Then write Momma. Private First Class! That will make Momma mighty proud and he was always her favorite, her baby, Lucky Thirteen she call him. Momma cry a lot the morning Daddy walk him out to the County Road to catch the pulp truck to Tallahassee and meet the Draft Man. Daddy cry a little too, tell him be a good soldier, write your Momma. He's not written much though. Writing is hard. He only schooled to sixth grade then quit to work in the fields. But if he make Private First Class.

Fat chance now though if his truck liberated! Fourth Platoon Leader Loo'tent Bannon most likely whup him or skin him. Pvt. MacArthur knows little of the Military Justice System but it's run by white men so assumes its punishments are harsh. Near tears, he limps across the alley, his first new shoes too big, blisters on his heels, and checks all the bumper numbers on the parked trucks. No.40444 is not among them. Cold fear curdles the beer in his belly. A tear rolls down his cheek. He wipes it away and limps back to the Goose & Feathers. Maybe, just maybe, Sgt. Washington, who knows just about everthing, can help him.

Technically, the Goose & Feathers, dim and relatively cool, is closed at 1330 hours, the street door locked, but the alley door is not locked and a dozen Negro GIs are enjoying that cheerful Empire custom called "Afters" as in "after hours" in the public room. The lounge behind the bar, where women are served, is empty. The licensee, Gimpy Callahan, can't legally sell drinks between noon and 1400 hours but he can give them away with the understanding those served will drop a quid note in the brandy snifter on the bar labeled Gallipoli Veterans Fund. Callahan's a Gallipoli veteran with his gimpy leg to prove it. He truly believes all blackfellows to be sub-human but the American sub-species seldom make trouble and he's got a bloody good thing going, the only pub in Townsville that will serve them, and treats them like he treats humans, friendly but reserved.

Sgt. Washington is sitting at the bar with two Third Platoon soldiers, Sgt. Franklin and former sergeant Kayo Jefferson, recently broken to private following a Mess Hall fight. The traces left by his former stripes still adorn his fatigues.

"Yo, Dugout," Sgt. Washington, who is from a place called D-troit and went to Big Ten College for two years to play football, just about the only black man ever did that, says. "I thought you were heading out to the docks, practice shifting?"

"Truck been liberate!" Pvt. MacArthur wails. Another tear rolls down his cheek.

"Oh shit!" Sgt. Washington says. "But you pulled the distributor arm. I saw you do it." Pvt. MacArthur nods and produces this arm from a pocket.

"That don't make no diffence," Sgt. Franklin, a thin man from a place called Clevelan with a scar on his face he got in a knife fight, says. "Muthafuck gonna liberate a truck, he come equip with a distributor om."

"What'll Ah do?" Pvt. MacArthur whines. He's ashamed to be seen crying but can't help it.

"Hey, don' worry, Dugout," former sergeant Jefferson, he's from a place called Philly and used to be a professional fighter, says. "Able Company movin' out t'night and Baker 'cept Foth Platoon. Things be so fucked up the Battalion nobody gonna know you deuce be missin'."

"But they be a trip-ticket wi' ma name on it," Pvt. MacArthur says, sniffling though perceiving a faint glimmer of hope.

In theory, no military vehicle in the Base Section leaves its unit or the Base Section Motor Pool without a trip-ticket noting its driver, destination, odometer reading and Time Out. Time In, odometer reading and fuel added if any are noted later and there's a copy on file. In fact, the Motor Pool sergeant caught flogging gasoline was apprehended when Capt. Dominic Raskovic, the CID commander, on Col. Web Allen's orders, spot-checked a few dozen trip-tickets and discovered the vehicles concerned seemed to be getting about four miles to the gallon.

"Douglas MacArthur be the name on that trip-ticket," former sergeant Jefferson says. "You think anybody Baker Company gonna call up Gee Hait Que and ast him what he done wi' that deuce?" He laughs and so does Sgt. Franklin.

"Kayo's probably right," Sgt. Washington says. "This outfit moves, it's like a Chinese fire drill. We'll be lucky if we don't lose ten trucks before we're in New Guinea. Besides, Baker Company C.O., Captain Helms, he'll likely be too drunk to count trucks. Captain Helms doesn't like the idea he's going to New Guinea."

"Nobody like that idea," Sgt. Franklin says. "They no poontang in Noo Ginny. I seen pitchers. Puss in Noo Ginny, they boobs look like goords, hang down like they gonna fall off, and they skin look like paint peelin'."

"That ain't all," former sergeant Jefferson says. "Fella was in Noo Ginny is in the Twelf Station tell me you poke one you prod turn white and fall off! We bettuh get us some poontang t'night. We be long time 'thout any. Less'n we draw sticks for the second cook. That light-skin boy. Or Dugout here."

"You let Dugout be," Sgt. Washington says. "Don't worry,

Dugout. I'll take care of that trip-ticket when we go back to the Company. Let's have another beer." He adds a quid note to the Gallipoli Veterans Fund and Gimpy Callahan draws four Foster's, a premium ale.

"We goin' back the muthafuckin Company?" Sgt. Franklin says.

"Hell no!" former sergeant Jefferson says. "Not'll it's time we movin' out. We all pack, ain't we, ready go? Let the muthafuck privates strike tents and load up." He turns on his bar stool and addresses four other members of the 404th QM Truck (C) drinking at a table: another large sergeant and three privates from Baker Company's Third Platoon. "Hey, Sar'ent Brown! You all goin' back the muthafuck Company s'afternoon?"

"Hell no!" Sgt. Leroy Brown says. "Not'll we movin' out. This be ower last night in civ'lization. We gonna 'joy owersells!"

"Relax, Dugout," Sgt. Washington says. "We'll go back to the Company when the movement starts. Nobody will notice you then. Fourth Platoon's going to be attached to Charlie Company and nobody in Charlie will know anything about your truck. If your platoon leader, Lieutenant Bannon, asks you anything, he's not very bright. You tell him Four-Oh-Four-Four-Four is on its way to New Guinea like it's supposed to be."

Former sergeant Jefferson drops a quid note in the snifter. "Four more, Mister Gallipolly veteran, you be so kind. Now less give some series thought how we gonna get some poontang ower last night in civ'lization."

Qualms still beset Pvt. MacArthur, but Foster's makes the world brighter and, no drinker, he's soon a little buzzed. He also feels pretty important. So some muthafuck liberate his truck. He's in high society or pretty near, drinking with three sergeants, all growed men. Well, two sergeants and a former sergeant. Momma be proud of him. Maybe.

* * *

Lt. Col. Parnell (Cob) Fogerty, the Base Section chief-of-staff, a muscular man gone to fat (5-9,195 pounds) with bristly black eyebrows and black hair cut short, wearing sweaty khakis but no necktie, sitting at the GI desk in his second-floor Base Section HQ office overlooking Hill Street, scowls at his In and Out and Hold baskets, all full, and silently curses Col. Webster R. Allen. Bastard left him all the paperwork. Goddamn National Guard officer. Weekend Warrior. A lawyer for chrissake, a civilian, while Cob Fogerty slowly climbed through the ranks in the peacetime Army. Stained too. A major relieved during the fighting at Buna Government Station a year ago, his subsequent promotions a mystery. That's the sitrep anyway from Maj. Pete Pulaski, another former chief warrant and one of Fogerty's Old Regular pals at Service Force HQ. Hopped on neckties too, this Allen. Says they make U.S. soldiers look like bellhops and grocery clerks. Not now though in Townsville, Uniform Regulations modified. Lt. Col. Fogerty feels half-naked without his.

But the goddamn Weekend Warrior, unfortunately, has one thing Cob Fogerty can't match. Allen was in combat, not long, about a month, but combat. Lt. Col Fogerty, twenty years in the Army, has yet to fire or hear a shot fired in anger and until and unless he does, which is unlikely, no one including him will ever know for sure just what kind of man Cob Fogerty is. Patriot or coward. And Allen knows that and knows Cob Fogerty knows it and the hell with it. Here comes more goddamn paperwork.

"Safe-in-hand mail, Sir," roly-poly Sgt. Costello, puffing after climbing the stairs from the ground-floor Message Center, says.

"Safe-in-hand mail, Sir." Lt. Col. Fogerty and Sgt. Costello.

Lt. Col. Fogerty grunts, the mail's a hefty bundle, and tells Costello. "Open the window, get some goddamn breeze in here."

Costello opens the window overlooking Hill Street, raising the lower half, trapping in the upper half a large black angry Australian wasp, which begins to buzz and beat its head against the glass. There is no breeze. Costello returns to the tiny office he shares with M/Sgt. Abbott and Fogerty attacks the safe-in-hand mail with the fixed bayonet on a miniature MI rifle. He finds:

Revised Instructions from Service Force HQ for the Salvaging of empty 55-gal. oil drums. Lt. Col. Fogerty scrawls "Salvage O" on the margin and tosses the Revised Instructions in his Out basket.

Unit War Bond Sales, Enlisted Personnel, 1-31 October (Revised). The Townsville Base Section is listed third from last. "Bond O, see me, PF" and into the Out basket.

Service Force Officer Promotions, 1-30 November, two mimeographed pages. Lt. Col. Fogerty scans them. Near-sighted, he reads without spectacles: has no spectacles in fact, reluctant to admit any physical decline. Two Old Regular pals are majors now and Pete Pulaski by god is a light colonel transferred to the Service Force HQ Transport Section.

Technical Modifications, 50-cal. Machine Gun Mounts, 3/4-ton Weapons Carriers. "Ordnance O" and into the Out basket.

Uniform Regulations, Revised. Cavalry Issue "Campaign Hats" no longer may be worn by Service Force personnel. No subordinate immediately coming to mind, it lands in the Hold basket.

An Order from the Service Force Commander, Lt. Gen. Bertram O. Auger: Pilferage continues to be a serious problem on the Swappa docks and all units concerned are directed to take appropriate action forthwith to reduce same. "Provost Marshal, advise me measures, PF" and into the Out basket.

A mysterious blank sheet of paper. A puzzle but best play it safe. Into the HOLD basket.

Revised Instructions for the salvaging of empty 55-gal. oil drums. Oops! Little mixup in the Service Force HQ Message Center. Lt.Col. Fogerty sighs, he's sweating like a pig, and bayonets another envelope.

GENERAL HEADQUARTERS
SOUHWEST PACIFIC AREA

Order No. 404:44   13 December 1943

1. It has come to the attention of this Command that U.S. Armed Forces personnel are transporting intoxicating liquors from the Australian Mainland to Forward Areas under this Command. This practice contravenes Australian Wartime Export Regulations and in view of the climatic conditions prevalent in the Forward Areas is deleterious to the speedy and successful prosecution of the war.

2. The transportation of intoxicating liquors from the Australian Mainland to Forward Areas under this Command therefore is prohibited, effective this date. Subordinate commands will implement appropriate action forthwith.

By Command of: Maj. Gen. Luther B. Haskett,
Gen. Douglas MacArthur   Adjutant-General

"Hot dickety dick!" Lt. Col. Fogerty bounds from his chair clutching GHQ Order 404:44 and dances a clumsy little jig his granddad used to dance expertly at Irish wakes. "Costello!" Sgt. Costello pops into the office. "We got the flyboys by the balls! Finally! Read this! No, read it later. I want copies. For the Provost Marshal. I'll give you a distribution list. Just run a lot of copies! Move!"

Costello grabs GHQ Order 404:44 and heads for the stairs. The mimeograph machine is in the Message Center. Lt. Col. Fogerty returns to his desk, sits and gloats. So GHQ's come to its senses, finally. There'll be no more goddamn ham-and-egg flights full of booze, just ham-and-eggs. The booze will stay in Townsville, as it rightly should. By god this calls for a little celebration. He opens his bottom desk drawer, removes the half-bottle of gin stashed there, pours a healthy snort in his coffee cup and sips it, gloating still.

There have been some bad times in Cob Fogerty's past. That time at Fort Sill for one when they ran out of everything including the vanilla extract and he wound up in the goddamn Infirmary in bed with green rats and hairy red spiders big as saucers. That awful time on the '41 Louisiana Manuevers when, a brand new second john, he was temporarily attached to Maj. Humphrey (Humpty Dumpty) Dumphy's umpires, Humpty Dumpty a goddamn rare Army teetotaler, and had to pretend he had terminal laryngitis and gulp some kind of cough syrup the label said was 20 percent alcohol by volume. Coming over on the boat was no fun either. Some cocksucker got into his valpak, a captain's valpak no less, and liberated half his Jim Beam. He had to ration himself severely the rest of the way to Sydney. Running out is a constant worry. But GHQ Order 404:44 will make things better. And he still has a jug of Gilbeys stashed under the bed in his room at the George Hotel and he'll get another jug or two tonight from Lt. Witters at the O Club. The Club is picking up its holiday booze today.

In fact, he observes through his open window, a deuce-and-a-half with the canvas top over its bed rolled down is clumsily backing up to the Burns-Phelps loading dock in the alley across Hill Street and two Burns-Phelps employees in baggy coveralls directed by a third with a clipboard are pushing two pallets stacked with booze in wooden cases across the dock. He can't spot Witters but an MP lugging a tommy-gun is climbing out of the deuce-and-a-half, ready to repel boarders. Skinny little fellow for an MP. They must be scraping the bottom of the barrel Back in The States.

Lt. Col. Fogerty pours himself another snort. What the hell, fresh supplies are at hand. And there's more safe-in-hand mail but to hell with it. He'll wade through it later or dump in on Allen's desk. But there's a small blue envelope mixed in with the safe-in-hand, addressed to the U.S. Army Commander, Townsville. Be dammed. The Weekend Warrior's got something going with an Aussie broad? Talk is he's screwing one of the Red Cross cunts. What the hell. In Allen's absence, Lt. Col. Parnell Fogerty is U.S. Army Commander, Townsville. He bayonets the blue envelope.

> Dear Mr. U.S. Army Commander:
> I live on N. Flinders St. next door by your Officers Club and sometimes my chickens they are White Leghorns get out and go over there and the officer there I don't know his name but he is a Leftenant chases them and they don't lay eggs and I think he killed 2. I try and keep them in but sometimes they get out. I work for Leftenant Col. Flapp your Quartermaster and I am all alone by myself since my husband Mr. Rooney went missing at Singapore. I hope you will say some thing to your Leftenant and also pay me for the 2 chickens he killed they were worth 2 quid 6p ea.
> Mrs. Dwight (Mickey) Rooney, Lemon Cottage, 2022 N. Flinders St.

Oh shit! Another Allied Relations Problem. Well, Allen can handle it. He's the goddamn diplomat. Husband missing at Singapore though? Lt.Col. Fogerty wonders how big Mrs. Dwight (Mickey) Rooney is? He likes big women and he's getting pretty tired of the skinny little maid at the George. Mrs. Rooney's letter lands in the Hold basket. He'll query Witters. Witters must know Mrs. Rooney's size if he's killing her chickens and he'll be back at the Club in a few minutes. The deuce-and-a-half in the alley across Hill Street, the skinny little MP perched on its tailgate, is pulling away from the Burns-Phelps loading dock.

White Leghorns. Cob Fogerty though not much given to introspection remembers his Ma had White Leghorns. Sold the eggs for pin money. Before Pa got sick and they lost the farm outside Moline and young Cob at twenty-one, nothing better to do, enlisted in the United States Army. Pa never got over it, losing the farm. Got a night watchman's job at the ADM grain elevator in Moline but hated the city, died within the year and Ma a year later. Some kind of cancer, both of them. Big brother Bill too in '35, not yet forty. He's the only one left not counting a bunch of cousins he wouldn't know if he saw them. Lt. Col. Fogerty raps his knuckles on his desk, though it's not wood, and sips his gin. So it goes, life. And what he ought to be thinking about, forget the White Leghorns, is implementing forthwith the appropriate action cited in GHQ Order 404:44.

Sipping his gin, gazing out his open window, Lt.Col. Fogerty thinks about that. Goddamn flyboys of course will try to evade, circumvent, GHQ Order 404:44. Bet on that. Goddamn island traders too no doubt. Burns-Phelps, Cummins & Campbell. Selling booze to flyboys at inflated prices suits them fine, screw GHQ and the Wartime Export Regulations. He'll send both firms copies of Order 404:44 though. Might do some good, they see MacArthur's name. Aussies think MacArthur saved their ass. Copy the RAAF joker runs Garbutt Field too, the one who hates Yanks. Start spot checks, random vehicles bound for the airfield.

What the hell!

Another deuce-and-a-half is backing up to the Burns-Phelps loading dock. A huge MP with a tommy-gun climbs from it. So does Lt. Bernie Witters: Looks like Witters anyway. Witters, if it is Witters, Lt. Col. Fogerty squints across the street, knocks at the dock door. The guy with the clipboard emerges and a discussion ensues. It grows heated. Witters, by god it is Witters, waves papers at the guy with the clipboard and the guy with the clipboard waves papers at Witters.

Cold fear curdles the gin in Cob Fogerty's belly. He leaps from his chair, sticks his head out the open window and bellows, his big parade ground voice, "Lieutenant! What the hell's going on over there!"

Lt. Bernie Witters, startled by this voice from on high that sounds like the wrath of God, executes a swift about-face, locates the voice and shouts, squeakily. "Sir! This m-man says we already p-picked up our liquor. I m-mean, somebody d-did, Sir."

"Get the goddamn sitrep and get over here! On the double!"

"Yessir!"

"I'll kill the goddamn flyboys!" Fogerty, swiftly surmising a terribly calamity has taken place, bawls. He pounds the windowsill. The raised window jars loose and falls on his neck like a dull guillotine. The trapped wasp, free, stings his right ear and Fogerty, trapped, howls. "Costello! Abbott!"

M/Sgt. Abbott pops into the office and struggles with the window. The wasp stings Fogerty's other ear and wings away. Lt. Witters jumps from the loading dock and starts across Hill Street at a fast lope. Two elderly Australian females, the Cummins sisters, rolling down Hill Street on their tandem bicycle, run him down. The front wheel takes Witters in the crotch and levels him. He squeals, the sisters squeal, the bicycle cartwheels and so do the sisters: a tangle of black cotton stockings, white petticoats, straw hats and wicker baskets. Witters is first on his feet though bent double. Clutching his crotch, he starts after his garrison cap, rolling down Hill Street, then stoops to assist one of the sisters, likewise rolling down Hill Street.

"Leave her!" Lt. Col. Fogerty, still stuck in the window, bellows. "Get your ass over here!" To hell with Allied Relations.

* * *

"We did it! We fuckin did it!" Saljeski says for the tenth or twelfth time, pounding the steering wheel on Pvt. Douglas MacArthur's deuce-and-a-half, bouncing through a pothole at 40 mph. "How you like the way I liberate this fuckin deuce? I had a stick a distributor arm in it."

"Oh you're a marvel all right," Billy Gote says. "But chrissake, slow down! All we need now is some MP nab us for speeding."

They're across the new bridge over the Ross River, no delay

this trip, luck with them, closing on Garbutt Field. Eddie Devlin's lying low in the back of the deuce with the booze and his tommy-gun, not loaded. The sweat rolling down Saljeski's face has cut wiggly tracks through his burnt cork. He looks like U.S. Rep. Festus Lee Claypool in black and white.

Saljeski slows a little, waits for a gap in the eastbound traffic and turns through the Main Gate into Garbutt Field. The RAAF sentry ignores them. They roll by the various quonsets and the Control Tower and out along the taxiway to the Lucky Lil's hardstand

"Oh shit!" Billy Gote says. "Shit shit shit!" The Lucky Lil's port wing has a distinct downward tilt and the port tire is flat. Billy jumps from the truck followed by Saljeski, Eddie Devlin drops from the tailgate with his tommy-gun and they survey this disaster. Bill Gote examines the flat tire. "Oh shit! It looks like the seal's busted and it's my goddamn fault! I let the dummy replacement land! Asshole bounced her in, busted the seal!"

"Can you fix it?" Saljeski says. He sounds scared.

"Christ, no!" Billy says. "I can't fix it! I'll have to call Second Air Depot. Get a new tire and get it mounted. Today yet if we're lucky. Then I'll clear for Woory and land on that old fighter strip. I won't fly with this tire. Depot might reseal it, pump it up, but it's prolly damaged. Might blow, I land with it." Billy Gote's a hot pilot but he's not stupid. "Oh why'd I let the dummy land!"

"What'll we do with the fuckin booze?" Saljeski says. "This fuckin deuce might be hot awready, fuckin coon report it liberated."

They discuss this briefly, they haven't much time, then load the booze into the not so lucky Lucky Lil. There doesn't seem to be anything else to do with it except abandon it along with the deuce-and-a-half and the booze, $64,000 worth at Nadzab prices, is their one great chance to get rich and pursue dreams After the War. And they may yet fly the Lil out of Townsville, with a new tire.

It's hard hot work, loading the booze into the Lil, but they get it loaded, well forward in the cargo compartment. They open one case and put four bottles of gin in Billy Gote's valpak. "Kill the pain, we got to RON," Billy says. They cover the booze and Eddie's tommy-gun and MP brassard, which he abandons, with a tarp Billy brought along, lash the tarp to the ringbolts in the cargo compartment floor and drop from the Lil onto the hardstand. Billy pulls the cabin door shut and hangs a red DANGER AMMUNITION sign he brought along on the handle. They squeeze into Pvt. MacArthur's truck and Saljeski drives back to the Red Cross Canteen and around behind it. There's a Red Cross jeep parked there.

"I'm gonna dump the fuckin deuce right here," Saljeski, he still sounds scared, says. "I aint leavin' no fuckin fingerprinsts either." He wipes the steering wheel and the knob on the shift and some of the burnt cork from his face with a dirty handkerchief and they get out of the truck. "Oh shit! Look!"

Two jeeps spilling MPs are parked at the Main Gate and a stocky MP captain and Sgt. Harry Parker appear to be arguing with the RAAF sentry and a RAAF officer in dress blues. Harry spots his co-conspirators. He looks puzzled, makes small flapping motions with his hands: why aren't they up up and away? Billy Gote shrugs, leaving Harry to wonder, and pounds on the Staff Only door. Flots opens it, says when asked, Sure, Billy can use the phone in the storeroom, and goes into the Canteen. Billy calls SAD, explains, requests, cites "high priority freight," pleads, slams the receiver down.

"Assholes!" he says. He also sounds scared. "They'll mount a new tire but not'll tomorrow morning and I got to go over there and fill out a goddamn requisition!"

Somebody's banging on the Staff Only door. Eddie opens it and Harry Parker joins them. "I'm supposed to check in the Canteen," Harry says. "Listen I hear anything about some booze was liberated. What happen you're still here?" Flat tire, they tell him, the Lucky Lil's got to RON. "Bad luck!" Harry says. "But I wouldn't worry too much. The shit be flying. Base Section knows the booze was liberated and figures it was flyboys liberate it. But the RAAF, bless 'em all, won't let us on the field so's we can search aircraft without a direct order from RAAF HQ. My C.O., Captain Raskovic, he's about ready and shit tacks. He's still argin' with the RAAF but he ain't gittin' nowhere. Base Sections gonna have to go through channels, Service Force HQ, GHQ, RAAF HQ, whatever, get a direct order we can search aircraft. That likely take about three weeks."

"I hope to christ you're right!" Billy Gote says, and they go into the Canteen, where his crew and a few field personnel are drinking coffee and Flots and Lt. Donald, off by themselves at the end of the counter, are deep into conversation.

"Awright, crew," Billy says. "Lissen up! We got a goddamn flat tire on the airplane. Seal prolly busted when we landed. So we're gonna RON. Air Depot will mount a new tire first thing in the morning. I'm going over there now, file a req. Porky, you be out here, oh-eight-hundred, see they do it right. Air Freight put the ammo aboard already. Airplane's closed up. Leave it that way. Our ETD is oh-eight-thirty. Use your jeep, Flots, fifteen minutes?"

"Where'll we stay?" Lt. Donald says. "I don't have my valpak." He's still embarrassed about his bad bouncy landing but beginning to think Lt. Gote should have given him more time in which to prepare for it.

"You and me," Billy says. "We'll check in the Transient Area, I get back. Sleep there, nothin' better turns up. You won't need your valpak, one night. You and Johnson be the Barrier Arms, Pork?"

"Roger," Porky says. "Got to check that Louise out."

Billy gets the key to Flots' jeep and departs for the Air Depot. Eddie and Saljeski join the loafers at the counter and order coffee. Harry Parker strikes up a conversation with some field personnel but doesn't hear anything about any booze that was liberated and departs, giving Eddie and Saljeski a discreet thumbs-up.

"Who's Louise?" Lt. Donald, who rather fancies himself a

ladies man, says.

"Maid the Arms," Porky says. "Her old man owns the dump. Louise prolly the last guaranteed government-inspected virgin in Australia. Fifteen goin' on thirty, her bilt."

Lt. Donald has no comment. He had in mind an older woman. His kid sister Carol back in Des Moines just turned fifteen.

"Hey!" Flots says. "You can come to the farewell party, Lieutenant. You and Billy. Any time after nineteen-hundred. Billy knows where the Manor is."

* * *

"I told the bastards," Capt. Dominic Raskovic, the Base Section CID chief, says. "I said it was high priority freight we had information was pilfered. But the goddamn RAAF. It's like talking to a goddamn wall! They're any kind Allies, I'm Clark Gable!"

"RAAF bastard runs the goddamn field prolly just being obstructionist," Lt. Col. Fogerty says. He's pacing the floor in his office where this council of war convened at 1600 hours, muttering like an angry volcano, glaring at Lt. Bernie Witters at each turn in his pacing and rubbing his red swollen ears. "Or RAAF might figured awready that high priority freight you mention is our booze. Every sonofabitch in the area prolly knows our booze was liberated by now. Burns-Phelps bastards know it. Prolly put it on the goddamn grapevine." The local grapevine spreads news with incredible swiftness.

"No, I don't think so, Sir," Raskovic says. "My chief investigator, Sergeant Parker here, he ran a little check at the field. He didn't hear anything."

Fogerty grunts. Raskovic's a stocky little man in sweaty khakis, 5-7, 185 pounds, with Slavic features, mean little eyes, a GI haircut and a former gymnast's muscular arms. A detective third grade in the LAPD's Hollywood Division in civil life, he often bores the regulars at the O Club with tales of the many sexual favors proffered him by stars of stage screen and radio he met in the course of his professional duties, but he's supposed to be good at his job.

"Maybe, Sir," Maj. Roger Dickinson, the Base Section Provost Marshal, says. "You could call the RAAF field commander, lay a little rank on him, cite that GHQ Order."

Dickinson's another peacetime Law and Order expert, a long indolent drink of water from West Texas, a former Texas Ranger who doesn't mind the heat, never sweats, wearing crisp khakis, snakeskin cowboy boots and a no-longer-authorized Cavalry Issue campaign hat, but that's of little import now.

"I did," Fogerty says. "RAAF duty officer said he was gone for the day. Bastard works short hours, I guess. Anyway, wing commander, he ranks me. And he's a goddamn hardnose. I tangle with him before. He ain't much an Ally. He won't get off his high-horse 'less he gets his own copy, that GHQ Order. Through channels. Might be a week, goddamn RAAF channels. I phoned Service Force HQ too. I got a pal there, just made light-colonel. I was gonna ask him there was some way and expedite that Order, lay it on the RAAF out the field, the goddamn wing commander. But my pal was gone for the day."

"Well, one thing we know," Dickinson says. "Our booze is still here. They didn't lib—I mean steal it until fourteen-hundred. I got the time from Burns-Phelps. There's no way they could drive out to the field, not with the traffic and the new bridge, and load it on their aircraft and take-off before fifteen hundred. Garbutt won't clear anything to Moresby, anywhere in New Guinea, after fifteen-hundred. Didn't either. I finally managed and extract that information from the Ops Office out the field. That's assuming the perpetrators were flyboys."

"Got to be goddamn flyboys!" Lt. Col. Fogerty says. "Nobody in this Base Section dare liberate that booze! I'd ship 'em off to some Infantry outfit so goddamn fast their heads swim! And they know that. Goddamn flyboys could fly our booze somewhere else though instead of Guinea."

"No, no way, Sir," Dickinson says. "Be their ass, they do. I got an all-points out, cites that GHQ Order. MPs will check every aircraft lands anywhere for contraband if it left Garbutt after fourteen-hundred. And Garbutt's the only field the RAAF runs."

Fogerty grunts, rubs one ear and winces. "Goddamn flyboys prolly know that too. You talked to Burns-Phelps, Provost. Why the hell they give the goddamn flyboys our booze anyway! Goddamn flyboy wasn't Witters. They know Witters."

"New man on the loading dock, they said, Sir," Dickinson says. "And the paperwork was all in order, they say. Requisition. War Authority endorsement. Purchase order with your signature."

"My signature!" Fogerty snarls. "Jeezuzz! Top everthing else then we got a goddamn case forgery!"

"Sir," Capt. Raskovic, former detective, says. "The way I see it, it prolly was goddamn flyboys lib—uh hijack our booze. But they must had some local accomplice. Or accomplices. They knew the time and the place and the Standard Operating Procedure and they had the paperwork."

"Where the hell is Flapp?" Fogerty snarls. "QM preps that req, p.o. How'd the goddamn flyboys get the paperwork?" Lt. Col Winston Flapp, Army Reserve, a Shreveport Cadillac dealer in civil life, is the Base Quartermaster. "Costello!" Sgt. Costello, he's been listening at the keyhole in their office door with M/Sgt. Abbott, pops in. "Where the hell is Colonel Flapp? You called him, told him be here?"

"Yessir! Duty officer said he was gone for the day."

"Oh for chrissake!" Lt. Col. Fogerty snarls "Gone for the day. Gone for the day! Who the hell's fighting this war! You tell his duty officer find him and tell him get his fat ass over here!" Costello departs. "Chrissake, men, we got a GHQ Order, you all seen it, prohibits the transport booze to Forward Areas and directs appropriate action forthwith. Besides I want our booze back, we are gonna look like a bunch assholes, that booze gets to Guinea!"

"We'll get it back, Sir," Dickinson, exhibiting false confidence, says.

Fogerty grunts, paces, rubs his other ear, winces and turns on Lt. Witters. "Goddamn it, Lieutenant, you been on time, pick up our booze, this wouldn't of happen. Why the hell were you late?"

"Sir!" Lt. Bernie Witters, his crotch throbbing, his prickly heat raging, says. "Chickens that Aussie woman lives next door the Club keeps, they got loose and they were uh defecating on my jeep, Sir."

"Forget the goddamn chickens, Lieutenant! I know all about the goddamn chickens!"

"Sir! Then we were on our way, pick up the MP rides shotgun, an MP stop us. Truck had a broken taillight, he said. He made the driver get out and look at it. Fact, Sir, the CID sergeant here, he."

"You were stopped for a busted taillight! And the goddamn flyboys got our booze! Oh for chrissake!" Lt. Col. Fogerty, appalled, shakes his head. A mistake, that makes his ears hurt.

"My man just doing his duty, Sir," Maj. Dickinson, the Provost Marshal, says.

"Duty, shit!" Lt. Col. Fogerty says. "Lieutenant, get the hell out of here. I'll see you later. And start rationing drinks at the Club tonight. Two per man per night till we get our booze back. Anybody bitches, tell them see me!" Lt. Witters scoots out of the office and Fogerty glares at the forces of Law and Order. "Another thing. How'd the goddamn flyboys get a deuce-and-a-half?"

"We're checking on that, Sir," Dickinson says. "No vehicle been reported lib—uh stolen. Or they might borrowed a vehicle. Second Air Depot maybe. Some truck unit. One the coon outfits maybe."

"Our best bet, Sir, way I see it," Raskovic says. "Is start with the QM. There's something funny there, way the flyboys, alleged flyboys, got the paperwork. See we can get a lead on some local accomplice. Or accomplices. And Sergeant Parker here, he heard there's a party tonight at that Red Cross female personnel billet up Hill Street. He says there's always a bunch flyboys at those parties and Sergeant Parker, he's got some contacts there. He's gonna check it out, maybe hear something."

"But what about our booze!" Lt. Col. Fogerty wails. "I want our goddamn booze back!"

"I'll put some men on Castle Hill, Sir," Dickinson says. "With binoculars. We'll keep the airfield under close surveillance."

"What the hell good will that do? Watch out booze fly away!"

Dickinson subsides, but Raskovic has an idea. "Another thing we could do, Sir, is get some those blue coveralls the RAAF EM wear. One-Hundred-Fourteenth Laundry does their laundry. Then put a couple of our men on the airfield. Undercover like. They can check some of the aircraft, keep their eyes open."

"By god, do that!" Fogerty says. "That's an order!"

"But the RAAF, Sir," Dickinson says. "They are mostly all little runts. My men are mostly big men. Except some my clerks."

"I seen one was a little runt was an MP," Fogerty says. "Or no, I guess not. That little runt was a goddamn imposter! So use a couple your clerks."

"Might create an Allied Relations Problem , Sir," Dickinson says. "I mean if the RAAF happen to find them on the airfield."

"Screw Allied Relations! I want our booze back! Chrissake, we got a GHQ Order, implement appropriate action forthwith. Look to me like you got a negative attitude, Provost."

"Oh no, no, Sir, not at all, Sir. In fact, I shall be launching a massive search, Sir. Forthwith. Just in case the perpetrators didn't make it to the airfield. We'll check the whole area, check vehicles."

"You do that, Provost! Use every man you got. All your men pulling double duty as of now till I say different or we get our booze back! That's an order! Pull all your details 'cept the traffic."

"All of them, Sir? There's a detail picks up the Red Cross female personnel when their Flinders Street Club closes, drives them their billet. For their safety. And one takes them to their Canteen out the field mornings."

"Pull those goddamn details!" Lt. Col. Fogerty says. "Puss can walk tonight! Ain't that far. Or call a cab. That's an order! I want our booze back! You find it, get a lead on it, you report to my sergeant here. He'll find me. Now move out!"

"Sir!" The forces of Law and Order, Dickinson, Raskovic and Harry Parker, salute and depart and Lt. Col. Fogerty digs the gin from his desk, it's damn near finished, gulps a swallow from the bottle, then another. Worst case develops, he'll close the Officers Club. And he pictures several flyboys tied to posts, puffing their last cigarettes while he jacks up the firing squad that will send them to Kingdom Come. But this picture, unfortunately, fades. He's got to catch the goddamn flyboys first.

"Sir!" M/Sgt Abbott pops into the office, evincing no surprise at finding an officer drinking on duty. "I just took a call. There a Congressman the George Hotel wants the Base Commander have dinner with him, eighteen-hunnert. But Colonel Allen, be nineteen-hunnert he's back here. So I guess that's you, Sir."

"What Congressman?"

"I dint catch his name, Sir."

"All right, I'll be there." Be some drinks there, no doubt. "Now listen up. You and Costello got the duty tonight. All night and no goddamn sleeping! I'll be the George at that dinner, then the O Club or my room, the George. You get a message for me from the Provost, I don't care what time it is, you call me."

"Sir!" Abbott, concealing his dismay, says. He was planning on taking in the nightly movie at Happy Valley, a new film called The Second Front starring Tyrone Power and Linda Lewis, that actress they call the Blonde Bombshell.

* * *

By 2100 hours, when a light snaps on in Jasmine Cottage at the top of Hill Street, which Jill Tucker observes from her Manic Manor bedroom window fifty yards down the street, the farewell party is working up a fair head of steam. Neither Boots Davis nor Rose Pearl Stevens, the farewellees, are present but they'll be along once they close the Flinders Street EM Club at 2200 hours. Flots and Jets are on hand though Jets, who doesn't much like boys, is sulking. Flots and Lt. Ronald Donald are getting on famously, sharing a Swappa sling in a jelly glass and reminiscing about the University of Iowa, where he was a Business major before enlisting and Flots was once a lively coed. Pops, the skinny old Australian who works for the Red Cross and is thought to have something going with Agnes Moore, is mixing drinks. Half a dozen other Red Cross female personnel and a dozen U.S. Armed Forces male personnel, officers and EM, various branches of service, among them Billy Gote and Eddie Devlin, are discussing with awe, glee, surprise and wonder the Great Booze Heist and, also, GHQ Order 404:44. The grapevine spread garbled news of both. Saljeski will be along once he's picked up the films he delivered earlier to the outdoor GI movies.

"You ever have Professor Panmander, Gwen, any your classes?" Lt. Donald says. "Really crazy old guy. American History and I think he was the advisor, the Rifle Club."

"No," Flots says. "But I know who you mean. I went with a guy for awhile was in the Rifle Club. He told me, the war started, Professor Panmander tried to enlist. In Canada. But he was too old."

Billy Gote and Eddie Devlin spent the hours after 1600, when they caught the GI bus into Townsville with Saljeski, picked up his truck and swung by the Flinders Street EM Club to tell Boots Davis her old friend Billy would be waiting for her at the Manor, holed up in Mrs. Dwight (Mickey) Rooney's house. Saljeski dropped them there, washed his hands and face, changed into his grubby suntans and left to make his movie runs. Billy and Eddie split an imperial quart of Foster's ale they took from the fridge, Saljeski said it was his, and watched a second john sitting at a window in the Base Section Officers Club nextdoor paw through papers, scratch his armpits and pound his head with his fists. Mrs. Rooney, a buxom wench at 5-4 and 13 stone, 182 pounds, came home at 1730 hours from her job at the Base QM, split another Foster's with them, said the QM was in a fair dinkum panic about some plonk some flyboys liberated and fixed them dinner, chicken and dumplings, after first firmly stating there'd be no funny business, get it out of their heads. She's a faithful woman, she said, faithful to Mr. Rooney missing at Singapore, and of course Arnold, meaning Saljeski, who came by after delivering his movies, got a big hug from Mrs. Rooney and drove them to the Manor.

Manic Manor Dec. '43

Most of the farewell party is in the Manor kitchen, males and females standing around or sitting at the kitchen table under a 40-watt bulb on a cord dangling from the ceiling. The males present also include a B25 pilot far gone in drink whose aircraft, now called Pistol Packin' Mama, SAD just fitted with a nose-mounted 75 mm cannon, a quiet little sergeant from the 12th Station Hospital supply room who came with a gallon of 190-

proof medical alcohol, a pretty good drink mixed with GI grapefruit juice, and USO entertainer Siggie Ferk, who somehow got wind of the party and turned up aching tooth and all, though without his accordion or Indian clubs, looking for Jill Tucker. The half dozen females include Betty Lou Fricker, who is thinking her former sorority sisters at Radcliffe will never believe the tales she some day may tell them. There are other males and females from here and there, more males than females, in the living room and on the patio, which are marginally cooler than the kitchen. There's a windup phonograph in the living room playing one record over and over again, an Erskine Hawkins blues with Billy Eckstine on the vocal.

The kitchen is very hot, 90-something F., no breeze, everybody sweating, the air thick with cigarette smoke. Winged insects including large Australian flying beetles bang into the 40-watt bulb at intervals and drop, dead or stunned, on the table. A tech sergeant from the Base Motor Pool, the Pool's acting first-sergeant since the former first was caught flogging gasoline, named by acclamation to the Bug Detail, clears these insects away and tosses them in the trash can beside the sink. Now and then an insect drops dead or stunned into somebody's Swappa sling. These are extracted and tossed in the trash. Nobody's going to waste gin though the supply tonight is relatively plentiful thanks to three bottles Billy Gote says he got off the 34th Squadron p.o. The theory is gin will kill any parasites the bugs may be vectoring.

A kind of census was taken earlier. One often is. The twenty-six persons present hail from eighteen states, the Territory of Hawaii, Australia (counting Pops) and the Sioux Nation. First Lt. Archie Hunker, the 34th Troop Carrier Squadron pilot who flys a general around, a husky swarthy young fellow from Rapid City, S.D., who claims to be one-sixteenth Ogallala, represents the Sioux.

The Great Booze Heist is the principal topic of conversation. A great many theories as to who did it and how have been advanced and the amount liberated reliably reported by a sergeant from the Garbutt Field Air Freight Detachment to be one-hundred cases. Unknown flyboys are considered the chief suspects and the big question is did they get out of Tville with the booze? The rumor is they did not. Whatever, and who ever, they are blessed in absentia. The overwhelming consensus is they're modern Robin Hoods and it couldn't have happened to a better bunch than the Base Section officers. Those officers are blamed in absentia ("Bastards got to MacArthur") for GHQ Order 404:44, which all the flyboys present consider a big joke.

"What are they gonna do?" Lt. Hunker says. "Snoop in every aircraft it's departing Tville? Fat chance. You know, though, somebody was to ask me, I'd tell them I wouldn't put liberating that booze past you, Billy Gote, I thought you could pull it off."

"Neither would I," Billy Gote says. "I thought I could pull it off. Say, somethin' I been meaning ask you, Hunk. Who's that Lucky Lil is on my aircraft you used to have?"

"Search me," Lt. Hunker says. "That was Hamsptead's aircraft before he got promoted and started flying a desk. Ask him. You know, I could pull it off, that booze. I mean that booze was on my aircraft I could fly it out of here. No sweat. Screw that GHQ Order. Nobody's going to mess with a general's aircraft. Except my general don't drink. Won't allow booze on his aircraft."

"Who the hell is your general?" Billy says.

"Brigadier-General Humphrey Dumphy. First Corps deputy commander. Humpty Dumpty, they call him. Or Short Stack. Not where he can hear it though. He's a fierce little fellow."

"Indeed he is," Agnes Moore, a heavyset woman with steel gray hair, the Manic Manor housemother insofar as it has one, says. "I met him once in Brisbane. What's he doing in Townsville?"

"He's not here," Lt. Hunker says. "He's in Brisbane. Some kind of conference. We had to put down here when my altimeter went belly up. Humpty Dumpty pulled rank and got himself on The Bataan, it went back to Brisbane."

"You don't need an altimeter," Billy Gote says. "Fly here to Brisbane the weather's good. Like today."

"I know that," Lt. Hunker says. "You know that. But Humpty Dumpty don't know it. Altimeter's fine. But there's a gal here I met last time I was here I like to see again. I'd seen her tonight except she had some family function she had to go to. She said. I prolly take a run by her house later."

"You got wheels then?" Billy says.

"Oh sure. First Corps deputy commander's entitled wheels. I use Humpty Dumpty's name and whine long enough, Air Depot gave me a beat-up jeep. When I went over there and went through the motions, filed a req they fix my altimeter ain't broken. Just in case Humpty Dumpty make some inquiries."

"What's your Indian name, Lieutenant?" Betty Jo Fricker says. "If you have one, I mean."

"Straight Arrow."

"You know what I think," Ann Silvers, a willowy Red Cross female personnel from Long Island (which she calls Long Giland) sitting beside Eddie, says. "I think whoever it was liberated that liquor, if they were flyboys, somebody here was in on it too. The flyboys couldn't just fly in and liberate it. Could they? Somebody here had to help them is what I think."

"I think Ann's right," Agnes Moore says. "But whoever it was helped them, I pity them if they get caught. I hear Colonel Fogerty is absolutely livid!"

"Fix me a sling, Eddie," Ann Silvers says, and Eddie jumps up to do that. He'd like to go to bed with Ann Silvers, short though their acquaintance be. Eddie's not been to bed, or in the backseats of cars, with very many girls. Count them on his fingers, but he keeps hoping.

"You're Eddie Devlin?" Agnes Moore says. They were introduced but Manic Manor introductions are often sketchy. "From Moresby? How's that big baby your wife had, we forward your telegram? My god, sixteen pounds!"

"Baby?" Eddie says. "Oh, yeah, baby. Fine. Great, last I

heard." Shit! Now Ann Silvers will think he's married, though that's not necessarily fatal in the middle of The War.

"What I think," a huge Samoan representing the Territory of Hawaii, a chief petty officer off the USS Little Rock, how he heard about the farewell party a mystery, says. "That booze was liberated."

A fat blonde ARC female personnel named Ima Score storming down the backstairs into the kitchen interrupts the chief. "Agnes!" she wails. "That goddamn Tucker's hogging the loo again! She's been in there an hour! Her and her goddamn ablutions! Get her out!"

"All right. I'll talk to her," Agnes Moore, this is an on-going problem, says, and goes up the backstairs with Ima. The chief opens his mouth but Saljeski's arrival cuts him off.

"Oh, man!" Saljeski says. "The fuckin feces is flying, that booze was liberated! There's fuckin MPs all over town. Stoppin' vehicles and searchin' them. They even stop me! They searchin' places too. They even search the fuckin Pro Station! They got fuckin dogs, that K-9 outfit out the horse track, sniffin' places. No fuckin stone unturn, K-9 guy I know told me! And there's a rumor they rationin' drinks at the fuckin O Club!"

"Watch your mouth, soldier," the chief says.

"Sorry," Saljeski says. "Hey! Who the fuck are you?"

The principal reaction to Saljeski's news about the O Club is glee, then Sgt. Harry Parker arrives wearing a fresh uniform and a helmet liner painted white, armed, a holstered .45 automatic at his hip, officially on duty.

"Howdy all," Harry says. "Ann, Flots, Betty Lou. I'm supposed to be up here gittin' a hot lead on which you goldurn flyboys liberate the Base Section O Club's booze. But I don't suppose I'm gonna git one." Some laughter greets this sally but the service personnel present who don't know Harry eye him with suspicion and distaste, the normal reaction to a MP. The frank manner however in which Harry described and assessed his mission and the laughter that evoked calm them.

"Nobody here but us chickens," Billy Gote says, which evokes more laughter.

"Fix me a short sling, Pops?" Harry says. Pops does that. "I'm on duty but what the hell. Everbody in the 301st, cooks and clerks and the Provost even, is on duty, view this major catastrophe." More laughter greets this report. Harry drinks his short sling. "Well, I got to get going. This booze thing keepin' us hoppin'. Say, though, Lieutenant Gote. That Samurai sword you was interested in. It's in my jeep, you want to take a look at it."

Eddie Devlin and Saljeski also evince a sudden interest in Samurai swords and so does the chief off the Little Rock, but Harry says, "I promise it the Lieutenant, Chief."

Outside, in the Manor's churned up backyard, slapping mosquitoes, no breeze blowing, the night hot and muggy, the conspirators huddle beside Harry's jeep.

"We got to try and git your girlfriend out of town, Sal," Harry says. "Some way or other. My leader, Captain Raskovic, he ain't exactly a dummy. He already been onto Colonel Flapp, the QM, tryin' and git a line on the req and purchase order and so on for the booze. I don't know he come up with Mickey's name yet. But I figger he will. Flapp prolly gonna involve Mickey. Try save his ass. Fogerty's after Flapp's ass. Does Mickey know what them extra req and so on she run off for you was for?"

"No," Saljeski says. "I just tell her I wonder what they look like."

"She buy that, you think?"

"Prolly. It ain't like Mickey's a fuckin brain surgeon, y'know. But she might got some fuckin idea now. What they was for."

"I don't exactly know," Harry says. "If Raskovic can git at her, Aussie civilian. But she works for us bloody Yanks. Raskovic will try though. Question her anyway, he gits onto her. Threaten git her fired maybe. Raskovic's a smart little varmint, I give him that. Your name comes up, Sal, you can kiss your ass goodbye.

So we better git her out of town. She got friends or relatives somewhere she can visit?"

"She's got a fuckin sister in Rockhampton," Saljeski says. "But she ain't got no fuckin dough, take a trip. Or me neither. I'm fuckin broke."

"I got some money," Harry says. "You got some money, Lieutenant? Eddie? How much it cost, the Q&NR to Rockhampton? I know there's a train leaves oh-eight-hundred."

Nobody knows but they pool their funds, mainly Harry's funds. "Twenty quid, that oughta be enough," Harry says. "Okay, Sal, you got wheels. Go see Mickey. Now. Scare her. Don't tell her any more than you have to but scare her. Tell her there's a bloody Yank captain wants to interrogate her and if he does she likely lose her job at the QM. And put her on the train."

"Roger." Saljeski pockets the twenty quid, hops in his truck and departs.

"You understand, Lieutenant," Harry says. "This just a precaution. You and Eddie be back in New Guinea tomorrow. But I want to save Sal's ass. Mine too, it comes to that. What'd Sal do with that deuce-and-a-half he liberated?" Left it out the field behind the Canteen, Eddie says. "Well, good a place as any, I guess. Raskovic thinks he gits a line on the deuce picked up the booze he'll have a hot clue. I'm gonna encourage that line of thinking. Keep his mind off the QM. Okay, I better report to my leader. Tell him there wasn't no information here regards that booze. I don't see you guys again, happy flying. And peddle the booze!"

Harry climbs into his jeep and departs and Billy Gote and Eddie return to the Manor kitchen, where Siggie Ferk is revealing a leading he-man film star's little-know preference for little boys and, it's past 2000 hours, some preliminary pairing-off is in progress. The Pistol Packin' Mama's pilot seems to think he's paired-off and bound for bed with Betty Lou Fricker, but is in for a big disappointment. There also are other female Red Cross personnel who do not for moral or other peculiar reasons pair-off except on rare occasions. Consequently, about eighty percent of the males present are in for a big disappointment and the pairing-off is highly competitive and quietly vicious. Harry Parker, wise in the ways of Maine moose, says it's like the rutting season "except the bucks here a little short in the rack department."

"It wasn't a genuine Samurai, Chief," Billy Gote says. "It look more like a leaf spring. Where the hell is Boots? And Rose Pearl? Ain't this their party? And they're gonna fly Seven-Mile with me in the morning but they don't know that yet."

"They'll be here," Ann Silvers says. "There's an MP detail picks them up and brings them home when the Club closes."

"Not Rose Pearl," Jody Foster, a medium-size Red Cross female personnel from somewhere in Kentucky, says. "Rose Pearl has a date. With real rank. That RAAF wing commander who runs Garbutt Field. The one who hates Yanks. Except Rose Pearl, I guess."

How'd Rose Pearl meet him? Nobody knows, another mystery, which triggers a discussion regarding Allied Relations. Several old Swappa hands present feel these Relations have deteriorated. "We got a couple GIs in our ER tonight," the 12th Station Hospital supply sergeant says. "Some AMF beat the shit out of them at the Rose and Crown."

More bugs bang the light bulb, fall to the table and are tossed in the trash. The last bottle of gin is opened. There's some Australian whiskey at hand but that's a last resort after the 190-proof is gone. The phonograph's still playing and Billy Eckstine's wailing, "It's gawnnn and started raininnn'."

Ann Silvers says Eddie can sleep on the patio though nobody will be going to be bed for hours yet and she won't sleep with a married man. A man she knows is married, that is. But more slings and the passing hours may change her mind.

Ima Score, she's from Richmond, says oot and hoose instead of out and house, bangs down the backstairs with her hair in rollers, followed by a weary Agnes Moore. "Somebody make me a sling," Ima says. "I'm gonna kill that goddamn Tucker!" Three male personnel leap up to make her sling.

"Oh put a sock in it, Score," Jill Tucker, a petite brunette in a white blouse full of bosom, seersucker skirt and spectator pumps, likewise descending the backstairs, says. That's a pithy Australian expression meaning shut-the-fuck-up.

"Jill baby!" Siggie Ferk says. "You're lookin' gorgeous! As allas. I been waitin' for you."

"Well, if it isn't Siggie Ferk, former vaudville star," Jill Tucker says, then ignores Siggie. "Is there somebody here with wheels? I need a ride."

All the male personnel not yet paired-off who have wheels promptly offer their services. Jill Tucker selects the quiet little 12th Station Hospital supply sergeant. They depart and those in the kitchen hear her tell him on the porch. "You understand you're just driving me, Sergeant. No funny stuff."

Ima Score gulps half her sling and turns mimic. "I need a ride, no funny stuff. Little slut could walk fifty yards, screw her goddamn colonel. I ought to short-sheet her bed!"

"No point in that," Ann Silvers says. "She won't be sleeping in it."

"Colonel, huh?" Siggie Ferk says, philosophically. You win some and lose some and his goddamn tooth is throbbing. "I guess there ain't no generals here."

"Flots," Lt Donald says. "Says I can sleep on the couch in the living room." Jets sneers, flounces out of her chair and bangs up the backstairs.

"Good for you, Loot," Billy Gote says. "Don't bounce Flots like you bounce my airplane. Where the hell is Boots? Whyn't somebody phone the Club, find out."

The phone's ringing in the living room. It rings again and again. The couple necking there ignore it. Ann Silvers goes and answers it. "Red Cross billet. Yes. What? I can't hear you. Just a minute." She silences Billy Ekstine. "Yes. What! Oh no! No! Oh no! Oh my god! Where? When? Yes, yes. Of course. Right away.

Oh my god!" She hangs up and returns to the kitchen, her expression stricken.

"What is it?" Agnes Moore says.

"Boots," Ann Silvers says. "Boots is in the 12th Station. She was raped! By a bunch of colored. They want two of us to come out there. Right away. Bring her some clothes, they said."

* * *

Col. Webster R. Allen, wearing the GI bedroom slippers, baggy seersucker pajama bottoms and red corduroy bathrobe he liberated when discharged from the 5th General Hospital in Brisbane, standing on the tiny brick patio outside his bungalow bedroom, whacking mosquitoes, surveys that portion of Townsville directly below him. There's not much to see. There's no blackout now in Townsville but there's a dimout said to save electricity for the War Effort. A few faint yellow streetlights line Flinders Street and here and there there's a lighted window, but most of Townsville goes early to bed. Lights still blaze along the docks, however. A supply convoy came in late in the day and the unloading and reloading of the sinews of war will go on through the night. Two vessels in the harbor are exchanging gossip or, conceivably, information vital to the War Effort with their Aldis lamps. The night is hot and muggy, heavy with the scent of jasmine, there are jasmine bushes all around the bungalow, and silent. For once, there's none of the usual racket at the Red Cross billet down the street, no scratchy old phonograph wailing, no bursts of raucous laughter, though somebody down there is grinding the starter on, no doubt, a military vehicle converted to personal use. There's a faint quarter-moon and a few dim stars above the black bulk of Castle Hill. Heavy clouds ripped at intervals by jagged lightening fill the eastern sky.

Web Allen, who when much younger wrote a few bad poems for the River Falls State College student newspaper, sees in that eastern sky a symbol of himself: a man with a mind heavily clouded ripped at intervals by jagged guilt. And thinks: oh god, Mert, what am I doing! Doing to you, us! And our wonderful daughters. Cheating. Smashing the Seventh Commandment. That's what. Yet awaiting with great expectation another wild assignation with Jill Tucker, young enough to my daughter. Who though it's ridiculous, I can't help it, I now love. Web Allen bludgeons his conscience. Rationalizes. His plump wife Mert, forty, Catholic as they come, a far better Catholic than the convert he is, is 10,000 miles away. She doesn't know. She'll never know. He'll see to that. And what she doesn't know (an adulterer's logic) won't hurt her. And it was such a long long time.

Web Allen recollects this extended period. Thirty-eight months since, not counting three brief leaves, the Division was activated. Twenty-one months since his last three-day pre-embarkation leave, when he last saw Mert and they last "made love," her phrase, in the usual fashion, a duty perhaps as much as a pleasure, both aware but submerging the grim thought it might be "the last time" they did. He was an Infantry captain then, the Fox Co. C.O., an MOS (Military Occupational Specialty) low on the actuarial tables, and the Division was in Ford Ord, beefing up with half-trained GIs dragooned from Basic Training camps up and down the West Coast, half-trained but warm and breathing, and Fox and the other rifle companies for once was getting first pick, the GIs in top half of the alphabet.

And he didn't subsequently hop into bed with the first woman ready willing and able to hop into bed with him. Or the second or the third either. God knows he might have. He had numerous opportunities. All the Americans did, still do, with sixty percent of the Australian males eighteen-to-forty somewhere, elsewhere, in their nation's armed forces. Many Americans, officers and EM, were asked to tea or over for a drink by lonely war widows in the first weeks after the Division disembarked at Adelaide and many of these Americans, Web Allen knows, drank their tea or gin-and-tonic, then, one thing leading to another thing, abandoned fidelity at an early stage. Including, this a well known fact, the Protestant chaplain, a previously staunch Methodist who within a month took up with a war widow on one of the farms near their first camp at Sandy Creek. The Catholic chaplain did not but he had a vow to keep. Web Allen of course also is beset by a vow. Forsaking all others. Well, one of these days he'll go to Confession like the good converted Catholic he's not.

The Americans don't get many invitations to tea now. Many Australians appear to be pretty tired of the bloody Yanks. Web Allen has little contact with Townsville's civilians. He did lunch once with Lord Mayor Hubert Applewhite, a retired ships chandler, and the City Council shortly after taking command of the Base Section, and he meets with Applewhite once a week, 1400 hours on Wednesdays in Applewhite's City Hall office, for a fairly useless discussion of on-going Allied Relations problems. They discuss GI traffic violations, GIs prone to relieve themselves in public, Applewhite's fond hope that all the bloody Yank blackfellows soon will be shipped off to New Guinea and the sticky wicket presented by local females married and unmarried pregnant by bloody Yanks married and unmarried. Tea or no tea, a good many bloody Yanks seem to be enjoying flourishing affairs in Townsville. Lt. Col. Fogerty for one is said to have something going with a skinny little maid at the George, a distant relative of Lord Mayor Applewhite's whose husband is a stoker in the Royal Australian Navy.

There's a scrawled observation in one of the stalls in the men's loo at the George Hotel, Web Allen recollects, a bad poem but a succinct sitrep. Breathes there a man with flesh so dead/He never to himself hath said/On crawling into some adulterous bed/Oh well what the hell, Jack, it's The War.

But that sitrep (hear this, conscience) does not apply to Web Allen. He loves Jill Tucker. Ought not to of course, it's patently ridiculous, but he does. Can't help it. Jill's a remarkable young woman. Bright, funny, articulate. So it's not just the sex though the sex is, well, sensational seems an apt word. His was a sheltered life, Web Allen's beginning to think, count on his fingers his previous sexual partners not including Mert, none of them very inventive. Jill says people who love each other ought never to be ashamed or reluctant to do anything that pleases the person they love. She's never actually said she loves Web Allen but in his lawyer's mind, given this statement, actions louder than words, demonstrates her love every time they tumble into bed. Or so Web Allen likes to think. He sometimes wonders why? Why him? An old by wartime standards married man twice her age. No raving romantic. But that's the way love is, he supposes.

It still surprises Web Allen. He met Jill Tucker a month ago at an Officers Only evening reception at the George Hotel for a male movie star out on a USO tour. Agnes Moore, the local Red Cross director, introduced them. Jill, she said, was "a new girl just up from Sydney." Perceiving at once that this new girl was attractive and intelligent and suddenly immensely lonely for intelligent conversation with an attractive American girl (well, woman), he presently suggested (but it was just a suggestion, adultery he truly believes far from his mind) they might after the reception have a nightcap at his bungalow.

Jill Tucker said she'd love to and they did, had a nightcap, then two more, he had some dubious scotch, and talked. He did most of the talking, rattling on in the presence of a good attractive listener. Talked some, not much, about the slipshod Base Section he was trying to whip into shape. Said he'd been in the fighting at Buna Government Station a year ago but did not pursue that. Spoke at greater length about the lawyer's life he found rewarding in West Cork, Wisconsin, pop. 2206, Before The War, suddenly immensely lonesome for that. Said he was married, that the honest thing to do, father of two daughters. Jill, somewhat more reticent, only said she's from Saugus, a Boston suburb. Her father, she said, is "in investments." One brother, Ralph, older: he's a B17 bombardier in the Eighth Air Force in England. Did not mention her mother but did say she has a B.A. "from

Radcliffe"and was though a woman "thinking about" law school, Harvard Law, when instead, The War on-going, she joined the American Red Cross, zipped through some orientation and was dispatched to Australia. Sydney. She thinks she may tackle law school After The War.

"Oh, you should," Web Allen said. "By all means. I think you'd make a fine lawyer."

"Mmmm," Jill Tucker said. "Tell me. I know it's none of my business but I'm curious. Have you been faithful to your wife?"

"Yes," Web Allen said. "I have. Twenty months, it's been. Faithful and celibate. Since oh-six-hundred hours ten March nineteen-forty-two."

Jill considered this information. "That's a long time," she said. "But I think The War changes things. Don't you? Would you like to fuck?"

The four-letter word though he'd heard it a million times, the Army couldn't function without it, surprised Web Allen, shocked him a little, but he recovered soon enough and in short order they were in his bed, inside his mosquito net, "making love" in the usual fashion before he exploded, then in his experience more unusual fashions. There were, often the case, two goddamn mosquitoes inside the net. They stung Jill twice ("Damn mosquitoes!" she said, slapping her naked behind) and Web Allen four times, none of which he noticed at the time. And thus their affair (but it's not just an affair, it's far more than that) began, at 2300 hours 20 November 1943, and within the week he was in love with Jill Tucker, ridiculous though that be. Jill's been to bed with other men, freely admits that, he wishes he knew how many, and this puzzles him some. Wealthy family apparently if her father is in investments. What was she doing sleeping around? Well, she's from the East of course. Web Allen, a true son of the Midwest, is suspicious of the East and its ways. Family with old Boston money, decadence setting in perhaps. None of which matters, as his grandmother used to say, a whit. Whatever a whit is. He's in love with Jill Tucker. And hopes she'll be along soon. It's been a long tiring day. He's ready for bed then sleep. The guy grinding the starter at the Red Cross billet is still grinding away.

A long tiring day. The JTC inspection (Col. Ives knows the drill) went well enough though. Hot as blazes and he was bitten by several ants but his prickly heat behaved and the noon meal (roast beef with mashed potatoes and green beans and apple pie) was surprisingly good. Special efforts taken to prepare it, no doubt. He gave the JTC an Excellent rating, which was what Col. Ives expected. That left Maj. Borgan beaming. And, surprise, the JTC has a landing craft now, an LCVP (Landing Craft, Vehicles and Personnel) Col. Ives won at seven-card stud with a queen-ten full house that beat the jacks-and-fives the ensign commanding the mysterious Navy Detachment in Woorammoolla thought a sure thing. A detail composed of JTC trainees, their training suspended, subsequently built a jetty at the edge of the mudflats and Borgan's learning to navigate the LCVP, takes it out at high tide and putts around in it.

Col. Ives, the old reprobate, happy old hedonist, also confided over drinks at the King Edward Hotel that his WENL's bastions have been breached. A "bonzer piece" is Mrs. Forbes-Fowler, Col. Ives said. He's picked up some Australian idiom. Her husband missing at Singapore also was an equestrian and Mrs. Forbes-Fowler thinks Col. Ives has a "bonzer saddlehorn." Those drinks and Col. Ives' reports delayed their departure for Townsville in the C60 but Sikorsky and his copilot, chatting up a couple of women in the King Edward's lounge, voiced no complaints. It was going dark when they took off from the Woorammoolla strip and 2000 hours when they touched down between the Garbutt Field runway lights. Fazoli, he still needs a haircut, was waiting at Ops with a garbled report on the day's big news. "Bunch of flyboys liberate the O Club's holiday booze, Colonel Fogerty is goin' nuts and they rationin' drinks at the fuckin Club!"

Web Allen heard more about this, more than he cared to hear, during a late dinner alone at the George Hotel when Maj. Abel Cain, the Base Section Adjutant-General, a thin former assistant district attorney from somewhere in South Carolina, came out of the bar with a long woeful tale regarding the day's disaster. Cain clearly is itching to prosecute the said flyboys, seek the death penalty, and clearly considers, he said so several times, rationed drinks at the O Club a devastating horror of war.

Web Allen heard more when Lt. Col. Fogerty emerged half drunk from one of the private dining rooms. "I jush had dinner with a Congreshman," Fogerty said. "You hear about what happen our liquor?" Yes, Web Allen said. Fogerty then goddammed the goddamn flyboys and the goddamn RAAF at great length, produced a GHQ Order he seems to think entitles him to shoot on sight flyboys who liberate liquor and outlined the many measures underway to recover the liquor, still thought to be in Townsville. "Shir, my opinion," he said. "Our besh move is you phone GHQ, talk the duty officer there, get thish Order expidished the goddamn RAAF out the goddamn airfied. Then we sersh all the goddamn airplanes out there."

Web Allen said he would: anything to calm his chief-of-staff. He also suggested his chief-of-staff go to bed, get some rest, but his chief-of-staff said, "No, gotta go the Club, make sure my man'ger there rashin' drinks," and went weaving out of the George calling for his driver.

Web Allen also met the congressman, a fat old drunk Democrat from Mississippi, U.S. Rep. Festus Lee Claypod or some name like that, when he and his party emerged from the private dining room and somebody identified Web Allen as the local U.S. commander. He was, Claypod said, "Motty please t'meet yawl, cuhnel," then went on about "Ah hopes yawl takin' good cay ma nee-uss litull Bootie Davis is servin' her cun'ree rot hee-uh inna Murkin Red Cross" until his aide, a tall young man in civvies, convinced the old fool it was bedtime. A captain and a lieutenant in natty uniforms with gaudy GHQ patches and three war correspondents traveling with Claypod were in the bar.

Fazoli then delivered Web Allen to his bungalow, where he peeled out of his scratchy pinks, his prickly heat staging a brief attack, got into his robe and pajama bottoms, phoned the 114th Portable Laundry Detachment and reamed the duty sergeant, who promised, word of honor, the detachment will find and deliver "the colonel's" missing khakis at 0700 hours.

The Great Booze Heist does not weigh heavily on Web Allen. Bad for discipline perhaps, grand theft technically, but good for troop morale, he surmises. The Base Section EM, no doubt, are laughing in their beer. Put it bluntly, he shares their glee. Base Section officers deprived of booze. That could not happen to a better bunch. He'll go through the motions of course, express dismay, let Fogerty and the Provost Marshal and the 301st MPs run around in circles, let Fogerty chew Lt. Col. Flapp's fat ass if in fact the Base QM was somehow derelict. But secretly Web Allen rather hopes the unknown flyboys, assuming it was flyboys and that's a reasonable assumption, get away with the booze. There's just a chance then, he thinks, a slim chance but a chance, that a few exhausted Infantrymen somewhere in the Forward Areas might get a bottle or two. The single bottle of foul Australian whiskey he packed all the way to the approaches to Buna Government Station, doled out by the dram while it lasted, was priceless. The late Sgt. Barney Clark finished it off before he took the patrol out.

Web Allen submerges that memory. He wants no part of the late Sgt. Clark's ghost and here at last is Jill Tucker, on foot, barefoot, carrying her pumps, accompanied by a small GI.

"Thank you, Sergeant, for the escort," Jill says. "You can go now." The GI disappears in the darkness. Jill crosses the yard and the patio. "He was going to drive me but his jeep wouldn't start. Did you hear about the liquor some flyboys liberated?"

"Oh yes, all about it. But I'm not going to lose any sleep over it."

Holding Web Allen's arm, Jill puts her pumps on and they go into his bedroom through the patio door. She'll wear her pumps but not another stitch while they roll around on his bed. That excites Web Allen, jump-starts the old libido so to speak.

"I had dinner with a Congressman," Jill says. "At the George. He's Boots Davis' uncle. Fat old man. Talks all the time but I hardly could understand him."

"Yes, I met him. From Mississippi. What's he doing here?" Web Allen dims the bedroom lights, removes his robe and sprawls on his bed inside the mosquito net. Jill joins him. She'll remove his pajamas presently. This also excites Web Allen, revs up the old libido, and neither his slipped disc nor prickly heat ever bother him at these times. There's a damn mosquito inside the net with them, circling. It looks like one of the Stuka dive-bombers featured in a recent Fox Movietone newsreel. Web Allen slaps at it but misses.

"Some kind of junket," Jill says. "He was on his way to Moresby in MacArthur's airplane but took sick. Something he ate, he said. Boots can't stand him. She says he's an old hypocrite, still chases women. He asked her to dinner and she asked me, join the party, so I did. Then Boots had to staff the Flinders Street Club. The old goat's aide and two GHQ flunkies and some war correspondents were there too. They're supposed to fly to Moresby in the morning. So was Colonel Fogerty. Believe me, he is fuming, that liquor the flyboys liberated! I heard they're rationing drinks at the O Club!"

"Yes, I heard that. Another horror of war."

Jill's kneeling between his legs and slowly removing her clothing: this also excites him. Immensely. "Boots is right. The old goat practically propositioned me." Likewise his aide, both GHQ flunkies and two correspondents. The fat correspondent was drunk.

"How'd you get back to the billet?"

"The old goat has a car. His driver took Boots to the Flinders Street Club and me to the billet."

"I heard somewhere the Red Cross is sending two of you to Moresby. Not you?"

"No. Boots and Rose Pearl. They're leaving in the morning. With a pilot who was at their farewell party at the billet tonight. I wish that goddamn Score was going." Naked finally, Jill straddles Web Allen hips and pulls at the drawstring on his pajamas. "Hey, your blue's fading. Oh hell!" The field phone on the floor beside the bed is ringing. "Don't answer it."

"Have to, this hour. Must be something. Maybe they caught the flyboys." Web Allen slides one arm out from under the mosquito net and lifts the handset from the field phone. "Colonel Allen here. Yes? Oh no! Oh my god! Oh hell!" Web Allen listens, expresses more horror, replaces the handset.

"What?" Jill says.

"Your friend. Miss Davis. She was raped! By some colored. That was the duty office at the 12th Station Hospital. They have her there. I better get out there. Get the sitrep."

"No, not now. They'll have her sedated. Wait until morning."

"No, I really should. Omigod! That damn Congressman! He's her uncle! He's Miss Davis' uncle! He'll blow a gasket, he hears she was raped. By colored! I've got to call my driver, get out there."

"No, wait! The Congressman won't know. He'll be gone in the morning. They're leaving for Moresby at first light. Then back to Brisbane and back to The States. He'll never know. Boots will never tell him. He might tell her mother."

"But he'll hear something. Might, the damn grapevine! Oh christ! This is all I need! American girl raped. By colored! And her uncle's a damn Dixie Congressman and he's here! What's the hell is that?"

That is a hard spatter of rain on the glass patio door. Lightening flashes. Thunder booms. Web Allen, clutching his pajamas, and Jill, both startled by this unexpected development, get out from under the mosquito net and stand peering through the patio door. More lightening illuminates Townsville and the harbor. Rain's pounding down, muffling the thunder. It's raining buckets, cats and dogs.

"The Bloody Wet!" Web Allen says. "The Bloody Wet's started!"

"Come on," Jill says. "Believe me, Boots will be sedated. I love to make love when it's raining!" She leads Web Allen back to his bed and, under the mosquito net, pulls at the draw-string on his pajama.

Web Allen hates himself, a little, derelict in his duty as he perceives it, American girl raped and a goddamn Congressman to boot threatening his sanity. But Jill's probably right. Miss Davis will be sedated and her dammed uncle, the Congressman, will be gone in the morning.

Unless the rain. The Bloody Wet may ground his airplane. Many airplanes. Forget it. Jill is performing an unnatural act she contends to be perfectly natural and two more ravenous mosquitoes have joined them inside the mosquito net.

* * *

Sgt. Porky Wallace, the Lucky Lil's flight engineer, huddled in the Pro Station doorway at the corner of Flinders and Dock Streets, soaked to the skin, sucking a wet Fleetwood, stares at the rain pounding down and curses his luck or lack thereof. He struck out! His Southern charm got him nowhere. His condoms still nest in his wallet. He had something going he's sure with two birds he chatted up on Flinders Street but they were on their way to the Australian Other Ranks Club on Front Street and two giant Allies in AMF battle gear on door duty there told him, "Fook off, y'bloody Yienk!"

He then gave the Flinders Street EM Club a shot but it was full of Base Section commandos and other air crew hustling maybe ten birds and he never did get anything going there. He heard a lot of talk about some booze some flyboys liberated and wondered briefly if Lieutenant Gote had anything to do with that but his mind was fixed on sex. He hung around until the Club closed and gassed for a while with the Red Cross gal called Boots but she declined his offer to walk her home, said an MP detail picked her up. He gave up on her finally and went looking for a pub serving "Afters" but couldn't find one, then was braced on Flinders Street, the third time, by two MPs, the town's crawling with MPs, who asked for his leave papers and studied his sacred air crew ID at length before grudgingly accepting he was air crew RON. The first two told him he was out of uniform wearing a tie and made him take it off.

Wending his way to the Barrier Arms then, Porky gave serious thought to is there some way he can get Louise the maid up to his room. But the sitrep is her old man, Biff Smith, locks her up after dark. These thoughts were interrupted by a sudden flash of lightening, booming thunder, a hard spatter of rain, then buckets of rain. He was soaked before taking cover in the Pro Station doorway. Not all bad though. If in fact The Bloody Wet's started and that's the way it looks, they'll likely RON until there's a break in the bad weather. Might be a week. That happened once during the last Bloody Wet a year ago. Time he got lucky but got the clap, broken to Private but remained air crew, kept his flight pay, Lieutenant Gote interceding on his behalf, had to work his way up to sergeant again.

Two GIs drunk as snakes, privates with no stripes, likewise soaked, stagger across Dock Street and push into the Pro Station. How in the hell did they!

"See your papers, soldier." A large MP, one of a pair in ponchos looming up out of the rain and the darkness, accosts Porky.

Wearily, Porky produces his air crew ID, explains he's RON. "Bunkin' the Arms. Just waitin' the rain lets up, I go over there. Might's well go now, I guess."

"Might's well, soldier," the MP says. "Rain won't let up, this the Bloody Wet's started. Hold it though. Convoy coming." The convoy, a jeep followed by sixteen GMCs with their tarps down, rolls out of Charters Road through the intersection and down Dock Street. Dimly visible beneath the tarps are dark faces, the whites of eyes, white teeth. "Part the Four-oh-Fourth QM Truck," the MP says. "Colored outfit. Goin' to Guinea. We gettin' rid a some the fuckin coons." The last truck rumbles by. "Okay, Soldier, on your way. Time you was in bed."

Porky crosses Flinders Street. He hates MPs and he's got a hard-on like a windsock in a Force 10 gale. But he won't jerkoff like Johnson, the Lucky Lil's radioman. Porky Wallace considers masturbation unmanly, like admitting defeat. And he has to get up at 0600 hours, catch the GI bus to Garbutt Field, watch the Second Air Depot clowns mount a new tire on the Lucky Lil. He'll set his infallible internal alarm clock. Or come to think of it, Louise will be along at 0630 with a pint mug of steaming tea, a little service the Barrier Arms provides. He may by god just grab Louise, take his chances with her old man.

* * *

The rain pounds down on Townsville, South Townsville, the harbor, the docks, Magnetic Island, Castle Hill, Garbutt Field, the 12th Station Hospital, the leaky pyramidal tents in Happy Valley and the 3rd Repple Depple. Pounds down all along the littoral, 1.5 inches in the first hour and more to come, soaking the parched land, reviving the Ross River.

The Bloody Wet. The AMF Bofors crews and beach guards seek cover as best they can. The 301st MPs hunting the missing booze slow their efforts. The 404th QM Truck (C) GIs bound for Oro Bay stand soaking in the rain on a Point Cleveland dock, waiting to board an LST, their officers and vehicles already aboard. The duty officer at the USAAC Meteorology Detachment in the Garbutt Field Control Tower phones the Air Freight sheds with a 24-hour advisory: rain continuing, ceilings and visibility well below minimums, all flights canceled. The Air Freight sheds shut down. The last light but one in the RAAF barracks, the one in the guardroom, winks out.

Two soaked 301st MP clerks in baggy blue RAAF coveralls take cover under the Lucky Lil and, squatting on their heels, oblivious to the high octane fuel over their heads, light damp Fleetwoods.

"Fuck this," Cpl. Elrod Finneman, a former Pine Bluff, Arkansas, hardware store clerk, says. "Wotta we care some flyboys liberate the fuckin officers' booze? Less call it a night. Hole up here and wait'll it's time Parker that asshole pick us up."

Pvt. Herbert Steussie, a former Hunger, Nebraska, feed mill employee, flicks his Ronson and consults his wristwatch. "Shit. It ain't even midnight yet. Four fuckin' hours we gotta wait then."

"You got a better idea?"

"No. But I thought we're supposed be clerks, the CID. Do office work. Not this undercover shit."

"You oughta know by now you do the fuckin' Army tells you. Relax. We're out of the fuckin rain anyway. We'll tell Raskovic we check a bunch airplanes, dint see no sign any booze. Or maybe we eliminate this one. It's got a fuckin flat tire."

"Awright. It was pretty fuckin dumb anyway, bring us out here inna dark. Whotta we gonna see inna fuckin' dark? Oh shit!"

A stubby Fiat truck's pulled up beside the Lucky Lil's hardstand. "Put them bloody smokes out!" a harsh Australian voice snarls. "Wot you bahstids doin' 'ere? Fook are youse anyw'y? Coom out so's we can fookin' see youse! Now! Fookin bloody move!"

3

17 DECEMBER 1943
GENERAL HEADQUARTERS, SOUTHWEST PACIFIC AREA
DAILY COMMUNIQUE

The Arawe area on the south coast of New Britain, where Allied Ground Forces under the command of Gen. Douglas MacArthur made a successful assault landing yesterday, was declared secured today but for scattered enemy resistance. Mopping-up operations are underway and are continuing also in the Finschafen area. Light Naval Force under Gen. MacArthur's command sank two enemy barges off Arawe. Other Allied Ground Forces under Gen. MacArthur's command continued their advance westwards in the Markham River Valley, liberating Loba and Wanga villages. Allied Air Forces under Gen. MacArthur's command flew 95 sorties, inflicting heavy damage to enemy positions and personnel at Wewak and Madang.

* * *

Sgt. Porky Wallace's infallible internal alarm clock goes off at 0630 and he wakes to find Louise the Barrier Arms maid with the morning tea, half a dozen heavy steaming mugs on a tray, at the open door to his room. This is a small room off the Arms' second-floor porch overlooking Garbutt Road, furnished with a metal bunkbed, a chair, a battered chest of drawers, a cracked mirror and a murky watercolor depicting an English garden. The Arms does not have many guests these days. GIs on leave head for Sydney's brighter lights or the new USAAC beachside R&R facility at MacKay fifty miles down the coast. Cpl. Johnson is alone in the next room.

It's still raining, a steady drizzle under heavy gray clouds, but there's enough daylight behind Louise to silhouette the lush young figure inside her thin cotton dress. Porky, who slept naked under a single sheet through the muggy night, studies this silhouette through the white mosquito net draped over his bottom bunk and wonders, Jeezuzz, is Louise wearing anything besides her dress and shoes! Yes, he deduces, panties, but no bra. He can see her nipples popping out. And he still has a mighty hard-on. It lifts his sheet like a tent pole.

"I brun yer tay," Louise, approaching the bunkbed, staring at the bump in the sheet, says, and wonders, What's the sar'ent's Thing look like? She's never seen a man's Thing. She's seen her sister Kate's little boy's Thing but he's just a baby, six months old, his daddy's a bloody Yank who vanished before he was born. His little Thing looks like one of the tiny white caterpillars that infest the eucalyptus. A man's Thing no doubt is much larger and sometime sticks straight up. Or so she's heard her girlfriends say when on rare occasiosn Da lets her go to the films. Two of these friends, they're seventeen, even claim to have Done It. Let a bloody Yank they met at "Desert Victory" put his Thing in them. Louise is not ready for that but she'd like to see a man's Thing. Curiosity killed the cat, Da often says. He also says, "Look wot 'appen to yer bloody stupid sister!" But Louise will take her chances, just looking.

"Put my tea on the chair," Porky says, and toys with an idea. Kick the goddamn sheet off, give Louise a big thrill. Him too. Porky rather likes to expose himself. But he has to get out to the airfield, see to the Lucky Lil's new tire. "Whyn't you bring my tea last some morning, Louise. So's we can talk."

Louise puts his tea on the chair and considers that. "I will t'morrer," she says. "Yer still 'ere," and backs out of the room with her tray.

Porky sighs, gets out of bed, finds his tea too hot to drink, gets into his uniform, goes to the loo at the end of the porch, where he wrestles with his erection, comes back, drinks his tea, still steaming, wishes he'd packed a poncho and goes downstairs to wait beneath the Arm's second-floor porch for the GI bus to Garbutt Field. The drizzle gives way to hard pounding rain. He'll check the weather at Ops but reckons they'll RON again. And he'll go on the prowl again. Louise is ready, ripe, hot to trot, is Porky's guess. But her old man, Biff Smith, an AIF sergeant in the Other Big War, bald as an egg, with a great flowing mustache, goes about 6-4 and 17 stone the way the Australians say it, 238 pounds, and he scares the hell out of Porky.

* * *

"All right, damn it, listen up!" Col. Web Allen, exhibiting leadership at 0800 hours in his former sugar warehouse office despite the way it looks, says. He looks like the Sad Sack cartoon in Yank Magazine. The khakis he's wearing, delivered as promised at 0700 hours by a 114th Laundry Detachment private, are not his khakis. They belong to some giant Enlisted Man. Nevertheless, his prickly heat off to an early start, he's wearing them, the lesser of two evils, instead of his scratchy pinks and, never mind the way he looks, treating his assembled subordinates like a bunch of green left-footed draftees. Outside, rain's pounding down, hammering the tin roof on the former warehouse. "I have two questions and by god I want answers! Whose bright idea was it to cancel the MP detail supposed to pick up the Red Cross girls at their Flinders Street Club? And whose equally bright idea was it to sneak two GIs in RAAF uniforms onto the airfield? Well?"

There is no immediate response from the subordinates: Lt.Col. Fogerty, who looks like death warmed over between his red swollen ears, Maj. Dickinson the Provost Marshal, Maj. Cain the Adjutant-General, and Capt. Raskovic the CID chief. Then Dickinson mumbles he was the one canceled the pick-up detail "on Colonel Fogerty's orders," and Raskovic admits "the undercover operation out the field" was his idea "but Colonel Fogerty gave me the OK."

"Just a minute there," Lt. Col. Fogerty, glaring at these snitches, says. "What."

"At ease, Colonel!" Web Allen, glaring at his chief-of-staff, says. "I guess we can thank you then, Colonel Fogerty, that poor girl was raped. Story I get, she was on her way home, walking up Hill Street to the Red Cross billet when four colored men, GIs, grabbed her and shoved her in a truck and took her out into the country. And raped her. That's what she told them at the 12th Station. Before they sedated her. And just in case any of you don't know it, this is the frosting on the goddamn cake. Her uncle's a Congressman. From Mississippi. And he's here! Right here in Townsville! He was supposed to fly to Moresby this morning but I assume you all know nobody's flying anywhere today. Not in this weather. So we'll have him on our hands. Colonel Fogerty, you met him. So you're the man's going to high tail it over to the George Hotel and tell the Congressman what happened to his niece and why. Before he hears it on the goddamn grapevine. I mean now, Colonel! That's an order. Move out!"

Fogerty, he's clutching a copy of GHQ Order 404:44, opens his mouth, closes it, says,"Sir!" and salutes and departs and Col. Web Allen, ignoring the salute, turns on Raskovic.

"As for you, Captain, case you don't know it, your undercover men are in the RAAF guardhouse. The field C.O., Wing Commander Hewlitt-Packard, phoned me at oh-six-hundred with that surprise. I didn't know what the hell he was talking about but he filled me in. He said he plans to charge your men with espionage and thinks they should be shot. Why not? They were in a Restricted Area in the uniforms of a nation and a service other than their own. I'll have to deal with that, Captain. You don't have the rank. But of all the dumbass ideas! You've been here long enough. You know, should know, the way the wing commander feels about Yanks."

"Sir," Dickinson says. "I said at the time that operation might provoke an Allied Relations problem. And I questioned the decision to cancel the pick-up detail."

"Sir," Raskovic says. "We were going to take those men off the airfield at oh-four-hundred. But my chief investigator, Sergeant Parker, he developed some information up at the Red Cross billet it might not been flyboys liberate our liquor. It might been the Navy. So we went down the docks, check that out. Didn't check out. Then we got the report, that girl raped. Sergeant Parker went out the field, pick up our undercover men, but they didn't show up. I guess uh by then the RAAF. But like I said, Sir, Colonel Fogerty, he authorized that operation."

"I'll take care of Colonel Fogerty, Captain," Web Allen says. "You've got that rape case and you damn well better get cracking on it!"

"Sir," Cain says. "I don't think the RAAF can make an espionage case stick, those two men. I know, the uniform thing. But chrissake, we're Allies."

"You want to talk to the wing commander? Tell him that."

"Well uh no, Sir. I don't have the rank."

"At ease then! All right. I gather it was the liquor was liberated set all this off. So hear this! I don't give a hoot in hell about the liquor! Forget it! Or learn distilling. Like the GIs in New Guinea. Our only priority is this damn rape. I understand your men are on double shifts, Provost. That stands until we get the bastards raped that girl. And reinstate those pick-up details. I got another call this morning, oh-six-thirty, from the Red Cross director. Your detail picks up the girls who staff the field Canteen didn't show up either. They had to call a taxi."

"Sir," Cain says. "I realize it's a terrible thing, that girl raped and all. But we've had rapes before."

"Not like this one, you idiot! American girl. Southern girl. Raped by colored. With an uncle who's a Congressman. From Mississippi. And he's here! Wake up, major!"

But Cain, who spends his evenings at the O Club, persists. "There was that nurse at the 12th Station. Said she was gang-raped."

"Said she was but changed her mind," Dickinson says. "Declined to testify. Our conclusion, that was just a gang-bang got out of hand."

"At ease, damn it!" Col. Web Allen says. "Forget the nurse. Forget the liquor. I want this rape solved. I want arrests and I want them yesterday!"

"But, Sir," Cain, he won't quit, says. "About the liquor. There's that GHQ Order says we're supposed to implement appropriate action forthwith."

"Major, shut up! I know all about the GHQ Order. It's not worth the paper it's written on. You think that order will stop the flyboys? They've got flight pay and procurement officers and aircraft. What's this appropriate action you'd like to implement forthwith? Shut down Garbutt Field?"

"Well uh, no, Sir. But."

"At ease then! Now listen up. These are orders."

M/Sgt. Abbott pops out of his adjoining office. "Sir, there's a phone call for Colonel Fogerty. From Service Force Headquarters. Lieutenant Colonel Pulaski. He says it's top urgent, Sir."

"Cain," Web Allen says. "Go see what that's all about." Cain, followed by Abbott, goes to see what that's all about. "All right. Captain, get your men together. Go see the girl who was raped and get going on that. I'm going to go see her too. We're done here."

"Sir," Raskovic says. "Two my men, I only got three. They're the ones the RAAF caught."

"Oh christ," Web Allen says. "Provost, give the captain here some men. Any help he needs."

"Colonel, S-Sir," Cain, emerging visibly shaken from Abbott's office, says. "That call. Colonel P-P-Pulaski. He's a friend, he said, of Colonel F-Fogerty. He called to advise Colonel F-Fogerty. Warn him like! Brigadier-General B-Bargle left Sydney this morning! On one of his inspection t-t-tours! In a airplane. It's not raining in Sydney. General B-B-Bargle is on his way here, Sir!"

"Oh shit!" Col. Web Allen says. Ordinarily, this frightening development would take precedence over all else (an ugly rape, lost liquor, a junketing Congressman, the speedy prosecution of The War) while the Base Section bends all its efforts to preparations for one of Brig. Gen. Sedgewick O. Bargle's dreaded unexpected inspections. But Col. Web Allen makes a courageous command decision. "All right, major. I'll tell Colonel Fogerty. He'll alert all units. But this rape case is still our number one priority. You concentrate on that, Captain. You too, Provost. Forget General Bargle. Forget the liquor. Just catch the bastards raped that girl! Any questions?" There are no questions. "Dismissed!"

The forces of Law and Order depart and Web Allen, abruptly close to what seems to be utter exhaustion though he did get a few hours sleep following another romp with Jill Tucker, slumps at his desk and massages his temples. So now he has an ugly rape and a dammed Congressman and Brig. Gen. S.O. Bargle, Service Force deputy commander, a world-class s.o.b., plucking at his sanity. A can of worms if ever there was one. He detests Brig. Gen. S.O. Bargle and Bargle doesn't like him either. Not since their little run-in at Service Force HQ. And Lord knows the Townsville Base Section is not ready for an inspection. Never will be. Brig. Gen. Bargle, no doubt, will find the Base Section wanting in many respects, enjoy tearing its operation to shreds, then no doubt chew Col. Web Allen's ass at great length and enjoy that too. Immensely. That's what the s.o.b. does best.

But The War, Col. Web Allen thinks, won't last forever. Years yet maybe but some day, eventually, it will be over, the Allies victorious, that's the assumption anyway, and he'll go home. Before The War is over, perhaps. There's a rumor the War Department is considering a Rotation Plan (subject to manpower requirements) based on "points" awarded for months of service, months overseas, wounds and decorations. Eighty-five points, the rumor is, will be the magic number, and he (without wounds or decorations) now has fifty-nine.

Web Allen's mind wanders. The U.S. Army Air Corps, naturally, has always had a Rotation Plan. Bomber crews fly fifty missions, then go home. Fighter pilots and transport pilots too. They fly more missions but also go home. In the middle of the war. Fifty missions. Fifty days in combat but they're not full days, six to eight hours most days, the way Web Allen views this. Infantry rifle companies put in twenty-four-hour days, the nights frequently worse than the days, but do not pile up any "missions." The rifle companies simply go on and on and their GIs and junior officers, presently, observing Tom and Dick and Harry and others killed instantly or mortally wounded, blown to pieces, in close proximity to themselves, no longer believe in their own immortality. They grow fatalistic, their best slim hope a cushy wound: no missing parts or ugly scars or permanent disability, but one bad enough (good enough) to get them evacced.

The late Sgt. Barney Clark, a realist, once (overheard by Web Allen) put that in a grim nutshell for several West Coast replacements claiming to be Quartermaster clerks and consequently vastly unhappy on finding themselves in Fox Co. "You assholes," the late Sgt. Clark said. "Might's well get ust the idea. The owny way you ever gonna get out a this outfit, get out a the fuckin' Infantry, is you get a arm or a leg or your balls or your fuckin head blowed off."

Some kind of premonition, that? Web Allen thinks it unlikely. There are numerous stories about premonitions: the GI who gives a buddy the silver cigarette case his fiancee sent him, then goes Over the Top (or wades through a swamp in Swappa's War) and gets himself killed. But the late Sgt. Clark was simply a realist and he doesn't want to think about the late Sgt. Clark anyway.

Web Allen sits staring out at the rain pounding down. Points or no points (the rumored Rotation Plan may be stillborn), he's pretty sure he'll survive The War. At some future point, no doubt, assuming The War goes well, the Base Section will abandon Townsville and relocate in some Forward Area where the risks are marginally greater. But, barring an unexpected airplane disaster or an errant bomb or a Jap torpedo or fatal auto crash if Fazoli remains his driver, all of which he considers unlikely, he's pretty sure he'll survive and eventually go home. Home to West Cork and live happily ever after. With Jill Tucker at his side. But that's patently ridiculous. Sheer fantasy. It's not a plausible scenario. Big city girl like Jill in West Cork. Not likely. He's told Jill something of West Cork, a quite little town but there's a lot going on there: the annual Pierce County Fair, a major Polka Fest. Great place to raise kids. Jill evinced no interest in that or motherhood, only said, "I really don't think anybody can plan anything, what with the The War and all." Besides which, a fact that looms up like Gibraltar, there's Mert, and his daughters. He'll not hurt Mert. Can't. Mert's a good woman, good wife, good mother.

Web Allen heaves a long hopeless sigh. His prickly heat erupts. He grits his teeth, resists the temptation to claw at his crotch, thinks about icebergs. His prickly heat subsides. You'd think the weather would be cooler with rain bucketing down but it's not. Yesterday was hot and dry. Today is wet and hotter. Muggy. Summer's coming on and the daily high in Townsville, he's heard, soon will hit 100 F. Prickly heat weather. There are times and this is one of them when Web Allen half wishes he'd never met Jill Tucker. His life would be a lot easier were that the case. But it's too late for that now. He loves, he's in love with, Jill Tucker. That's patently ridiculous, but she seems to be always or almost always in his thoughts and he the happier for that.

But not exactly estatic. Not in the giant EM's khakis, the pant legs rolled, his hands lost in the shirtsleeves. Col. Web Allen phones the 114th Portable Laundry Detachment. The C.O., a first john, is not there, his whereabouts unknown. Web Allen reams the corporal who answers the phone, gets another abject apology and another promise: the colonel's khakis, clean and pressed, will absolutely be delivered to the colonel's billet no later than 1100 hours. Web Allen phones his billet and instructs Pvt. Cerna: call me when my uniforms come and send the big ones back to the 114th.

These operations vital to the speedy prosecution of The War complete, Col. Web Allen sits staring at the rain pounding down and the thick gray clouds low in the sky above Burns-Phelps Pty. Ltd. But that's of no assistance to the speedy prosecution of and he has a duty to perform, unpleasant though it be, never mind he looks like the Sad Sack. "Sergeant Abbott!" Abbott pops in. "Go find my driver. I'm going out to the 12th Station. See that poor girl who was raped."

Web Allen hates rape, rapists and rape cases. He tried a few when assistant Pierce County prosecutor. The proceedings were always harder on the victims than the sullen defendants and he always thought about his daughters. Outside the rain's slowed to a steady drizzle. No doubt the Ross River is rising fast and the damn bridge over it is far from finished. But that's just a detail under the circumstances.

* * *

Alison Culpepper (Boots) Davis (tall, tanned, slender, her dark hair chopped short) wakes woozily at 0900 hours in one of the private rooms usually reserved for majors and other higher ranks in the Officers Ward, a quonset hut, at the 12th Station Hospital, the EM ward are in tents, and wonders: Where am I? There's a small unfamiliar window wet with rain in the curved wall beside her bed. She's wearing baggy blue GI pajamas and the mosquito net draped over the bed is olive drab. She sleeps in her cotton panties and the nets at Manic Manor are white. Then everything, the terrible thing that happened to her, comes flooding back, sweeping over her like a tsunami.

Raped! She was raped! Raped twice! Fucked! By two nigras! Kidnapped and raped! She feels bruised, used, incredibly dirty. Dirty dirty dirty! She'll never feel clean again. And her life is over. In ruins. Finished at twenty-five. But did it really happen? Yes, it really happened. She was raped. Twice. By two nigras. She hopes they burn in Hell! She'd like to watch that. Watch them burn, twist and scream. It's still hard to believe. But her jaw hurts. Where one of them hit her. The big one.

There's a knock at the door and a Medical Corps captain comes in, a short man with his shirtsleeves rolled, hairy arms, a stethoscope around his neck. He lifts half the mosquito net, pulls up the only chair and sits beside the bed. Outside, rain's pounding down, streaming down the window.

"I'm Captain Sussman," he says. "How are you feeling?" Boots mumbles, Not so good. "No, I guess not. You had a bad time, Miss Davis. A very bad time. Traumatic. You may still be a little fuzzy. We sedated you. But you're all right, physically. Nothing broken, I mean. You took a pretty good whack on the jaw. It'll be sore for a few days but it wasn't fractured . You're a tough lady. The other thing. Well, there'll be some MPs here pretty soon. They want to question you. Hard, I know. But has to be done, I guess. Meantime, if you have any questions I can answer."

Boots takes a deep breath. "Disease," she says. "Do I have a disease? And oh god! I might be pregnant! It's that time."

"They didn't use condoms? If you know, I mean. I mean you've uh well uh had previous sexual."

"Yes. No. They didn't use condoms. The bastards!"

"Don't worry, Miss Davis. I know that's a dumb thing to say. But we took smears. It'll be a few days, we know about any disease. But don't worry. There's a new drug, Penicillin. You may have heard of it. Penicillin will take care of that. Pregnancy? I doubt that's the case but if it is, you are. Well, I can do a d-and-

c. Or we can send you to the 5th General in Brisbane. They do early abortions there. On the q.t. If that's what you want."

"Oh god, yes!"

"All right then. Don't worry. I know that's a dumb thing to say. But I'm an ear nose and throat man. Treating prickly heat and gunshot wounds. I really don't know what to say in these circumstances."

"Sussman?" Boots, who doesn't want to think about these circumstances, her circumstances, says. "There was a Red Cross Field Director, Sussman, in Brisbane."

"My brother Melvin. He's in Port Moresby now. Doesn't like it much."

"Oh god! I'm supposed to go to Moresby! New Guinea. Was, I mean. Today! Oh, damn it! Goddamn them!" And Boots begins to cry.

"Oh there there," Capt. Sussman, wishing he were somewhere else, says . "You can still go to New Guinea, Miss Davis. Day or so here, I'm sure we'll discharge you. Nobody's going to New Guinea today. Nobody's going anywhere. All the airplanes are grounded. I guess what the natives call The Bloody Wet's started. Oh hell!" Medical School didn't teach him to treat, counsel, rape victims. "Are you hungry? Would you like some breakfast or anything?"

Boots stifles her sobs. "Just coffee. And a bath. Or a shower. I feel so damn dirty!"

"I'll see to it," Capt. Sussman says. "Might take awhile. Showers are Red Lined. Kitchen too. There's a general coming. For an inspection. We're getting ready for that." He lifts the rest of the mosquito net, drapes it on its frame and escapes. Did the best he could, he thinks, but what the hell can anybody do in these circumstances?

Outside, the rain slows to a drizzle. The coffee arrives, delivered by a Limited Service GI ward boy who surveys Boots with great curiosity, then departs. Moments later, three visitors wearing wet raincoats arrive: Colonel Allen, Jill Tucker's boyfriend, Agnes Moore the Manor housemother and Ann Silvers.

They stand around in their wet raincoats. Nobody much knows what to say. Boots puts up a pretty good front: she damn well won't cry in front of everybody. Then Agnes says she and Ann came right out to the hospital last night, soon's they heard, and brought Boots some clothes and loafers, the hospital said one of her shoes was missing, but Boots was sedated then. Her clothes are in the chest of drawers, her loafers are under the bed. Colonel Allen says he's terribly sorry, can't begin to say how sorry he is, this thing happened, and explains. There was a mix-up with the MP pick-up detail but that will never happen again, those responsible severely reprimanded. But a fat lot of good any of that does. He also says, "We'll catch the men did this, Miss Davis, you have my word on that, and try them and convict them and by god hang them! Sentence them to hang anyway. Sentences might be commuted." But a fat lot of good that does. Hanging too good for the bastards anyway, too easy, too quick. Everybody says anything she wants just name it.

At which point Uncle Festus, U.S. Rep. Festus Lee Claypool, and his aide, the swifty who made a play for Jill Tucker, roll in. Boots was dreading this but expecting it, sure the grapevine swiftly spread the juicy report: bunch of coons humped a Red Cross girl! The aide helps Uncle Festus out of his raincoat and holds it and Uncle Festus embraces Boots or tries to, smelling of whiskey, drooling on her GI pajamas.

"Oh ma pore litull Bootie, this turrble turrble thang!" Uncle Festus says, nine or ten times, then turns his wrath on Web Allen. "This be uh diss-grace, Cuhnel, this turrble turrble thang! Ma pore lil nee-uss. Murkin gurl doin' her bit. Ohmee all 'round her and Ah toll yawl yawl taken good cay of her and this turrble turrble thang happen! Gahdamn nigras! They ott uh oll be castrate! Ah allas said that. Yawl light cuhnel as had dinnuh with me lass night and come see me the ho-tel this mawin, waken me opp and tell me this turrble turrble thang happen, he say they be uh mix-up, some dee-tail sposed pick litull Bootie up derelic' in they duty! Ah be hole yawl puhsonally ree-sponsbul foh that, Cuhnel! Yawl bettuh cotch them gahdam nigras done this turrble turrble thang! Cotch them and hangs them high! Or Ah get back in Wash'ton Ah by god gonna call onna Congress for uh in-ves-tee-gay-shun!"

"We'll catch them, Sir," Web Allen says. "Catch them, court-martial them, convict them and hang them. Well, sentence them to hang. Sometimes, Sir, those sentences are commuted."

"Not if Ah can helps it!" U.S. Rep Claypool says. "Them gahdam nigras done this turrble turrble thang ain't nevuh evuh gonna be commuted! Make uh note that, Calvin! Oh what om Ah gonna tell yawl pore Mama, Bootie? This turrble turrble."

"Nothing!" Boots says. "Not one word! You ever tell Mama anything, Uncle Festus, I'll kill you!"

"Theyuh theyuh now, litull Bootie," Rep. Claypool, patting Boots' hand, says. "Fonn wi' me, that the way yawl wants it. Ah can unnerstan' that. Ah nevuh tell yawl pore Mama nuffin'. Not nuffin. Ah promiss, word uh gennemum, membuh The Congress."

He moves to embrace Boots again and drool on her pajamas but Capt. Sussman arrives and intervenes. "There are MPs here," he says. "They want to question Miss Davis. I'll have to ask you people to leave."

Rep Claypool, noting he's a "long stannin' membuh the Missis-sippi bah," thinks he should remain "wholl pore litull Bootie is question," but is dissuaded. He has a ten o'clock meeting with the Lord Mayor, Mister Applecart, Calvin Winsome reminds him, and bundles him into his raincoat and out of the room with the others.

"Are you ready for this?" Capt. Sussman says. "Talk about it?" Ready as she'll ever be, Boots says, and Capt. Sussman de-parts, leaving the door open for Capt. Dominic Raskovic and Sgt. Harry Parker, both in wet raincoats. Raskovic closes it.

"Hi, Boots," Harry says.

"Harry!"

"You two know each other?" Raskovic says.

"Manner of speaking," Harry says.

"Well, make it easier then," Raskovic says. "Maybe." He sits on the chair beside the bed in his raincoat. "I'm Captain Raskovic, Miss Davis. Criminal Investigation Detachment. And I tell you this. I interrogate a number of uh well rape victims I was with LAPD and there prolly eight-hundred things I rather do. But it got to be done, we're gonna apprehend the perpetrators. So just tell us what happen. You take notes, Sergeant."

Harry digs a notebook and pencil from inside his raincoat. Boots takes a deep breath. This won't be easy but if helps catch the bastards.

"I closed the Flinders Street Club at twenty-two-hundred. Rose Pearl Stevens, the other girl, left early. Her date picked her up. I waited for the MP detail that picks us up but it didn't come. There was an air crew sergeant hanging around said he'd walk me home but I knew if he did I'd have a hassle with him. I told him there were MPs coming and he left. What a joke, huh?"

It's a joke so funny Boots begins to cry. Raskovic and Harry wait in silence. Boots wipes her eyes and takes another deep breath.

"So I waited but the MP detail didn't come and I decided to walk. It's only eight blocks to the billet. I was halfway up Hill Street when a truck pulled up beside me and stopped and this damn big nigra jumped out of the cab and two more jumped out of the back. They grabbed me and the big one threw a blanket over my head. It all happened so fast I couldn't do anything. I couldn't even yell. The big one had his hand over my mouth. They picked me up and put me in the truck. The front. The big one got in with me and there was a driver and I suppose the other two got in the back."

"Did they," Raskovic says. "say anything?"

"The big one, he had his mouth right up against my ear, said, 'We just gonna have some fun, baby. Don't make no trouble and you won't get hurt.' He had one arm around me and he was holding me tight and he still had his hand over my mouth. He was strong. He'd been drinking. He wasn't drunk but he'd been drinking. Beer, I think. I could smell it on his breath." Boots takes another deep breath. "The driver turned the truck around in the middle of Hill Street and we went down Hill Street and along Flinders Street and out Charters Road, I'm pretty sure. I heard a train whistle anyway. Then out into the country. Not very far. Then turned left over some railroad tracks and down a bumpy road a little ways and stopped. I think it was a place there was a camp once. There was a cement slab there anyway. They pulled me out of the truck. I still had the blanket over my head."

"Did you," Raskovic says. "Say anything?"

"I said Please don't. The big one said, 'Shut up.' I knew what they were going to do or wanted to do and I was afraid they'd make me do, well, other things too. And I was afraid they'd kill me. Afterwards. They pushed me down on the cement. On my back. Two of them, I think the two that were in the back, held my arms and held the blanket over my head. The big one, I know it was him, pushed my skirt up and tore my panties off. And raped me. It didn't take him very long."

"Did you," Raskovic says. "Well uh resist? Struggle?"

"Some. A little. It didn't do any good. I guess by then I mostly just wanted to get it over with. I was still afraid they might kill me."

"Did the big one," Raskovic says. "Well uh ejaculate?"

"Oh yes! He did. The bastard! Then when he was finished he held one of my arms and another one raped me. One of the ones that was in the back, I think. Not the driver, I'm pretty sure. It didn't take him very long either. He went off too. The bastard! Then I think it was the other one was in the back was getting ready for his turn when I guess they saw headlights or something coming down the bumpy road. The big one said, 'Motherfuck, somebody coming, let's haul ass!' I yelled Help! That was when he hit me. I think it was him, the big one. On the jaw. I guess he knocked me out. Just for a minute. When I came to and got the blanket off my head they were gone and there was a jeep, I could just make it out in the dark, parked across the road. I yelled Help! again and the people in the jeep, they were a captain and a nurse from the 12th Station, came and found me and brought me to the hospital."

Boots shuts her eyes. Tears roll down her cheeks: she can't help that. She, Alison Culpepper Davis, raped! Twice! By two nigras!

"We'll talk to them," Raskovic says. "The captain and the nurse. I can't begin to tell you, Miss Davis, how sorry we are this thing happened." A fat lot of good that does. "But we'll apprehend the bastards. I promise you that. Did you hear any names? Did they call each other anything at any point?"

"No. When they pulled me out of the truck the big one said, 'Don't nobody say no names, we just be numbers and I be Number One.'"

"Smart bastard," Raskovic says. "Did you see any number or anything on the truck, we might ID it?"

"There was a number on the front bumper but I only saw it for a second when they grabbed me. It think it was four-zero-four something."

"Sonofagun!" Harry Parker says. "Four-oh-Fourth QM Truck! That's a Colored outfit. Moved out last night. Part of it."

"What time?" Raskovic says.

"Don't know. Late. Easy find out."

"We'll check it. Tell me, Miss Davis, did you touch anything in the truck? I'm thinking fingerprints."

"I think," Boots says. "I put one hand on the dashboard up by the windshield. And on the seat beside the driver when we were on the bumpy road. And the door, when they pushed me in. But I'm not sure."

"Would you recognize any of those men if you saw them again?"

"Oh god," Boots says. "I don't ever want to see any of them again! I don't know. It was dark and I only saw the big one and the driver for about a second before they put the blanket over my head. The driver was sort of skinny. But nigras all look the same to me." Boots closes her eyes and a tear rolls down her cheek. "I might recognize the big one's voice. He didn't say much but he didn't sound Southern. If you know what I mean. He sounded more like a Northern nigra."

Raskovic doesn't know what Boots means but nods. "Well, I guess that's all for now, Miss Davis. You've been a big help. Really. We might want to question you again and we'll have to get a formal statement from you but that can wait. You think of anything else might help us apprehend the bastards you let us know. And I am really sorry this happen to you. I really am. Really really sorry."

He really is sorry, Boots guesses, but a fat lot of good that does. "I lost one of my loafers. And my panties. They might still be there where."

"We'll check it out," Raskovic, rising from the chair, says. "The other uh clothes you were wearing, Miss Davis, we'll have to take those. For evidence. Hospital must have them. There's kind of a forensics lab, GHQ, and you never know. You got other clothes you can wear?"

Boots nods. Harry steps to the bed and squeezes her hand. "You're okay, Boots," he says. "Just hang in there." Harry's touch does a little good, not much. Steady rain is falling outside the window.

The captain and nurse who found Boots, Capt. Carlton Brooks, an orthopedist by trade, and First Lt. Jan Peters, a sultry surgical nurse, prove of little value when Raskovic and Harry question them in Brooks' office.

"We just wanted to get away from the hospital for a little while," Capt. Brooks says. "But christ, I'm a married man. I wouldn't want my wife hears that and takes it wrong, you know. She's in Minneapolis but you never know. We had a case here, a head case. Perfectly innocent friendship but we evacced him Back to the States, he phones the wife. We just wanted to get away from the hospital for a little while."

A likely story, Capt. Raskovic thinks. Wasn't it Lt. Peters was involved in that gang-bang or whatever? But he calms the orthopedist. "I understand that, Captain. That's none of our business anyway. Red Cross girl you found was raped is our business. But maybe you and the lieutenant here can give us some help, apprehend the bastards raped her. That's if you saw anything, the scene the crime."

But all Capt. Brooks and Lt. Peters saw was a deuce-and-a-half tearing up the road they were driving down, that road where the colored Dock company was camped before it moved out, the colored called it Lenox Avenue. The deuce-and-a-half damn near hit their jeep but it was just a deuce-and-a half, hundreds like it in Townsville. Then they drove on a little ways and parked, just to have a cigarette, and heard somebody yelling "Help!" and found Miss Davis and brought her to the hospital, the ER.

"She wasn't exactly hysterical but she was pretty shaken up," Lt. Peters says, and that's her contribution to the investigation.

"You won't want us for witnesses or anything, will you?" Capt. Brooks says. "I mean we actually didn't see anything and like I said, I'm a married man. And I'm pretty busy. We're expecting casualties from, where is it, Arawe? And I've got to update my charts. There's a general coming, inspect the hospital."

"Probably not," Raskovic says. "But we'll let you know." Let the bastard with the wife in Minneapolis sweat a little.

Outside then, in their jeep with Military Police on the front bumper, Harry at the wheel, rain hammering the canvas top, Boots' skirt and blouse and bra and left loafer in a paper sack under the dash, Raskovic says, "We'll check the scene the crime. You know that road, Lenox Avenue? Find her panties maybe, shoe, blanket she mention. Tire tracks too but rain prolly wreck them. No sense cast them anyway. All the goddamn trucks got the same tires. We got something else put evidence in?"

"There's more sacks under my seat," Harry says, driving out of the 12th Station Hospital parking area (a dozen GI ward boys in wet ponchos are raking its gravel and washing the little white stones that border it) and south on Charters Road, full of puddles hiding potholes, past Happy Valley (where GIs in wet ponchos are tussling with the ropes on wet pyramidals, pulling them taut) then brakes to a stop. There's a long line of deuce-and-a-halfs halted ahead of them, some kind of tie-up.

To their right is the 3rd Repple Depple, two-hundred wet sagging pyramidals. GIs in wet ponchos are raking the walkways between the pyramidals and washing the little white stones that border the walks. The Rep Dep HQ is a quonset hut in a stand of eucalyptus close to Charters Road. There's a staff car parked under the eucalyptus and four GIs in wet ponchos huddled beside the quonset.

"What the hell," Raskovic says. "Those GIs doing sitting in the goddamn rain?"

"Bird Patrol," Harry says, and explains. The Rep Dep C.O., Lt. Col. William Farmer, got his hands on that staff car when it turned up in a September supply convoy. He parks it under the eucalyptus, keep the sun off it. But kookaburras, large black-and-white birds with a raucous cry, Australia's national bird, roost in the eucalyptus and shit on the staff car. Or would if the Bird Patrol organized by Lt. Col. Farmer, four Rep Dep GIs picked at random, roused at 0400 hours when the kookaburras wake, armed with metal slingshots manufactured by the 330th Ordnance Co. and a pail full of ball-bearings, didn't pepper the kookaburras with ball-bearings and drive them off. In fact, there's a lone kookaburra coming in for a landing now on one of the eucalyptus. The GIs stand, unlimber their slingshots, load and fire.

"Be dammed!" Raskovic reports. "They hit it!" The kookaburra squawks and flies away, the traffic ahead moves and Harry drives on. "I wonder what those GIs gonna tell their kids, they ever have any, kids ask, What you do in the war, Daddy? Shot birds? Hell, me too, I ever have any kids. I never seen a goddamn

Jap. Prolly never will. I ain't gonna tell them I spent lots my time catching guys was pissing in the street." But Raskovic's not much given to introspection. "Okay, we'll check the scene the crime. Then take a little run the Base QM. Interrogate that Aussie broad Flapp says typed the p.o. and so on for the O Club booze the goddamn flyboys liberate."

"Booze?" Harry says. "I thought you said this rape case our Number One Priority?"

"Yeah, well, it is," Raskovic says. "But I got a call from Colonel Fogerty, the office, you were gasssin' up the jeep. Fogerty says the booze our Number One Priority. He quote me that GHQ Order again. Said the Red Cross girl prolly been fucked before. Many times. Colonel Allen, though, he made it pretty clear. Forget the booze, he said, apprehend the bastards raped that girl. So whatta you think we do, Sergeant?"

"Well, hell. Allen's got the rank. He's the Base Commander."

"I know that. But Fogerty's a vindictive bastard. And I hear we got officers going nuts at the O Club. Two goddamn drinks and they got to call it a night. Cain, the A.G., he call me too, quote me that GHQ Order. Fogerty prolly put him up to it."

"What's the Provost say?"

"Hnh!" Raskovic snorts. "Provost takin' cover. He says I'm in charge all the investigations. Use my own judgment." They ride for a time in silence, the rain pounding down under thick gray clouds, looking for Lenox Avenue, while Raskovic mutters then makes a command decision. "Way I see it, Chief Investigator, we got to work both these goddamn cases. Apprehend the bastards raped that girl. And find the goddamn booze. Apprehend the goddamn flyboys liberate the booze too, but Colonel Fogerty mostly just wants the booze back. The other thing, case you don't know it, is the goddamn RAAF caught our undercover guys. Finneman and what's his name, Steussie?"

"I wonder what happen to them," Harry says. "When I went and get them up and they dint show up. But I figger they prolly just piss off and walk back the company. I dint have time this morning, inquire they was back the company."

"They dint show up because they was in the RAAF guardhouse. RAAF bastard runs the field, the one hates Yanks, he phoned Allen. Bastard claims they're same as spies. But Allen's gonna handle that. Spring 'em, I hope. We are gonna be up to our ass in paperwork, this goddamn rape. You know anybody else the company can type?"

"There's a kid name Redhardt in Second Platoon. Lionel Redhardt. He's a pretty good blackjack player and I hear him say once he can type."

"I'll ask the Provost give us him, t d y. Hey, that the road?"

It's a narrow muddy road winding into the scrub on their left beside a tall eucalyptus with a faded sign, Lenox Avenue, nailed to its trunk. Harry turns onto this road, bumps over the Q&NR track and shifts the jeep into four-wheel drive.

* * *

RAAF Wing Cmdr. Haines Hewlitt-Packard, the Garbutt Field commander (a tall thin man in his early fifties with a long bony face, a long thin nose and sparse gray hair, RAAF Reserve, an assistant bank manager in Sydney when the Pacific War began and he was called up) observes the rain pounding down outside his barracks office and a portion of his command: the Air Freight sheds, the ATOP without its usual frieze of servicemen awaiting air transport, the bloody Yanks' Red Cross Canteen, the Control Tower and Ops Office manned by bloody loafing Yanks probably playing poker. There's a lone B25 bomber with Pistol Packin' Mama on its nose, silly bloody Yank name, parked on the apron, but it's not going anywhere. Nobody's going anywhere today, everything socked in, Brisbane to Nadzab, ceilings near zero, visibility little better. Bloody Yanks' first ATC C54 direct from their bloody States won't be landing today either as scheduled.

The Bloody Wet's off to a roaring start, no break in it foreseen for thirty-six to forty-eight hours, say the weather boffins.

So, Wing Cmdr. Hewlitt-Packard happily surmises, the plonk somebody, bloody Yank airmen no doubt, lifted off the bloody Yanks' O Club, is likely still in Townsville. Very likely, in fact, that plonk, still missing at last report, is aboard one of the dozen or so Dakotas, bloody Yanks call them C47s, parked on his airfield. The two bloody Yanks in RAAF coveralls his security patrol caught hiding under a Dakota in the dead of night pretty well proves that theory.

Wing Comdr. Hewlitt-Packard smiles a rare small tight smile. Bloody Yanks lost their plonk and he in a manner of speaking most likely has it. Can't immediately lay hands on it, unfortunately, though that's something to think about and he bloody well will think about it. He's the field commander but his men can't search bloody Yank aircraft. No authority. Bloody Yanks can't lay hands on their plonk either though. Not with extra sentries posted, orders issued, no unauthorized personnel allowed near aircraft. Sentries kept a close eye on the Second Air Depot crew mounting a tire on a Dakota at 0800 hours. Bloody Yank air crew that liberated the plonk is authorized of course. He can't keep air crew from their aircraft. But that crew's not going anywhere today. Or tomorrow. Not with the Bloody Wet. They must be sweating, aircraft full of plonk they can't fly anywhere. Two he has in custody are sweating too. Told they'll face spy charges, likely be shot, one began to bawl. Bloody Yank cry baby. Can't hold them forever of course, bloody Allies. Long enough though, make them and other bloody Yanks squirm.

Hewlitt-Packard smiles another small tight smile. He hates the bloody Yanks and well he should. It was a bloody Yank B25 bombardier on leave after flying five missions or some such minimal number got his only daughter, Sybil, just turned nineteen, preggers. Only daughter, only child now, Jeremy killed at El Alamein. On July 4, Sybil thinks, bloody Yank holiday. Bloody bombardier named Petr Syzmonski. Bloody

Middle Europe mongrel short a vowel. Promised to marry Sybil of course, next leave, lesser of two evils though barely. Then bloody Syzmonski got himself killed, his B25 hit by flak over Wewak with a full bomb load. Blew up, no survivors. That was the story Sybil got anyway, bloody letter from one of Syzmonski's mates. Hewlitt-Packard suspected this mate might be lying, protecting Syzmonski's bloody arse, used his connections and finally, bloody Yanks reluctant to admit aircraft losses, confirmed that. Bloody Syzmonski is dead all right. Sybil is six-months preggers and pretty soon now Hewlitt-Packard will be the grandparent of a bloody little half-Middle Europe mongrel bastard, male or female as the case may be.

Bloody stain on the family name. Good old Australian family name. First ancestor came out on a prison ship. Guard though, flogged a few Irish en route. Plain Hewlitt then, good English name. Next ancestor hit it big in the New South Wales gold strike, put the family into banking, added Packard. Went to America with his gold, came home to Melbourne with a Packard automobile. Bloody Yank automobile but very prestigious, those days, only one in Melbourne. Well, nothing wrong with a new name. Other than bloody Syzmonski.

The rain lets up a little. Hewlitt-Packard watches a plump bloody Yank Red Cross girl with a raincoat over her shoulders come out of the rear door of their Canteen and study the lorry parked there, kind the Yanks call a deuce-and-a-half. Parked there since yesterday, Hewlitt-Packard thinks. Bloody Yanks park them anywhere, go off and leave them. The Red Cross girl goes back into the Canteen.

Hewlitt-Packard smiles another small tight smile. Bloody Yank Red Cross girl he met at the All Forces Officers reception for a bloody Yank film star out to entertain troops seems willing. Rose Pearl Stevens. Odd name, Rose Pearl, but Stevens is a good English name. Tall blonde, fairly bonzer figure, suits his plan. Impressed by the Australia Club and his personal transport, an Afrika Korps command car captured in the Western

Desert, left to him when the RAAF squadron that captured it was shifted to one of the airstrips outside Port Moresby. R.P. Stevens also has orders for Moresby but nobody's going to Moresby, anywhere in New Guinea, today. Time to strike, though. He'll pick her up at 2130 hours at the bloody Yanks' other ranks club. Last night just a reconnaissance. They'll have a late dinner, drinks and wine at the Club. More drinks in his room there. Bloody Yank got Sybil pregnant. He'll do the same for one of them. With a little luck. Hortense, wife, no doubt not approve. But it's his plan, not her's, one he's been crafting for three months.

The rain's pounding down hard again. Wing Cmdr.Hewlitt-Packard decides it's time, going on noon, he phones the bloody Yanks' Base Section commander again. Colonel Allen, equivalent rank. They've met several times. Allen seems a decent sort considering he's a bloody Yank and he's phoned three times, put off by the duty sergeant. Wants his bloody spies released, no doubt. Bloody nuisance phoning though, military phone system. He'll let the sergeant do it, ask Allen to lunch at the Australia Club. Might as well, nothing going on at the field, rain all the bloody day. Buy the bloody Yank a good whiskey, probably needs one. Heard he has another bloody rape on his hands, Red Cross girl, bloody Yank blackfellows. Bad show. Find out what the bloody Yanks know about their missing plonk too, rumor there's a GHQ Order might give them some clout, rumor they'll go running to GHQ, bloody MacArthur, for help. Best be forewarned. "Sergeant Keeney!"

Sgt. James Keeney (a scrawny little man with battered knuckles and a mighty mustache, wearing RAAF dress blues, some of whose ancestors were flogged by Hewlitt-Packard's, a first-class aircraft mechanic in the Other Big War, Leftenant Hewlitt-Packard's mechanic before the Leftenant, shot down on his third sortie, wound up in a Jerry POW camp) pops in from his adjoining office, stamps his foot, salutes and shouts, "Sir!"

"Sergeant, phone Colonel Allen for me. Bloody Yank Base Section commander. Ask him to lunch with me at the Club, oh-twelve-thirty, discuss Allied Relations Problem. His bloody spies. And raise my driver. I'll lunch there in any case. Be all quiet here today, The Bloody Wet."

"Sir!"

"Further orders. My considered opinion, Sergeant, that plonk the bloody Yanks are crying about is aboard one of their Dakotas on our airfield. Must be, bloody Yanks itching to search aircraft yesterday. But there'll be no Dakotas going anywhere today. Or tomorrow. Take some men and undertake a little reconnaissance. Should you locate the bloody Dakota of which I speak, I would not be adverse to a little sabotage. Ground the bloody aircraft. Leave that to you. I know you're a sly one. Bugger all the bloody Yanks then. Bloody Yanks who lost their plonk. Bloody Yanks who hope to transport it somewhere. Be a bonzer day then."

"Sir!" Sgt. Keeney, stamping his foot and saluting, says. "Orders received and understood!"

* * *

USAAC Col. Robert (Big Bob) Betrandus, the Second Air Depot commander (a big man with a big pale face, perfect teeth and wavy blond hair, wearing crisp pinks, both his medal ribbons, American Defense, Asiatic-Pacific, and small silver wings that date to his airline days but some think denote a pilot), is having lunch, fresh fish and french fries awash in ketchup, with his principal subordinates at the table by the picture window reserved for them in the Air Depot Officers Mess. Second Air Depot (which reports to Air Service Command in Brisbane, the Fifth Air Force supply arm) has an arrangement with two local fisherman: the fishermen get petrol from the Depot's tanks and the Officers Mess gets fresh fish. This mess, also the Depot Officers Club, occupies one end of a long sturdy frame building set on short pilings with termite guards. Its eight tables have tablecloths. The Depot EM eat at bare picnic tables in the other end. A single kitchen between them serves both ends but, barring a record catch, the EM do not get fresh fish. Outside the picture window rain's pounding down on the half dozen large quonset huts that house the Depot's repair shops, the hundred pyramidal tents scattered among the eucalyptus trees for its EM, the officers share a barracks, and the putting green Big Bob had built. But there'll be no putting today for pound notes, at which Big Bob excels.

The subordinates, whose current duties are not particularly surprising given the Armed Forces' personnel policies, are Lt. Col. Bert Gerber, the Depot chief-of-staff, a partner in his daddy's Boise, Idaho, restaurant supply business in civil life, Maj. Lew Richall, the Engineering officer, a peacetime Tucson florist, and Maj. Jason Reeves, the personnel chief, a Denver bulk oil dealer Before The War. They have discussed with Big Bob the latest local rape, a juicy one, Red Cross girl gang-banged by eight coons, finding it deplorable, and agreed with Big Bob, they always agree with Big Bob, it's high time GHQ shipped all the coons to New Guinea. "More like their natural habitat" in Big Bob's opinion. Not so deplorable (Second Air Depot and the Base Section, in fierce competition for what passes for fun and games locally, are barely Allies) is the fact the rape victim's uncle is a Congressman stuck in Townsville now The Bloody Wet's started.

"My judgment," Big Bob says. "The goddamn Base Section has a plate full. American girl gang-banged by coons. Southern girl to boot, my information. And her uncle, a goddamn Dixie Democrat, is here! Expect he's raising hell, chewing some Base Section ass. Hear they got a surprise inspection coming too. And somebody, most likely some our gallant flyboys from up in New Guinea, liberate their O Club booze! Incidentally, how are we fixed?"

"We're okay for a week," Lt. Col. Gerber, who in addition to his other duties monitors the Depot officers' liquor supply, says. "Better lay on a mission to Sydney though, the weather breaks."

"Jeezuzz," Big Bob says. "This goddamn weather could last a week. Did once last year."

"Meteorology," Maj. Richall says. "Thinks there'll be a break in it, thirty-six, forty-eight hours. There is, that first ATC 54 Direct from The States will come in. Ops chief told me it's in Noumea. Landed there yesterday. Would of been here today except the damn weather."

"I should meet that Fifty-Four," Big Bob says. "But those meteorology guys are wrong more than they're right." His plate's clean. He tells the GI waiter standing by, Bring more fish and fries. "You know, men, I been thinking. Assuming it was some our gallant flyboys from up in New Guinea liberate that Base Section booze, and I take that to be a logical assumption, and they didn't get out of here with it yesterday. Where is it? No aircraft left here today or will. How about yesterday before fifteen-hundred? Or after? What I'm saying is, that booze might still be here! My information , the goddamn Base Section mounted a major search but didn't find it. So where it might be, by god, is aboard one the aircraft on the field. A bomber maybe. More likely though, one the Forty-Sevens. That's the case, by god, there ought to be a way we can locate that aircraft!"

"Makes sense to me, Sir," Gerber says. "We can check there were any departures yesterday after, say, fourteen-thirty."

"Hey!" Richall says. "There was a Forty-Seven pilot called yesterday p.m. from the field. Had a flat. Wanted a new tire mounted. Right away. Gave my lieutenant a hard time. Pilot might been a patriot though. Said he had ammunition aboard, priority clearance. But we couldn't mount a tire then. Too damn busy. We put a new tire on his aircraft this morning."

"Christ," Big Bob says. "I never encounter a Forty-Seven pilot in a big hurry to get back to New Guinea! Ammunition or whatever. You get his name, aircraft ID?"

"Be in my office, Sir."

"Dig it up," Big Bob says. "And check departures. What time was it, that booze was liberated? How much was there?" Nobody knows the time but the sitrep, Reeves says, is the flyboys (assuming it was flyboys) got away with more than a hundred cases. "Damn! That's a nice round figure! You know, men, this goddamn weather lasts, we can't lay anything on to Sydney. Well, I don't like to deprive our gallant flyboys up in New Guinea a little libation, but it's every man for himself, this war. We find that booze, I got the rank. I'll take care the gallant flyboys. I'll lay that crazy GHQ Order on them. Or make a deal. Let them have the Australian whiskey, there is any."

"Might be a little problem though," Gerber says. "Locate the aircraft, Sir. Goddamn RAAF runs the field won't let us Yanks except air crews roam around on it. Won't let us, except we have an ERO. Emergency Repair Order. They make us tow the aircraft over here. Fact, I heard the RAAF said Up Yours to the Base Section MPs wanted to search aircraft yesterday. After the booze was liberated. Then caught two prowling around the field last night and have them locked up."

"Goddamn RAAF," Richall says. "Gave my men a hard time, they went over the field this morning with an ERO, mount a tire on that Forty-Seven. We couldn't tow it with a flat. Goddamn RAAF always gives us a hard time."

"Shit!" Big Bob says. "That hardass RAAF joker runs the field. What's-his-name, Hewitt-Pecker? He might be thinking same as I'm thinking about that booze. Say, though, isn't there some general's aircraft on the field needs something?"

"Yes," Richall says. "Forty-Seven with an instrument malfunction. It's Brigadier-General Dumphy's aircraft. He's First Corps deputy commander. His pilot was in and got a req and we gave him a jeep. But Dumphy's not here now. He's in Brisbane, some kind of conference. Hitched a ride on The Bataan, Ops told me. We're going to tow the aircraft over our shop."

"No you're not," Big Bob says. "Write up an ERO. Take some men and go over the field. Fix the aircraft and take a look around. Check that other Forty-Seven you mention. All the Forty-Sevens. Christ, you got a ERO for the First Corps deputy commander's aircraft. RAAF got to let you on the field for that. I'll call what's his name, Hewitt-Pecker, and clear it. Or no, I won't. Sonofabitch might get ideas, I make a big thing out of it. Might have ideas already. Like I said. RAAF gives you any shit, Engineering, tell them our shops are full. Hey, there's a will there's a way. That's my motto, live by. Where the hell are my fish and fries?"

"Take a little while, organize it," Richall says. "Have to find the req for the general's aircraft, case the RAAF asks for it. They do, sometimes. And I got a high priority job in the shop, two new engines on that Air Service Command Twenty-Four."

"Twenty-Four can wait," Big Bob says, "It won't be going anywhere today. Or tomorrow, this weather. You get over to the field, Engineering. Take a look around. Well, finally!" His fish and fries arrive and he slathers the fries with ketchup.

"But what about the Base Section, Sir?" Reeves says. "I mean, well, the Base Section O Club bought that booze. Technically it's like it's, well, their booze. Isn't it? I mean if we locate it, Sir. Won't the O Club or the Base Section claim."

"We locate it," Big Bob says. "That'll be Top Secret. Besides, I'm SOPD here, American Forces. All we'll be doing, we locate that booze, is our duty, that GHQ Order. Preventing the transport of intoxicating liquors to Forward Areas. Implementing appropriate action forthwith." That gets a laugh, Gerber and Richall decide they'll have more fish, whatever it is, it's a nice fish with firm white flesh, and Big Bob changes the subject. "Understand the goddamn Base Section gave our softball team another shellacking yesterday. Nineteen to six or something? That's four in a row they won, right? What the hell's the matter with our team anyway?"

"Nineteen to seven, Sir," Reeves, the SAD softball team manager, whines. "But our team's not that bad, Sir. It's that goddamn Radke the Base Section got out of the Rep Dep. He's a professional baseball player. Was, I mean. He hit three homers and a triple with men on yesterday. He hits three or four homers every time we play them. He hit two yesterday when we were trying to walk him."

"Damn it all," Big Bob says. "It don't seem fair. Base Section's got a professional in its lineup. Was a professional. You ever talk to this Radke, Major?" Some, Reeves says. "Talk to him some more, next game we play the Base Section. Find out he might like a transfer. Tell him the Base Section probably be in New Guinea pretty soon, but we, the depot, likely be here for the Duration."

"I'll do that, Sir," Reeves says, "That's an excellent idea, Sir." Outside, the rain's pounding down, tearing up the putting green.

* * *

Capt. Raskovic and Sgt. Harry Parker are sitting in their jeep, rain hammering the canvas top, outside the Townsville Constabulary, a squat two-story red brick building on Front Street overlooking the harbor. The CID, which often works with local law enforcement in cases involving GIs, has two small second-floor rear offices in the Constabulary, overlooking the trash cans in the alley behind the Wong Fu Chinese restaurant next door to the Flinders Street EM Club.

"There's somethin' goddamn funny goin' on," Raskovic says. "I wish I knew what. First she don't come to work the QM today, this Missus Rooney old Flapp says types up the req and so on for our booze. This Missus Rooney I'm just about ready and bet my ass was in cahoots with the goddamn flyboys liberate our booze. Called in sick, her girlfriend the QM says. But we go out her house, she ain't there, house all locked up. Then back the QM, the goddamn girlfriend remembers Rooney went to Rockhampton this morning, see her sick sister. I don't know the goddamn girlfriend is just dumb or was in cahoots with the goddamn flyboys too. But I know one thing. It is mighty fucking convenient for somebody, we suppose this Rooney was in cahoots with the goddamn flyboys, she happens to be in Rockhampton in the middle our investigation. I could phone Rockhampton CID but I don't know anybody there and then the story, flyboys liberate our booze, be all over Swappa in about an hour. If it ain't awready. Besides, Rockhampton CID don't know the questions ask this Rooney."

"We kind of come to a dead end then, I guess, Sir, the booze," Harry says. "So what are we gonna do now? Concentrate on the rape case?"

"Yeah. But first I'm gonna talk to this Rooney's dumb girlfriend again. Lean on her some. Find out this Rooney got any Yank boyfriends. Flyboys or whatever. Like I said before, I bet my ass the goddamn flyboys had an accomplice here the Base Section. Maybe several. We ID this accomplice or one of them and lean on him or maybe it's a her hard enough we'll get a line on the goddamn flyboys. And the booze. If it's still here. Which it prolly is. Fogerty says there's no way the goddamn flyboys got out of here with it yesterday. And they ain't going anywhere today. Or tomorrow, this weather. I'm gonna check with the lieutenant runs the O Club too. Witters. Club's next door this Rooney's house. He might seen some flyboys or GIs there. He ain't very bright though, Witters, my estimation."

"Sir, due respect," Harry says. "We ought a run a check on the Four-oh-Fourth QM Truck too. That colored outfit. Maybe get a lead on the bastards did Boo—Miss Davis."

"We will, we will. I know that's gnawing on you, Sergeant. Hell, you know the girl. It's gnawing on me too. I hate rapes. And I know the booze prolly ain't very high on your list priorities. It ain't your booze. But I got Fogerty on my ass. So drop me the QM. I'll interrogate the dumb girlfriend again and call Witters. Somebody the QM'll give me a ride the Company, I get a sandwich or something. All I had for breakfast was coffee. You too prolly. All the damn cooks are doing is clean up the kitchen, this goddamn inspection. You lock up the evidence we got and go eat. Then start on our Initial Report, the rape. Finneman and Steussie still in the RAAF slammer, far as I know. I'll ask the Provost give us that

Redhardt you mention. I don't think Davis' panties, shoe, that blanket gonna do us much good. Except we found them, the scene the crime. Alleged scene. Forensics too complicated for the Constabulary. They do prints is about all. Forensics, we got to send the evidence to Brisbane, GHQ. But we'll get Davis ID her panties, shoe. Sign a statement. You and me, we can testify we found them, the scene the crime. Alleged scene. Okay, drop me the QM. Pick me up the Company, thirteen-thirty. Then we'll hit the Four-oh-Fourth Truck."

Harry starts the jeep. The Base QM is in a cluster of quonset huts on what used to be the local cricket grounds a block beyond the George Hotel on North Flinders Street. The 301st MP Co. and Base Section Stockade are under canvas a bit farther on in Victoria Park, now closed to the public. Finneman and Steussie usually write the CID reports. Capt. Raskovic is verbal enough but prone to writer's block when confronted with reports. The rain's slowed to a steady drizzle. Low clouds hide half the harbor.

* * *

"Well, I guess it's an idea, Sal," Billy Gote says. "But there's a goddamn big if in it. It's if can we trust this friend your's keep his big mouth shut, he puts two-and-two together? He could make a lot of points, y'know, he wants to be a goddamn hero."

"No, Booney's okay," Saljeski says. "I know him quite awhile. We been drunk together. Besides, I awready told him it's gonna be like a fuckin Installment Plan. Just for a precaution."

"By god you're a shrewd one, Sal," Billy Gote says. "And I expect there soon be various parties pokin' around the airfield. If they ain't already. Lookin' for a airplane full of booze. Prolly be a good idea, there's some way discourage that."

"Any chance the rain will let up?" Eddie Devlin, clutching at a straw, smothering a yawn, says. "Just long enough so we can get out of here."

"Not today," Bill Gote says. "Garbutt Ops won't clear anybody to any where today. I mean any where northbound. There ain't any where. Weather's socked in all the way to Nadzab. Might be a break in it, day, day and a half, the weather guys say. But those dummies just guessing. You sure your friend's coming, Sal? He might got tied up, this inspection you mention."

"No, he'll be here. I promise him a fuckin jug and two more later."

It's 1300 hours. They're sitting at a table for four in the public room at the Barrier Arms, ponchos draped on their chairs, drinking Foster's. Big Biff Smith, shirtsleeves rolled on his massive arms, and his daughter Louise are busy serving "Afters" to thirty-odd air crew grounded by the weather. The public room is warm and Eddie, who did not get into bed with Ann Silvers, is half asleep.

Ann Silvers still thinks Eddie is married and was all wrought up in any case when she and Agnes Moore, they took the ARC jeep, returned to Manic Manor from the 12th Station Hospital with a few sketchy details regarding Boots Davis' traumatic experience. Billy Gote very much wanted to go with them but Agnes Moore said No, absolutely not, there wasn't anything useful Billy could do and it was women's work. Pops by then had carved the turkey and everybody ate some but nobody, thinking about Boots, had much appetite. Lt. Hunker heard the sketchy details, ate some turkey, expressed sympathy for Boots, left to see his girlfriend and was not seen again. Neither was Saljeski. Billy Gote and Eddie finally slept badly, wrapped in o.d. blankets on two deck chairs on the Manor patio, fair game for ten-million mosquitoes, but nobody went to bed until 0300 hours, Boots' traumatic experience discussed at great length

They were roused at 0600 hours when Jill Tucker returned to the Manor and got into another fight with Ima Score over the loo while Agnes Moore was trying to raise a taxi for the Canteen crew, Flots and Jets, who also were having a cat fight, when the MP detail supposed to pick them up failed to appear. Eventually though things quieted down, all the Red Cross personnel gone to their various posts. Billy and Eddie had coffee they made and Fleetwoods for breakfast and spent the forenoon at the Manor, playing rummy, cursing The Bloody Wet and commiserating though not much with Lt. Ronald Donald, whose pants are missing. He removed them before screwing Flots on the living room sofa, then fell asleep and when he woke up they were gone. Flots thinks Jets took them and said she'll get him another pair, somewhere, after the Canteen closes. Lt. Donald whined a lot while sitting around in his o.d. issue skivvies and uniform shirt. He has another pair of pants in his valpak but that's aboard the Lucky Lil.

Saljeski turned up in his truck at 1230 hours, bringing ponchos for Billy and Eddie, full of what he'd heard about Boots and his idea. "It wasn't fuckin easy," he said. "Convince Mickey she should go visit her fuckin sister. But I did finally and put her on the fuckin train to Rockhampton." He also said, "The fuckin Base Section is in a fuckin panic on account of some fuckin general is comin' for a fuckin inspection," then drove them to the Barrier Arms. They left Lt. Donald whining at the Manor.

They discussed Boots' traumatic experience again on their way to the Arms and devised various prolonged and painful deaths for the bastards did her. Billy plans to visit Boots later at the 12th Station. If he can. Outside, rain's pounding down. Inside, big Biff Smith is scowling. The day's trade is below average. The bloody Base Section Yanks who usually crowd the Arms' public room between noon and 1400 hours for "Afters" (and contribute to the AIF Widows' Fund, Biff's favorite charity) are absent, busy preparing he's heard for a bloody inspection, some bloody Yank general on his way to Townsville. And the bloody Yanks present, as always, are eyeing his daughter Louise with lust in their bloody hearts.

Sgt. Porky Wallace, nursing a Foster's at the end of the bar, is one of those, but sure now they'll RON again Porky's busy planning his evening campaign, no place in it for Louise. He'll hit the Flinders Street EM Club early, pick up a bird, any bird, hustle her back to his room, that's all right with Biff so long as the bird's not Louise. They'll no doubt be wet, have to peel right out of their clothes.

A tall soldier in a wet poncho and a wet no-longer-authorized campaign hat, chewing tobacco wadded in one leathery cheek, enters the public room through the rear door, spots Saljeski, joins the conspirators, sits in the fourth chair, removes his campaign hat, shakes it free of rain and puts it on again tipped low on his forehead.

Saljeski makes the introductions. "This Sergeant Daniel Boone. He's a handler, that fuckin K-9 Detachment. Lieutenant, Eddie here friends a mine, Booney. You bring the fuckin dog?"

"You bring the booze?" Sgt. Boone says. "Dog's out in back in my three-quarter-ton."

"You'll get the fuckin booze," Saljeski says. "But first you got to swear an oath, Booney, on a fuckin Bible if we had one. You never fuckin seen us. You don't fuckin know us. You don't know fuckin nuthin' about the booze you're gonna get either. It fell out a fuckin tree on you."

Sgt. Boone, munching his chew like a ruminating Holstein chewing its cud, considers this, puts two-and-two together and expresses awe. "Fell out a fuckin tree on me? Like shit! Jeezuzz! You the guys liberate the O Club booze!"

"Booney, I don't know what the fuck you're talkin' about!" Saljeski says. "It just happen the Lieutenant here got a airplane full of ammunition he don't want anybody fuckin with it, blow up the fuckin airfield. Booze you're gonna get is mine. I got a pretty good connection, Burns-Phelps. I'm just doin' the Lieutenant here a fuckin favor."

Sgt. Boone considers this explanation and chews his way to a conclusion. "I think you ought a gimme a case booze then, Sal, you doin' people fuckin favors."

Saljeski, Billy Gote and Eddie consider this proposition. Billy Gote doesn't like it. He'd like to strangle Saljeski and his bright ideas but it's too late for that now and they'd best placate this shrewd sonofabitch. "I think the Sergeant's right, Sal. You ought a give him a case now. Then we're out of here with the ammo without blowing up the airfield, two cases. That's about a thousand quid worth, Sarge, Nadzab prices."

A thin smile creases Sgt. Boone's leathery face but he drives a hard bargain. "What I heard, it was like two-hunnert cases booze was liberated. Three don't sound like much."

Negotiations stall. Sgt. Boone chews for a time in silence then turns salesman. "He's a mighty good dog, Attila. Nobody gonna go near your airplane, Loo'tenant, all that ammo, Attila is guardin' it. I by god guarantee you on that. But I am thinkin' more like five cases. Two now and three the airfield don't blow up."

"Oh shit." Billy Gote says. "Roger. We prolly put you in for a medal too, Sarge. You and your dog prevent a major disaster out the airfield. Except this all Top Secret. Roger?"

"Roger," Sgt. Boone says. "And I tell you what. I'm a pretty good Suth'ren Baptist. I pertend like we got a Bible. I swear I never seen you guys and this moonshine we talkin' about, it fell out a fuckin tree on me. But how we gonna get Attila out the airplane? I hear the RAAF makin' it tough, get on the airfield."

A problem but they devise a solution. They'll take Saljeski's truck. The RAAF know Saljeski: he often puts films bound for New Guinea on a C47. Boone and Eddie, masquerading as air crew, will ride in the back with Attila. "He prolly won't attack nobody I'm with him," Sgt. Boone says

Billy Gote borrows Porky Wallace's sacred air crew ID and sends him upstairs to get Cpl. Johnson's, said by Porky to be "readin' comicbooks, prolly jerkin' off." Billy offers no explanation but Porky, it's understood, will always owe Lt. Billy Gote for the business with the clap and Porky's flight pay.

Porky returns with Johnson's ID and in the yard behind the Barrier Arms at the end of a gravel driveway leading to Garbutt Road, a steady drizzle falling, Mrs. Biff Smith keeps a few chicken there, they load Attila, a black 120-pound Rottweiler in a heavy wire cage, into Saljeski's truck. Attila growls, bares his fangs, snaps at Eddie. "I told you he's a good dog," Sgt. Boone says.

At which point Sgt. Harry Parker wheels into the yard in his jeep and, still in the jeep, while Boone soothes Attila, confers with Saljeski, Billy and Eddie. "Constable give me your message you was gonna be here, Sal," Harry says. "But we been busier'n hell, Boots and all. What's the idea, the dog?"

"That's a K-9 dog," Saljeski says "It's gonna guard the airplane 'til the fuckin weather breaks. Keep the fuckin snoopers clear."

"Well, that's an idea, I guess," Harry says. "But let's hope the goldurn weather breaks. Colonel Fogerty, he's still rarin' to get the booze back, shoot some flyboys. It's a goldurn good thing you got Mickey out of town. We already interrogate her girlfriend the QM, Sadie Bailey, once, and Raskovic interrogatin' her again, right now, and prolly leanin' on her pretty hard. Hard as he can, she's a Aussie civilian. You know this Sadie, Sal? More important, she know you? She know you're Mickey's boyfriend?"

Saljeski pales beneath his freckles. "Shit! I don't fuckin know! I don't know this Sadie except Mickey mention her a couple times. I don't know what Mickey might told her. Told her my fuckin name!"

"Well, don't panic yet," Harry says. "This Sadie probably don't know anything incriminating. She sound pretty dumb the first time we interrogate her. And I got a call from Flots out the Canteen. That deuce-and-a-half you liberate and dump there is blocking the backdoor, the Canteen, Flots says. You happen to know, Sal, what outfit was it you liberate that deuce from?"

"No. Some fuckin coon outfit prolly. But I don't fuckin know."

"Reason I ask," Harry says. "Is we got a suspicion it might been some coons in the Four-oh-Fourth QM Truck, that's a coon outfit, did Boots. She seen a bumper number anyway was like a Four-oh-Fourth number when they grab her. If that deuce you liberate happen to be a Four-oh-Fourth deuce, that be somethin' Raskovic can chew on. Keep his mind off the booze. I'm gonna steer him out the Canteen anyway. If I can. Take a look at that deuce. Colonel Allen, his orders, he told Raskovic forget the booze, get the bastards did Boots. I keep reminding Raskovic that. But Fogerty is on his ass, find the booze, and I think he's more scared Fogerty. We found Boots' panties, one her shoes, where they did her, and we're gonna hit the Four-oh-Fourth anyway, later on. Ask some questions. Some them shipped out last night for Oro Bay but not'll midnight. Well, I got to wheel. Pick up Raskovic. I'll keep you posted. Stop by the Manor tonight with a sitrep if I can. Flots says there's gonna be another farewell party for Rose Pearl Stevens. Let's hope the goldurn weather breaks."

Harry departs and they all climb into Saljeski's truck, Boone's still calming Attila, and head for Garbutt Field. Rain's pounding down hard again. Garbutt Road is full of puddles: many hide potholes. They're halted by an MP in a wet poncho at the new bridge over the Ross River while eastbound traffic splashes by. The bridge construction appears to have been halted. The engineers are piling lumber in neat stacks in preparation for Brig. Gen. Bargle's inspection. Muddy water running swiftly to the sea is halfway up the Ross River's low banks.

They get a break at the field's Main Gate. The RAAF sentry on duty in a wet raincoat recognizes Saljeski. He inspects the air crew ID presented by Billy Gote, Sgt. Boone and Eddie and is preparing to wave them on when Attila growls, a noise like a gut-shot bassoon. The sentry peers into the truck. "You got a fookin dog wit you!"

"Just givin' him a fuckin ride," Saljeski says. "He likes rides."

"Bloody great beast he is," the sentry says. "I likes dogs," and waves them on. The rain's slowed to a steady drizzle.

Saljeski drives by the Control Tower, no sign of life there, and out along the taxiway full of puddles to the Lucky Lil's hardstand. The Lils' wings are level, a new tire on the port wheel. The revetment like a great gray jello mold protecting the hardstand has turned to black mud. The DANGER AMMUNITION sign still hangs on the Lil's cargo door. There's a stubby RAAF Fiat truck parked farther along the taxiway. Sgt. Boone opens Attila's cage, says "Good dog" and clips a nylon rope to Attila's studded collar. Attila jumps from Saljeski's truck, growls and displays his fangs.

"I'll tie him that brace there over the wheel," Sgt. Boone says. "He be out of the rain there but he can reach the cargo door. I tell him, 'Guard the door, Attila,' he chew on anybody dumb enough and go near it."

"No," Billy Gote says. "Not this airplane. My airplane. Anybody see Attila guardin' this airplane they are gonna figure there is something goddamn valuable aboard, ammo ain't that valuable, and start puttin' two-and-two together. Tie him the next airplane. The general's airplane. Straight Arrow Hunker's airplane but what the hell. Confuse the issue like, any snoopers come snoopin'."

"Ever you say," Sgt. Boone says. "You the ones payin' for Attila."

"What if somebody," Eddie says. "Comes and checks the general's airplane?"

"Attila chew on them up, I guess," Billy Gote says. "Come on, let's get this over with, give the Sergeant his down payment and get out of here. I think there some snoopers in that Fiat truck snoopin' already."

Sgt. Daniel Boone and Attila.

They walk through the drizzle to the next revetment. Sgt. Boone leads Attila to the fuselage door on Brig. Gen. Humphrey Dumphy's airplane and says "Guard, Attila!" Then ties Attila to the port wheel strut and instructs Saljeski. "You got to feed him once a day, Sal. Couple pounds meat. He likes a bone in it. He's okay today. I feed him awready, and okay for water, all the puddles." Attila's lapping one up. "There ain't puddles, bring him water. Just set it down where he can reach it. Same his meat. He prolly won't attack he thinks you got something for him. Just don't go near that door." Attila, settled on his belly on a dry spot beneath the aircraft, growls and displays his fangs. "Now I wanna see my booze."

They return to the Lucky Lil. The rain's pounding down hard again. Billy Gote unlocks the cargo door, boosts Eddie into the Lil and climbs in himself. They pull the tarp off the booze and remove three cases of gin and two of Tanundra brandy.

"What the hell," Billy Gote says. "Let's take some more gin, long's we're stuck here. Put four jugs in my valpak and Donald's.

We'll take them too. Poor bastard needs pants." They do this and replace the tarp and Eddie grabs his musette bag and recalulates the riches they'll divide: $59,776 or $14,944 each. Still sums hard to imagine. They drop from the Lil. Billy closes the cabin door and straightens the DANGER AMMUNITION sign and they get into Saljeski's truck with Sgt. Boone, his booze, their booze, the valpaks and Eddie's musette bag and drive back through the rain pounding down to the Barrier Arms, delayed at the bridge, the muddy water higher on the Ross' banks. In the yard behind the Arms they shake hands with Sgt. Boone and he loads his down payment into his three-quarter-ton.

"Don't you forget now, Booney," Saljeski says. "You took an oath, swore on a Bible or next fuckin thing to it. And you still got three cases comin' on a installment plan, the fuckin airfield don't blow up."

"I never seen you guys," Sgt. Boone says. "But you take good care them three cases, Sal."

"Hey, it's none of my business, Sarge," Billy Gote says. "But how you gonna explain, your C.O. asks, Attila ain't in his kennel or whatever?"

"I just tell him Attila prolly smell a bitch in heat and run off. He done that once before. But my C.O. got his head up his ass right now, gettin' ready this goddamn inspection. He prolly never miss Attila."

Sgt. Boone departs in his three-quarter ton. Billy, Eddie and Saljeski return to the Arms' public room, the rear door unlocked at something after 1400 hours. Biff Smith and Louise are serving legal drinks to the air crew present. Billy Gote gives Porky Wallace the air crew ID he borrowed, gets three Foster's and joins Eddie and Saljeski at a corner table.

"All we can do," Billy says. "Is sweat it out. Hope the goddamn weather breaks. Hope the RAAF don't let anybody near my airplane. Hope your pal Boone don't get patriotic and shoot his mouth off. Hope that goddamn GHQ Order don't give the Base Section any leverage. Hope and sweat."

"Hope that fuckin Sadie the QM don't know me," Saljeski says.

"You know," Billy says. "I hate and say this, what happen to Boots. But we really be up that old shit creek if Harry's C.O., this Captain Raskovic, dint have that on his plate."

"What are you going to do with your share the money, Sal?" Eddie, striving for a brighter note, says. "Be call it fifteen-thousand bucks now."

Saljeski perks up: this is a brighter note. "Well, I tell you. There's a fuckin bar in West Philly, Girard and Fifty-Second Street, I got my eye on. Fazio's. Neighborhood bar. I been in it many times. I know the old guinea owns it. He owns the fuckin building. Two apartments upstairs. He's about ready retire. I figger I can buy it, the fuckin license, the works, maybe fifteen grand. Give the old guinea five and a contract-for-deed. Fix it up some. No fuckin coons allowed but it ain't a coon neighborhood. I be fixed for life then. Be better maybe I was a fuckin guinea. It's a guinea neighborhood. But I can talk some guinea. There's some think I am a fuckin guinea. Northern guinea. Some fuckin Kraut barbair'n one my ancestors." Dreaming his dream, Saljeski drinks his Foster's.

"How about you, Lieutenant?" Eddie says.

"Oh, I don't know," Billy Gote says. "I think I'll wait'll I get it, I make any plans." Billy Gote has a plan but $15,000 won't swing it. Be a start though. He'll invest that money, finish college, a business major, study the Stock Market, bonds, whatever, watch his investment grow and one day buy the First State Bank of Onamee, Kansas, walk in, say I'm the new owner and fire the president, old Jeremiah Grabb. Give him fifteen minutes, clear the premises. It was old Grabb foreclosed on the family business, Gote Farm Implement & Fertilzer, in 1935. Dad gave too much credit of course, farm customers all broke, The Depression going strong, two-year drought, fields all blown to Missouri, gone with the wind. Old Grabb delivered a little lecture on credit, sound business practices, in Billy Gote's hearing, Billy then sixteen, the day they went to the bank and Dad asked, begged, for more time. No dice: Old Grabb foreclosed. Dad couldn't take it, losing the business, three generations in the family. Drowned himself in the Onamee River a week later. Fell from his bass boat, never learned to swim. Accidental death, the County Coroner ruled. Pretty smart some ways though, Dad. Billy as instructed burned the "Personal" letter addressed to him that came a week later forwarded by one of Dad's former fishing buddies then living in Florida. "Can't go on," it said, "Don't want to, lost the business, best for everybody, there's insurance, don't tell your mother, take good care of your mother." Mother however took care of herself, married again within the year Mr. Nelson Riddle, not the bandleader, asshole owned a Ford dealership in Wichita, took both his younger sisters with her to Wichita. Billy stayed with Granny Gote in Onamee, finished high school and joined a harvest crew. Insurance company stalled of course, suspected chicanery, but finally paid up, $25,000. Mrs. Riddle kept most of it. Did give him $2,000 for college, Kansas State, but he spent another season with the harvest crew first, Texas to Canada and back, hard work but he liked it, liked tearing up small Great Plains towns on Saturday nights, popping local maidens with a little luck. KSU kind of slow compared to that. Then The War started, Poland or someplace, and he dropped out of KSU and enlisted in the U.S. Army Air Corps. Couldn't hack fighters but 47s are all right. Orders of magnitude better than the miserable Infantry anyway. And some day by god he'll even things up with old Grabb. Buy the bank and bounce him. Lecture him maybe, sound business practices. Billy hopes the old bastard lives long enough, face this day of reckoning. Grabb won't be dead broke like the old man was but you can't have everything: $15,000 is just a start. Also, another post-war plan, divorce the former Beverly Biddly, High School sweetheart. Why'd he ever, home on leave, marry her in a hurry anyway? Well, only way she'd screw him for one thing and numerous classmates, war looming, were getting married. They honeymooned in an upper berth on the Atchison Topeka & Santa Fe en route to Kingman, Arizona, and 47 flight school. Bev didn't like Kingman, living in a cheap motel, her chief entertainment trips to the laundromat where other Air Corps wives, she said, described in detail their various husbands' peculiar sexual desires. Bev would not accede to his peculiar sexual desires, went home to Onamee when he shipped out for Swappa, no longer writes. No doubt she's spending the $50-a-month allotment he foolishly wrote in stone and, perhaps, acceding to some 4F's peculiar sexual desires.

"Whatta you gonna do, Eddie?" Saljeski says. "With your share?"

"Oh I don't know." Eddie's not actually given this much thought. "Buy a car, I guess, I get home. Packard convertible maybe." A car that will cost, Eddie thinks, close to $2,000 (at '41 prices) but what the hell. It will pop a few eyes in his hometown, Winatchee Falls, a medium-sized dot on the Minnesota Prairie. And a house for his parents perhaps. They've been renting cheap apartments, Eddie an only child, since his Uncle Tim Heaney, the executor of Grandpa Heaney's estate, half a millionaire on paper, lost the estate and everything else in the 1929 Stock Market Crash. Every dime and the Devlin's house, Grandpa's old house in nearby Stiles, title to same part of the estate, mortgaged by Tim. Well, it's not "lost" exactly. The house is still there but the First National Bank of Winatchee Falls foreclosed on it and somebody else lives in it now. Uncle Tim is still around, the bookkeeper at the Dobermann Hotel, the best hotel in Winatchee Falls. He sometimes gave Eddie two-bits when half a millionaire on paper. Eddie's sure his mother would like a house and his dad, an auto mechanic, doesn't make much money. His mother after Uncle Tim's malfeasance surfaced often wailed, "We'll always be poor now!" But Eddie will soon fix that. The Packard convertible will be sky blue and loaded (radio, spotlight, white sidewalls) and the passenger when he tools it down Broadway in

Winatchee Falls with the top down will be Merrilee Pretzell, just about the richest girl in Winatchee Falls. Her father, Dr. Wayne Pretzell, and his brothers own the Pretzell Chiropratic Clinic, said to be world famous, Winatchee Falls' chief claim to fame. Eddie laid siege to Merrilee's virture on and off for four years Before The War (but did not breach her defenses) and still writes her now and then, though she's not written him lately.

"Harry," Saljeski says. "Harry says he's gonna buy a fuckin boat and go fishin' for fuckin lobsters. What Harry really wants though is he shows his old man he's just as fuckin smart his old man was. His old man was a fuckin rum-runner there was Prohibition. He had a fuckin boat went like a bat out of hell and he went out the fuckin ocean in it and bought booze off ships come from Ireland or some place and bring it back the shore. There's about a thousand fuckin places the shore Maine, Harry says, you can hide a fuckin boat and his old man knew ever one. There was fuckin Prohibition agents after him but he allas bring the booze a different place and they never caught him. Then he load it on a fuckin truck and cover it with potatoes and haul it Boston or else New York and sell it. His old man made a pile of dough, Harry says, it was Prohibition. He lost most it bettin' on fuckin horses but still got enough he can live on, he's retired. He throw a fuckin fit though when Harry decide a be a fuckin deputy sheriff. Harry wants to show his old man he can make some fuckin dough too, sellin' booze."

"Speaking Harry," Billy Gote says. "It ain't any my business. But I never hear him mention he's got a girlfriend here."

"Oh, he's got one," Saljeski says. "But it supposed to be a big fuckin secret so don't tell him I told you. He's gettin' it on with a nurse out the 12th Station. A fuckin lieutenant. So they ain't suppose to fraternize, but he knew her from Before The War. She's from Bangor. A banger from Bangor."

"There's a sergeant in our squadron got that problem too," Billy Gote says. "But him, it's his wife. She's an Air Evac nurse.

First lieutenant. They fratenize some though. Chaplain up at Wing, he's one them Unitarians, lets them use his tent, he's conducting services."

"Y'know, " Eddie says. "Something I been wondering about. Hey, we need some beer." He goes to the bar and returns with three Foster's. "What are we going to do with our money when we get it? I mean it likely be a wad of quid choke a horse like they say. There no banks in Guinea and a Aussie bank, you prolly have to come back After The War and get it."

"Roger that," Saljeski says. "What me and Harry done, the guy the fuckin Bakery Company fixes Harry's uniforms is makin' us money belts out a old shirt we can wear under our fuckin shirts. Then we're gonna buy money orders, the fuckin Base Section Finance Office, and send it home. Three, four hundred a shot like it was dough we fuckin won playin' poker or shootin' craps. Take awhile but what the hell. Harry's gonna send his his uncle. The one's the fuckin sheriff. I'm gonna send mine my mother and she better not fuckin spend it! You prolly can do that too. Buy money orders the fuckin Moresby Finance Office. You want money belts, tell Harry tell the guy at the fuckin Bakery Company. They're two quid and you got to get him a old shirt but it owny takes him about a hour." Billy Gote and Eddie say they may do that. "Incidennly, Lieutenant. You understand I ain't worried about it. But just how you figger to sell the booze anyway?"

"I prolly just leave it on my airplane, I land Seven-Mile," Billy Gote says. "Then give my C.O. his scotch. Roger it with him and fly on up to Nadzab. Tell Ops, the strip there, I got a few jugs booze in my airplane I'll sell. That'll draw a crowd, believe me. Half a day, maybe less, it all be sold. Say, you drive me out the 12th Station, Sal? I want to see I can see Boots. I'll catch the GI bus back."

"Roger." They finish their Foster's. Eddie doesn't want to see Boots, given her circumstances. He really doesn't know Boots. He'll go with Saljeski on his movie delivery runs if there are movies, they may be cancelled while the Base Section prepares for Brig. Gen. Bargle's inspection, eat somewhere with Saljeski, probably Happy Valley, meet Billy later at Manic Manor in time for Rose Pearl Stevens' farewell party. Rain's still pounding down.

* * *

"You hadda wait awhile, I guess," Capt Raskovic, climbing into the CID jeep at the entrance to the 301st MP camp, says. "But I had another go-around with Fogerty and Cain and the Provost. They was in the Provost's office. Fogerty's about ready he shits tacks. Allen phoned GHQ, he says, requested authority to search aircraft. But it dint come through yet. Goddamn RAAF still got Finneman and Steussie. That's the bad news. I wish there was some good news."

"There might be, Captain," Harry says. "I got a call the office. There's a deuce-and-a-half out the airfield behind the Canteen. Been there since yesterday, the Red Cross girl called me thinks. Like it was abandoned. She wants it moved but I told her wait. Maybe we should take a look at it. Those flyboys liberate the booze must had a truck. Most likely, they just leave it somewhere. Be the one they had, we might get a lead."

Raskovic considers this. "Well, possibility maybe. But somebody abandon it, it most likely was liberated and there been no deuce-and-a-half Stolen Vehicle Reports since Tuesday. I check that. But, hell, we'll go take a look at it. Might's well. I got zippo, that dumb broad the QM, Sadie. She thinks Rooney has a Yank boyfriend but she don't know who he is. I believe her. I lean on her pretty hard. Hard as I could, goddamn Australian civilian. That dumb Witters, the O Club. Another washout. He's seen a GI at Rooney's house but wouldn't recognize him, he says. He mostly just bitch about Rooney's chickens get loose and shit on his jeep. I told him that's an Allied Relation Problem. How come the Red Cross gal call you instead the Provost?"

"I guess because she sort of knows me from a couple parties I was to up at their billet."

"I been told those pretty good parties. Lots of loose quiff. You ever get any that, Sergeant?"

"No. They're pretty good parties but there ain't that much loose quiff. There's eight, ten Red Cross gals at them but some them don't put out. They ain't very patriotic. And there's always four, five guys after ever one will. Mostly flyboys. Some Base Section guys."

"Goddamn flyboys," Raskovic says, more or less automatically, "Okay, lets take a look at this deuce."

They drive slowly through Townsville, the rain pounding down has not thinned the military traffic, and out Garbutt Road, splashing through the potholes, held up at the new bridge, the Ross River still rising, convince the RAAF sentry at the Main Gate they're on legitimate business vital to the War Effort, pull up beside the deuce-and-a-half parked behind the Canteen, get out of their jeep, the rain's changed to a slow drizzle, and study this vehicle. It's just a wet war-worn deuce-and-a-half with a dirty windshield, a few dents here and there, its windows closed, the canvas top over its bed soaked black, Bumper No.40444.

"Hey!" Harry says. "That's the number Boo—Miss Davis seen! Thinks she seen anyway. This a Four-oh-Fourth QM deuce, Captain! That colored outfit. It might be the deuce those bastards."

"Doubt it," Raskovic, peering through the passenger window, says. "Keys in it. All the Four-oh-Fourth vehicles got that bumper number. Besides, what's it doing here? That don't make any sense."

"They might had some air freight they deliver. Afterwards. Why they leave it here?" Harry shrugs. "You often tell me, Captain. The criminal mind is hard to fathom."

"True. Lemme think a minute." Chewing his lower lip, oblivious to the drizzle, Raskovic thinks a minute. "Your theory prolly crazy, Sergeant. But there ought a be a trip-ticket, this vehicle.

Bumper number, we can ID the goddamn driver. Let's find out the Red Cross knows anything."

They bang on the Staff Only door. Flots opens it and they follow her through the storeroom into the Canteen, where numerous field personnel ducking the rain are drinking coffee, but learn little. Flots thinks the truck was there yesterday when she closed the Canteen but she's not sure. It was there this morning though, 0700 hours, when she opened the Canteen, late because the MP detail supposed to pick them up at Manic Manor didn't come and she and Jets had to take a taxi. Nobody's been near it since, far as she knows, but she wants it moved. It's blocking the rear door and the Canteen is expecting a delivery: flour, lard, a new doughnut machine.

"We'll move it," Raskovic says. "But not yet. I'm gonna call the Provost. Get a detail out here. Use your phone, Miss uh?" Miller, Flots says, phone's in the storeroom. Raskovic goes into the storeroom and Harry orders coffee.

"What's up?" Jets says.

"Can't say," Harry says. "Captain don't allas confide in me. Might be something though, connected what happen to Boots "

"You guys MPs, huh?" a field personnel in greasy fatigues says. Harry's wearing his brassard. "You ever catch them eight coons did that Red Cross girl you ought a cut their goddamn balls off!" All present agree that's a good idea. It's amazing, Harry thinks, not for the first time, the speed with which the grapevine spreads news, though often garbled, through the military in Townsville. All it took of course in this case was one ward boy at the 12th Station Hospital.

"You find that booze was liberated yet?" the curious field personnel says. "Catch the flyboys liberate it? Bless 'em all."

"No," Harry says. "No hide or hair that booze. You know they rationing drinks at the Base Section O Club?" Many present knew that, all the news spreads swiftly, but are pleased to hear it confirmed by a reliable source and find Harry's update, no hide or hair the missing booze, delightful.

"All right," Jets says. "Enough. Nobody's flying today. I'm going to close the Canteen. You all get out of here." Reluctantly, the field personnel depart to find somewhere else out of the rain. Jets locks the front door. Flots is busy wrapping leftover doughnuts. "There's a damn flyboy," Jets tells Harry. "Making a play for Flotsie. But I fixed his wagon. I swiped his pants."

Raskovic comes out of the storeroom. "Detail on its way," he says. "Gimme a cup coffee, black." Flots draws a cup from the big urn behind the counter and along with Jets get busy cleaning up. They're not speaking, a lovers' quarrel, but work well together.

The MP detail, a sergeant and three privates, arrives twenty minutes later in a jeep and Raskovic and Harry assemble them beside the abandoned deuce-and-a-half.

"This vehicle might be evidence, that rape case," Raskovic says. "So chrissake don't touch it. Don't let anybody touch it. I want two men on it all the time, all night, now'll you're relieved. Sometime tomorrow prolly. You bring rations? Okay. You can take turns, hole up out the rain in the storeroom there. Red Cross girl give you the key when she leaves."

"Sir!" the sergeant says and salutes.

Raskovic returns the salute and gets into their jeep and so does Harry. "Me and you, Chief Investigator, we are gonna go see the Four-oh-Fourth Truck. You know where it is?" Harry nods, starts the jeep and drives out the Main Gate. "You know, the more I think on it the more I think we might by god have something, that deuce! Why they dump it out the field, I don't know. But like I tell you, the criminal mind is hard to fathom. Anyway, we'll get Miss Davis take a look at it tomorrow. I think she be able. See she can ID it. Then I'll get the Constabulary, check it for prints. I maybe could do that but I'm kind of rusty, prints. You ever lift any prints, Sergeant?"

"No." Fingerprints were seldom a factor in the usual crimes (break-ins at service stations, stolen lobster pots, DWIs) in

Hancock County, Maine. Following break-ins and lobster pot thefts, Uncle Wilbur the Sheriff simply rounded up the usual suspects. Uncle Wilbur knew something about fingerprints, he'd been to the FBI School, but didn't tackle them himself. If he wanted prints, the Bangor police or State Crime Agency lifted them. But in no case in Harry's experience while a deputy did fingerprints solve a Hancock County crime. Nor will any prints the Townsville Constabulary may lift from the deuce-and-a-half solve Boots' rape. Raskovic, though he doesn't know it, is headed down a dead-end road. But that's all right. That's just fine. No doubt, his detective's instincts aroused, Raskovic would like to apprehend the bastards did Boots. Be a feather in his cap if he did and so long as he's wrapped up in that the booze aboard the Lucky Lil and Billy Gote's ass and Saljeski's and Eddie Devlin's and Harry's too are somewhat safer then they otherwise would be.

They cross the new bridge without delay, the Ross River still rising, reach Townsville and splash through the potholes on Charters Road past the 12th Station, Happy Valley, the Rep Dep and Lenox Avenue. Harry knows the way. He had a look at their Top Secret Base Section map.

The 404th QM Truck Battalion (C) camp is deep in a patch of scrub on a muddy track off Charters Road just beyond Lenox Avenue. Rain drips through the scrub. They find the Battalion C.O., Major Shiloh Bragg, on the phone in his headquarters, a leaky pyramidal tent, chewing somebody's ass. Battalion commanders usually are light colonels but (C) outfits often do with less.

"Some my men?" Maj. Bragg, says, when Raskovic explains their business. "Jeezuzz! Ah hopes not. That's all Ah need. That and this gahdamn in-spection. Nevuh know though. I got some hod cases, this outfit. Nothen nigras. Foh-oh-foh-foh-foh be a Bakuh Company vee-hicle but Bakuh, it ship out lass not foh Oro Bay, 'cept Foth Platoon. Foth Platoon be attached Chollie

Company now. Chollie rot on down the road a piece. Cap'n Smiley, Loo'tent Bannon, he Foth Platoon leader, they be glad and hep yawl. Ah got this gahdamn in-spection git ready foh. Yawl lemme know, any ma men involve in this turrble thang."

Raskovic and Harry drive on down the road a piece past square bare patches amid the scrub, turning to mud now, cluttered with junk left behind, where the Able and Baker Co. tents used to be, and a Motor Pool, where several Colored working under a tarp are disembowling a deuce-and-a-half. A Caucasian second john is watching them work. Most of the officers in (C) outfits are Southerners. The Army theory is they know how to "handle" colored.

The Charlie Co. HQ is another leaky pyramidal. Capt. Smiley, busy checking Red Line reports, professes no knowledge of Baker's Fourth Platoon, it was only attached to Charlie at 0200 hours, but tells a corporal, "Go fetch Loo'tent Bannon. He on that clean-up de-tail."

Second Lt. Stanley Bannon, a rail-thin cracker, a sharecropper's son risen to great heights since surviving pellagra, says when he arrives Bumper No. 40444 "show nuff be Foth Platoon vee-hicle but it on it way to Oro Bay." Advised by Raskovic that it is not, 40444 is parked behind the Garbutt Field Red Cross Canteen, Lt. Bannon expresses surprise and dismay and scurries off to find the trip-ticket issued 40444 yesterday.

He returns to confess, "Ah cain't fonn no trip-ticket, Suh, that vee-hicle. It prolly juss be miss-laid. It be purty hectic hee-uh yesstiday and lass not. Movin' out and everthang. And we lock cats onna hot tin roof now, this gahdam in-spection. Ah sure they be uh trip-ticket, Suh, but mott take a while and fonn it."

"Jeezuzz, Lieutenant!" Raskovic says. "You realize this a rape investigation! And the girl was raped, case you don't know it, her uncle's a Congressman! From Mississippi. And he's here, raising hell!"

"B-but ma Platoon Sar'ent," Lt. Bannon says. "He say he

know who drivin' that vee-hicle yesstiday, Suh. It be Private MacArthur, Suh. Douglas no-middle-initial MacArthur."
"What! Who!"
"Ah knows, Suh. We gets that reaction alla tom. But that be his name. Private Douglas MacArthur."
Raskovic digests this startling information. "You sure, Lieutenant? You goddamn better be. You might be a witness one of these days, this uh Private MacArthur was driving that vehicle. You said it was on its way to Oro Bay."
"Ah know, Suh. Ah did, Suh. Ah said that, Suh," Lt. Bannon babbles. "Ah thought it was, Suh. It s'posed to been. But mah Platoon Sar'ent, he say."
"Where is this Private MacArthur then? On the high seas on his way to Oro Bay?"
"No, Suh. He on KP now. He belong ma Platoon and he miss Re-treat lass not and Ah put him on KP. They about a dozen ower men miss Re-treat. Some them gahdamn nee-uh miss movement."
"Where were they? What were they doing? They say?"
"No, Suh. Well, they say they juss drinkin'. That Goose and Feather place. On account it they lass not in civ'lization, Suh."
"Awright," Raskovic says. "You go find that goddamn trip-ticket, Lieutenant! Any the rest of this outfit on movement orders?" No, Capt. Smiley says, just rumors, two-three weeks maybe. "Okay, the Lieutenant here stays here. He might be a material witness. I'll get an order, make that official." This is not the worst news Lt. Bannon ever heard. "Me and you, Sergeant, let's go talk to this Private MacArthur. Where's the Mess Hall?"
It's on down the road a piece through the scrub, a long plywood structure set on short pillings. They find Pvt. Douglas NMI MacArthur in stained fatigues in the kitchen with his head in one of the ovens, scraping grease.
"Out, boy!" Raskovic, giving Pvt. MacArthur a little kick in the butt, says, then orders the mess-sergeant, cooks and other KPs out of the kitchen. Pvt. MacArthur backs out of the oven and stares up at these white mans, a short one who looks mean

and a big one who also looks mean and the big one anyway is a MP! He wearing that thing on his arm MPs wear. They stare at Pvt. MacArthur without saying anything. The short one looks meaner'n a mad bobcat, and Pvt. MacArthur jumps to a conclusion. They know his truck was stole and they come for him!

Capt. Raskovic, Harry Parker and Pvt. Douglas MacArthur.

"We're MPs, boy," the short one says, confirming Pvt. MacArthur's worst fears. They both MPs! "We know you driving that deuce-and-a-half four-oh-four-four-four yesterday. We know you miss Retreat. We figure you're one the bastards grab that girl. White girl, boy! And rape her! Now you are gonna tell us who else was with you! Their names, boy!"

"Nuh! Was lib'rate!" Pvt. MacArthur wails. "Ma truck lib'rate!" He'll admit to that. But the white girl! He heard all about the white girl, the mess-sergeant, the cooks and KPs talking. Another KP, former Charlie Co. Cpl. Willie Badger, discharged this morning from the Colored ward at 12th Station Hospital, where they stuck him with needles because he had the clap, broke to private and put on KP for that, came back to Charlie this morning with the whole story he heard at the hospital. White mans hangs colored people for what happen that girl. Or burns them. With gasleen. White mans burns and hangs his Uncle Jonah MacArthur, say Uncle Jonah do that to a white girl. "Honess, Mister mans! Ma truck lib'rate. Honess!"

Capt. Raskovic, scowling, studies Pvt. MacArthur for a time then makes a decision. "Cuff him. We'll take him downtown and interrogate him. Let him sweat awhile first. Think about it. Then by god he'll give us some names, his goddamn buddies!"

Harry produces handcuffs, cuffs Pvt. MacArthur in the approved manner, hands behind his back, and hoists him to his feet and they hustle him out of the Mess Hall and into the jeep's rear seat while the mess-sergeant, cooks and KPs watch, wide-eyed.

"We're goin' downtown, boy," Raskovic says. "And later on we are gonna talk and you are gonna tell us who your buddies rape that white girl are. Or else I really hurt you, boy! And don't you even think you jump out this jeep, boy! You jump out this jeep, boy, we come back and run over you!" Raskovic dealt with young blacks in the LAPD. He knows the drill: scare the shit out of them. "Jeezuzz, Sergeant, I got something I tell my kids now, I ever have any, they ask, What you do in The War, Daddy? I once apprehend Douglas MacArthur!"

Harry starts the jeep, turns it around and away they go. The rain's pounding down, tears are rolling down Pvt. MacArthur's cheeks and he just wet his pants.

"Jeezuzz!" Lt. Stanley Bannon, peering from his Fourth Platoon HQ, another leaky pyramidal, says. "They taken MacArthur!" Then turns on his Platoon Sergeant. "What the hell happen that gahdamn trip-ticket foh foh-oh-foh-foh-foh?"

"I honestly don't know, Sir," Sgt. Ackroyd Bannister, a Tuskegee Institute graduate and New York City school janitor in civil life, says. "I know we had it. I wrote it up. For MacArthur and Sergeant Washington, Company Headquarters. Washington was MacArthur's driving instructor. He came in last night just before the move-out and went through the trip-tickets. Said he had to sign-off on it. It was here then."

"Whar he now? Sar'ent Wash'ton."

"On that LST, Sir. En route to Oro Bay. He went with the Forward Echelon."

"Shit! Well, rot one up then. Trip-ticket foh foh-oh-foh-foh-foh foh yesstiday. That gahdamn MP cap'n, he chew ma ass when Ah couldn't fonn it! He tell me Ah mot be uh widness too. Ah ain't goin' to Guinea! Rot one up. Thass an order! Ah toll that gahdamn cap'n Ah fonn it foh him."

Sgt. Bannister doubts this order is as they say in New York strictly kosher but an order is an order. He digs a blank trip-ticket from his field desk.

* * *

Col. Web Allen sits squirming at his gray metal desk at 1530 hours, fiddling with paperwork, squirming because his prickly heat's raging and the khakis he's wearing are crushing his genitals. The 114th Laundry Detachment delivered these khakis, a shirt and trousers, as promised. Pvt. Cerna phoned to so report and Fazoli drove Web Allen to Jasmine Cottage to change uniforms. But these are not his khakis. They belong to some midget EM. He can't button the collar or waist, the pants expose his ankles, the crotch fits like a vise. They are however his only uniform. Pvt. Cerna, quick to send laundry out, grabbed the giant EM's khakis and sent them back to 114th along with his scratchy pinks. Pvt. Cerna also shines Web Allen's shoes and makes his bed. May wonder why the bed's a wreck, sheets all tangled, flung about. May think his colonel has nightmares but probably not. Pvt. Cerna probably knows all about his colonel and Jill Tucker.

The paperwork is the usual waste of time. Web Allen shoves

it aside and phones the 114th Laundry Detachment. The first john who commands the detachment is not there, his whereabouts unknown. Web Allen blisters the duty sergeant and gets more abject apologies and promises but he can't wear those and sits staring out at the rain pounding down.

So's his poor head, pounding. He's not used to four drinks said to be twelve-year-old scotch with his lunch: lamb chops, parsley potatoes, creamed asparagus, some kind of pudding, "savory" on the menu. The Australia Club does well by its members. There are only a dozen, the senior Australian officers in Townsville: most billet there. Wing Cmdr. Hewlitt-Packard insisted on the drinks, matched him scotch for scotch with no visible effect. Persnickety old joker in a strange uniform: dress shirt, tie, blue jacket with two tiny ribbons, one for each war apparently, khaki shorts, dark blue socks on his skinny legs, bony knees exposed. Stares at people through half glasses on his long thin nose as if detecting an unsavory odor. Seems to think he's British aristocracy, landed gentry. Web Allen's never met a British aristocrat but he's seen the British upper classes depicted in films.

Tried to pump him, the persnickety old joker, about the missing booze, any Base Section plans to enlist GHQ assistance. Not much visible reaction when told Web Allen "doesn't give a damn" about the booze. Did say, "Bad for officer morale," but surmised there wasn't much of that anyway. "Seldom find it, L-of-C troops." Dismissed Miss Davis' rape in six words. "Bad show, bloody blackfellows always trouble." And did agree finally, following a lot of balderdash about Allied Relations, to release the two MPs his sentries caught "in a Restricted Area." Said he'll see they're returned to the 301st MP Co., still in their RAAF coveralls, "assuming there'll be no further attempts to invade my airfield."

Web Allen reassured him on that point, guesses the lunch was not entirely wasted, wonders if M/Sgt. Abbott has any aspirin. The rain's still pounding down and there's a leak in the ceiling over his desk. "Sergeant Abbott!" Abbott pops in. "Bring me two aspirin if you have any. And help me move my desk. There's a damn leak. Get a pail or something, catch it. Preparations for the inspection well underway?"

"Yessir! Far as I know, Sir. Colonel Fogerty's phoning, checking units. No aspirin, Sir. Sorry. I have a letter for you, Sir. It was mixed in with the safe-in-hand mail."

They move the desk. Fogerty's been sulking since packed off to see U.S. Rep. Festus Lee Claypool but is functioning, apparently. The letter's a V-mail from Mert. Web Allen, awash in guilt, he's not written Mert for two weeks, hangs his spectacles on his ears, opens the V-mail, squints at the tiny print. Mert types her V-mails.

> West Cork, Dec. 2. Dearest Web: I trust this finds you well. We are all fine. Barbara has a major part in the High School Christmas Pageant. She's the Virgin Mary. Betsy will be in the orchestra. She really is getting quite good on her flute. Practices every day and I don't even have to tell her! Some of the teachers thought this year's Pageant should have a Military Theme, but I'm glad they finally decided to stick with a Religious one. It seems to me what with the war and all we really should continue our old customs and Celebrate the Birth of Our Lord the way we always do. It's what you men, all our boys, are fighting for, I think. Bob and Mary Weller's boy Ben is Missing. He was at that Anzio place in Italy and they think he might have been taken prisoner by the Germans but they're not sure. They haven't heard anything. He was, or is, only 20. You might remember him. He had a terrible "crush" on Barbara when she was just a freshmen and he was a senior. Speaking of that, I don't want to worry you, Web dear, but I think you know we have an Army Glider School here now. I'm sure I told you that. They are in the Armory for their Ground School. They're from all over the country and most of them are 19 or 20 but some of them are older and Barbara has a terrible "crush" now on

one of them. He's 24! His name is William Holmes and he seems a nice enough young man. He's been over to the house two or three times and says his father is an Eastman Kodak executive. But he's from Rochester, N.Y., so far away, and he's so much older! I do worry some about Barbara, Web. She's only 17 and she has that rebel streak in her. Like you used to have. I worry she might do something very very foolish. She's supposed to be the Virgin Mary. She's hard to handle sometimes. Part of growing up, I suppose. But you mustn't worry, Web dear. I can handle her. Perhaps though you could write her, a personal letter. Just give her some good advice. When you have time. I know you are very busy, a major command and all. We are all very proud of you. But I do hope you can write her. All for now. I love you very much. Keep safe. Mert.

Oh and I'm just the one to do that, write Barbara, Col. Web Allen thinks, still awash in guilt, and sums up his situation. It's a dismal sitrep. Southern white girl technically under his command raped by Colored. Her Dixie Uncle, a Congressman, at hand, raising hell, voicing threats. The damn booze, its whereabouts unknown though suspected. Brig.Gen. S.O. Bargle coming down the pike to inspect his command. And married but in love. With a woman young enough to be his daughter. Sex with whom torpedoes all his scruples. Sorry, folks, but that's the way it is. And he still loves Mert too, though in a different way. Mert's a good woman. Good wife. Good mother. Loyal, honest, kind, reverent, trustworthy. Everything a wife (or Boy Scout) should be. Mert doesn't deserve this, what he's doing. The fact she doesn't know, never will, has nothing to do with it. And his daughters. He loves them, God knows, in a different but equally powerful way. Should anything "bad" happen to either, what would he do? And now he must write one of them, Barbara the rebel, tout fidelity, saving one's self for one's true love, etc., etc. Write Mert too, somehow. Then engage in more natural and unnatural acts with Jill Tucker before this day is over.

Web Allen remembers a line from William Faulkner's "Wild Palms." "Between the grief and nothing, he would still take the grief." But that protagonist's grief did not include a double-barreled rape, a fat congressman, lost booze, Brig.Gen. Bargle. What the hell did that protagonist know about grief?

There's a knock and Lt. Col. Fogerty enters the office. He seems to be over his sulks though his ears are still red and swollen. In fact, he's beaming. No doubt he's been nipping at the gin in his desk.

"Good news for a change, Sir!" Fogerty says. "Light colonel I know, Service Force HQ Transport Section, just phoned me. General Bargle's stuck in Brisbane! Weather's got him grounded. Might not be here for three, four days. We'll go on with our preparations of course. I'll have this outfit up to snuff, time he gets here. You hear anything yet from GHQ, Sir? We can lower the boom on the goddamn RAAF?"

"No, not yet," Web Allen says. "Brigadier I talked to said it might take awhile, work through the Command Structure, Allied Relations and all. I'll let you know, Colonel, minute I hear anything."

Fogerty grunts. "Well, our booze ain't going anywhere today. Or tomorrow, not in this weather. So we got some time. I'm gonna check some units, see they're ready for inspection." Fogerty departs. He must have had several nips, accepting this delay in his plan to search all the aircraft on Garbutt Field with such equanimity.

The rain's changed to a slow drizzle and another leak's developed near the windows. There's a tin pail Abbot found under the other one. Web Allen finds a V-mail form, he prints his V-mails, prints "Dear Mert," and there stalls, dead in the water. There's no way he can write Mert. Or Barbara. Not now. He'll write them tomorrow. He crushes the form and drops it in his wastebasket and his prickly heat stages a brief assault, raking his crotch. You'd think the prickly heat would ease off in view of the rain but it's not. The rain's pounding down hard again and the new leak's dripping. "Sergeant Abbott! Find another pail."

* * *

U.S. Rep. Festus Lee Claypool, his party and Siggie Ferk the World Greatest Juggling Accordionist are playing poker at a corner table in the George Hotel public room, dealer's choice, draw or stud, no crazy games, three-quid limit on bets, three raises. Outside the rain's changed to a steady drizzle.

Claypool, a shrewd old boy when it comes to cards, and James Enders, the UP man, veteran of many a late night newsroom poker game, are the big winners. Siggie Ferk, INS, Calvin Winsome and the GHQ flunky captain are hanging in there. The flunky lieutenant doesn't play poker and is off somewhere getting another sitrep on the weather. David Dudley Hull, beset by a mean hangover, dropped out an hour ago after losing twenty quid ($64) but remains at the table nursing a dubious scotch he bought himself and thinking of ways to put the $64 on his expense account. Old Claypool bought a couple of rounds when the game began but is hoarding his winnings now. They all commiserated with him earlier, terrible thing happened to his niece, but he seems to have put that behind him, though now and then muttering, "Turrble turrble thang."

It's Claypool's deal. "Five cod draw," he says. "Jacks uh bettuh," and deals, the cards flipping fast from his fat fingers. "Calvin, yawl hee-uh that cap'n the next table, we havin' ower lunch, one say he was uh weathuhman, say this gahdamn rain mott lass uh week? That be the case, Ah mott have to and change ower plans. Cancel ower trip Up The Front. Be motty dis'pointin' Ah miss seein' ower boys Up The Front. But they be some impotent votes comin' up in The Congress Ah got to be back in Wash'ton foh."

"Rain might last a week, Sir," the flunky captain says. "This is the rainy season here. But I understand the Meteorology Detachment out at the airfield thinks there might be a break in the weather within thirty-six to forty-eight hours."

Enders, lying in the weeds, bets a pound. Siggie Ferk, Calvin Winsome and the flunky captain see that and INS raises a pound.

"Ah be two days behin' skeddle then," Claypool says. "That be cuttin' it motty thin. Ah am seein' and raisin' I guess this uh pond. Fact be, Ah thank Ah juss bettuh cancel ower trip Up The Front and git rot back to Bris'bn and fly rot on home. Yawl take cay that, Captain? Range us some transpotation? Mistuh Fook, yawl welcome accompany us Bris'bn, yawl be so minded."

"Well, thank you, Congressman," Siggie Ferk says. "I appreciates that. You sure got my vote, I ever domicile in Mississip."

"I'll call the GHQ Transport Section right now, Sir," the flunky captain, happily throwing his hand in, says. He never was wild about a trip to Port Moresby anyway, even a day-trip.

David Dudley Hull gulps. If he has to fly on alone to New Guinea the airplane he'll be in will not have a fighter escort, which the flunky captain said Claypool's would. Enders also is disappointed. He has to stick with old Claypool. But he's been disappointed before, newswise, many times, on other junkets, and he's been picking INS' brains, getting a feel for the Real War. INS claims to have flown eight combat missions in various kinds of bombers. And Enders is sitting on a natural full-house, Jacks-and-fives.

Siggie Ferk and Calvin fold. INS and Claypool take two cards each and Enders raises a pound. INS folds, Claypool sees the raise and checks and Enders says, "Let's separate the men from the boys. Three pounds. How much is that in real money, ten bucks?"

Claypool ponders and Enders composes in his head the lede he'll cable, embargoed though it be, from Brisbane. "Somewhere in Australia: A major tropical storm that grounded aircraft throughout the Southwest Pacific Area forced U.S. Rep. Festus Lee Claypool (D-Miss) to abort his planned tour of the U.S. Army's fighting fronts in New Guinea. He was deeply disappointed by this change of plan, Rep. Claypool said, but impressed with the high morale he found among the many GIs with whom he spoke in Australia blah blah blah." Which no doubt is what Claypool would say had he spoken with any GIs and Enders has been putting quotes and syntax in congressmen's flannel mouths for years.

Claypool throws his hand in. "Yawl too rich foh mah blood, Mistuh Enduhs." Enders scoops up the skimpy pot, another disappointment. Outside, rain's pounding down. The wet bedraggled palm trees David Dudley Hull observes through the public room's tall windows look as miserable as he feels.

* * *

The first unit Lt. Col. Fogerty checks is the Base Section Officers Club. He drives there himself in his jeep, leaving his driver to drink coffee and discuss women with other loafers in the Red Cross Canteen across Hill Street. He finds Lt. Bernie Witters counting bottles on the shelves in the Club storeroom.

"I hope they count up," Lt. Col. Fogerty says. "Because I got a little jolt for you, Lieutenant. Nitpicker that asshole is gonna inventory you tomorrow, fourteen hundred. I tried and stall the asshole but he quote me some AR I never heard of he says gives him authority, him being the Finance Officer. I just come warn you, get your records in order. And I need a couple jugs. We ain't locate the booze the goddamn flyboys liberate yet but I reckon it's still here. Prolly out the airfield on their goddamn airplane. But their goddamn airplane ain't goin' anywhere today, this weather. Or tomorrow. And Colonel Allen phoned GHQ, requested authority we tell the goddamn RAAF go take a flying fuck. Then we start searchin' the airplanes. Today yet maybe, we get the word, or else tomorrow."

Fogerty moves to pluck two bottles of gin from a shelf but Lt. Witters intervenes. "No, don't take those, Sir! We got two bottles

Gilbey's Select in November, Sir, and I put them away for you." Witters produces these bottles from beneath the bottom shelf.

Lt. Col. Fogerty expresses surprise and pleasure but he's somewhat puzzled. "Hey, Select! Whyn't you gimme them before?"

"I was saving them for you, Sir. For Christmas. But it's almost Chritsmas. Uh, Sir. There might be a little problem, you know, the inventory? I mean the stock I, you. Well, it's sort of added up, Sir."

"Breakage," Lt. Col. Fogerty says. "You're bound to have some breakage, Club this size. Quite a lot prolly. Write up some breakage reports. Tell Nitpicker stick 'em up his ass. Or your bartender. What's his name, Dugan? He looks shifty. He might liberated a few jugs. Turn Nitpicker loose on him. And get this place cleaned up. General Bargle's stuck in Brisbane, the weather. Doubt he'll inspect the Club anyway. But you never know, that s.o.b. How's the rationing going?"

"There's an awful lot of complaints, Sir. Seems like everybody blames me. And those goddamn chickens, Aussie woman lives next door, Missus Rooney. I think I mention them, Sir. They get loose about ten times a day and poop on my jeep."

"I know all about the chickens, Lieutenant. Tell me, this Missus Rooney. You seen her, I guess. What kind of broad is she? Looks like, I mean."

"Well she's not bad looking, Sir. Big though. Not so tall but I bet she weighs two-hundred pounds. Oh, there's another thing, Sir. That MP stopped the truck yesterday, I was on my way to get the liquor. Said it had a broken taillight? I'm pretty sure, Sir, he was the CID sergeant was in your office."

"So?" Lt. Col. Fogerty's mind is elsewhere. "Chickens, they're an Allied Relations Problem. I'll handle it. I'll go talk to this Missus Rooney, I get a chance. I got to roll, check units gettin' ready for this goddamn inspection. Nitpicker's a pain in the ass but you write up some breakage reports, sic him on Dugan, you be okay."

Lt. Col. Fogerty departs with his Select and Lt. Witters, dropping into a broken chair in the storeroom, buries his head in his hands. He doubts fictitious breakage reports and any shenanigans he can blame on Dugan will account for the Club's missing booze: sixty-odd jugs appropriated over the months by Fogerty and a few more, not replaced, he must have peddled to transient officers. He just checked all his reqs and purchase orders again, with a growing sense of doom.

* * *

"Sir!" RAAF Sgt. James Keeney, stamping his foot, his wet pants slapping his skinny ankles, snapping off a salute in Wing Cmdr. Hewlitt-Packard's barracks office at 1700 hours, says. "Permission report." Outside, rain's pounding down. Hewlitt-Packard nods and Sgt. Keeney reports:

He took four men and they reconnoitered the field at length but did not unfortunately discover the bloody Yanks' missing plonk. There wasn't any way they could look inside the parked C47s without climbing on a wing where it says No Step and Sgt. Keeney, who treats all aircraft like a mother hen with chicks, wouldn't let his men do that. They did however observe "one bloody suspicious haircraft wit a dog, great bloody beast 'e is," tied to it. A Dakota with a star on its nose, some bloody Yank general's Dakota. They also saw some bloody Yanks, a major and other ranks, cruising the field in a Second Air Depot three-quarter ton. Those bloody Yanks, observed through binoculars misted with rain from the Fiat lorry on permanent surveillance on the taxiway, stopped at the bloody general's Dakota but the great bloody beast kept them at bay. Those Yanks had an ERO, Sgt. Keeney checked with the Main Gate sentry. They were supposed to repair an instrument on the general's Dakota. So they may be back. And the bloody Yank Dakota parked next to the general's is loaded with ammunition, so posted. "Where we caught the bloody spies, Sir, smoking. They might blowed us all to bloody kingdom come, Sir." Sgt. Keeney also queried the bloody Yank

MPs guarding the bloody Yank lorry behind the Canteen, but that's nothing to do with the missing plonk. MPs said the lorry may have something to do with "the blackfellows as 'umped the bloody Yank Red Cross sheila."

Wing Cmdr. Hewlitt-Packard digests this intelligence, discards some of it. "Got to be the bloody general's Dakota with the plonk aboard then, Sergeant. Great bloody dog there. Air Depot Yanks sniffing around. Bloody Air Depot Yanks are looking for the plonk too! Get their plonk in Sydney but want more. May be short, worried, the weather. Or bloody greedy. Good work, Sergeant. Come night now, I should think the bloody general's Dakota might have a flat tire. Case the bloody weather breaks."

"But the bloody dog, Sir."

"Take a Fiat. Rev it up. Put a bullet in the bloody tire. Oh-three-hundred, I should think. One shot, all souls abed, no one the wiser. Leave it to you, Sergeant. I'll be at the Club tonight. All night. Best you get out of those wet trousers now. Then deliver the bloody Yanks spies to their unit. Told Colonel Allen we would."

"Sir!" Sgt. Keeney stamps his foot, salutes and departs. Hewlitt-Packard has a room in the barracks but it's furnished with a camp bed. His room at the Australia Club has a double-bed. The rain's still pounding down.

* * *

Col. Big Bob Betrandus and his subordinates are as is their custom enjoying cocktails in the Air Depot Officers' Mess at 1730 hours. Outside the rain's slowed to a steady drizzle and the putting green's awash in mud-colored water.

"Goddamn dog," Maj. Richall the engineering officer says. "Rottweiler, I think. Savage animal anyway. No way we could get a look in the aircraft, Sir. One of my men tried to get up on the wing and look inside. The goddamn dog came after him, damn near got him, tore his pants. But I'll bet a month's pay that's the aircraft with the Base Section booze. General Dumphy's airplane. We didn't see anything, any other aircraft, indicate there was booze aboard."

"Makes sense to me," Lt.Col. Gerber says.

"Me too, I guess," Big Bob says. "But what about the Forty-Seven that pilot called yesterday, hot to get a new tire mounted?"

"That one's loaded with ammunition, Sir," Richall says. "So posted and it is ammo. One of my men got up on the wing and looked inside. Mortar rounds, he said."

"By god then," Big Bob says. "I agree with you, Engineering. It's got to be the General's airplane has the booze on it! His crew, they're the culprits! Or the general is. I'll be dammed! First Corps deputy commander liberating booze! Where's First Corps HQ now anyway?"

"Rockhampton, Sir," Maj. Reeves says. "But there's a Forward HQ in Dobodura. Or maybe it's in Nadzab. Somewhere in New Guinea anyway."

"Personnel there be in the market for booze," Big Bob says. "Where the hell's the general's crew? They must be here, their aircraft is. Shacked up maybe. Let's find them. You get a name, Engineering, the pilot, he req what was it?"

"Altimeter repair, Sir. Be in my office."

"Go find it," Big Bob says. "We'll call the Transient Area, say we need the pilot, some problem with his aircraft. Be some first john probably. I'll lay rank on him. Scare the bejesus out of him with that GHQ Order. Make a deal with him."

"Sir!" Richall swallows his martini, grabs his raincoat and heads for his office. The rain's pounding down hard again.

* * *

The squad room in the Townsville Constabulary on Front Street is fairly crowded at 1900 hours. The four-to-midnight shift commander, an elderly sergeant with a fat pink face, he looks like Santa Claus with a shave, is at his desk, puffing a pipe and reading reports of minor crimes turned in by the eight-to-four shift. Four constables in ankle-length raincoats and bobbie helmets are standing around awaiting their opposite numbers, four AMF Field Police and four U.S. MPs, before beginning the evening foot patrols. The patrols are joint forces because most of the crimes they encounter, scuffles between Allies, urinating in public, are likely to involve military personnel. Outside, rain's pounding down.

Capt. Raskovic, Sgt. Harry Parker, Cpl. Elrod Finneman and Pvt. Herb Steussie are studying the wanted posters, most of which depict Aborigines sought for sheep stealing. They all had a meal of sorts earlier in the 301st MP mess, lemonade and spam sandwiches (actually canned pork shoulder but the GIs call it spam) while rain drummed the mess tent. The kitchen, all cleaned up for Brig. Gen. Bargle's inspection, was closed, but now the inspection's been delayed, they heard, there'll be a hot breakfast. Finneman and Steussie, back in their khakis, gobbled up the sandwiches, said all the goddamn RAAF gave them was water and hard biscuits.

The opposite numbers arrive and the foot patrols depart, going out into the rain, but they'll soon find cover under the awnings along Flinders Street.

"Constable Sergeant," Raskovic says. "Be dinkum we use your basement awhile? We aim to interrogate that blackfellow we got locked up. He might make a little noise and we don't want to disturb you."

"Welcome to it," the Constable Sergeant, who truly believes all blackfellows to be sub-human, says. He tosses Raskovic a heavy key. "He one the ones rape that girl?"

"We figure he knows something about it," Raskovic says. "Okay, men, let's go to work." He leads his command into the cellblock behind the squadroom, where they encounter a strong smell of urine and disinfectant. There are four windowless cells behind heavy bars, two each side of a narrow passageway, bare but for iron cots with stained mattresses. Constabulary prisoners are let out at intervals to use the loo at the end of the passageway. There's a town drunk asleep in one, snoring. Two are empty. Pvt. Douglas MacArthur, handcuffed still, lies curled in a fetal position on the cot in the other one with his eyes shut, mumbling prayer. He opens his eyes and cringes when Raskovic unlocks the cell door.

Oh mama! They back! The little mean white mans, the big one and two more and the little one look like he prolly like to burns and hangs Color boys!

"Get him up," Raskovic says. It was his idea to lock MacArthur in the Constabulary cellblock and leave him there to think and worry rather put him in the 301st Stockade where other prisoners might commiserate with him, and his idea to bring Finneman and Steussie along for the interrogation. Numbers are frightening and he'll find work for them. He also phoned the 404th QM Truck (C) for a sitrep on MacArthur's 201, which he found pleasing. Nineteen-year-old kid from the Deep South, no known previous arrests, no experience with big city police methods.

Harry Parker pulls Pvt. MacArthur to his feet and they hustle him down into the Constabulary basement, a damp dark windowless place with a concrete floor lit by a single 40-watt bulb on a dangling cord when Raskovic hits the light switch. It's cluttered with traffic barricades, No Parking by Order of the Constabularly signs and old Air Warden gear. Muddy water is seeping across the floor in one corner: the basement sometimes floods during The Bloody Wet.

"Take the cuffs off," Raskovic says. "Strip him. Lay him on the floor." Harry, Finneman and Steussie carry out these instructions with some help from Pvt. MacArthur, who unties his shoes. He's not going to make no trouble for these white mans. "Pull his arms over his head and hold his wrists, Sergeant. Tight. Finneman, you and Steussie spread his legs and hold his ankles."

Harry squats on his heels behind Pvt. MacArthur and

Finneman and Steussie kneel at his feet and comply with these instructions. Pvt. MacArthur, naked, terrified, spread-eagled on the cold concrete, is shaking like a leaf in a strong autumn wind. Capt. Raskovic steps between his spread legs, plants an 11D GI shoe on Pvt. MacArthur's shriveled black scrotum and applies a little pressure. Pvt. MacArthur squirms and moans.

"This the way the Russkies do it," Raskovic, sharing some interesting information and a little anecdote with his men, says. "Don't leave any marks. They did it my Uncle Vladimir, you believe my old man. Tough cookie, Uncle Vladimir. Held out half a day. Then he was ready and confess he been screwin' Stalin's wife, that's what they wanted to hear. Let's see how long this little cocksucker holds out." He applies some additional pressure, crunching poor Pvt. MacArthur's testicles. Pvt. MacArthur squirms and moans. "That just a sample, boy! Now, our information, you maybe dint actually rape that white girl. But we know you drivin' that deuce-and-a-half when your goddamn buddies grab that white girl! So you just as guilty as your goddamn buddies did rape her. You in on it, boy! We prolly hang you too. But you tell me your buddies, their goddamn names, we maybe go easy on you. You don't tell me, we are gonna stay here all night, boy! Who with you, boy? Who the bastards grab that white girl and fuck her!"

Pvt. MacArthur squirms and whimpers. "Nuh! Ah din! We din! Ma truck lib'rate! Honess! Ooooooh! Please, mans! You hurtin' me!"

Raskovic applies more pressure. "You report your truck liberated, boy?" Pvt. MacArthur moans and shakes his head. "In just about a minute, boy. I am gonna fix you so you never rape another white girl. You never fuck another girl." This may not be true: Raskovic's not been to medical school, but neither has Pvt. MacArthur "Then we gonna cut your black cock off!" Raskovic applies more pressure. Pvt. MacArthur sobs and squeals. "You tell me some names, boy! Who your goddamn buddies? Who rape that white girl?" Raskovic applies more pressure. Pvt. MacArthur screams and sobs. Tears stream down his cheeks.

"Captain, Sir," Finneman says. "I don't like doing this. I'm afraid I'm going to be sick."

"You barf, Finneman," Raskovic, applying more pressure, says. "You're gonna be a goddamn private! Or else I ship you off some Infantry outfit. Hold his goddamn ankle!" Some infantry outfit! Fear produces a rush of adrenaline and Finneman tightens his grip on Pvt. MacArthur's ankle "Who, boy! Who your goddamn buddies fuck that white girl? Gimme some names!"

"Nuh! Truck lib'rate!" Pvt. MacArthur wails. "Honess! We din! They din. Oooooh! You hurtin' me!"

"You ask for it, you black bastard!" Raskovic, squashing poor Pvt. MacArthur's testicles, says. Pvt. MacArthur howls. Raskovic goes right on squashing his testicles. "I told you, boy! You tell me goddamn names! Or else we stay here all night!"

Pvt. MacArthur screams. He's had enough. He's no Uncle Vladimir. "Sar'ent Washin'ton. Sar'ent Franklin. Ust to be Sar'ent Jefferson. But they din! Oh oh oh! Oooooh! You hurtin me!" Sobs choke him. Tears stream down his cheeks.

"What!" Raskovic, appalled, no history buff but he knows those names, says. Then, suspicious, squashes Pvt. MacArthur testicles. "You think you're funny, you little black bastard! You gimme your goddamn buddies names! Right names! Real names! All their names, boy! Or I am gonna make jelly out a your black balls!"

Pvt. MacArthur screams, howls, writhes and in a rush and tumble of words between sobs blubbers, "Is they names! Honess! Sar'ent George Washin'ton. Sar'ent Benjamin Franklin. Was sar'ent Thomas Jeff'son."

"Holy Christ!" Raskovic, appalled still but convinced, his 11D shoe he surmises the equal on any truth serum, says. "Okay. Christ! Okay. That's who then. And you all grab that white girl and two you, two them, I don't care who, fuck her! Then you dump that deuce-and-a-half you drivin' out the airfield. That right?"

Pvt. MacArthur howls and blubbers. "Yassuh. Yassuh. We do that. Oooooh! Please, Mistuh mans! You hurtin' me awful bad!"

"Where those bastards now?" Raskovic keeps the pressure on. "Out the battalion?"

"Nuh," Pvt. MacArthur moans. "They on a boat. They goin' Noo Ginny."

"Shit!" Raskovic says. "We'll get them though. Jeezuzz! Washington. Franklin. Jefferson. Awright, boy." He lifts his shoe from Pvt. MacArthur's scrotum. "You done the right thing, boy. You get dressed now. Let him up, men. Cuff him, Sergeant." Relief and continuing pain trip Pvt. MacArthur's bladde and he urinates, can't help it, a thin arching stream "Oh shit! He piss on me! I ought a kick his!" But that might leave a mark. "Anyway, we got what we came for. We'll take him the Stockade now. You understand, boy? We are gonna write up everthing you told us. That's we call a confession. Then you are gonna sign your name on it. Means it's true! You change your mind, what you told us, we come back here and the sergeant, he's bigger'n me, he's gonna stand on your balls! You understand that, boy?"

Pvt. MacArthur, still in great pain, struggling into his fatigues, bobs his head. He understands the part about coming back to the basement anyway. And he won't ever say his deuce-and-a-half was lib'rate again. The little mean mans is awful mean, just about the meanest mans he ever meet or ever wanna meet. But Sar'ents Washington and Franklin and former Sar'ent Jefferson, they prolly safe from him. They on a boat on they way to Noo Ginny.

They hustle Pvt. MacArthur, dressed and cuffed, shoes unlaced, still in pain, up the stairs through the cellblock into the squadroom. "He one the ones?" the Constabulary Sergeant, puffing his pipe, says.

"Looks like it," Raskovic, tossing the sergeant the cellblock key, says. "We got a confession out of him anyway. Finally. Kind of a surprise." But those names would mean little to the sergeant.

"Good on youse! Thought you was. Heard him yodeling. Bloody blackfellows allas bloody trouble."

"Truer word was never spoke," Raskovic says. "Say, Sergeant. You think we can borrow your fingerprint expert tomorrow? Sometime the afternoon prolly? We wanna check a vehicle we figure might been involved for prints, there are any, and I'm kind of rusty, prints."

"Sure, glad to be of assistance." The Sergeant consults the duty roster. "That be Constable Crowe. Jack Crowe. He be on the day shift, off at four."

"We'll pick him up," Raskovic says. "Appreciate your help, Sergeant. Okay, men, let's go." They hustle Pvt. MacArthur out of the Constabulary and into CID jeep's the rear seat beside Steussie. The rain's still hammering down. "Prisoner here goes into solitary, the Stockade, and you're gonna babysit him, Steussie. Make sure nobody talks to him. Finneman, you go up the office and write up his confession. You heard what he said and you can look at Sergeant Parker's Initial Report, some the details. You and me, Sergeant, we're gonna hit the Four-oh-Fourth QM Truck again. Find out where those bastards we got their names gonna disembark. Prolly Oro Bay. Jeezuzz! Washington, Franklin, Jefferson! Me and you prolly fly up there, take them inna custody. You know, men, we wrap up this rape in record time, get it off the board, we will be the white-haired boys around here!"

"But uh, Captain, Sir," Cpl. Finneman says. "His uh well confession, Sir? It was sort of like. Well, you know, Sir. Extorted? What I mean is. Well, will it hold up in court, Sir?"

"Finneman." Raskovic says. "You let me worry about that. You just get your ass in gear and write up his confession. There's times, Finneman, I don't think you're cut out for police work."

* * *

The second farewell party at Manic Manor, centered again in the kitchen, bugs banging the light bulb and winding up in the trash, wet ponchos here and there, all the usual suspects present, was initially somewhat subdued, but by 2200 hours it's working up a fair head of steam. The census counted twenty-two persons from sixteen states, the Territory of Alaska (the chief off the Little Rock is missing) and the Sioux Nation. Outside, rain's pounding down. Neither farewellee is present. Boots Davis is still in the 12th Station, though Agnes Moore heard they may discharge her in a day or two, and what happened to Boots, still fresh in everybody's mind, put a damper on things for awhile. Rose Pearl Stevens has another date with her RAAF brass. The sitrep is he took her to the Australia Club again for a good meal and some twelve-year-old scotch. Rose Pearl won't be going to Seven-Mile in the morning, not with the weather.

Those present include Billy Gote, Eddie Devlin, Saljeski, Lts. Hunker and Donald, Flots, Ann Silvers, Betty Lou Fricker, Pops, the 12th Station supply sergeant, who finally got his jeep started and brought another gallon of 190-proof to this party, and assorted flyboys. Jets is upstairs in the room she shares with Flots, sulking. Ima Score is in the loo, beating Jill Tucker to it, and Jill's doing her hair in the room she shares under duress with Ima. Lt. Donald's fully attired, wearing the pants that were in his valpak. He found his other pants on the awning over the patio and retrieved them with a branch torn from the broken hedge but they were soaked and, hung on a floor lamp in the living room, aren't dry yet. He and a flyboy are comparing short-snorters (paper bills in small denominations from various nations, taped together and signed by persons encountered in the service) though Donald's doesn't amount to much. The flyboy's is three-feet long.

"Hey, Donald," Lt. Hunker says. "What you gonna tell your kids, you ever have any, they ask, What you do in the war, Daddy? I got a stick and fish my pants off a awning in Townsville, Australia?"

"Oh put a sock in it," Lt. Donald says. He doesn't much like Hunker, who's making a play for Flots, who seems to have lost interest in Lt. Donald and may at this very moment be kneading Hunker's thigh or something under the table. Lt. Donald, proving he's a man, is drinking 190-proof lightly laced with GI grapefruit juice.

Pops is drinking something he calls a Swagman, gin plus a secret ingredient, and urging Agnes try one. She'll stick to Swappa slings, Agnes says. There's plenty of gin. Billy Gote brought three jugs he says he got it off the 34th Squadron p.o. Billy Eckstine's wailing, appropriately enough, "It's gawnnn and started raininnn." Eddie Devlin's sharing a sling with Ann Silvers and telling her for the ninth or tenth time he's not married, that telegram about the sixteen-pound baby was just a joke. Saljeski's idea of joke. Saljeski's confirmed that and Ann Silvers appears to be half-convinced. Saljeski, with Mrs. Rooney out of town, is making a play for Betty Lou Fricker, mixing her slings, intent on her knickers.

"I went out the Twelfth Station and saw Boots," Billy Gote says. "She seems okay. Consider what happen to her, I mean." Then decides this is nobody else's business. Boots was glad to see him. Said she was anyway. They talked for a while, mostly about Guinea and Seven-Mile Strip. Boots still wants to go there. But when he tried to hug Boots, give her a friendly kiss, she withdrew, went rigid, froze right up and said, "No! Not now, Billy!" He can understand that, more or less, in view of her circumstances. Take awhile no doubt before she wants to sleep with him, sleep with anybody, again. Goddamn it, though! He really likes Boots. They hit it off real good. But life goes on. Billy Gote surveys the field. Ann Silvers is a good-looking girl but he won't shoot Eddie down. Eddie's a good kid. Or compete with Saljeski, though he reckons Saljeski's target, Betty Lou Fricker's knickers, will as they say in the bomb squadrons be aborted. Betty Lou's a cold fish. Score, if she turns up? Built like a barrel but what the hell. Score with Score. But his heart's not in it. Damn! He really on short acquaintance had something going with Boots. Not just the sex either. He really likes Boots. Then this, that, had to happen!

Billy Gote goes to the sink and is building a sling, a big strong sling, when Sgt. Harry Parker rolls in with the news they've all been waiting for, more or less.

"We might got the bastards did Boots," Harry announces. "Captain Raskovic thinks so anyway. Know who they are, I mean." Who, everybody wants to know. "Well, you prolly won't believe this but our information they are George Washington, Benjamin Franklin, Thomas Jefferson and Douglas MacArthur." Startled exclamations greet this revelation. "Four coons the Four-oh-Fourth QM Truck. Two sergeants. Washington and Franklin. Private MacArthur. Jefferson was a sergeant but been broke to private. We got MacArthur, Douglas, in custody. I swear that's his name. He pretty much confess, Raskovic lean on him a little. Well, quite a little. The other three ship out last night for Oro Bay. They had time and do Boots before they embark though. We went out the Four-oh-Fourth and got their serial numbers and all. Raskovic's on the ACS, trying raise the LST they on. Get them clapped in irons, I guess. Raskovic and me, we be flying up to Oro Bay and bring them back. Soon's the weather breaks."

Exultation greets this news. It calls for a drink all around. Somebody builds Harry a sling. Boots doesn't know any of this yet, far as Harry knows, but Raskovic will call the 12th Station, he's off the ACS, and somebody there will tell her.

"Raskovic," Harry says. "Thinks we might got the deuce-and-a-half they use too. Our information, MacArthur was the driver and they dump it out the airfield behind the Canteen. Why they dump it there we don't know but Raskovic says criminal minds are hard to fathom."

"That was their truck!" Flots says. "Oh my God!"

Billy Gote, Eddie and Saljeski exchange startled glances and Saljeski opens his mouth but notes Harry winking and closes it.

Why muddy the waters? And the booze, Priority One, is still aboard the Lucky Lil, nowhere to fly it with the weather socked in. Outside, rain's pounding down.

"What's the latest," Billy Gote says. "That booze was liberated?"

"Well, that's kind of on hold, the time being," Harry says. "RAAF" won't let us on the field, search a bunch airplanes, without they get a direct order from RAAF HQ. Base Section is workin' on that. Raskovic says Colonel Allen called GHQ. Requested somebody there speed things up, lean on RAAF HQ. But that ain't happen yet. Prolly take awhile, go through channels and all. Booze kind of a Mexican stand-off."

Jill Tucker, wrapped in a terrycloth robe, stamps down the backstairs and says Score's got the loo tied up. Agnes Moore says wearily she'll talk to Ima and goes up the back stairs with Jill. Betty Lou Fricker yawns, says it's time she went to bed, she's got the early Canteen shift, and follows them, leaving Saljeski dry-docked. He accepts Pops' offer of a Swagman. Somebody asks will the four coons be court-martialed and when? Technically, Harry says, the case is "still under investigation." Ima Score comes banging down the backstairs goddamning Jill Tucker. Billy Gote surveys Ima like a man who might buy a horse and decides he'll get a good night's sleep, good as he can on the patio. Lt. Donald, conceding Flots to Lt. Hunker, wonders will somebody give him a ride to the USAAC Transient Area? Saljeski says he will but it's early yet. Ann Silvers, making Eddie's day, whispers she guesses he is not after all married and can sleep in her and Boot's room. Billy Eckstine wails, though nobody needs this information, "It's gawnnn and started raininnnnn'."

Jill Tucker comes down the backstairs, dressed, seeking a ride up the street. The 12th Station supply sergeant volunteers, vows his jeep will start and there'll be no funny business.

"Hey, Tucker," Ima Score says. "I hear your old boyfriend's coming to town. How are you going to handle that? Not that I give a damn."

"Former old friend," Jill says. "If you are referring to Brigadier-General Bargle. He's in Brisbane, waiting for a break in this weather. He called me. Don't worry, Roomie, I'll handle it. Let's go, Sergeant."

Jill and the sergeant go out into the rain. "Will some kind person," Score says. "Provide me with a very large sling?" Lt. Donald springs up to do that. The USAAC Transient Area is a dismal place, he spent a week there one night as the saying goes on his arrival in Swappa, and Score come right down to it is not all that obese.

Harry Parker yawns, drinks his sling, says it's been a long day, he's ready to hit the sack, but he's got another Samurai sword in his jeep if Lieutenant Gote wants to look at it, and the other two Samurai enthusiasts present, the chief off the Little Rock is absent again, also express an interest in this artifact.

They huddle on the Manor's back porch, out of the rain, it's slowed to a steady drizzle, batting at the ususal horde of mosquitoes.

"I don't exactly know what the hell is going on," Harry says. "But after Flots call me about that deuce-and-a-half you dump behind the Canteen, I steer Raskovic out there. Keep his mind off the booze and Colonel Allen's on him, get the bastards did Boots. Now Raskovic's got a bug up his butt that's the deuce the coons did Boots had. He's gonna check it for fingerprints."

"I wipe the fuckin steerin' wheel," Saljeski says. "Shift too."

"Good for you," Harry says. "But you know and I know that ain't the deuce the coons did Boots had. Not unless they went out the field and got it and took it back and dumped it there and that don't make any sense. Coon we got, MacArthur, claim his deuce was liberated. I figger it was and it prolly the one you liberate, Sal. We track MacArthur down with the bumper number and his lieutenant, the Four-oh-Fourth, couldn't find a trip-ticket but says it was MacArthur drivin' that deuce. And MacArthur confess it was him, or two his buddies, did Boots. But

I might confessed that too, Raskovic was jumpin' on my balls. I don't know what to think."

"Well, hell, whatever," Saljeski says. "They just fuckin coons, Harry. Whatta we care?"

"True. But Raskovic got this idea in his head and a confession and somethin' funny up his sleeve, I think. I don't know what exactly. Confession might be a bust, anybody finds out how he got it. And you be happy to know, Sal, that dumb Sadie the QM don't know who you are."

"Bless her fuckin heart!"

"Anyway, that deuce and gittin' fingerprints and git MacArthur sign his confession and all prolly keep Raskovic busy tomorrow. I don't know what the hell he thinks prints are gonna prove. There prolly coon prints all over that deuce. But he's gung-ho, get some. Them other coons, the three MacArthur ID, they ain't been charged or apprehended yet unless the skipper, that LST they on, lock them up already. And we just holdin' MacArthur, time being. Be a hell of a thing though, they ain't the coons did Boots."

"Harry," Saljeski says. "They just fuckin coons! We got the fuckin booze we fuckin better worry about!"

"Sal, I know that! I ain't gonna spoil Raskovic's fun. Rain on his parade. We're goldurn lucky he's gung-ho, get what happen to Boots off the board like he says. Colonel Fogerty's till ridin' his ass, find the booze or the criminals took it. What's the sitrep, the weather?"

'Thirty-six hours," Billy Gote says. "Weather guys say there prolly be a break in it. But they just guessing like always."

"We better say some prayers then, we know any, they guessing right," Harry says. "That Mexican stand-off I mention prolly ain't permanent. There's that goldurn GHQ Order for one thing. Somebody up GHQ likely remember it and GHQ move pretty fast sometimes. Screw channels. Might lay it right on the RAAF out the field they got to let us search airplanes. I like and see you, Lieutenant, and Eddie the hell out of here with the booze.

Then make us all rich. I'll try and check with you tomorrow, anything else develops."

Harry scoots through the rain to his jeep and departs, splashing through the muddy yard, and the Samurai enthusiasts return to the party. It wasn't a genuine Samurai, Billy Gote says. Outside, the rain's hammering down. Inside, Billy Eckstine's wailing, "It's gawnnn and started raininnn."

* * *

Sgt. Porky Wallace, soaked again, rain pounding down, puffing a damp Fleetwood on the Barrier Arms' groundfloor porch, peer through the drizzle past the Tivoli Cinema, the busy intersection, no traffic there now, and the Pro Station at the two MPs in ponchos enforcing the Off Limits outside the Dock Street cathouses. If those MPs weren't there. It's hard to believe but he struck out! Again! His condoms still nest in his wallet.

The Flinders Street EM Club was virtually deserted, nobody there but air crew, all the Base Section commandos, he heard, busy preparing for some inspection. But there weren't any birds there either, practically speaking. Stayed home no doubt in view of the fucking rain. What good's the fucking rain, RON again, if he can't get laid? The Rose & Crown was serving "Afters" but there were no birds there either, just a bunch of Aussies, and he got into a little tiff with one of them, a big AMF asshole who made fun of his medal ribbons (American Defense, Asiatic-Pacific, Air Medal with Stars). "We 'ears youse bloody Yienks," this asshole said. "Gits yer bloody medals int boxes yer bloody cornflikes." Porky let that slur pass and left the Rose & Crown. All the asshole's big buddies were itching for a punch-up with a bloody Yank.

Down the street, a GI in wet khakis crosses the intersection and pushes into the Pro Station. How in the hell! Porky (amazed, envious, disgusted), he knows the drill, pictures this lucky GI in the Pro Station. The station's staffed around the clock, two 12-hour shifts, two medics on each. They play a lot of rummy. One medic will leave the game long enough to give the GI a large syringe full of thick brown stuff said to kill VD bugs, a big needle attached, a tube of black salve said to kill crab lice and their eggs and, if the GI needs them, some instructions. The GI will go into one of the cubicles at the rear of the station and carry out these instructions and the medic will go back to his rummy game. Those medics are pulling soft duty. But Porky woudn't want it. What are those medics gonna tell their kids, they ever have any, kids ask, What you do in the War, Daddy? I was on pecker patrol?

Porky flips his Fleetwood into a puddle and goes into the Arms through the tiny deserted lobby and up to his room. He's got a hard-on like a telephone pole: which, the way it feels, may explode at any minute. They'll RON again, no break in The Bloody Wet immediately foreseen, and at 0600 hours Louise will be along with his tea. Big fucking deal. Porky doubts she'll jump into his bed. The rain's pounding down again.

* * *

Col. Web Allen, sprawled on the bed in his bungalow bedroom at 0100 hours, sharing his mosquito net with Jill Tucker and three hungry mosquitoes (though they ought to be sated by now), is unable to perform despite Jill's ministrations and, kneeling naked over his naked body, she's getting a little bit miffed.

"Damn it, Colonel," she says, she rarely calls him Web. "What seems to be the matter?"

"I don't know," Web Allen says. He's seldom felt so miserable or useless. "Lot on my mind, I guess. Too much." His prickly heat's raging. He slaps at but misses a hovering mosquito. Outside, rain's pounding down.

"What?" Jill slaps at but misses the same mosquito. "You don't care about the liquor the flyboys liberated. You're worried about the inspection? General Bargle scares you? But I heard he's stuck in Brisbane. And the MPs know who raped Boots."

"Yes. Think so anyway. Captain Raskovic called me. Four colored men from a QM truck outfit. He said they match Miss Davis' descriptions and one's in custody and confessed. The other three shipped out last night for Oro Bay. But they'll be arrested, brought back. We'll court-martial them. I don't know how much good that will do Miss Davis. She'll still have to live with it. Fact she was raped. And testify. That'll be hard on her. I know. I prosecuted some rape cases. Always hard on the victim. But at least her damn uncle the congressman is off my back. I called him at the George. Old fool congratulated me. He wants their names, the perpetrators. Well, suspects. Technically. He's not going to New Guinea, he said. He's going back to Brisbane if the weather breaks. I heard it might."

"Well then," Jill, launching another attempt to revive Web Allen's flaccid equipment, says. This proves useless and she gives up.

"I guess I'm worried about my daughter. Oldest daughter. She thinks she's in love with a glider pilot." This scarcely is the time or circumstances in which to discuss family matters, but he is worried. Naturally.

"Letter from your wife?"

Jill's evinced little interest in Mert or his daughters other than to note when he showed her the girls' school photos Mert sent that Barbara was "very attractive." The 1938 photo he had of Mert was lost along with the rest of his personal effects somewhere on the way to Buna Government Station. Mert's not replaced it. She's reluctant to have her photo taken. Just as well. He'd not want Mert's photo watching him cavort with Jill Tucker. Have to put it in a drawer, out of sight out of mind.

Jill did find humorous the intimate fact (he's now vaguely sorry he shared) that his and Mert's infrequent couplings, which he took to be normal, were ruled by the Rhythm Method reluctantly approved by the True Church. Jill uses a diaphragm. Mert knows that's a terrible sin, an invention of the Devil. But Jill's never evinced much interest in his life Before The War (or After

The War) or the fact that, family legend has it, one of his ancestors twice removed was Ethan Allen, Revolutionary War hero, led the Green Mountain Boys. Jill says there's no sense planning anything while The War lasts. No matter. He loves her. Loves her mind: quick, perceptive, skeptical, bit cynical perhaps. Many no doubt think Jill brash, self-centered. He prefers to think her independent, sees in her the rebel streak he used to have. He did not however find humorous the intimate fact she shared, which was she first slept with somebody, not identified, when seventeen. Barbara's age. And some unknown number since then. Jill's quoted, paraphrasing, one of John O'Hara's salty characters. Fucking is just about the friendliest thing two people can do.

"Why don't you take a little nap," Jill, rolling onto the bed beside Web Allen and pulling up the sheet, says. "Get some rest. Don't worry about your daughter. The glider pilot will soon be off to The War. Is there anything to read around here?"

She plans to stay apparently and have as the Australians say "another go" at him later. Web Allen finds a Field Manual. Jill adjusts the lamp beside the bed and soon finds the proper manner (illustrated) in which to prepare a footlocker for inspection, extra socks here, toothpaste and toothbrush there, razor blades beside them, somewhat hilarious.

Web Allen turns on his side. Lord knows he could use a little nap but doubts he'll enjoy one. He'd like to sleep until Brig. Gen. S.O. Bargle is back in Sydney. Or better yet the victim of an air disaster. His prickly's heat still raging. Outside, rain's pattering on the jasmine bushes. Like the rain pattered on the ferns and jungle canopy the night the late Sgt. Barney Clark took the patrol out. But that's not a memory likely to encourage sleep, and the field phone on the floor beside the bed's jangling.

"Lord!" Jill says. "Can't we do something about that damn phone? Let it ring. Don't answer it."

"Have to, this hour," Web Allen says. He sticks one arm out from under the mosquito net and collects the handset. "Colonel Allen here."

"H-Headquarters d-d-duty officer, Sir," the party calling stutters. "I t-tried and c-c-call Colonel F-Fogerty, Sir. B-But he, I, well, I guess he's asleep, Sir. I d-d-didn't get through to him."

"All right. What is it?"

"B-Brigadier General B-B-Bargle, Sir! He's here! At the G-George Hotel. He came up on a t-train, Sir! He c-called for a car. And he's ordered a c-car, Sir. Oh-seven-thirty. To b-b-begin his inspection, he said!"

"Alert all units!" Col. Web Allen, combat veteran, says. The goddamn Japs at Buna Government Station often sprang nasty surprises in the night. "Call all the duty officers. Reveille will be at oh-four-hundred. I'll rouse Colonel Fogerty."

There'll be no nap now or fun with Jill later. Brig. Gen S.O. Bargle, snoring away no doubt at the George Hotel, dreaming no doubt of the Articles of War and stern disciplinary measures, puts a terminal damper on Web Allen's libido.

"What happened?" Jill says.

"General Bargle! He's here! He came up from Brisbane on a train! His inspection is on again!"

"Well I'll be dammed. What a resourceful old bastard. You have to give him that."

4

18 DECEMBER 1943
GENERAL HEADQUARTERS, SOUTHWEST PACIFIC AREA
DAILY COMMUNIQUE

Allied Air Forces under the command of Gen. Douglas MacArthur flew a record 152 sorties, inflicting heavy damage to enemy positions and personnel at Wewak, Madang and Saidor in New Guinea and Cape Gloucester on New Britain. Allied Ground Forces under Gen. MacArthur's command pursued scattered enemy forces at the western end of the Markham Valley and in the Finschafen area and continued mopping up operations at Arawe on New Britain. Light Naval Forces under Gen. MacArthur's command sank two enemy barges off Cape Gloucester on New Britain and shelled enemy positions ashore, inflicting heavy casualties to enemy personnel and destroying a fuel dump.

* * *

Brig. Gen. Sedgewick O. Bargle, a wiry little fellow in his early fifties, 5-8, 148 pounds, with a face like a skull, very little hair, that he has cut to a quarter-inch, an expert with the epee at West Point, stripped to his baggy olive drab GI shorts, paid $500 a month with his longevity, is ripping through his fifty daily push-ups, counting them off, at 0630 hours in his room at the George Hotel, after ripping through his fifty daily sit-ups, fifty daily deep knee bends and other calesthenics. Outside, a slow drizzle is falling.

Finished with his push-ups, hissing "fifty," Brig. Gen. Bargle springs to his feet, puffing a little, not much, digs a fresh khaki uniform from his valpack, every stitch he wears issue, pulls on his socks, pants and GI shoes and gets busy transferring his stars and medal ribbons to the shirt. In Sydney his orderly does this, three times a day some days, but in "the field," which is what Brig. Gen. Bargle considers Townsville, he dispenses with an orderly and does this himself. It takes awhile. He has two rows of ribbons (none of which reflect valor under fire) including the one the French gave him for yeoman work on the docks at Bordeaux when he was a first john in the Other Big War, and several for short sojourns in areas later considered worth a ribbon.

Many are impressed by this display. But then Lt. Col. Webster R. Allen, Brig. Gen. Bargle remembers (a bird colonel now, God help us!) was not.

His ribbons transferred, Brig. Gen. Bargle goes into the bathroom, a rare private bath at the George Hotel, and gives this more thought while stropping his straight razor. Allen, a failure at command himself or so the story was, a National Guard officer relieved at Buna Government Station, "combat fatigue" his 201 said, was the deputy PX officer at Service Force HQ, but recently mysteriously promoted to light colonel, when at lunch with three junior officers in the Officers Mess in mid-July he spouted off like a military analyst. Brig. Gen. Bargle overheard him, distinctly. "Most of the troops," Allen said, "actually fighting this War are civilians in uniform." Thus impugning in Brig. Gen. Bargle's considered opinion the dedication, long years of low-paid faithful service, bravery and courage of all those officers, many it is true Regular Army officers, whose important duties do not happen to expose them to combat.

Combat. The tip of the spear, an officer Brig. Gen. Bargle much admires, Lt. Gen. C.H. (Court House) Lee, the Service Force commander in the ETO, calls it. But what good is a spear without a sturdy shaft? The men behind the men at the front who train, supply and support the men at the front? A captain at Allen's table wisely brought that up. Then Allen had the temerity, gall, bad taste, to call the dedicated personnel at Service Force HQ "the men behind the men behind the men behind the men behind the men behind the men at the front."

Well, Brig. Gen. Bargle remembers with relish, he promptly braced Lt. Col. Allen, right there in the mess, and chewed his National Guard ass pretty good, citing the 96th Article of War (Brig. Gen. Bargle knows the ARs by heart), anything construed detrimental to military discipline grounds for swift disciplinary action. Army thinks officers should be chewed out in private but he wanted to embarrass Allen. Did too and enjoyed it. Heard no more from Lt. Col. Allen about who's actually fighting this War. Then, a major screw-up somewhere, War Department Personnel Office apparently, Allen was promoted again to bird colonel and shipped off to command the Townsville Base Section when Brig. Gen. Bargle's old classmate, Col. Martin Ballsup, was transferred to Tasmania, the big island below Australia, to command the several huge truck farms just established there to produce fresh vegetables for the U.S. Armed Forces in Swappa. They've not produced any yet but that's the plan.

Shaving, Brig. Gen. Bargle nicks his chin, blames Allen, the man upsets him! But he'll have another whack at Allen shortly. His inspection no doubt will find this Base Section wanting in many particulars and he'll gleefully thereafter chew Allen's National Guard ass again. In private perhaps but loudly. Allen's clerks will overhear this and spread the word. He'll add to Allen's other woes, the booze some flyboys heisted and a nasty rape case, Red Cross girl gang-banged by a dozen colored. The grapevine brought garbled word of both those disasters to Brisbane.

Brig.Gen. Bargle closes the nick on his chin with a styptic pencil and treats himself to a small smile that nearly cracks his skin: he's not much given to smiling. And he'll give Jill Tucker another ring. The sitrep is she's sleeping with Allen and Jill Tucker in his experience is pretty much faithful to one man at a time. Though there was talk, a rumor, she had it on with a USO entertainer once when he was on an inspection tour. But he'll give her a ring. Red Cross will track her down again, brigadier-general calling, and you never know. There's a faint stirring in Brig. Gen. Bargle's skinny loins. Mrs. Bargle is sitting out The War in D.C. and their only offspring, Sedgewick Jr., is a captain pushing paper and denying requisitions at the Ogden, Utah, Quartermaster Depot.

It is perhaps unfortunate, Brig.Gen. Bargle sometimes thinks, thinks now, that the nation's wars mostly are fought by civvies in uniform. But where would those civvies be without the professional soldiers, dedicated men like himself, true patriots, who train, instruct, supply and support them? Blundering around like lost sheep on a stormy night, that's where. But that's a metaphor Brig. Gen. Bargle would like to rephrase.

Once upon a time a long time ago, just out of the Point in '14, Second Lt. Sedgewick O. Bargle was an Infantry platoon leader who three times in succession during night maneuvers on dark wet rainy nights got his platoon hopelessly lost on the rolling prairie outside Fort Riley, Kansas. There's an entry deep in his 201, "Unfit for combat command," followed by his transfer to the Quartermaster Corps.

But Brig. Gen. Bargle, who at the time blamed his platoon sergeant and a faulty compass, has pretty much managed to forget all that. Thirty-three years on what's called active service counting his years at the Point, a major facing retirement when the Jerries (who he rather respects, respects their military prowess anyway) started World War II and saved his career, Brig. Gen. Bargle has yet to hear a shot fired in anger (or fear) and, the last time he tackled a rifle range, in 1939, failed to qualify. But Brig. Gen. Bargle does not dwell on any of that either. He has a job to do and he's doing it and there also are some "Superior" and "Excellent" ratings in his 201. It's just fate Allen, damn his National Guard civilian ass, was in combat, if but briefly. It's no big deal.

Brig. Gen. Bargle, clean-shaven, gets into his shirt with the stars and ribbons and his issue necktie, tucked in between the third and fourth buttons, picks up his trenchcoat and goes down to the George Hotel dining room, where he gives the GI waiter his usual breakfast order: one hard-boiled egg, toast, black coffee and a newspaper. The newspaper is the daily Coast Times. The War seems to be going well. The Russkies are sticking it to the Jerries near Kiev. Jerries still hanging tough in Italy. Another island he never heard of wrested from the Japs in the Central Pacific. Another German city obliterated if you believe the Brits' Bomber Command and the U.S. Eighth Air Force.

But something is nagging at Brig. Gen. Bargle's highly-trained brain. Was the sleepy GI driving the staff car that finally picked him up at the Q&NR depot wearing a necktie? Hard to say. The GI was wearing a filthy raincoat buttoned to his chin. The waiter arrives with Brig. Gen. Bargle's breakfast and he clearly is not wearing a necktie. His khaki shirt is open at the throat under his stained white jacket.

"Where's your necktie, soldier?" Brig. Gen. Bargle, cranking up his snarly general's voice, says.

"I uh," the waiter stutters, this is the first general he's encountered up close. "We uh don't wear ties any more, Sir. New Base Section Uniform Regulations."

Brig. Gen. Bargle, appalled, waves the waiter away. Is Allen out of his mind! The Service Force Uniform Regulations are written in stone, so to speak: All Personnel in Rear Areas will wear issue neckties at all times with the Class A khaki uniform. Brig. Gen. Bargle pulls a notebook and pen from his shirt pocket and scribbles. He had to wait twenty minutes at the Q&NR depot for the car dispatched by the Base Section Motor Pool, meanwhile, the depot closed, taking shelter from the rain pounding down in a phone booth once occupied by the mysterious Kilroy. That's a black mark. Unilaterally amending, the Service Force Uniforms Regulations. That's a big black mark! The day is starting well.

Done with his breakfast, Brig.Gen. Bargle leaves the George, the rain's pounding down, and waits under the porte-cochere for the staff car he ordered. It arrives ten minutes late, a '41 Dodge splattered with mud, it's not flying a brigadier's pennant, three more black marks, and the driver, who hops out, snaps off a sloppy salute and opens the rear door, needs a haircut and he's not wearing a necktie under his raincoat.

"Sorry I'm late, Sir," this driver says. "I had a help paint stones at the Motor Pool."

"Where's my pennant?"

"We uh couldn't find one, Sir."

"What's your name and rank, soldier?"

"Stefanelli, Sir. Giuseppe NMI Stefanelli, Sir. I'm a p f c, Sir."

"You're on report, soldier! You're out of uniform. No necktie. And you need a haircut." Might as well start now, shape up the Townsville Base Section. He'll ream Allen, that civilian in uniform, later. No neckties!

"B-But, Sir," Pfc. Stefanelli, he's not very bright, arguing with a brigadier-general, says. "New Base Section Uniform Reg—"

"At ease!" Brig. Gen. Bargle, climbing into the Dodge, snarls, and gets busy with his notebook. "First unit I want to look at is the Base Motor Pool."

"Yessir!" Pfc. Stefanelli, closing the door on Bargle's trenchcoat, says. "Oh! Sorry, Sir." He opens the door, closes it again without trapping the trenchcoat, lopes around the Dodge and slides behind the wheel. The rain's slowed to a drizzle.

* * *

Sgt. Porky Wallace, who did not set his internal alarm clock, wakes at 0700 hours with a hard-on like a redwood tree. Louise, he can hear her chirpy voice, is somewhere down the porch with the morning tea. Beyond his open door rain's pounding down. No doubt they'll RON again and local maidens and older women too by god better look out!

Louise enters the room with a single steaming mug on her tray. She's wearing a light sweater, he can't see her nipples, but the rest of her is clearly outlined beneath her thin dress. "Hi brun yer tay last like yer said," she says.

Porky's erection throbs. He's naked to his navel, his sheet shoved down. Louise peers through the mosquito net at the bump in the sheet. Blimey! The sar'ent's Thing is moving! And it must be as big, bigger even, than the bangers, sausage laced with breadcrumbs, the Smiths often have for supper.

"Put it on the chair, it cools," Porky says. Louise does that and, holding her tray like a shield, continues her inspection. In just about a minute, Porky thinks, he'll kick the sheet off, give them both a big thrill. But a little light conversation will prolong the pleasure of anticipation. "You got a boyfriend, Louise?"

"No," Louise, inspecting still, says. "Da says I ain't old enough yet. Not'll I'm sixteen, he says. In July." Even in absentia, Porky won't argue with big Biff Smith. But he's not going to wait until July either. He raises his knees, grips the sheet with his curled toes.

"Louise!" Biff's big voice booms up from below stairs. "Har yer finish wit' the bloody tay yet! I needs yer down 'ere!"

"Hi got t'go," Louise, with a last lingering look at the bump in the sheet, says. "Da wants me." And scoots from the room. Porky moans.

Later, up, in uniform, gone to the loo, where he wrestled with his erection, and back, Porky takes his steaming tea out onto the porch and drinks it. Steady rain is falling. Down Dock Street, two MPs are patrolling outside the cathouses. Two more are bracing a GI outside the Q&NR depot and one's directing traffic through the busy intersection. All five look especially spiffy, brassards on their raincoats, helmet liners white as snow. The Pro Station medics are polishing the green bulb over the station's door. The inspection he heard about, Porky deduces, some fucking general with a reputation for making trouble, must be on. But that's nothing to do with him, he still has a mighty hard-on and a long empty day stretches ahead. There might be some birds though at the Flinders Street EM Club in the afternoon. He's never had any luck there in the afternoon but the situation, his situation, is fast becoming desperate. He'll give it a shot. The Club opens at noon.

* * *

The situation in his office, Col. Web Allen thinks, but for the fact everybody is dry and fed and nobody is shooting at anybody, resembles those situations he encountered at Buna Government Station while waiting for the Allied Forces' puny artillery bombardment to lift before sending his Fox Co. GIs forward again until stopped cold again, some dead, some wounded, by fire from previously undetected Jap bunkers largely impervious to 75mm artillery fire. Situations you could sum up in a single word: dread.

Web Allen's at his desk, puffing a Fleetwood. Outside, rain's pounding down, hammering the leaky tin roof. Three pails are slowly filling with drips from the ceiling. And somewhere outside, producing the dread in his office, Brig.Gen. S.O. Bargle is presumed to be busy inspecting and, no doubt, finding numerous faults and shortcomings. Lt. Col. Fogerty, both his ears still red and swollen, likewise puffing a Fleetwood, is pacing the floor between the leaks. So is Maj. Cain, a nervous type who doesn't smoke. Lt. Col. Winston Flapp, the Base Quartermaster, a large stolid man with a large stolid face, is sitting in one of the office chairs, fiddling with his pipe. Maj. Dickinson the Provost Marshal is in the other one, wiping rain from the plastic cover on his garrison cap. His beloved campaign hat, no longer permitted by Service Force Uniform Regulations, is hiding in his bedroll.

All four, prepared should they encounter Brig. Gen. Bargle, are wearing clean crisp though slightly damp khakis and their medal ribbons, though these in total are no match for Bargle's. Web Allen's wearing the giant EM's Sad Sack khakis, delivered again at dawn by the 114th Laundry Detachment, still searching for his, and along with his ribbons (American Defense, Asiatic-Pacific, Papuan Campaign) his cherished Combat Infantry badge, a long silver rifle on a blue field. The rebel streak he used to have surfaced while he was dressing and, finding that badge in his dresser drawer, he put it on. Because Brig. Gen. Bargle doesn't have one.

Web Allen dressed at 0500 hours after getting no sleep to speak of and again failing to perform despite Jill Tucker's best efforts. He then found in a closet a pink Oriental parasol left (or abandoned) by the bungalow's owners and walked Jill down Hill Street through a steady drizzle to the Red Cross billet. She usually goes home by herself without waking him but he was awake and felt he owed her that after failing to perform. They kissed briefly at the billet's back door. A first john sporting gaudy Fifth Air Force patches was asleep in the kitchen with his head on the kitchen table.

"Don't worry about it, Colonel," Jill said. "These things happen. And don't let General Bargle spoil your day. He's an old bastard or so I've heard but he'll soon be back in Sydney. I'll see you tonight."

He wouldn't worry about it, Web Allen mumbled, then walked back to his bungalow through the drizzle pattering on his parasol, worrying, and wondering: what in God's name he, once a respected Wisconsin attorney, was doing walking through the rain beneath a pink parasol in Townsville, Australia, with a mind like an attic full of junk, a jumble of sex, Jill Tucker, Brig. Gen. Bargle, Mert, Barbara and her glider pilot and that constant nuisance, the late Sgt. Barney Clark's ghost? He put the parasol back in the closet, called for his car and came early to his office, skipping breakfast, he didn't feel like eating, having instead a mug of Sgt. Costello's lethal coffee and cigarettes.

Lt. Col. Fogerty arrived some minutes later at for him a record early hour, pretty shaky until he had coffee no doubt laced with gin, then came into Web Allen's office, rubbing his red swollen ears, to report, "All our units ready as they ever be for this goddamn inspection," and ask, "Any word yet, Sir, from GHQ?" Not yet, Web Allen said, truthfully enough. "Jezuzz," Lt. Col. Fogerty said, "I wish they get off their dead duffs down there!"

Then Maj. Cain, he has a ground floor office in the HQ warehouse, and Flapp and eventually Dickinson wandered in. This council of war if that's what it is wasn't convened, it just happened, produced in absentia by Brig. Gen. Bargle. It truly is amazing, Web Allen thinks, the way one scrawny little one-star general can disrupt the speedy prosecution of The War. He's seen this before of course, The War on hold for an inspection. The GIs' explanation for this and other military mysteries is simply, "That's the fuckin Army for yuh, Jack."

"Well, one thing anyway," Dickinson, a Texas optimist, says. "It looks like my men got that rape case cleaned up. ID the perps anyway, I mean. Got one in custody. My men did a bang-up job on that, I say so myself. I might just put Raskovic in for a Legion of Merit."

"I wouldn't do that yet," Cain, former prosecutor, pausing in his pacing, says. "It's not the strongest case I ever saw. I know Raskovic got a confession. I'm not going to ask him how he got it. And I'll prosecute the bastards. Don't you worry. But I wish I had some corroboration. Victim identify those coons or something, we get them back here. But she don't sound like she be too sure about that, the Initial CID Report I saw."

"What's Raskovic doing today?" Fogerty, pausing in his pacing, says. "You ain't forgot we got another major crime here, Provost?"

"He's going to question the rape victim again," Dickinson says. "See if she can ID that deuce-and-a-half the coon we got in custody was driving."

"Christ, can't that wait?" Fogerty says. "I don't want Raskovic tied up all day. I want him lookin' and ID and apprehend some goddamn flyboys. We might get the word any minute from GHQ. Give us authority lower the boom on the goddamn RAAF and start searchin' aircraft for our booze. Ain't that right, Sir?"

"Hard to say," Web Allen says. "I told you. Brigadier I spoke with said it might take a while, work through the Command Structure, Allied Relations and all, and get us that authority. Especially on the weekend. And I want any loose ends, the rape case, tied up."

"Shit!" Fogerty, resuming his pacing, says. "I check with the Weather bozos this morning. They think there might be a goddamn break in the weather tomorrow. There is, we can kiss our booze goodbye! What the hell's the matter with GHQ anyway? It's that GHQ Order we're trying and enforce. Implement appropriate action. You hold off on that Legion of Merit, Provost. See Raskovic finds the goddamn flyboys and we get our booze back."

Col. Web Allen smothers a yawn, lights another Fleetwood, calls on Sgt. Costello for more coffee. He's not up to another lecture on priorities. In fact, he rather suddenly realizes, he doesn't much care, give a damn, what happens, the rape or the booze, and remembers what it was like crawling out of a wet hole at dawn in the jungle outside Buna Government Station following a sleepless night filled with the usual alarms and the fear the damn Japs might mount another banzai attack. Bitter black coffee and a damp cigarette if anybody had any got The War started again then, more or less. And he's suddenly, he also realizes, tired to death of all his subordinates, none of whom knows anything about wet holes or banzai attacks, their only "field" experience if any some silly peacetime maneuvers.

"All right. Enough," Col. Web Allen says. "All this talk isn't getting us anywhere. Let's get on with our duties. Back to our posts. We'll work until seventeen-thirty today, impress General Bargle if he turns up." Ordinarily, the Base Section knocks off at noon on Saturdays. "But Bargles come and Bargles go, men. The

War won't last forever. Like our allies say, or sing. Oh there'll be no promotions this side of the oceans, so cheer up my lads, bless 'em all, the long and the short and the tall, bless 'em all! Dismissed!"

The subordinates depart, somewhat puzzled, to pretend should Brig. Gen. Bargle turn up they're all dedicated to the speedy prosecution of The War. They've not heard their commanding officer cite or sing that sad rollicking Australian marching song on any previous occasion.

Web Allen, flipping his Fleetwood into a pail full of rain, humming "Bless 'em all,the long and the short and the tall," digs a V-mail form from his desk and prints:

> Dearest Mert: Have your letter of 2 Dec. and was pleased to get it. I am well and very proud of both our daughters. Be sure to tell them that. As to Barbara, I'll write her but I don't think you should worry. The glider pilot

And there stalls, dead in the water, no longer humming, his rollicking mood evaporating. What the hell has he got to sing about? He crumples the V-mail, drops it in his wastebasket, lights another Fleetwood, he's smoking too much but so what, and sits staring out at the rain pounding down. It's raining cats and dogs. A new leak in the ceiling is dripping on his Out basket. The contents thereof when dispatched will be wet but who cares? Not him.

* * *

Breakfast at Manic Manor at 1000 hours likewise is coffee and Fleetwoods. Billy Gote, Eddie Devlin, Lts. Donald and Hunker have it at the kitchen table. Outside, rain's pounding down. Donald and Hunker compare notes, though perhaps lying, on their and Flots' and Ima Score's earth-shaking sexual encounters. Eddie might join in this symposium, his encounter with Ann

Silvers was by his standards earth-shaking, but doesn't want to talk that way about Ann Silvers, the way the local swordsmen used to talk about their sexual conquest at Black's Billiards in Winatchee Falls. Eddie on short acquaintance is half in love with Ann Silvers.

Billy Gote leaves the kitchen to try phoning the Meteorology Detachment at Garbutt Field again, no easy task given the local phone system, half civilian, half military, the interface shaky. The detachment phone's been busy all morning, everybody checking the weather. Billy gets through this time though and returns beaming. "Hey! Weather guys say there might be a break in the goddamn Wet! Late tonight, early tomorrow. They guessing like always. But I better tell my crew, the Arms, alert 'em. So they don't disappear. You too, copilot, you're alerted. When Saljeski say he pick us up?"

"Noon about," Eddie says. "Depends though. He might have to stay in his office. Pretend he's working until the goddamn inspection is over." Jill Tucker, first thing in the morning, told the Manor residents and guests the inspection is on again, Brig. Gen. Bargle in town in all his glory and in full cry, blame the Q&NR.

"Shit!" Billy Gote says. "We might not have wheels then. I ain't keen on walkin' all the way the Arms. I can try and phone but."

"I got my wheels," Straight Arrow Hunker says. "I'll give you a lift. My crew's the Arms too. I better alert them and my copilot. And I better check my airplane. Weather breaks, Humpty Dumpty prolly be back here rarin' we get back to Dobo."

"Who's your copilot?" Billy Gote says. "He shacked up somewhere?"

"No. He's the George. Copilot's Moneybags Shelden. You know him. That rich little sucker. His old man's the president some railroad. He sends Moneybags couple hundred a month so Moneybags can live in a style he been accustomed, he gets a chance."

"Oh, sure, I know Moneybags. Know who he is. What kind a pilot is he?"

"He's okay. But it don't make much difference. I do the flying. He only gets to sit in his bucket we're taking off and landing. Humpty Dumpty likes to sit there the rest of the time. Moneybags rides in the cargo with the steward."

"Steward! What are you flyin'? The Pan Am Clipper?"

"Well, orderly. Humpty Dumpty's orderly. He's a corporal carries Humpty Dumpty's valpak. He's the Arms with my crew. Hey, I'm gonna take a little nap. That Flots wear a man out. Then we'll go the Arms."

"Me too," Lt. Donald says. "Man, that Score, she's a load! Say, I notice Jets dint swipe your pants, Hunker. How come?"

"Flots warn me. I hid my pants under the couch. We dint see any sign, Jets."

"Jets was out on the patio awhile," Billy Gote says. "Fact, we had a heart-to-heart, slut Flots is, sleepin' with guys. Kept me up half the night. What happen to that gal here you were gonna see, Straight Arrow?"

"That mission been aborted," Hunker says. "She finally told me. She's shackin' up with a goddamn Base section commando. First john's the C.O. some laundry outfit."

Hunker and Donald hit the sacks in the living room, two spavined sofas, and Billy Gote and Eddie share the last of the coffee and light Fleetwoods.

"If the goddamn weather breaks," Billy says. "We are gonna blaze out a here so fast Ops'll think the Lucky Lil's a Pee-Thirty-Eight. I don't much like the idea there's a goddamn general in town. He might throw his weight around. Lean on the RAAF out the field let the goddamn Base Section search aircraft. Shit! We had it made, Eddie. Except that dumb thing I did! Let that asshole Donald more less crash land my airplane and bust a tire. Then the goddamn weather. Bloody Wet had a start early! But the weather breaks and we get out a here tomorrow. Hey, we all be rich pretty soon!"

Eddie nods. He might, he thinks, worst comes to worst, escape retribution. Technically, he was, is, just a passenger aboard the Lucky Lil. But that's a technicality the Base Section, bent on revenge, well might ignore. And where, he wonders, is Capt. Clapham Panmander, his C.O., these days? Still at Arawe, he hopes. He doesn't want the old coot killed or wounded, the old coot takes pretty good care of Eddie, but if the old coot returns to Seven-Mile Strip and finds Eddie missing. AWOL. Eddie's MOS is still Rifleman. Old coot said he'd get that changed to Clerk but hasn't yet. Technically, Devlin, Edward T., Pfc., is still an Infantry replacement. God help him!

Eddie lights another Fleetwood and decides he'll say a little prayer the damn weather breaks. Won't do any harm. Outside the rain's pounding down.

* * *

"I got another call from Colonel Fogerty," Capt. Raskovic says. "He give me till noon, wind up the rape case. Then we better get cracking on the booze, he says. Doing what, I don't know. Fogerty says we're just waitin' on some brigadier at GHQ that Colonel Allen talk to. Brigadier's supposed to get us the authority, stick it to the goddamn RAAF and start searching airplanes."

"Hell with Allied Relations then, I guess," Harry Parker says. They're in the CID jeep, rain hammering its canvas top, bound for the 12th Station Hospital but stuck in traffic behind a tanker at the busy intersection, the Pro Station there ready for inspection, a clean green light bulb over its door.

"But we can't get that constable," Raskovic says. "Lift any prints off that deuce till sixteen-hundred. I dint tell Fogerty that but we are gonna do that. The other thing Fogerty says is I got to stay here, we recover the booze, and try and nail the goddamn flyboys liberate it. Them and anybody here was in on it. Their accomplices. So I guess you, Sergeant, and couple guys the Company gonna fly Oro Bay, the weather breaks. Apprehend the goddamn perps and bring 'em back here."

"Roger," Harry, though his heart's not in it, says. The heavy hand of GHQ poised to strike is bad bad news. The MP on traffic duty at the intersection blows his whistle. The traffic moves and Harry follows the tanker through the intersection onto Charters Road. They're going to pick up Boots Davis, see if she can ID the deuce-and-a-half still under guard behind the field Canteen. "Colonel Allen though, Captain, Base Commander. I guess he still wants we should concentrate on the rape, collect all the evidence. Right?"

"Yeah, I guess," Raskovic, beset by conflicting orders, says. "But Allen actin' kind a strange, Fogerty says. Singin' Aussie songs. Sang one they had a meeting this morning."

That intelligence is a mystery to Harry. They drive the rest of the way to the 12th Station in silence. Boots is waiting in the Orderly Room, back in uniform, clean blouse, seersucker skirt, her other loafers and a raincoat Ann Silvers delivered. She gets in the jeep and they drive to Garbutt Field through a steady drizzle, held up at the new bridge, the Ross River full of muddy water rushing to the sea. Boots seems okay, normal. Capt. Sussman told her they'd identified the men who raped her and have one, who confessed, in custody, the other three on an LST on their way to Oro Bay.

"I raised the captain that LST on the ACS," Raskovic says. "He lock them three in his brig. We'll have to ask you to identify them, Miss Davis. If you can. When we got them in custody here. Be a few days. I know you're supposed to go to New Guinea. But you'll have to stay and testify too, you know, their court-martial. Be hard, I know. But I'm sure you want to see these men get their, well, just desserts. Major Cain, the A.G., he told me he'll convene a court-martial soon as he can. And he'll want to talk to you, he's preparing his case."

"I have to wait for some tests anyway," Boots says. "But Capt. Sussman said he'll discharge me today. I can go back to our billet this afternoon. If I want to. I think I will. The hospital's expecting casualties from some place. Arawe, I think."

They cross the bridge, reach the airfield, convince the RAAF sentry they won't go near any aircraft, park beside the suspect deuce-and-a-half and get out of the jeep.

"Take ten," Raskovic tells the two MPs guarding the deuce. They go into the Canteen. "Now you take a good look at this vehicle, Miss Davis. See there's any way you can identify it's the one they jump out of and grab you. One you was in."

Boots surveys the deuce and shrugs. "God, Captain, I don't know. The number on the bumper is the same. I think. Part of it anyway. But it was just a deuce-and-a-half. That's all I really saw."

"You told us," Raskovic says. "You think you grab the door when they push you in the cab. Show me where. Then we look inside." Boots shows him, one hand under the handle on the passenger door, then Raskovic opens the door and she climbs in the cab. "Show me where you brace yourself, the dashboard there, and the seat, you were on the bumpy road." Boots does this, right hand on the dashboard behind the windshield, left on the worn seat beside the indentation formed over the months by many colored drivers weighing in excess of two-hundred pounds. "You see anything else you recognize?" Boots shakes her head and they help her out of the cab. "Well, I thank you, Miss Davis, take this time and assist us in our investigation. We'll drive you back the hospital."

Raskovic routs the MPs out of Canteen and gives them orders, the deuce-and-a-half will remain under guard, nobody gets near it, and they drive back to the 12th Station Hospital through hard pounding rain, held up a long time at the new bridge. An Engineer lieutenant prone on its planks is peering at the bracing in the swift-running muddy water.

Is Raskovic, Harry wonders, dumb? Or dumb like a fox?

Harry's investigative experience is limited. Uncle Wilbur the Sheriff sometimes shared some of the expertise he gleaned at the FBI School, but that's about it. Keeping the crime scene inviolate though was one bit of expertise Uncle Wilber shared. But Raskovic was an LAPD detective for eight years or so he says. A real expert. Whatever, Boots' fingerprints are on and in the deuce-and-a-half now. The rain may destroy those on the door, Harry's not sure, but Constable Jack Crowe, the fingerprint expert, no doubt will find those in the cab without any trouble. Be another nail then in Pvt. MacArthur's and his three pals' coffins. A crooked planted nail. But like Saljeski said, they're just a bunch of coons.

They drop Boots at the 12th Station. "See you tonight at the Manor maybe," Harry says. "I guess there be another farewell party for you and Rose Pearl."

"Probably," Boots says. "Except I'm not going to New Guinea yet." She seems to Harry to be okay, normal enough, though scarcely the happy-go-lucky girl she used to be. He can understand that.

"Let's roll," Raskovic, putting an end to this conversation, says. "We got some time yet before we pick up the fingerprint constable and Fogerty told me check with him. Ever hour on the hour. See we got the word yet from GHQ. So's we can search the goddamn airplanes."

* * *

U.S. Rep. Festus Lee Claypool and most of his party, which now includes Siggie Ferk, are enjoying a wet lunch, steak-and-eggs and a dubious bourbon the flunky captain finally broke down and dug out his valpak, in the George Hotel dining room. The exception is David Dudley Hull. His steak is tough, his eggs are runny, his spirits are low and fear has wrecked his appetite. The word is there might be break in the weather tomorrow, in which case, he assumes, he'll be flying to New Guinea. Without a fighter escort. While Claypool, the old fart (whose self-serving quotes, if ever hey reach the Milwaukee Herald, Executive Editor Jake Jasper no doubt will spike) and everybody else flies back to Brisbane. The flunky captain says he'll have an aircraft laid on the minute the weather breaks.

"Ah be motty dis'pointed," Claypool whines. "Ah won't see ower boys opp The Front." Since nobody believes this, nobody pays his whine much attention. His afternoon program, he says, is Calvin Winsome will visit the 12th Station Hospital, "Tell ma nee-uss pore litull Bootie Ah not be fergit her," then they'll play some poker: draw, stud, no crazy games. The flunky captain says he'll lay on a staff car for Calvin. "Who that fella theyuh that table by hisself? He ain't et nuffin. He juss seem t'be drankin' his lunch."

"That's the Base Section commander," Calvin Winsome, paid to know these things, says. "Colonel Allen. You met him night before last, Sir, here. And he was at the hospital."

"Ah, so Ah did. Ah wonduh is that a good thang. Omee commander drankin' his lunch?" Rep. Claypool often holds others to standards higher than his own.

"Well, I heard he has an inspection on his hands today," the flunky captain says. "Some Service Force general up from Sydney. Here to find fault and chew ass. Inspections are always traumatic, Sir."

"Wish him well then," Festus says. "He seem lock uh nice 'nuff fella, Ah was talkin' him. Foh uh Yankee. And his men, he phone me, they cotch them gahdam niggers did pore litull Bootie purty quick." Festus waves a fat hand, catches Col. Web Allen's attention and lifts his bourbon in a friendly salute.

Web Allen lifts his whatever, a strong gin-and-tonic, he thinks, in response. He's had two whatevers, should order his lunch, but decides he'll have another. He's in good spirits again, humming "Bless 'em all the long and the short and the tall" at intervals. He'll write Mert and Barbara the minute he's back in his office. And show Jill Tucker a thing or two tonight. What after all can Brig. Gen. S.O. Bargle, that one-star sonofabitch, do to him? Chew him out? He's been chewed out before by other experts. Fire him? Not hardly. He's a temporary bird colonel in the Army of the United States. Transfer him? Where? Doesn't matter though he'd miss Jill Tucker. He corrals a GI waiter, orders a Bless 'em all.

"Beg pardon, Sir," the waiter says.

"Drink," Web Allen says. "Whatever I'm drinking. You need a haircut, soldier! Next time I see you, a haircut. Oh cheer up my lads, bless 'em all, the long and the short and the tall."

* * *

Wing Cmdr. Haines Hewlitt-Packard, lunching at his desk in his barracks office at 1300 hours, tea and a meat pie Sgt. Keeney brought up from the mess, observes at intervals the rain pounding down on his airfield. Heavy gray clouds hide the horizon. They look the way his brain feels. But by god he bloody did it! Popped the tall blonde bloody Yank Red Cross damsel with the good English name in his room at the Australia Club! Twice! Bloody remarkable, man his age. After drinks and a good English dinner: pot roast, jacket potatoes, brussels sprouts, nice savory, wine. Damsel didn't eat her sprouts. Bloody Yank tastes hard to fathom. Drank her wine though and more in his room. Little difference of opinion then. Bound he'd use a bloody rubber, spoil everything. Finally saw it his way, more wine in her belly. Cried out satisfactorily enough, both times, when he exploded. Might take, might not. Gave it his best bloody shot anyway, evened things up (perhaps) with the bloody Yanks, bloody Petr Szymonski.

And he's still got the bloody Yanks' stolen plonk, so to speak, no flights out of Garbutt Field since 1700 hours Thursday, that a C60 bound for Brisbane, and there'll be no flights today. Wish he'd had more sleep though. Four hours not enough, man his age. Drove the damsel to her billet then, 0530 hours. Saw a bloody Yank looked like Colonel Allen plodding up Hill Street under a pink bumbershoot. Strange business. Out for a morning constitutional perhaps? Pink bumbershoot scarcely fitting though for a military man. Last thing the damsel said, "I wish to god you'd used a rubber, Commander."

Bloody awful thought! Does she know something, some bloody disease with which he may be infected? Been sleeping with numerous bloody Yanks, no doubt.

Wing Cmdr. Hewlitt-Packard submerges that bloody awful thought, time will tell, decides he'll take a little nap in his barracks room. Might as well, bloody rain still falling, field shut down. Best get a report though on the bloody Yank aircraft with, he's all but certain, the missing plonk in its cargo compartment. "Sergeant!" Sgt. Keeney pops in, his mighty mustache freshly waxed, stamps his foot and salutes. "Any developments, reference the bloody Yanks' plonk? The weather?"

"Sir! Haircraft in question 'as flat tire has directed. Bloody great beast still tied hit. Werry bad temper, my men sigh. No sign the bloody crew. Continuwing keep haircraft hunder hobservation. Rine continuwing, 'ole bloody die. Moight be a brike int t'morrer."

"Bloody busy day then. Possibility. I shall be taking a little nap, Sergeant. Any activity relative that bloody aircraft, wake me."

"Sir!" Sgt Keeney stamps his foot, salutes, exits and back in his office curls up with the old Air Aces Magazine a bloody Yank gave him. It's full of tales of derring-do in the Other Big War, His War, The War in which he spent his youth. Outside the bloody rine's pounding down.

* * *

Porky Wallace is not at the Barrier Arms, in his room or in the public room, when Billy Gote, Lt. Hunker and Eddie arrive there, wet, the canvas top on Hunker's beat-up jeep leaks and rain's pounding down. Biff Smith's behind the bar in the public room, his massive arms folded, scowling at the world. Louise is washing glasses. The public room is empty but for Hunker's crew, Brig.Gen Dumphy's orderly and a few more air crew nursing Foster's and playing poker for matches. The air crews trapped in Townsville by The Bloody Wet are pretty well tapped out and the Base Section commandos who usually come for "Afters" at this hour are absent in view of Brig. Gen. Bargle's inspection.

Lt. Hunker alerts his crew and the orderly. A poker player says "Sar'ent Wallace reconnoiterin' the Flinders Street Club" and Hunker, an accommodating fellow at loose ends, drives Billy Gote and Eddie there. They have a little trouble getting in. It's an EM club, the surly MP in a wet raincoat on door duty says. Billy Gote says he has a matter vital to the War Effort to discuss with his flight engineer. The MP is not swayed but agrees to ask the Red Cross girl-in-charge, see what she says. Rose Pearl Stevens, pale and shaky, her freckles stark as bullet holes, tells the MP it's all right, let the Lieutenants in.

The Club, a peacetime International Order of Moose Lodge, likewise is virtually empty, the Base Section commandos with free time who usually crowd it dry-docked by the inspection. A few air crew are importuning the afternoon volunteers, two Australian grandmothers, but Porky Wallace Red Lined those old broads in short order: they were showing guys their goddamn grandkids' snapshots. Porky's slumped in a chair at the rear of the Club puffing a Fleetwood and leafing through a six-month-old Newsweek.

"Look alive, Pork!" Billy Gote says. "Sitrep is there might be a break in the weather, first light or pretty soon after. There is, we are out a here. ETD like oh-seven-hundred. So you're on alert. Tell Johnson. You be outside the Arms ready to roll, oh-six-thirty."

"Roger," Porky says. "Shit. Tell you the troot, Loo'tent, I'm about ready get out a here. I ain't had no luck." Billy Gote shrugs: that's an on-going problem. "Say, them parties up that Red Cross billet I hear you talk about sometimes. There any loose gash there? Like I said."

"Depends. Some looser than others. Competition's pretty stiff though. Why?"

"I like and go one them parties, Loo'tent, that's roger with you. Tonight maybe. I don't mind a little competition. Like I said. Well, shit! I been struck out!"

"Sure. Roger with me. I'll tell the Red Cross girl here invite you. Those parties sort of invitation only. You know where the billet is? Always helps you bring a jug."

"Jeezuzz, Loo'tent, you know what's it's like find a jug here since that booze was liberated? Twenty quid and that's you can find any. It's like fuckin Guinea. But I guess I can find one. I wunner it was anybody we know liberate that booze?"

"I wonder too, Pork. See you later then."

"Roger." Porky puts his mind to where he can get a jug if that's what it takes. He still has twenty-five quid and four condoms in his wallet.

Billy Gote tells Rose Pearl, Ask my sergeant there to your farewell party tonight, and goes out into the rain with Eddie and Hunker. They might as well go back to Manic Manor, they decide, have a drink, play some rummy, call Meteorology at intervals for updates on the weather, then pick-up some Wong Fu take-out for an evening meal. They've nothing better to do. Hunker says he'll check his aircraft in the morning. Be soon enough. "Humpty Dumpty be back here tomorrow, the weather breaks, but not right away." It's four hours by air in a C47, Brisbane to Townsville. There's a Townsville Constabulary parking violation ticket on Hunker's jeep. He tears it up.

* * *

Maj. Warden Nitpicker, the Base Section Finance Officer, arrives at the Officers Club in a jeep at 1500 hours accompanied by two second johns who early in their Army careers convinced somebody they were budding accountants in civil life and thus gained admittance to Finance School. One john is driving, the other riding shotgun. Nitpicker as befits his rank is alone in the rear seat. A thin bony man in a trenchcoat, wearing spectacles and a permanent scowl, Nitpicker in civil life was a claims adjuster for the Cornbelt Insurance Co., famous for denying claims filed by fraudulent farmers who on finding their corn crops in shreds following severe thunderstorms claimed to have suffered hail damage.

The john driving parks the jeep close to the Club. Nitpicker and the johns climb out and scoot through the rain pounding down into the Club, scattering a dozen White Leghorns pecking gravel in the driveway. They find Lt. Bernie Witters in his office, the bungalow's former kitchen, puffing a damp Fleetwood. There's an ashtray full of butts and a messy jumble of paperwork on the kitchen table.

"All my records, Sir," Witters says. "You'll find them all in order, I think, Sir."

Nitpicker wrinkles his nose. He does not smoke and considers those who do lacking in moral fiber. "Take a walk, Lieutenant. Go chase those chickens off the premises."

"Sir!" Witters says and departs, reluctantly. He'd like to stay, offer some explanations he feels might be useful, but wouldn't mind killing a couple of goddamn chickens. And he has a little ploy going, he hopes. He subtracted from his inventory records the holiday liquor the Club did not get: the eighty cases the goddamn flyboys liberated.

"Start with the date the Club opened," Nitpicker tells his johns. "If you can find it in this mess. Check the requisitions and purchase orders. Balance those against the reported receipts for the pertinent periods. Then we'll inventory the spirits in the storeroom. I'll have a look at his Breakage Reports. Always suspect those."

Eighty minutes later, by which time Lt. Bernie Witters has not managed to kill any more goddamn chickens but has smoked six Fleetwoods and treated himself to two stiff gins in the Club bar, Nitpicker sticks his head out the kitchen window, spots Witters investigating something under a jasmine bush and snarls, "Lieutenant! I want you in here!"

"Sir!" Witters scurries into the Club and up to the former kitchen, where Nitpicker and the johns stand waiting, both johns scowling.

"Lieutenant," Nitpicker, he's not had so much fun since last denying a claim for alleged hail damage filed by a fraudulent farmer facing foreclosure, says. "As near as we can ascertain, and believe me it wasn't easy, you're short approximately seventy bottles of spirits. That's taking into account your claimed breakage. Though I frankly suspect that figure is padded."

"Oh no, S-Sir," Witters stutters. "It g-gets pretty wild here some nights, Sir. I mean, everbody drinking."

"At ease!" Nitpicker snarls. "I'm not finished. For awhile there my men here thought you had more inventory than your records indicated. You fooled them. But you didn't fool me! You can't for god's sake subtract from inventory, I refer to the spirits that were stolen, spirits you did not place in inventory. What do you take me for anyway, Lieutenant? Speak up!"

"Uh well I uh well uh, Sir," Witters stutters and splutters, while the second johns he fooled for awhile eye him with distaste.

"Very well," Nitpicker, who knows a fraud when he sees one, says. "You have no explanation. I frankly did not expect one."

"S-Sir," Witters stutters. "My b-bartender, his name's Dugan, Sir. I think he steals."

"At ease!" Nitpicker snarls. "I detest an officer who won't stand behind his men! Well, I can't deal with you directly, Lieutenant. Unfortunately. But you can bet your bottom Breakage Report I shall apprise Lieutenant Colonel Fogerty of our findings. Forthwith. He'll deal with you. All right, men, we're finished here."

"Major, Sir," one john says. "You wondered about the bottles with the marks?"

"Oh, yes, so I did. There are a number of bottles in your

inventory, Lieutenant, with scribbles on the labels. What the devil's that all about?"

"Oh uh n-nothing, S-Sir. I mean that's just so me and my bartender. We uh know which is the uh old stock, Sir. So we uh use it up first, Sir."

Nitpicker grunts, that's a minor matter, leaves Witters with the cheering message, "I wouldn't want to be in your shoes, Lieutenant!" and departs with his johns.

Witters hears one wail, "Oh, darn it, Major! A damn chicken pooped on your seat! Wait, Sir, I'll wipe it off."

Lt. Bernie Witters finds that small comfort. What, he wonders, will Lt. Col Fogerty do when he gets Nitpicker's report? Step forward like a good guardian angel and tell Nitpicker it was he, Lt. Col. Fogerty, who drank most of the missing liquor? Bernie Witters, though no great judge of character, finds this difficult to imagine. He's somehow pretty sure Fogerty's guardian angel days are over. Finished. And, an awful thought: Witters, Bernard C., 2nd Lt., Inf., is still technically an Infantry replacement! God help him! His Club job was and is ds tdy.

Bernie Witters goes behind the Club bar, lights another Fleetwood and pours himself a stiff gin. Maybe it's time he dug up the money in the cookie tin under the jasmine bush. But on the other hand, a straw to clutch at, Fogerty's always been pretty good to him. And he's been pretty good to Fogerty. Wait and see then? What else can he do?

Well, he can tell Lt. Col. Fogerty he's absolutely sure now. The MP sergeant who stopped the Club truck for a broken taillight the day the liquor was liberated and the CID sergeant he saw in Fogerty office, who's supposed to be helping solve that terrible crime, are one and the same. A pretty suspicious coincidence. If it is a coincidence. Lt. Col. Fogerty evinced no interest in that or its implications earlier, but if he brings it up again. Or maybe it was the same sergeant and he was only, like the Provost Marshal said, doing his duty as regards the taillight. But it's another straw to clutch at. Bernie Witters adds gin to his gin. Outside, rain's pounding down, blowing through the lattice-work. There are two White Leghorns in the Club doorway. Nitpicker left it open.

"Shoo!" Bernie Witters squeals. "Goddamn chickens!" And hurls an empty glass at the Leghorns. It misses, sails out the door and skids across the driveway. The Leghorns shit on the doorsill and withdraw.

* * *

Col. Robert (Big Bob) Betrandus, seated at the massive desk in his Air Depot office at 1600 hours, bare but for a phone, a pen set, a B17 Flying Fortress model in a shallow dive and a bit of paper work, pauses in his paperwork, which is toting up the liquor on hand as reported by Lt. Col. Gerber, and stares out at the rain pounding down. It's destroying his beloved putting green. War is hell all right. They'll have to resod the green once The Bloody Wet winds down. There's a knock, Maj. Richall pops into the office and salutes: Big Bob' a bear for military courtesy during office hours.

"What's up, Engineering?" Big Bob says.

"Made another reconnaissance, the field, Sir," Richall says. "No dice. Goddamn dog's still tied to that aircraft. Still mean as hell. But the aircraft's got a flat tire."

"Well I'll be dammed! That's two flats in two days on Forty-Sevens. Is that a coincidence or what? Anybody req a tire? You get a line on the pilot?"

"Not yet, Sir. Req a tire, I mean. The pilot's First Lieutenant A. Hunker. I got his name from Ops. But nobody knows where he is, Sir. Or his crew. They're not in the Transient Area. I checked. Pilot's probably shacked-up somewhere."

"Well, we know who he is anyway. Good work, Engineering. Keep trying, the pilot. We're getting a little low, Gerber's figures.

This Hunker's a flyboy I want to talk to! He'll have to surface sooner or later, req a tire. Anything new on the weather?"

"Latest sitrep, Sir. Meteorology thinks there'll be a break in it early tomorrow, Sir. First light or a little after. There is, that ATC Fifty-Four will come in. First one Direct from The States! Fact, Ops has a tentative ETA, oh-eight-hundred. You know who's on it, Sir?"

"No. How the hell would I know that?"

"Linda Lewis, Sir! The movie star. Ops got a manifest on the ACS. I guess she's making one of those USO tours. Entertain the troops."

"No kidding! The one with the big boobs? Monster boobs. Wasn't she in the movie the other night? The one with Tyrone Power?"

"That's right, Sir. The Second Front. She was the gal in the French Resistance helped Tyrone blow up the Krauts' command bunker, all the Krauts' big guns, clear the way for the invasion. The Blonde Bombshell, they call her, Sir."

"Tell Gerber," Big Bob says. "Lay on my car, oh-seven-thirty. We'll meet that Fifty-Four, the weather breaks! You, me, Gerber. I was going to meet it anyway. Maybe we can get Linda Lewis over here for some drinks. Entertain us."

"Sir!" Richall says, salutes and departs, pleased to have pleased Big Bob with the news about Linda Lewis, The Blonde Bombshell.

Big Bob picks up his phone, calls the Depot duty officer, leaves orders for his orderly: press his best pinks, shine his RAAF flight boots. USO entertainers of the stature (so to speak) of Linda Lewis usually are accompanied by a flunky USO officer sent along to guard the said entertainer's virtue. But Big Bob, he rubs his big hands, will outrank that flunky, he is after all U.S. Armed Forces SOPOD in Townsville. Outside, the rain's pounding down, wrecking the putting green.

* * *

"Goddamn rain prolly destroyed any prints, the outside," Capt. Raskovic says. "But do the best you can, Constable. Under the handle there, passenger door. We really appreciate you taking the time and assist us."

"Glad to help, Sir, bloody bad show, rape," Townsville Constable Jack Crowe says. He's a tall thin man in his early sixties, still in uniform, a bobbie helmet and a raincoat down to his ankles, retired after thirty-five years on the force when The War began but back on duty now, volunteered for that, do his bit. Volunteered for this bloody job too, more or less, give the bloody Yanks a hand on his own time.

The rain's slowed to a steady drizzle. Constable Crowe removes from under his raincoat the biscuit tin in which he stores his fingerprint equipment and studies the deuce-and-a-half behind the Red Cross Canteen. Raskovic and Harry Parker watch. The MPs guarding the deuce are taking ten in the Canteen storeroom. The Canteen closed early, nobody in it all day but field personnel.

Constable Crowe, he's got a delicate touch, brushes black powder on the spot in question, then watches it wash away. "Afraid it's no bloody use, Sir."

"Figured that," Raskovic says. "Let's try inside the cab, be dry there." Constable Crowe climbs into the deuce-and-a-half and proceeds with these instructions. Harry and Raskovic watch, standing in the drizzle. Time passes. Constable Crowe's a methodical man. Whistling a tuneless tune, he delicately brushes powder here and there. He's always preferred the black powder to the red, he says. "Try on top the dash there by the windshield," Raskovic says. "They likely put their hands there."

Some did, Constable Crowe reports. Whistling, he brushes more powder here and there, studies his work, gets the tape from his kit and carefully lifts the prints he dusted. More time passes. Finished finally, the tape in his biscuit tin, he climbs from the cab.

"Bloody prints everywhere," he says. "Some good, some not

so good. Blackfellows all over this vehicle, my deduction. One bonzer set top the dasher where you suggest. Small ones. Not a one on the bloody steering. Don't know why. Think there would be. Might been wiped."

"Prolly was," Raskovic says. "Suspects in this case pretty goddamn smart, some ways. What about the seat there next where the driver sits?"

Constable Crowe shakes his head. "Bloody porous surface. No prints there be worth anything. Shall I try the bed, Sir?" No, Raskovic says, Not now, another time maybe. The rain's pounding down again. Constable Crowe stows his biscuit tin under his raincoat. "I'll take photos the ones I got and mount them, I get back the Constabulary. You'll be wanting matches then, Sir?"

"Yes. We'll bring the victim the Constabulary and print her, you be so kind. Tomorrow prolly. We'll print the bastards did her, I mean suspects, once we got them all in custody. I thank you again, Constable, help us out. Now lemme take care this vehicle."

Raskovic calls the MPs from the storeroom and instructs the sergeant. Take the deuce, key's in it, to the 301st MP Impound Lot, post guards, nobody gets near it, drop Constable Crowe at the Constabulary en route. The sergeant and Constable Crowe climb into the cab, the other MPs climb in the back, the sergeant starts the deuce and away they go.

"Hot damn!" Raskovic, whacking Harry Parker's shoulder, says. "It look like we prolly find Miss Davis' prints in that vehicle! Constable Crowe find them, I mean. I know prints some but now we got an independent source, find them. He prolly find some MacArthur's too. Some his buddies. We got the goddamn coons by the balls, Chief Investigator! We'll print Davis tomorrow, coons like I said. Let's get back the office. I got to call Colonel Fogerty, see they hear anything yet from GHQ, lower the boom on the goddamn RAAF. I told you, dint I, Provost got a detail ready, search all the goddamn airplanes? Whole platoon MPs on standby, ready to roll! Provost extend the traffic details, put it together. C'mon, let's go! I'll drive."

They jump in their jeep. Raskovic sometimes likes to drive when he's wound up and he's wound up now. He zips the jeep through the Main Gate, startling the RAAF sentry, onto Garbutt Road, bound for Townsville at 40 mph, splashing through the potholes, over the new bridge with no delay. The Ross River is up to its banks. Harry Parker's worn conscience squeaks a little. It looks like Raskovic may indeed have the four coons, guilty or not, nailed dead to rights with Boots Davis' planted fingerprints and some of theirs perhaps in the deuce trip-ticketed to Pvt. MacArthur, coupled with Pvt. MacArthurs' confession. Guilty or not. But like Saljeski said, they're just a bunch of coons.

"By the balls!" Raskovic says. "By the balls!" Rain's pounding down, streaming down the windshield, the wipers overwhelmed, but he's still going 40 mph.

* * *

Brig. Gen. S.O. Bargle, northbound through South Townsville on Charters Road in his '41 Dodge, bouncing through potholes full of rain, rain hammering down, by the 3rd Repple Depple, Happy Valley and the 12th Station Hospital, is though this is not evident in high spirirs. It's been a good day. Better even than he expected. In a word, or ten words, the Townsville Base Section's gone to hell in hand basket. Col. Webster R. Allen's not up to running it and he'll soon be telling Allen that and happily chewing Allen's National Guard ass. Specifically. Brig.Gen. Bargle refers to his notebook:

The white stones bordering the drives and pathways at the Base Motor Pool were by no means white. "We j-just p-painted them, Sir," the captain running the Motor Pool whined. "B-But the rain washed it all off, Sir." No excuse. The stones ought to have been painted before the rain began.

In fact, the white stones bordering the drives and pathways

all over the Base Section generally were in deplorable condition and a number of units, on his orders, are even now digging them up and realigning them and painting them, in the rain. But that's not something the Service Force deputy commander should have to see to!

A number of signs nailed to trees, purportedly locating various units in the scrub south of Townsville which he wasted a lot of time trying to find, apparently were posted by units now elsewhere. Those signs should have been removed when the units departed. That's elemental and would have saved him a lot of time.

Some 212 empty 55-gallon oil drums, he made Pfc. Stefanelli count them, salvageable but not salvaged as directed in the recent Revised Instructions for the Salvaging of, are rusting in the rain in a former fuel dump deep in the scrub. Criminal!

An area vacated by a portion of the 404th QM Truck Battalion (C) now en route to Oro Bay was a disgrace, not yet policed, floor boards no doubt pilfered and sundry other junk and equipment left by the departing troops soaking in the rain. The battalion commander, a Major Bragg, was promptly put to leading a detail rectifying that situation, though he's probably put a lieutenant in charge by now.

A former sergeant in the 330th Ordnance Co., now a private on KP until further notice, was though ostensibly on duty using a metal lathe the Property of the Government of the United States to fashion a fake Samurai sword out of an automobile leaf spring, likewise no doubt the Property of the Government of the United States, and the reason perhaps this '41 Dodge rides like a Conestoga wagon.

Six 2.5-ton GMC trucks were parked outside the Colored EM's Red Cross Club quonset and inside their drivers, supposed to be on duty, were rolling dice. Shooting craps. But those drivers won't shoot any more craps today, Brig. Gen. Bargle grimly surmises, and the ARC Swappa HQ in Sydney will hear about that too.

The 3rd Replacement Depot's pyramidal tents were by no means properly aligned or as taut as prescribed in the Field Manual and the general dismay and helplessness displayed by the troops there with the nearby river over its banks and beginning to inundate those tents bodes ill for the speedy and successful prosecution of The War.

Four GIs fooling around with slingshots and a pail full of ball-bearings outside the Rep Dep HQ were unable to explain their function to his satisfaction. It somehow involved kookaburras, the Australian national bird, and in fact one of the GIs dropped a kookaburra with his slingshot before he put them all on report and sent them packing back to their tents. Another Allied Relations Problem no doubt, the damn bird, but he'll dump that on Col. Webster R. Allen. If, that is, Allen is still functioning following the chewing-out Brig. Gen. Bargle is contemplating with great anticipation.

The Base EM camp pyramidals were reasonably taut but badly aligned, their realignment is underway, and the half dozen he actually inspected contained many items that were not issue: gas lanterns, cots with comforters, rough furniture built with lumber no doubt pilfered, etc. One had (though not any more) electric lights using power, a stupid private proudly explained, siphoned from Townsville's civilian grid. Another Allied Relations Problem. Brig. Gen. Bargle is well acquainted with GIs' irresistible impulse to make their lives more comfortable but truly believes only officers of field grade and above are entitled to electric lights in their quarters in wartime.

The 12th Station Hospital, which ought to have been preparing for long-term casualties evacced from Arawe, likewise appeared paralyzed by the muddy water seeping into its ward tents.

The Special Services Office was another disaster, its softball, basketball and volleyball records (how many were there, which units had them) a shambles. The SSO, a Capt. Forney, could only babble about a new system he was installing, something to do with the way dry-cleaners keep their records, that a mystery to Brig. Gen. Bargle. Then he came across a former sergeant, now a private, asleep in the equipment room. Asleep while on duty! But the former sergeant said that was his duty. "Got to rest up for the game," he said, "Case it ain't rained out." Another mystery. Just about the only thing spoiling the day was the SSO Motion Picture Section, all its films neatly shelved, its distribution records up to date and, so far as he could tell, correct. Motion picture non-com seemed to know what he was doing. Slovenly soldier though, grubby uniform, needs a haircut.

One of many. There were slovenly soldiers everywhere, pockets unbuttoned, haircuts long overdue. A number obviously had not shaved at dawn. Yet they were supposed to be ready for this inspection. Word of his coming no doubt preceded him. It always does. And nowhere, anywhere, on a soldier in khakis, the Class A uniform, officer or EM, did he see a necktie!

Brig. Gen. Bargle closes his notebook, puts it in his shirt pocket, buttons the flap, smiles a mean smile. Matter of minutes he'll be chewing Col. Webster R. Allen's National Guard ass like it's never been chewed before. The rain's slowed to a steady drizzle.

* * *

The MP on traffic detail at the busy Flinders Street intersection, Pvt. Leonard D. Poole, in civil life an indifferent suburban cop in Upper Darby, Pa., where his paternal grandfather Dante Gambino is a power in local politics, stands fidgeting and sweating inside his wet raincoat. He can't wait any longer. He was supposed to be relieved at 1400 hours but his duty tour was extended, nobody's come to relieve him even to pee and if he doesn't pee right now, he pees in the Pro Station, he'll pee in his pants! The MPs on cathouse patrol who sometimes give him a pee-break are busy derailing the hopes of two GIs and the MPs on AWOL patrol are ducking the drizzle inside the Q&NR depot.

Pvt. Poole scans the four streets he controls. For once there's scarcely any traffic, just a jeep approaching on Garbutt Road and a staff car on Charters Road, both a good ways off, and makes a command decision. Leaving his post, he dashes into the Pro Station plucking at his fly, startling the Pro Station medics at their rummy game and advising them, "Jeezuzz, I got to pee!"

He's enjoying the pleasure of a pee long delayed at the Pro Station urinal when he hears in rapid succession auto horns blowing, a faint inarticulate human cry, a resounding crash, metal banging metal, glass shattering and another inarticulate human cry.

Pvt. Poole, dribbling down his pants, his fly and raincoat flapping, dashes from the Pro Station, expecting the worst and finding it. There's a '41 Dodge staff car crosswise on the sidewalk outside the Pro Station, its left rear quarter crumpled, the glass in that door shattered, its left rear tire torn and flat, and an MP jeep with a broken windshield, a bent bumper and mangled grill down on its front axle in the middle of the intersection, water leaking from its radiator, its right front wheel still slowly spinning ten feet away beside a large crumpled body in a GI raincoat with an MP brassard on its arm. A dozen air crew, ignoring the drizzle, are tumbling out of the Barrier Arms and the MPs on the cathouse and AWOL patrols are lumbering down and across Dock Street.

Pvt. Poole peers through the staff car's shattered window and sees, this far worse than his worst fears, a skinny dazed bareheaded brigadier general with a GI haircut and a bony bloody nose sprawled across the rear seat, swearing. The GI driver, likewise dazed but conscious, is sprawled across the front seat, babbling "had the right-of-way."

The body in the street is Sgt. Harry Parker. He, it will develop, flung himself from the CID jeep after once yelling uselessly, "Captain! Look out!" an instant before the collision, when it clearly was inevitable, rolled when he hit the street and escaped with skinned knuckles, a lacerated cheek and a bruised right shoulder. One cathouse MP helps Harry sit up and insists he remain sitting. The other looks to Capt. Raskovic and yells, "Somebody call a amblance!" Capt. Raskovic is out cold, slumped across the jeep's steering wheel, the impact with which removed four of his front teeth before his head cracked the windshield.

Pvt. Poole, smart enough to take cover, scoots into Pro Station and phones the 12th Station Hospital for an ambulance and the 330th Ordnance Co. for a tow-truck. The other MPs and the Pro Station medics, peering through the staff car's shattered window, watch Brig. Gen. S.O. Bargle slowly sit up, locate his garrison cap, pull it from under his butt, clamp it on his head, fish an o.d. handkerchief from his pants pocket and clamp it on his bloody nose. He also has a cut lip, he'll soon have a world-class shiner, there's blood all over his trenchcoat and he can't though he's trying open either rear door on the Dodge.

"You men!" Brig. Gen. Bargle snarls, his big general's voice muffled but imperious. "Goddamn it! Look alive! Get me out of here!"

Easier said then done. The doors on the Dodge, sprung by the collision, will not open. An MP scurries into Q&NR depot and returns with a crowbar. Willing hands pry the right-rear door open and Brig. Gen. Bargle, observed by all present, crawls out of the Dodge onto Flinders Street. Pfc. Stefanelli also crawls out, climbing over the front seat. The point of impact was behind Stefanelli. He was flung about when the Dodge, stove in and briefly airborne, spun through 180 degress, its engine stalling, and slammed onto the sidewalk, but escaped with bruises, a chipped tooth, some psychological residue and, he fears, a big black mark on his driving record. The goddamn jeep was on his left. He had the right-of-way. But it's an MP jeep, Military Police in big white letters on its bent bumper. The fucking MPs no doubt will blame him. Maybe not, though.

"Who," Brig. Gen.Bargle, on his feet beside the Dodge, snarls through his bloody handkerchief in his big though muffled general's voice. "Was the idiot driving that jeep? I want that man!"

"Captain Raskovic, Sir," the MP commanding the AWOL

patrol says. "He's the CID chief, Sir. It look like he's hurt pretty bad, Sir."

"Good!" Brig. Gen. Bargle snarls. Marching through the drizzle to the jeep, he snarls at Raskovic's inert figure. "You're on report! You! You maniac!" Then stands glaring at the assembled troops while blood soaks the handkerchief clamped to his nose and hard rain starts pounding down.

A 12th Station Hospital ambulance arrives. The driver and the medic aboard ease by Brig. Gen. Bargle and lift Capt. Raskovic out of the jeep onto a stretcher and into the ambulance. They help Harry Parker to his feet and into the ambulance and gingerly approach Brig. Gen. Bargle. He will not, Brig. Gen. Bargle snarls, require immediate medical attention. The ambulance crew back off, climb into their ambulance and depart. Brig.Gen. Bargle stands in the rain, ignoring it, fuming. A 330th Ordnance tow-truck arrives and hooks onto the CID jeep. The MPs but for Pvt. Poole, still taking cover in the Pro Station, the Pro Station medics and the air crew from the Barrier Arms observe all this but chiefly are interested in Brig. Gen. Bargle. It's not every day, this a real treat, they see a one-star general in a bloody trenchcoat with his nose in a bloody handkerchief, so mad he could spit.

"What are you men doing!" Brig. Gen. Bargle, glaring at these observers, snarls. "Return to your duties! Now! Disperse! That's an order!" The air crew slowly retreat into the Arms. Bargle glares at the MPs present. "Where's the MP supposed to be on traffic duty here? I want him!" No one seems to know. Pvt. Poole's still in the Pro Station, buttoning his fly. "All right! You're all on report! I'll find him! Driver, will this car run?"

"I'll see, Sir," Pfc. Stefanelli says. He climbs into the Dodge and gets it started. "I think so, Sir."

Brig. Gen. Bargle, soaked, his nose is still bleeding but the flow is slowing, climbs into the Dodge. "Base Section Headquarters, driver. You wait for me there." MPs ram the right-rear door shut. Stefanelli bumps the Dodge off the sidewalk, turns it around and drives slowly, the flat tire whop-whop-whopping, along Flinders Street. Brig. Gen. Bargle pulls his notebook from his shirt pocket. Like himself, it's bloody but unbowed.

* * *

Col. Web Allen, slumped at his desk in his Sad Sack uniform at 1700 hours, his prickly heat raging, a Fleetwood smouldering in his heaped ashtray, a crumpled V-mail form in his fist, staring out at the rain pounding down on Hill Street, the steady drip drip drip from the leaky ceiling, four leaks now, plucking at his sanity, is down in the dumps again.

Jill Tucker phoned ten minutes ago, he still was more or less euphoric then. She will not after all see him tonight. Her often irregular period's started. That's always traumatic. Jill takes to her bed, very bitchy, lets others do her bit. That was the case the other time anyway, shortly after they began their affair. But it's not an affair or just an affair. He truly loves Jill Tucker etc. etc. Which no doubt is why her phone call left him so devastated. Destroyed his euphoria. He won't see Jill tonight. He'll miss her, terribly. Her and their steamy fun and games. Confounded period takes precedence.

Web Allen's not felt so bad, so sad, so hurt since, well, comes oddly to mind the time a quarter century ago when Melanie Svensen, then seventeen, on whom he had a terrible crush at the time, turned him down for the West Cork High School Senior Prom. She went instead with Bernard (Barney) Clark, the football captain. Barney Sr. And married Barney Sr. a year later, a week after her graduation, pregnant by him at the time, and lived unhappily ever after. Or maybe not. They're still married, Melanie and Barney Sr., parents of eight. Well, six, Sean and Barney Jr. no longer with us. Always poor though. Barney Sr. peaked in High School, thereafter drove trucks, worked now and then at the ADM elevator, sought work with faint determination when unemployed and drank. He's working steady now though at the Twin Cities Arsenal, this a report from Mert.

Melanie. He's not thought of her since, well, a year ago, when he wrote her, had to write her, her and Barney Sr. "Regret to inform you . . . son Bernard killed in action against the enemy . . . liked and respected by all his buddies . . . did not suffer." A kindly lie. The late Sgt. Clark's ghost looms up. Web Allen bids it begone and lights another Fleetwood. Faint sounds of useless activity, ringing phones, typewriters clacking, reverberate through the former sugar warehouse. Base Section HQ is speedily prosecuting The War. Or so it will appear should Brig. Gen. Bargle appear.

M/Sgt. Abbott explodes into the office. "Sir! General Bargle, Sir! He's here! I seen him drive up! MP on door duty hadda help him out his car. Open the door. Car's all banged up. Like it been in a wreck. You want I should empty the pails, Sir?"

"No, leave them." Who cares? Abbott withdraws and Brig. Gen. Bargle, wasting no time knocking, stamps into the office from the hall, stamping as best he can with a pronounced limp, blood all over his trenchcoat. His nose looks like a ripe tomato and there's a large purple bruise beneath his left eye. "My god, Sir! What."

"Stand at attention!" Brig. Gen. Bargle snarls. "Superior officer addressing you!" Web Allen rises and snaps to attention. "One of your men ran into my car! A Military Police captain! But that's just the frosting on the cake. Your command, Sir, is a disgrace! And that's just an outline! You're at attention!" Web Allen stiffens. Bargle also stood him at attention while chewing his ass in the Service Force mess. "Now I'll give you the details. You incompetent!" Brig. Gen. Bargle removes his bloody trenchcoat, tosses it on a chair and pulls a small notebook smeared with blood from his shirt pocket. "Item One!"

Brig. Gen. Bargle flips through this notebook, item after item, for what seems to Web Allen, standing rigid at attention, his buttocks clenched, a very long time. Through Item Sixty-Six. Miss

Davis' rape is cited at one point, likewise the booze the flyboys liberated, both in Brig. Gen. Bargle's view "clear evidence of a total breakdown in discipline." There's also a lot about dirty white stones, sagging pyramidal tents, empty oil drums rusting in the rain, Colored transport personnel rolling dice, signs on trees, Government Property converted to private use, GIs with slingshots shooting kookaburras, a former sergeant sleeping on duty, troops who need haircuts. Web Allen lets it all roll over him. He's better off than the late Sgt. Clark anyway. Barney Jr. Why's his ghost popping up again? Earlier memories of Melanie, his mother, probably. Funny the way the mind works, his mind anyway. No doubt Abbott and Costello, ears to their office door, Fogerty too perhaps, are enjoying Brig. Gen Bargle's performance.

Brig. Gen.Bargle pauses, cracks a deathhead smile. Time to taunt Allen. "There's more and I'll get to that. Heard you're shacking up with a Red Cross girl. Jill Tucker. I knew Jill in Sydney. Intimately. She ever tell you that? Give you that line about Radcliffe? Her old man's in investments? I've got friends in Beantown. I ran a little reconn on Jill. When I was thinking about a more permanent. Well, never mind that. Radcliffe, hell! Her old man's in the junk business. Holy terror in bed though. I guess you know that. I'm going to sample some of that. Again. Tonight. She call you? Have to wait your turn, I'm out of town. You're at attention, Sir! Item Sixty-Seven. Last but not least. Just who the hell do you think you are, unilaterally amending Service Force Uniform Regulations! No neckties! I'm going to recommend you be relieved, Sir, that matter alone! And I by god want your men in Class A uniforms in neckties! As of now ! Have you got a necktie?"

"Yes, Sir!" Web Allen dropped his issue necktie in his top desk drawer the day the unilaterally amended Uniform Regulations took effect.

"Put it on! Now! That's an order! Chrissake, look like a soldier. Get a decent uniform. You look like that Sad Sack cartoon. And take off that goddamn Combat Infantry Badge! You're in the

Quartermaster Corps now. You're not entitled to wear that goddamn badge!"

"Sir!" Col. Web Allen opens his top desk drawer, picks up his issue tie, grasps it by both ends (Jill lied to him or Bargle did and the hell he's not entitled), steps from behind his desk, loops the tie over Brig. Gen. Bargle's head, crosses it over his prominent adam's apple and pulls it tight, then tighter.

"Wark!" Brig. Gen. Bargle gargles, grabbing Web Allen's wrists. "Stop! You're choking me! Wark! You're insane! Wark! HELP!"

Abbott, Costello and Fogerty burst into the office but skid to a halt, monentarily paralyzed. Never in their eighty-odd years of combined service have they seen a colonel choking a general with a necktie.

"HELP!" Brig. Gen. Bargle gargles. "Gagh! Wark! HELP!" His bony face is turning purple and his mean little eyes are bulging.

Abbott, Costello and Fogerty snap out of their paralysis. They grapple with Web Allen, pry his right hand off the necktie and Brig. Gen. Bargle, clutching his throat, swallowing air, backs out of its loop. Costello clamps a full-nelson on Web Allen. Abbott steps in a pail full of rain and knocks it over. Web Allen drops the tie and sings, merrily, "Oh there'll be no promotions this side of the oceans, so cheer up my lads, bless 'em all, the long and the short and the tall, bless 'em all."

"This officer," Brig.Gen. Bargle, his general's voice cracking and squeaking but imperious, snarls. "Colonel Allen. Is relieved of command! Herewith! He's under arrest! Assaulting a superior officer. No, he's insane! He's a Section Eight! I want him locked up! Who are you, Colonel?"

"Fogerty, Sir, Parnell," Lt. Col. Fogerty says, and salutes. "I'm the chief-of-staff."

"You're the acting Base Section commander. As of now. Call the Provost. Tell him send some men. Get an ambulance. This man, Colonel Allen. He's insane! I want him locked up in the Nut Ward at the 12th Station Hospital. Forthwith!"

"Sir!" Fogerty grabs the phone on Web Allen's desk and shouts into it. "Get me the Provost and the 12th Station Hospital. On the double!"

"You can let me go, Sergeant," Web Allen says. "I've done my bit." Costello gingerly removes his full-nelson. Brig. Gen. Bargle backs away. Web Allen sits in one of the office chairs, digs a crumpled pack of Fleetwoods from his shirt pocket, lights one with his Zippo, offers Bargle the pack.

Brig. Gen. Bargle, rubbing his throat, shakes his head. "I smoke cigars. When I can get any. Good god, Sir, you are insane! You're a Section Eight! And you're sitting on my trenchcoat! Get off my trenchcoat!"

Outside, rain's pounding down. Another leak develops in the ceiling. It drips on Web Allen's head. He ignores it, hums "Bless 'em all, the long and the short and." His War, he vaguely surmises, soon may be over. A Section Eight is the Army nomenclature for one unable to cope. Cope mentally. So what? Jill Tucker lied to him. Or Bargle did.

"General, Sir," Fogerty says. "Provost on his way, Sir. Ambulance too. Uh, Sir, there's something I like and discuss with you, you have a minute. When we're uh well finished here, I mean. Major matter morale you might say, Sir."

"Your liquor some flyboys liberated," Brig. Gen. Bargle says. "I heard about that in Brisbane. Very well. When we're finished here."

* * *

The concrete floor in the huge Second Air Depot quonset in which engines are repaired is damp but a dozen SAD GIs are shooting craps there at 2000 hours, there because the quonset has electric lights. Outside, rain's pounding down. Other GIs directed by a sergeant are disassembling an engine on a B24, working late because it's a high prioity job. Pvt. Claude (Frenchie) LaCroix, a swarthy young man from upstate Vermont, no longer is in the game. He wiped out rolling craps while seeking a Big Eighter from Decatur. His buddy, Pvt. Dade Brewer, a fat GI from Hunger, Idaho, also wipes out while seeking a Bix Six from Salt Lick.

"C'mon, Brew," Frenchie says. "Let's hit the sack." They head for the door but pause there, waiting, the rain may let up. Frenchie makes sure no one is within earshot. "Brew, lissen. I know where that fuckin booze the flyboys liberate is!"

"What!" Pvt. Brewer says. "Chrissake, where?"

"That Forty-Seven I look in for that prick Richall. The one next the one wi' the fuckin dog tied it."

"You said it was full ammunition."

"Fuckin aye I said it was full ammunition. I ain't gonna tell Richall it's full booze. But I seen a pile cargo with a tarp over it and a box wasn't all covered said Gilbey's gin on it!"

"Jeezuzz! It's like two-hunnert cases booze those flyboys liberate! What I heard. But cripes, Frenchie. There ain't anyway we can get it. Is there? Goddamn RAAF got the field locked up tight."

"Hey, I been bustin' my fuckin brain, Brew! Tryin' figger a way we can get that booze. You try too. We get that booze, we be rich! But keep your mouth shut. Fuckin officers find out, they'll grab it."

* * *

Considerable revelry is in progress, it's a special occasion, at the Base Section Officers Club at 2100 hours while outside a slow drizzle falls. That horror of war, the two-drinks-per-night-per-member-limit, has been lifted, at least temporarily, Lt. Col. Fogerty's orders, and many toasts drunk to Fogerty's sudden promotion to Acting Base Section Commander. Capt. Raskovic's unfortunate collision with Brig. Gen. Bargle also has been discussed, briefly, and Col. Allen's "crack up," based on Fogerty's description ("He damn near choke the old bastard to death, I didn't intervene") and subsequent incarceration in the 12th Station Hospital Nut Ward at greater length, the consensus on that, also offerd by Fogerty, "Goddamn Weekend Warrior never was up to the job."

Lt. Col. Fogerty downed all the toasts and has reached that degree of intoxication he most prefers, still functional, happy and horny. Acting Base Section Commander: everything's coming up roses. And it's not every night a light colonel bends elbows with a real live Congressman. U.S. Rep. Festus Lee Claypool and his entourage (minus David Dudley Hull, who's repacking his gear) arrived an hour ago. Claypool wished to hobnob with some of the boys he considers Up Near The Front. He and the entourage joined Fogerty and Maj. Cain at their table and Cain's fawning over Claypool. Siggie Ferk, mistrustful of Townsville dentists, he'll soon be in Brisbane, find a dentist there, is treating his throbbing molar with gin.

Be happier still though, Lt. Col. Fogerty thinks, if he had a big woman waiting. He goes to the bar and queries Lt. Bernie Witters, who in view of so much revelry is helping Pfc. Dugan mix drinks. "Yo, Lieutenant. You seen your neighbor Mrs. Rooney lately? I promise you I talk to her about her shickens and by god I will."

"Who? Oh, no," Witters says. "I think she might be out of town." He drops the drink he's mixing, swears, another glass broken, gin all over his pants. Witters, Lt. Col. Fogerty deduces, has been drinking. Hell, he's drunk. "Colonel, Sir, Major Nitpicker, he said he was gonna send you a report, the inventory?"

"Yeah, he send it me. I only glance it, Allen crack up and assault General Bargle and all. But it look like your inventory come up short. I dint know better, I think you might been peddlin' booze."

"Oh, no! No, Sir!" Witters whines. "Not me, Sir! It's just we did have a lot of uh breakage, Sir. And what I uh well gave you, Sir. It's sort of counted up, you know, Sir. And Dugan. Like you said. I think he steals."

"Yeah, well, lucky for you maybe, Lieutenant, I'm Acting Base Section commander. I'll take care that asshole Nitpicker. But just between you and me, it look like we prolly get our booze back! Don't say nothin' yet. But General Bargle, I talk with him and he called GHQ. He's got more clout there then Allen. He request GHQ tell the goddamn RAAF out the airfield go take a flying fuck at theirselves and let us search the goddamn airplane. Implement appropriate action forthwith like that GHQ order direct us."

"Sir," Witters says. "Speaking that liquor. I mention this before, but now I'm sure. Real sure. That MP sergeant stopped the truck it had a busted taillight and our liquor was liberated. He was the same CID sergeant was in your office. The one supposed."

"So?" Lt. Col. Fogerty, his thoughts riveted on a big naked woman, says. "I don't see no connection. General Bargle thinks the goddamn RAAF prolly get the word from GHQ first thing tomorrow. We got a platoon MPs on standby, ready search the goddamn airplanes. We get our booze back, Lieutenant, you prolly can fiddle your inventory, make Nitpicker happy. No sweat, right? Gimme a bottle gin. I take it my table."

Four junior officers belly up to the bar seeking Swappa slings. Lt. Witters, drunk, Nitpicker and the mysterious sergeant still troubling him but somewhat relieved in view of Fogerty's news about the booze, discovers there's no gin at hand. "Dugan, go get some gin and a bottle for Colonel Fogerty. Storeroom's open."

Lt. Col. Fogerty waits, gets his gin and returns to his table. He's reached the point at which he prefers his gin straight. He pours hefty shots for himself, Cain, Claypool and his entourage and offers a garbled toast "to the great state Mishishippee." Then gulps his shot, chokes, gasps, splutters and roars, "This's WATER!"

More or less simultaneously the junior officers discover their

Swappa slings are grapefruit juice and water and emit loud cries to that effect.

Lt. Col. Fogerty leaps from his chair with his alleged gin in his fist, charges the bar, grabs a handful of Lt. Witters' shirt with his other hand, shakes the alleged gin in Witters' face and bellows. "What the hell's goin' on here! This's WATER! What happen the gin! Gimme a report, you asshole!"

"I uh oh no oh, Sir, I uh it." Lt. Witters can only stutter.

But Pfc. Dugan proves helpful. "All the booze inna storeroom there wi' marks on the labels prolly just water, Colonel."

"Jeezuzz H. christ!" Lt. Col Fogerty, tightening his grip on Witters' shirt, bellows. "You lie me, you little shit? You tell me you ain't peddle any booze? Our booze!" Witters gurgles and stutters. "By god we are gonna find out!"

Lt. Col. Fogerty gives Witters a hard shove and charges into the storeroom followed by Cain and sundry other officers confronting another horror of war. They quickly sample several jugs with marked labels, confirming Dugan's information.

"Put him on charges, Sir?" Cain says. "Misappropriation of Government Property. Well, it's not exactly Government Property, I guess. But I'll think of something."

"No," Lt.Col. Fogerty says. "I pick the crooked little shit for Club manager. I'll unpick him! He's relieved his d s t d y. Herewith! We'll ship him back the Repple Depple. Infantry replacement. I want three volunteers with a jeep, take the little prick. Forthwith!"

Five minutes later, all the time Fogerty gives him to get his belongings together, Lt. Bernie Witters departs for the 3rd Replacement Depot in a jeep with three fellow officers who do not speak to him en route though eyeing him with great hatred. His money's still buried under the jasmine bush and Lt. Col. Fogerty's phoning the Rep Dep duty officer with orders. "I'm sendin' you a little asshole second john. Witters, Bernard C. He's a Infantry replacement. You tell Colonel Farmer I want him shipped out, some Infantry outfit the hell up in New Guinea. Forthwith!"

Lt. Col. Fogerty then calls for a volunteer to help Dugan tend bar. Lt. Stanley Bannon of the 404th QM Truck (C) steps forward. That settled, the revelry resumes, though somewhat muted by the knowledge that more Club booze (some seventy bottles, Cain estimates) is gone with the wind. Fogerty, clutching a bottle of Gilbey's with a pristine label, muttering imprecations, rejoins Rep. Claypool and his entourage and Claypool proposes a toast. "To Cuhnel Fogerty. Ah allas lock and see a officer taken swift actshun, mattuh dis'pline."

Lt.Col. Fogerty accepts this accolade with suitable modesty and waxes sadly philosophical. "Jeezuzz. You try and do somebody a favor. Be nice them. Then they kick you in the balls!"

Rep. Claypool, veteran of a many a political back-stabbing, concurrs. "Offen true, Cuhnel. Turrble turrble thang but offen true." They drink to that. Outside, a slow drizzle is falling.

* * *

The revelry at the third Manic Manor farewell party (sixteen states, Puerto Rico and the Sioux Nation represented) also is somewhat muted at 2200 hours though both farewellees, Boots Davis and Rose Pearl Stevens, are present and everybody's trying hard. Outside, a thin drizzle is pattering down. Inside, the usual bugs are banging the light bulb and Billy Eckstine, though his articulation is getting pretty scratchy, is wailing, "It's gawnnn and started raininnnn."

Boots of course, though a farewellee, won't be going to New Guinea. She has to wait for the results of her tests for social diseases and the court-martial presumed to be coming along shortly and she's supposed to go down to the Townsville Constabulary tomorrow, where a Constable Jack Crowe will fingerprint her. Sgt. Harry Parker told her that when she ran into him in the 12th Station Hospital Orderly Room, where she was waiting for Capt.

Sussman. Harry said he'll take her to the Constabulary and also told her about Capt. Raskovic's collision with Brig.Gen. Bargle. Harry, declared fit for duty following a cursory examination, his cheek only scraped, his knuckles lightly bandaged and his bruised shoulder taped, was waiting for a 301st MP jeep supposed to pick him up. It's bad enough, Boots thinks, she was raped by two goddamn nigras, now they're going to fingerprint her. Like a common criminal. But if that helps nail the bastards raped her, she'll do it. Rose Pearl Stevens will be going to New Guinea. The plan now is she'll fly there with Billy Gote in the Lucky Lil. If the weather breaks.

Boots got back to the Manor at 1800 hours, delivered by Capt. Sussman, and took a long hot soaking bath, everybody leaving her the loo. It proved another useless effort to feel clean again, but she's not said anything about that and no one's mentioned her traumatic experience. Everybody's trying, Boots surmises, to pretend it didn't happen, whether for her sake or their's is unclear. She wishes she could pretend. She's trying though. Carry on. Join the party. Billy Gote's being solicitous, mixing her drinks, killing her with kindness. She's drinking too much but what the hell. She's done that before.

And there are other subjects of great interest to discuss. Col. Web Allen's crack-up, abrupt dismissal and subsequent incarceration in the 12th Station Hospital Nut Ward, for one, and Capt. Dominic Raskovic's collision with Brig. Gen. S.O. Bargle. Several garbled versions of both events originating with various Base Section HQ and 12th Station GIs and one offered by Sgt. Porky Wallace, who actually almost witnessed the collision, saw the goddamn general get out of his staff car with a bloody nose and blood all over his trenchcoat anyway, have been dissected. One version has Col. Allen trying to push or throw Brig. Gen. Bargle out of a second-story window at Base Section HQ. Another has Bargle wishing to shoot Capt. Raskovic on the spot.

"I saw Colonel Allen," Boots says. "When they brought him

to the hospital. I was just getting ready to leave. He looked all right to me. I mean he wasn't violent or anything."

"The quiet ones are the ones you have to watch out for," Agnes Moore, once employed at a state mental institution, says.

"What will our Jill do now?" Rose Pearl Stevens says. "No cuddly colonel to keep her warm."

"Ha!" Ima Score says. "Don't worry about her. Little slut's got a date tonight with General Bargle! I heard her on the office phone, he called. They used to shack up in Sydney."

"Get the sitrep from her then," Saljeski says. "What fuckin Allen did to fuckin Bargle." Watch your mouth, Agnes says. "Sorry," Saljeski says.

"Maybe," Ima Score says. "You want to wait until morning. But she probably won't tell us. My guess, Rose Pearl, Allen's out of the picture, General Bargle's back in Sydney, little slut will make a move on your Wing Commander. She'd like the Australia Club, way you describe it."

"More power to her," Rose Pearl, who still wishes the damn Wing Commander had used a condom, says. Stupid to let him without one, her in mid-stream.

"There was a lootenant in our outfit took a poke at a major," Porky Wallace says, but no one evinces any interest in this story. Porky subsides and asks Betty Lou Fricker if she'd like another sling? Just one more, Betty Lou says, a small one. Lieutenant Gote was right. The competition at the Manor is pretty stiff but Porky figures he's Number One with this Betty Lou Fricker. She's kind of a cold fish but he's commandeered the chair beside her's and is mixing her slings. There's plenty of gin. The last two jugs Billy Gote says he got off Asshole Nadler, the 34th Squadron p.o., stashed away, were broken out in honor of Boots' homecoming. No one's touched the Australian whiskey Porky Wallace bought for twenty quid from Biff Smith, publican turned highway robber.

"Speaking generals," Lt. Straight Arrow Hunker says. "I got

to get my butt out the field first thing in the morning. Take a look at my airplane."

"Is your general's the one from First Corps?" Agnes Moore says. Hunker nods. "We had a phone call for you today. At our office. Second Air Depot is looking for you. Colonel Betrandus there wants to see you." Hunker wonders what for? "Something about your airplane." Hunker shrugs.

Somebody wonders what will happen to Colonel Allen and, this of lesser interest, Captain Raskovic? Nobody knows, but the 12th Station Hospital supply sergeant thinks they'll ship Allen off to the 5th General Hospital in Brisbane. "For an evaluation. See he's a Section Eight. They got a bunch of nut doctors there. Story I heard, he was there once before. That's they don't court-martial him."

Eddie Devlin, whispering, wonders if Ann Silvers and young Mr. Devlin might "sleep" together again tonight on the patio, but Ann Silvers doesn't think so. There'll be other people on the patio, she whispers, and anyway she thinks she should sleep in her room. So Boots won't be alone.

Billy Gote, whispering, proposes he and Boots "sleep" together somewhere later on, but Boots declines this proposal. The last thing she ever wants to do again is "sleep" with anybody! And she wonders: does Billy really want to or is he just being nice? Trying to make her feel better, still desired and desirable. No matter. Billy's a nice enough guy. But he's a goddamn man!

"Any you blokes try a Swagman?" Pops, the skinny old Australian, busy adding his secret ingredient to one, says. No one rises to this challenge and the discussion turns to nut doctors, the Army shrinks, what they do, how they do it. Many, the consensus is, are pretty nutty themselves.

"Remember you enlisted or were drafted," Lt. Donald, who seems to be back in Flots' good graces, says. Jets is up in their room sulking and Hunker has his eye on Ima Score, variety the spice of life. "Army shrink asked you, You like girls? You said Yes, you were in. You said No you liked boys better, you weren't?"

"I wish the fuck I know that then!" Saljeski says. "Sorry, Agnes."

Similar regrets are voiced by other male personnel present and the discussion turns to the popular belief (or rumor) that numerous queers lied to Navy shrinks and are enjoying life afloat.

This discussion is interrupted when Sgt. Harry Parker arrives (favoring his right shoulder, a bruise on his cheek, his knuckles bandaged) with the latest sitrep. The 12th Station Hospital discharged him, he says, because it's making room for casualties evacced from Arawe, and he has a new jeep the 301st Motor Pool gave him. Captain Raskovic has a concussion and four front teeth missing. He more or less came to for a minute in the ambulance but doesn't remember the collision. Thinks they were struck by lightening. He'll likely be hospitalized four or five days and the 12th Station Dental Section will build him a partial denture. What will happen to him then? Who knows? Up to Brig. Gen. Bargle, most likely, who immediately following the collision sounded like he wanted Raskovic's ass on a platter. First Lt. Garth Ziese, the 301st MP supply officer until two hours ago, an Arkansas hog farmer in civil life with a degree in swine husbandry and an ROTC commission, is the acting CID chief. Major Cain, the Base Section A.G., has taken personal charge of the rape investigation and wants the three suspects on their way to Oro Bay apprehended there and returned to Townsville forthwith.

"LST they're on supposed to land Oro Bay day after tomorrow," Harry says. "I'm gonna take a detail up there, two men, take them into custody and bring them back."

"Retrograde amnesia, Captain Raskovic," Agnes Moore says. "That's often the case following severe trauma." Boots Davis wishes she had some of that.

Jill Tucker arrives with Brig. Gen. Bargle's driver, Pfc.

Stefanelli, in tow. "You're home early, Roomie," Ima Score says. "Early for you. What happened to your date?"

"As you no doubt know," Jill says. "General Bargle was in an automobile accident. He hurt his back. Your information, Roomie, I gave him a rubdown and put him to bed and his driver was kind enough to bring me home. Will somebody make Steffie here a drink? Any more questions?"

In fact, the old goat couldn't get it up. Moaned about his back and his nose and his black eye and the shocking fact that "your crazy boyfriend assaulted me!" Then described with evident pleasure the way he promptly relieved Colonel Web Allen and had him locked up. Said, "You're boyfriend's insane! We'll Section Eight him. Kick him out of the Army. Or maybe I'll court-martial him." Vindictive old goat. Jealous perhaps. Served him right, he couldn't get it up. She didn't give him any help. Sidetracked his pleas, citing his injuries, she "play" with him. He'll be leaving Townsville, he said, minute the weather breaks. So, write the old goat off? All he ever had going for him were his general's perks. But he wields some clout, not much, at Red Cross HQ in Sydney and she's getting pretty of tired Townsville and Ima Score. Reason she agreed to see him. Left the old goat with the idea she'd like a transfer, Brisbane or Sydney. Write Colonel Web Allen off too, the way it looks.

Jill surveys the males present. Pfc. Stefanelli with his nose in a sling is a good-looking lad: young, blond, muscular. Just a kid though. Her interest wanes, replaced by lethargy. Her damn period may in fact be starting.

And Score, trust her, has another question. "What about you're other old boyfriend, Roomie? They say he's locked up."

"So they say. Might be your big chance, Roomie, you go see him and he's in a straightjacket."

"You're a bitch, Tucker."

"Takes one to know one."

"Girls, girls!" Agnes Moore says. "I won't have this bickering."

"By the way," Jill says. "That liquor the flyboys liberated.

General Bargle phoned GHQ this afternoon. He has friends there. He told me GHQ is putting an order through RAAF Headquarters to the RAAF here to let the Base Section search the airplanes on the field. First thing tomorrow, he thinks."

Fear and consternation though not evident greet this news in some quarters. "Oh, shoot!" Ann Silvers says. "I was hoping the flyboys would get away with that liquor. Stick it to the O Club."

"What'll they do, you think," Saljeski says. "Guys took the booze, they fuckin catch them? Sorry."

Nobody knows but the best guess is hang them high if Lt. Col. Fogerty, Acting Base Section commander, has his way. Lock them up anyway, years and years, hard time in the Flat Mountain Stockade then Leavenworth or some other federal prison.

"Well, I'm going to bed," Jill says. This is not her problem.

"Me too," Betty Lou Fricker, shattering Porky Wallace's hopes and plans, says. She goes up the backstairs with Jill. "I heard somebody say you went to Radcliffe, Jill. When were you there?"

"No," Jill says. "I went to Bennington."

"Shit!" Porky Wallace says. "Hey, old man, I'll try one them Swagman."

"Say, Lieutenant," Harry says. "I got another them Samurai swords in my jeep. Better one, you like and take a look at it."

"Sure, I'll take a look at it," Billy says. Eddie and Saljeski also evince a continuing interest in Samurai swords and a hasty council of war convenes on the back porch. The rain's slowed to a light drizzle.

"Might be we got a problem," Harry says. "What Jill said. That goldurn General Bargle my leader run into. He been in touch with GHQ all right. Fact, Provost got a goldurn platoon MPs on standby. Ready search airplanes minute Bargle gets the word."

"Might got a problem!" Billy Gote says. "Jeezuzz! Is there any goddamn way we can get the booze off my airplane? Just dump it somewhere? Save our ass. My ass."

"Doubt it," Harry says. "Wish there was. But the goldurn RAAF still got the field locked up tight. Roving patrols and all. I mean I prolly can get a truck and the RAAF got to let you on your airyplane. But they see its booze you're unloading. Well, forget it."

"Fuckin Air Depot got a finger in the pie too," Saljeski says. "I heard a fuckin rumor anyway, I deliver their movie. Colonel Betrandus there like to get his hands on the fuckin booze. But what I heard, Air Depot thinks the booze is on the fuckin general's airplane. Where we tie the fuckin dog."

"I wish now we tie him my airplane," Billy Gote says. "He maybe delay this goddamn search some."

"Maybe the weather will break," Eddie Devlin, clutching at his favorite straw, says. "Then we can get out of here. Tomorrow's Sunday. You think GHQ works Sunday? Do whatever so the Base Section can start searching airplanes?"

Nobody knows. The general assumption is GHQ doesn't prosecute The War much on weekends and the Base Section except in unusual circumstances runs at half-speed weekends. But Lt. Col. Fogerty no doubt considers the missing booze an unusual circumstance.

"Possibility maybe, the weather," Billy Gote says. "Hell! All we can do is hope and sweat. Maybe, everbody got the idea the booze is on the general's airplane, Hunker's airplane, dog'll delay things awhile. What good that'll do, I don't know. Shit! Maybe I'll just get drunk!"

"Jeezuzz!" Saljeski, slapping his forehead, says. "I forgot a feed the fuckin dog!" But that's of little consequence under the circumstances. "Hey, what happen!"

The light drizzle's petered out, that's what. It's not raining. The Bloody Wet is taking a breather. The clouds are thinning. Two faint stars twinkle in the sky above Castle Hill.

"I got to call Meteorology!" Billy Gote says, and they charge back into the Manor. Billy commandeers the phone in the living room and the farewell party takes on new life. If in fact this is the long-awaited break in The Bloody Wet, many present will be flying tomorrow. Rose Pearl Stevens reels up the backstairs, sling in hand, to pack, and Boots goes with her, help her pack.

"ETD for Moresby is oh-eight-hundred!" Billy Gote, back in the kitchen, says. "Strips there still socked in but they'll clear, the weather guys say. We're gonna be up up up and away inna the wild blue yonder! Make me a goddamn sling, somebody."

"Hey, Lieutenant!" Harry says. "Maybe I can fly with you. Me and my detail I mention. Far as Moresby. Then we'll catch something, Oro Bay. Take them suspects inna custody."

'Well, yeah, I guess," Billy Gote says. "But you sure you and your detail want to ride in a airplane full a ammunition? I don't want anybody fooling with that ammo."

"No sweat," Harry says. "My detail won't fool with that ammo. We got Five-A Travel Priorities but it still gonna be a son-of-a-gun get out of here tomorrow, everthing all backed up."

"Roger then," Billy Gote says. "What the hell. Meet you at Ops, oh-seven-hundred. Sal, you come with your wheels and get me and Rose Pearl and my copilot and Eddie, here the Manor, oh-six-thirty?" He will indeed, Saljeski says. "Roger that then. Porky, we'll pick you and Johnson up at the Arms, say oh-six-forty. You be ready. Sooner we get out the field, sooner we'll get clearance."

"Roger," Porky says. Betty Lou Fricker left him high and dry but Louise will be along with his tea at 0600 hours and he's got a hard-on like a 155mm Long Tom artillery piece and time is running out.

* * *

Col. Web Allen peers out through the hurricane wire on his window at the 12th Station Hospital. The officers' Nut Ward is actually a single room. He's barefoot, wearing GI pajamas. The room is warm and dark. Somebody turned off the single ceiling light in a wire cage, the switch in the hall, an hour ago. And he took the sleeping pill the ward boy gave him but it did not put him to sleep. It's stopped raining but rain's still dripping from the eaves above the window. The clouds have thinned. Two faint stars twinkle in the sky over Castle Hill. The emblems of rank worn by Brig. Gen. S.O. Bargle.

What in God's name, Web Allen wonders, swept over him, producing an irresistible impulse to assault the old bastard and choke him to death? Damn near did too. Striking a superior officer is a court-martial offense. Trying to strangle one with a necktie no doubt's considered equivalent. But he's not under arrest, just locked up. Old bastard evidently thinks Webster R. Allen really is insane. Said so in fact, several times. May be right. Somewhat unbalanced anyway. But the old bastard impugned Jill Tucker's character, veracity, fidelity. Assuming the old bastard was lying. And sneered at his Combat Infantry Badge. He can't truthfully say he's sorry he tried to strangle the old bastard. Sorry he failed maybe.

Web Allen wonders: will he see Jill Tucker again? Not for a time, that seems certain. A Captain Sussman, some name like that, said they'll evac him to the 5th General Hospital in Brisbane via FAMOCA for an "evaluation." Psychiatric evaluation, that means. Talk to shrinks again. Then what? Who knows? A court-martial no doubt is still a possibility, though few colonels face those. Higher ranks facing court-martials are thought to be bad for discipline, troop morale, likely to raise questions about the Army's leadership. Medical Discharge maybe, ranking officers often so treated. A Section Eight good-of-the-service discharge perhaps. Find out soon enough. No doubt a 12th Station desk commando is even now whacking out an evac order with a 5A Travel Priority.

Web Allen sighs. His prickly heat flares, rages. Nobody's watching, he claws at his crotch, a substantial pleasure. His War, he again surmises, soon may be over. Well, he lost heart for The War a long time ago. More than a year ago. What's today, it's past midnight, 19 December? Yes, more than a year ago, give or take a day, and the late Sgt. Barney Clark's ghost still haunts him.

There were two stars in the sky that night too, just visible through the jungle canopy, when Sgt. Clark, Barney Jr., Melanie's firstborn, took the patrol out.

Five months earlier, in July, the Japs, unaware apparently that the U.S. Navy had halted their drive south, landed 10,000 troops at Buna Government Station, a government building and a Methodist mission church in thatched huts on the northeast New Guinea coast, eighty miles from Port Moresby on the other side of the Owen Stanley Range. Those troops, subsequently reinforced, launched a drive into, up and over the Owen Stanleys, defeated scattered AMF units and by mid-September, coming down out of the mountains into the foothills, were a scant thirty-two miles from Moresby and its airstrips. A desperate situation calling for desperate measures. The 32nd Infantry Division was alerted and its 128th Infantry Regiment dispatched to defend the Moresby airstrips: dispatched by air in C47s and other assorted aircraft, the first U.S. troops ever airlifted to a battlefront or so they were told. In fact, confronted by a mixture of AIF forces back from the Western Desert, the Jap drive stalled thirty-two miles from Moresby and the surviving Japs troops, all starving, presently began to retreat. Few made it back to Buna Government Station but more Japs, landed there, still held the station and nearby Dobodura village and GHQ was determined to drive them from both. The regiment, a company at a time, was put aboard a variety of small ships and sailed around the eastern tip of New Guinea to Oro Bay on the northeast coast thirty miles from Buna Government Station. They went the rest of the way on foot, a two-day march with full packs on a series of native trails through the jungle in 95-degree heat, discarding much of what they carried along the way, stuff the natives snapped up, took a day off and on the fourth day the 1st and 3rd Battalions, 2nd

Battalion in reserve, launched an attack through the big coconut grove east of Buna Government Station.

This attack was stopped cold by a bunch of bunkers in the coconut grove. So was another, three days later, led by 2nd Battalion, in which Fox Co. suffered its first casualties. They withdrew then to regroup and extend their front inland and westward without opposition but for a some sniper fire. By then, reinforced, they were mixed with some AMF units in something called Warren Force, Warren a brigadier dispatched by GHQ. Torrential rain drenched them daily. The daytime temperature was in the high nineties, the humidity about the same. Their GI shoes and fatigues were beginning to rot. They were eating cold C rations, dividing eight-ounce cans between two men. Less than 1,000 calories a day, the Battalion surgeon estimated. Everybody in short order was hungry, exhausted and sick: malaria, dysentery, fungus infections, blackwater fever, dengue fever, FOU (Fever, Origin Undetermined). Their "supply line" was a joke. C47s and B24s based at the Moresby strips dodged the thunderstorms over the Owen Stanleys but most of the stuff they dropped fell behind the Jap lines. Small ships, island traders with worn sails and wheezy gasoline engines, based at Oro Bay, crept up the coast on moonless nights through the uncharted coral reefs, but Jap aircraft often sank them. Native Papuans recruited in the coastal villages were the one reliable link, humping up the jungle trails from Oro with boxes on their heads.

The Japs, it eventually became clear, were still holding a defense in depth in the bunkers in the coconut grove and more bunkers in the jungle and head-high kunai grass around the New Strip, a fake airstrip built by the Japs, clever little bastards, on which many allied bombs were wasted. One, falling short, inflicted more Fox Co's. casualties: two dead, two wounded. Nobody knew how many bunkers there were but there seemed to be a great many. Three more Warren Force attacks launched with high hopes failed to make any visible dent in these bunkers though producing many casualties. The rifle companies, 1800 officers and EM or just under half the Regiment's initial strength, took 90 per cent of the casualties.

It was mainly the native carriers who kept Warren Force going but they had to be fed too, Cs, or they quit and went back to their villages. Pvt. Oscar Olhoff, who in civil life, driving a tank truck, delivered gasoline to Pierce County service stations, assessed this situation one day. "Chrissake," Pvt. Olhoff said. "It's like I deliver gas and the fuckin truck burn up half it!" This generally was thought to be the smartest thing Pvt. Olhoff ever said. He was killed, eviscerated, later that day when a Jap knee-mortar round exploded between his legs while he was crawling through the kunai grass in a futile attempt to stuff a grenade through a firing slit in one of the bunkers beyond the New Strip.

The bunkers were shallow holes, the water table there amid the tidal creeks a foot down, built up with coconut logs and 55-gallon oil drums filled with sand, firing slits cut in the logs, roofed with more logs, three or four layers, covered with dirt and vegetation, impervious to mortars, machine-guns, rifle fire and the light artillery with which Warren Force was equipped, which often had no shells anyway. The bunkers were difficult to detect, some were fake bunkers, until they opened fire and the fire usually came from adjacent bunkers. They had interlocking fields of fire and there were snipers up in the coconut trees. Based on a few body counts, there were half a dozen Japs in each bunker, all as sick and hungry as the GIs who killed them.

There was a lull in the fighting after the last failed attack then orders came down from Warren Force HQ eleven miles down the coast in another world, said to be enjoying one hot meal daily. The rifle companies were directed to launch night patrols and pinpoint the location of the bunkers holding up The War.

Maj. Web Allen, former Fox Co. commander, was the Second Battalion S2 (Intelligence Officer), just so assigned and promoted, a battlefield promotion, when the former S2 was evacced to Moresby with a fungus infection, dysentery, FOU and a 105-degree temperature. Troops with 104-degree temperatures stayed on the line gulping aspirin if there was any. Web Allen took the patrol order down to Fox Co., dug-in in wet holes along the New Strip, a quarter-mile hike on a muddy trail, at dusk. Fox in view of its location was the logical choice to mount one of those patrols. He took his precious Australian whiskey, half a bottle, with him. The new Fox Co. commander, a first john Web Allen did not know, transferred from another unit, was not thrilled with the patrol order. His men, he said were "awful tired" and there were only 98 left out of 189 on the roster "when this fucking operation started." But an order was an order. The john called for volunteers, passing the word along the Fox Co. holes.

There were no volunteers. Then Sgt. Barney Clark, drawing rations for the First Platoon at company HQ, said, "Shit, I'll take it," and induced or dragooned four wet weary hungry First Platoon GIs, all privates, to join him.

The patrol formed up and waited, huddled under the HQ shelter-half, most of those abandoned, too much to carry, while slow rain fell, dripping through the jungle canopy, and mosquitoes hummed in the dark. "We'll wait'll the fuckin Japs go to sleep," Barney Clark said. "That's the fuckers ever do." Web Allen waited with them, sharing his whiskey, sip at a time. The first john was half asleep in a nearby hole and two members of the patrol fell asleep sitting up. Web Allen knew them, both were National Guardsmen, Pierce County farm boys in civil life. The other two were Draftees (Enlistees in their right minds with a choice of service never chose the Infantry) dumped in the Division just prior to its embarkation, a stocky little Mexican, Pablo Something, and a tall skinny kid, Robert NMI Douglas. The front was quiet but for occasional rifle fire when somebody detected or thought they detected suspicious sounds. Patriotic Japs sometimes infiltrated Warren Force in the night.

Barney Clark, presently, began to reminisce. "You remember all the times you persecute me, Captain?" He still called Web Allen captain. "Me and Sean? And times you defend us. I guess me and Sean some your best customers, back then."

"You were," Web Allen said, and so they were, Barney Jr. and his brother Sean, a year younger. Chips off the old block, Barney Sr., as the saying goes, hard drinkers in their late teens, wild drivers, quick to take offense and start fights in rural beer-joints. Which they generally won or Barney Jr. won, stepping in to reinforce Sean, who was small but had a big mouth. Barney Jr. was a Sectional Golden Gloves champion three years running, moving up from lightweight to middleweight, but trounced in the Regionals by some black kid from Milwaukee who could box a little. Barney Jr. was a puncher. Web Allen when assistant Pierce County district attorney "persecuted" both brothers half a dozen times for simple assault, DWI, speeding, disorderly conduct. Convicted them too, then sometimes paid their $10 or $20 fines. He figured they'd had a hard life, growing up in a violent household with Melanie and Barney Sr. Later, in private practice, he defended both pro bono in paternity suits and got them off, before Sean departed this world, killed instantly when, drunk, alone in Barney Jr's. hopped-up '34 Ford, he hit a bridge abutment on a county road at 85 mph.

Barney Jr., shortly thereafter, enlisted in the National Guard, Fox Co's. First Platoon in West Cork. He seemed to like soldiering, made Expert on the Rifle Range, proved a natural-born leader, a trait much admired by the Army, though a miserable peacetime soldier: slovenly, late for drills, AWOL on occasion. He made sergeant twice but was broken to private, the last time for absconding with the Company command car and smacking a rural mailbox during the Carolina Maneuvers. He still was paying for that at Buna Government Station, $10-a-month deducted from his sergeant's $78-a-month on a Statement of Charges. Capt. Web Allen promoted Barney Jr. to corporal again in South Australia and to sergeant in the Division camp outside Brisbane. The practice in Guard units was to promote Guardsmen if warm and breathing, but Barney Jr. was a natural-born leader as well and, it turned out, when they encountered enemy fire, one of those rare soldiers, tough as nails, impervious to discomfort, blessed with immense stamina, utterly confident of their own immortality, who thrive in combat. Technically, Sgt. Barney Clark was the First Platoon leader that night, leading 26 men out of an original 48, both the second johns and staff-sergeant who'd previously led them wounded and evacced to Port Moresby.

The slow rain petered out. Moonlight filtered through the jungle. Barney Clark inquired as to the time. Web Allen had the only wristwatch still working: 2300 hours by its luminous dial. "Fuckin moon," Barney Clark said, then roused the sleeping farm boys and the first john. The patrol looked to its gear, discarding things likely to make noise, and the first john passed the word down the line. Hold your fire, there's a patrol going out.

"Thanks for the drink, Captain," Barney Clark said and, rather a surprise, shook hands with Web Allen, then led the patrol, single-file, crouched low, into the kunai grass grown up on the New Strip.

The firing began thirty minutes later, Jap rifles cracking, a Nambu ripping off, U.S. M1s booming, grenades exploding, subsided, resumed without the M1s, died down. Scattered fire erupted elsewhere along the Warren Force front and somewhere along the line a precious flare went up. In its eerie light Web Allen saw GI helmets retreating through the kunai on the New Strip, their number initially unclear. The number was three: the little Mexican, Robert Douglas and one farm boy. They were carrying the other farm boy, his legs shattered by a Nambu, his helmet lost, when they stumbled out of the kunai and collapsed.

"Oh Jesu!" the little Mexican said. "Dey hit Sar'ent Clark and this fella and the other fella! Dey really rake us! Sar'ent Clark hit in his leg. I try help him but he say, No get out a here, Mex, go! We all way round behin' a bunker. Sar'ent Clark right by it door. Den anudder bunker shoot! Dey might got Sar'ent Clark and he still alive! But he tell me go!"

A medic rousted from his hole shot the farm boy full of morphine and bandaged his legs and they put him on a litter and four GIs rousted from their holes started down the muddy trail to the Battalion Aid Station with him. The scattered fire along the front subsided and for a time the night was a very quiet. Web Allen queried the surviving patrol members as to bunker locations but they could only say they'd spotted two, maybe four, in the jungle beyond the New Strip.

Then the screams began. Muffled but clearly audible, they continued for a time, it seemed a long time, then subsided. "Oh Jesu!" the little Mexican said. "Dey got Sar'ent Clark!"

He could, Web Allen was sure, ask for volunteers, he'd get them, go in with grenades, knives, M1s and tommy-guns and rescue Barney Clark. But which and where exactly was the bunker in which Barney Clark apparently was a prisoner? Adjacent bunkers would cut them down. Web Allen, helpless, cursed The War and his helplessness.

There were more muffled screams at intervals throughout the long night. They triggered ragged rifle fire all along the line until the word was passed: don't waste your ammunition. Web Allen spent those hours crouched beneath the Fox HQ shelter-half, wide awake, helpless, dreading the screams and the silences while awaiting more screams. At 0530 hours a gray dawn crept through the jungle and the screams began again, continued for a time, grew fainter and ceased.

Web Allen returned to Battalion HQ, where he learned the farm boy with the shattered legs was DOA at the Aid Station, a George Co. patrol though losing two men had more or less located several bunkers and another Warren Force attack would jump off at 1000 hours supported by four Australian Bren guncarriers. Web Allen returned to Fox Co., ostensibly to collect any Jap documents the attack might uncover and interrogate any English-speaking Japs captured, though that was unlikely. The Japs preferred to die and go to heaven with their Emperor's blessing and the Warren Force troops preferred to speed them on their way. They'd taken only three prisoners, all wounded, and only one, a private, spoke English. He claimed to have been a UCLA senior visiting his parents in Kobe when drafted in the summer of '41 and knew nothing of military value.

The attack, Web Allen trailing along behind it, was by Warren Force standards a success. By 1500 hours, when it petered out, all the Brens destroyed or disabled, their crews KIA or WIA, and numerous other casualties suffered, the attacking troops had gained nearly 200 yards, sent about a hundred Japs to their heaven and overrun a dozen bunkers. One of them, the little Mexican and Pvt. Robert Douglas were pretty sure when Web Allen caught up with them, both exhausted but unscathed, was the one where Sgt. Clark was hit. They approached this bunker and found at its low rear entrance four dead Japs, the other farm boy, likewise dead, and Barney Clark's head. Or what was left of it. The Japs (before beheading Barney, presumably) had gouged his eyes out, cut off his nose and ears and pulled half his teeth.

Web Allen, the little Mexican and Robert Douglas went into the bunker, cautiously, looking for booby-traps, but there weren't any. They were expecting some further horror. They'd all seen the body of a GI briefly held prisoner by the Japs then dumped in the kunai grass. The bunker was damp and dark but there was daylight spilling through the firing slits and the door. It smelled like a shithouse, the little Mexican said. There was shit piled in one corner and two scrawny dead Japs eviscerated by their own grenades on a rough wooden bunk. What was left of Barney Clark lay face up on the dirt floor in a large puddle of drying blood. He was naked but for his torn fatigue pants, those pulled over his rotting shoes. His left knee was shattered. He'd been raped several times judging by the condoms on the floor, emasculated, his genitals lay in the dirt and (before he was decapitated, presumably), disemboweled. His intestines trailed across the floor and there were ants crawling all over them, his shattered knee, other wounds and gaping belly wound.

Pvt. Douglas and the little Mexican killed both the dead Japs again, emptying an M1 clip into each. The bunker Japs, Web Allen surmised, starving to death on a handful of rice a day soaked in swamp water, doomed to die, were not entirely sane. But they died quickly. He tried to imagine Barney Clark, blind, unable even to see the next horror he'd suffer but knowing there'd be one. The Japs no doubt, moonlight filtering through the firing slits, could see what they were doing. Then bitter regret and a sudden disinclination to pursue the speedy prosecution of The War overwhelmed Web Allen. The thing on the floor was Melanie's first-born and he, Web Allen, clearly was responsible for the terrible way it died. He ought never to have let Barney Clark take the patrol out. He had the rank. He ought to have said, No, Sergeant Clark, you're the First Platoon leader, you stay with your platoon. But nobody else had volunteered and the Warren Force patrols order was, well, an order. A damn order. To be obeyed. Or the Army would fall apart.

They pulled Barney Clark's pants up, left most of his intestines in the bunker, found his fatigue jacket, his dogtags in one pocket, wrapped his head in the jacket, carried both parts of him back to the new Fox Co. HQ, where GIs observing his remains cursed as if praying, and buried both parts with little ceremony in a shallow grave marked with a stick, his dogtags tied to the stick. The First Corps GRU (Graves Registration Unit) would dig him up later, along with the other Warren Force dead, and bury him and them again along with the flyboys, bomb victims etc. in the new American military cemetery at Three-Mile Strip.

Maj. Web Allen returned to Battalion HQ but did not though exhausted, curled up on a stretcher beside the Aid Station, a slow drizzle falling, racked by chills and fever, a classic malarial attack, and memories of the late Sgt. Barney Clark in and outside the bunker, sleep at all that night either. "You was sort a deleerus," a medic told him in the morning. "Talkin' about somebody name Melnie."

And at 0900 hours, Maj. Gen. Ernst Schultz, a big man in excellent health wearing crisp fatigues, up from First Corps Advance HQ in Oro Bay to relieve the Warren Force commander and take command thereof, arrived at Battalion HQ on a tour of the front, accompanied by two aides and other Corps brass. There'd be no more lollygagging up on the line in his command, Maj. Gen. Schultz told the weary assembled Battalion staff in his big booming general's voice, and night patrols mounted by the rifle companies would continue in preparation for "the final attack" on Buna Government Station.

"No, I don't think so, Sir," Web Allen said.

"What!" Maj. Gen. Schultz, appalled, said. "Who the hell are you?"

"Major Allen, Sir," Web Allen said. "Battalion S Two. No more patrols, Sir. I lost three good men, last one I sent out. More patrols, we'll just lose more good men."

Maj. Gen. Schultz as the saying goes looked Web Allen up and down, saw something, perhaps several things, he did not like and, no man to waste time, said, "The major here is relieved." Then told one aide, a first john, "Take him to Dobodura. Put him on an airplane to Port Moresby, the 7th Station. I'll have a recommendation." And told the other aide, a captain, "Stuart, you're the S Two now, this sorry battalion."

The first john rounded up a jeep and drove Web Allen to the Dobodura airstrip, an hour's drive over a muddy track, some of it corduroy road, in the course of which they did not converse much, and by 1300 hours Web Allen was asleep as if dead on a cot in the Officers Ward at the 7th Station Hospital beside Seven-Mile Strip.

Some days later, the badly wounded had priority, he was in a real bed in a locked ward at the 5th General Hospital in Brisbane, awaiting his first session with the shrink. The shrink was a fat captain in a natty uniform, ten years younger than Web Allen, who wore glasses with heavy black frames he liked to remove and tap his front teeth with. They had three more sessions over the next three weeks: the shrink claimed to be pretty busy. Web Allen went on at some length initially about the late Barney Clark, the terrible way in which he died and the fact that he, Web Allen, might have prevented that.

The shrink's treatment of choice was, "Best put that behind you, Major. You were only doing your duty. I feel you've vented your anger, your grief and, perhaps, some normal guilt. I find that encouraging. It's best we not submerge anger or other strong emotions. But I believe it's time now you put that event behind you. A traumatic experience, I grant you. Combat is traumatic. Essentially, it's far beyond the parameters of our previous experience. The War in and of itself is traumatic for all of us. In fact, I'm working on a little monograph, I believe that explains the wide use of profanity in the services. Without profanity, few service personnel have vocabularies adequate to describe the traumatic events, real or imagined, they encounter."

Traumatic anyway, and real, for the late Sgt. Barney Clark Jr. And the goddamn shrink, a real asshole, had the gall to include himself in this litany of woe. What did he know about trauma? Or, safe and dry and fed regularly in a General Hospital in Brisbane, combat?

The shrink also said something puzzling at their last session. "I understand, Major, you're a close friend of the governor in Wisconsin. I did some graduate work in Madison." Had Web Allen confused perhaps with his brother Alvin, a deputy commissioner in the Wisconsin Department of Revenue? Web Allen had no comment and the shrink's diagnosis and prognosis finally was "Combat Fatigue, improving." Coupled with it was Maj. Gen. Schultz's promised recommendation: "Unfit for combat command." Swiftly thereafter came a GHQ Order transferring "Allen, Webster R., Maj., Inf." to the Quartermaster Corps and the Post Exchange Section at Service Force HQ in Sydney. Where, in June, along came a War Department Order promoting "Allen, Webster R., Maj., QMC" to lieutenant colonel. In July he ran afoul of Brig. Gen S.O. Bargle in the Officers' Mess and in September along came another WDO promoting "Allen, Webster R., Lt. Col., QMC" to bird colonel, with which rank he was the logical choice, despite Brig. Gen Bargle's objections, to command the Townsville Base Section following Col. Ballsup's transfer to Tasmania.

Is there, Web Allen wonders, somewhere in the United States Army, an unfortunate Maj. Webster R. Allen with a serial number like his but for one digit wondering why the hell he's never been promoted? It's possible. Likely in fact. One explanation anyway. Maybe the only explanation. Whatever, four stars are peeping through the ragged clouds over Castle Hill. Like the four stars worn by Maj. Gen. Schultz.

* * *

Saljeski halts his panel truck at the Barrier Arms at 0230 hours. Garbutt Road is still full of puddles and a late-comer to the Manor party reported the Ross River over its banks, but there's been no rain since 1100.

"Thanks for the lift," Porky Wallace says. "Fuckin party was a bust, huh? I give my left nut for a piece ass! I struck out this whole fuckin trip! And now we flyin' back to Guinea and I got a hard-on like I don't know what! You gonna give us a ride out the field, right?"

"Roger," Saljeski says. "I'm gonna pick up Lieutenant Gote and them and Rose Pearl, the fuckin Manor, oh-six-thirty, then you and your radio guy."

"Maybe that Rose Pearl like to join the Mile-High Club," Porky says, but doubts his luck is that good. "Say, y'know that booze was liberated? I wunner was Loo'tent Gote in on that? He was all fired up, load and fly right back to Seven-Mile, we land. But then we got that flat on the airplane and it start rainin' and all."

Saljeski shrugs. "I don't know nuthin' about that fuckin booze. I'm ready hit the sack, my fuckin tent ain't under water. See you inna morning."

"Roger." Porky gets out of the truck and goes into the Barrier

Arms: Louise will be along with the morning tea in less than four hours.

Saljeski makes a U-turn on Garbutt Road, zips through the busy intersection, the last MP on traffic detail there off duty at 2000 hours, and heads for Happy Valley. He's supposed to leave his truck at the Base Section Motor Pool overnight but the Motor Pool duty sergeant, a basketball freak Saljeski recently presented with a basketball removed from the SSO's athletic supplies, will check it in and out on paper and Saljeski will need it first thing in the morning for the run to Garbutt Field.

Splashing through the potholes on Charters Road, Saljeski decides he won't dwell on the MP platoon said to be standing by ready to search aircraft and starts spending the $14,000 and change he'll soon, with just a little luck, have. He won't change the name at Fazio's but he'll put a sign on the door, Under New Management, install a new jukebox with lots of flashing lights, dump the old Italian songs, who needs opera, aim for a younger crowd, offer a Happy Hour, half-price drinks. All the nearby neighborhood bars will hate him, he starts a Happy Hour, but what the hell.

5

**19 DECEMBER 1943
GENERAL HEADQUARTERS, SOUTHWEST PACIFIC AREA
DAILY COMMUNIQUE**

Allied Ground Forces under the command of Gen. Douglas MacArthur continued mopping-up operations at Arawe and in the Finschafen area and launched long-range patrols in the Markham Valley. Allied Air Force under General MacArthur's command flew 105 sorties inflicting heavy damage to enemy positions and personnel at Wewak and Madang and at Cape Gloucester on New Britain. Light Naval Forces under Gen. MacArthur's command sank two enemy barges off Arawe.

* * *

Sgt. Porky Wallace, his internal alarm clock set, wakes at 0600 hours with a hard-on like a Long Tom loaded, not locked and ready to fire. Outside the sun is shining and Louise is at his bedside with his tea, the only mug on her tray, she's a little early, staring at the bump in his sheet. Porky grips the sheet with his toes and pulls it down to his navel. He'll be out of the Arms, long gone, in thirty minutes, safely out of Biff Smith's reach.

"You want to see it, Louise?"

"See wot?"

"This!" Porky yanks the sheet to his knees. Louise stares, wide-eyed, and gurgles. Blimey, it is as big as a banger! Looks like one too, though somewhat lighter in color. Like a banger somebody peeled the skin off one end. Louise leans for a better look. Her tray tilts, the mug slides across its tin surface, tips and dumps a pint of tea at a temperature slightly below 212 F. through the mosquito net onto Porky's genitals.

Porky screams. The mug falls to the floor. Louise squeals, grabs the mug and scoots from the room and below stairs Biff Smith bellows, "Wot the bloody 'ell's goin' on up there!"

Porky stifles another scream, moans, grabs the sheet, wraps it around his scorched equipment and hears Louise explaining, somewhat hysterically, "Hi drop the Sar'ent's tay, Da. But 'e don't want henny now."

Cpl. Johnson pops into the room in his skivvies. "What happen? You yell."

Porky, grounded in a puddle of steaming tea, writhes and moans. "Oh jeezuzz! She spill tea on me! I'm all burnt!" He lifts the sheet. His cock looks like a shriveled red pepper, it's sprouting white blisters and so are his balls. "Oh jeezuzz! I'm all blister! I need help! Help me, you asshole!"

Johnson helps Porky get out of his bed with many moans and stifled screams and into his uniform (pants unbuttoned, shirttail out, shoes unlaced), then scrambles into his own uniform and they go down the backstairs, dodging Biff Smith, by the Tivoli Cinema and across Flinders Street to the Pro Station, Porky moaning the while, bent double like a man with severe abdominal cramps.

"Jeezuzz!" the Pro Station medic who examines Porky says. "I never seen nuthin' like this before! Your dong just one big blister, Sar'ent! We ain't equipped, handle this. You better go the 12th Station."

"How, f'chrissake!" Porky says. "I can't fuckin walk!"

"Those prolly third-degree burns," the other medic, taking a look and offering his professional opinion, says. "I guess maybe we can call a amblance."

"You do that!" Porky says, and the medic goes to the phone. "Go back the Arms, Johnson. Loo'tent Gote comes, tell him what happen. I'm all burnt. I'm inna hospital. I can't fuckin fly." Johnson departs and Porky sits, gingerly, there are blisters on his butt, on the bench in the Pro Station, squeezing his genitals. Squeezing them seems to ease the pain, a little.

"Sar'ent Wallace, he had a accident!" Cpl. Johnson, babbling through the passenger window on Saljeski's truck outside the Barrier Arms, says. "Pretty bad accident! He's the 12th Station. Girl brings the tea spill it on him! All over his uh, well, you know, private parts? He's burnt pretty bad! He can't fly. We went the Pro Station and they call a amblance for him!"

"Oh shit!" Billy Gote, in the front seat with Rose Pearl Stevens, says. Eddie Devlin and Lt. Ronald Donald are in the back with everybody's baggage, the movies in cans and the broken projector. "Well, christ, we'll fly without him then. Go get your stuff, Johnson. His too. Check out. On the double! Field's gonna be a goddamn madhouse next couple hours. We ain't got time, commiserate with Porky. Eddie, you're gonna be a flight engineer this trip. Work out better maybe, they checkin' Travel Priorities. They be too busy, check air crews IDs."

"I ain't got enough money, pay our rooms," Johnson says.

"Oh christ, here." Billy gives Johnson a ten-quid note. Johnson scoots into the Arms, settles with Biff Smith, tells Biff when queried Sergeant Wallace went out the airfield already, returns with his and Porky's musette bags and climbs in with Eddie and Lt. Donald.

Saljeski finds a gap behind a 12th Station ambulance in the heavy traffic bound for Garbutt Field and away they go, splashing through the potholes still full of rain. They're held up well short of the new bridge. The Ross River is over its banks, muddy water spread across the flat ground on both sides of Garbutt Road, the AMF Bofors crew marooned with their gun on the small rise that's an island now. Billy Gote, impatient, worried, drums the dash with his fingers while eastbound traffic splashes by.

A face appears pressed against the glass in one of the windows in the ambulance's rear doors. "My god!" Rose Pearl says. "That's Colonel Allen!"

"Hey! We're movin'," Saljeski says.

They follow the ambulance over the bridge, posted 5 MPH now, muddy water splashing its planks The RAAF sentry waves them through the Main Gate. Garbutt Field, shut down for two days by The Bloody Wet, is indeed a madhouse. A dozen deuce-and-a-halfs are competing for parking space at the Air Freight sheds. There's a double frieze of servicemen of two nations laden with gear milling about outside the ATOP. Flots and Jets, blonde hair awry, and Pops are wrestling a new doughnut machine into the Canteen. Wing Cmdr. Hewlitt-Packard and Sgt. Keeney, standing beside their Afrika Korps command car adjacent to the Canteen, are directing traffic on this busy morning. Two B24s and a C60 are running their engines up on the apron, battering all present with noise. There's no room to park outside the Ops office at the base of the Control Tower, jeeps and staff cars and the ambulance transporting Col. Allen crowding its Western fence. Sgt. Harry Parker and two massive MPs with slung tommy-guns and musette are waiting there.

"Drive around, Sal," Billy Gote says. "Wait for us. C'mon, Rose Pearl. I got to get clearance and put you and Harry and them MPs on my manifest."

Easier said than done. Ops is jammed. U.S. Rep. Festus Lee Claypool and party are there along with a great many other hopeful passengers. Calvin Winsome, the flunky GHQ captain and two dozen pilots seeking clearances are crowding the counter and the captain who runs Ops is fighting them off, his current place in the "Origin of Species" forgotten.

"Awright! Congressman's party!" the Ops captain shouts. "There's a C-Sixty on the apron you can board." Rep. Claypool and his entourage, which now includes Sigge Ferk, gather up their considerable baggage and push out of Ops. "The rest you, listen up! Just wait, goddamn it! I know you all got high priority travel orders and priority freight. But wait! I got a general I got to get out of here and another one coming in I got to get out and he's got a flat on his airplane. Sergeant, call the Air Depot again, get their ass over here, fix that flat! Lieutenant Martin! You're cleared to Sydney with that Service Force general, he shows up. I got a Five-A nut case going to Brisbane I got to get out of here too and the courier plane. I maybe put the nut case on that. And I got that ATC Fifty-Four, first one Direct from the States, ETA in thirty-minutes. I get them I mention out of here, Fifty-Four lands, then you people can fly. So line up, goddamn it! I take you one at a time for ETDs."

Billy Gote and Rose Pearl, jumping the line forming, push up to the counter and Rose Pearl, a female, gets special attention, though quickly disappointed.

"Jeezuzz, lady," the Ops captain says. "Two-A Priority. You ain't got a chance here. I got orders, load everything northbound Fours and Fives. I doubt you got much chance at ATOP either, but that's where you got to go, lady. Wish you luck. Okay, Lieutenant, where you bound?" Seven-Mile, Billy Gote says. "Roger. How many passengers you can take?"

"I'm loaded," Billy Gote says. "Fourteen-thousand pounds ammo, full crew. I guess I can take these MPs, they all Five-As. Put them my manifest. Parker, Harold, Sergeant, and uh."

"Benson, Carl, Private," Harry says. "Jukes, Ercell, Private."

"Them and one more," the Ops captain says. "I got a war correspondent. Real pain in the ass. You take him. Mister Hull!" David Dudley Hull emerges from the crowd lugging a great deal of baggage. INS told him the 20-pound Forward Area limit is seldom enforced.

"I can't take him," Billy Gote says. "He's got too much stuff!

I be overweight."

"No you won't," the Ops captain says. "Or you can wait. I put him on somebody else's airplane, I'll clear you, ETD maybe fourteen-hundred. Take him, I clear you now, ETD maybe oh-eight-thirty. Check with the Tower on that. You happy take the asshole?"

Billy Gote shrugs. "Roger, you say so, captain." Time's ticking away. There's that MP platoon standing by to search aircraft and Sunday though it be the heavy hand of GHQ may expedite that at any moment. The sooner the Lucky Lil's up up and away into the wild blue yonder with the booze the better.

"Mister Hull," the Ops captain says. "You flying with Lieutenant Gote here. Next!"

Billy Gote, Rose Pearl, Harry, Pvts. Benson and Jukes and David Dudley Hull, struggling with his baggage, leave Ops and flag Saljeski, circling the ramp in his truck with Eddie Devlin, Lt. Donald and Cpl. Johnson aboard. They somehow all pile into the truck, Hull's baggage a real nuisance, drop Rose Pearl at the ATOP and drive out along the taxiway, the truck low to the ground with nine people aboard, three of them very large, to the Lucky Lil's hardstand.

"Where are you from in The States, Lieutenant?" David Dudley Hall, a journalist hard at work, always on the ball, says. He hopes this pilot though he looks like he might be a hot-rod is in fact a careful cautious pilot with lots of experience. His airplane, David Dudley Hall heard him say so, is full of ammunition!

"Kansas," Billy Gote says, and that's that, no story there.

Saljeski halts his truck outside the hardstand, muddy now with the dirt the rain washed off the revetment. They climb out, but for Saljeski, lugging their baggage. The sun's beating down, glittering off main runway's steel matting, and the temperature's rising fast.

"Thanks for the lift, Sal," Billy Gote says. "I'll be in touch."

"I'll stick around, wave you a fuckin goodbye," Saljeski says. He'd like to see the booze aboard the Lucky Lil up up and away

"Whatever," Billy Gote says. He leads everybody else across the muddy hardstand, removes the DANGER AMMUNITION sign and opens the Lil's cabin door. "Okay. Our ETD's damn near an hour yet and it prolly pretty hot in the airplane. But you all get in. Don't fool with that ammo. You do the cockpit pre-flight, copilot. I'll check the flaps."

Lt. Donald, Johnson, Eddie, Benson, Jukes and David Dudley Hall climb into the Lil, careful not to fool with the ammunition. The B24s take off, roaring down the main runway one behind the other and Billy Gote begins a cursory pre-flight inspection, checking the flaps.

Harry joins him. "Look like we got it made, Lieutenant! But we might be cuttin' it pretty thin. That goldurn general, Bargle, and Colonel Fogerty was in the Provost's office when we leave the Company and what I heard, they was expectin' word from GHQ any minute give them authority they can stomp all over the RAAF and start searchin' aircraft."

"Hell with the pre-flight then," Billy Gote says. "Let's get in the airplane."

A jeep full of air crew whizzes by and pulls into the adjacent hardstand, where Brig. Gen. Humphrey (Humpty Dumpty) Dumphy's C47 waits. Profanity and exclamations of dismay promptly follow and Straight Arrow Hunker appears around the end of the Lucky Lil's revetment.

"Jeezuzz!" Hunker says. "There's a goddamn dog tied my airplane! He was there when I come out and check my airplane, oh-six-hundred, and he's still there! He like to chew on anybody goes near the airplane! He damn near chew on Moneybags Sheldon. And I got a flat tire! Goddamn Air Depot. I call them but they ain't come and fix it yet! And my general, I check with Ops, he's on his way. Left Brisbane at first light in a goddamn A-Twenty!" That's a speedy light bomber.

"Well, you got your problems, Straigth Arrow," Billy Gote says. "I got a ETD, oh-eight-thirty," and climbs into the Lucky Lil with Harry.

"Your men at the ready, Sergeant?" Wing Cmdr. Hewlitt-Packard, directing a deuce-and-a-half loaded with 81mm mortar rounds and displaying a DANGER AMMUNITION sign to the Air Freight sheds, says.

"Sir!" Sgt. Keeney says. "Hat the ready, Sir. Six harmed men in one the Fiats hup the taxiw'y. Other reports, Sir. Bloody great dog still tied the suspect haircraft. No sign yet, Hair Depot Yanks wi' a tire for hit. Lance Jack Binsley monitoring bloody Yank communications."

"Good work, Sergeant," Hewlitt-Packard says. "We'll be waiting for that bloody general, he tries to board his bloody aircraft. Bloody Yank will have the rank, but we'll wave that bloody order, MacArthur's Headquarters, came yesterday. Implement appropriate action forthwith. Confiscate the bloody plonk!"

"Saddle up!" Maj. Dickinson the Provost Marshal bawls. Sixty 301st MPs, belted and buckled and armed, start climbing into four deuce-and-a-halfs parked at the Company gate behind Dickinson's command jeep and a spanking new staff car, a '41 Ford with Pfc. Stefanelli, somewhat hungover, at the wheel. Brig.Gen. S.O. Bargle and Lt. Col. Parnell Fogerty jump in the staff car. Fogerty's ears are still red and swollen. Bargle's nose still looks like a tomato and his shiner's a deep purple. The word came through less than a minute ago, a direct call, GHQ to Brig. Gen. Bargle in the 301st Orderly Room.

"You know something, Colonel?" Bargle says. "I don't think Allen ever did call GHQ, relative your liquor problem. There's no record he did anyway on the phone logs. I think he was just pulling your chain."

"Bastard!" Fogerty says.

"And I had difficulty. Everybody at GHQ goes to the beach weekends. Except MacArthur. I finally got hold of a classmate. Major General Oliver Blunder. In Coolangatta. We used to call him Blunderbus at The Point. He went to bat for you. Authority's verbal but RAAF HQ in Brisbane is supposed to inform the RAAF runs your airfield. Via teletype."

"What the hell's holding us up?" Fogerty wails. "Goddamn flyboys swiped our booze might be taking off awready! With our booze!"

"Doubt it," Bargle says. "Aircraft I ordered will have priority. And the one laid on for that congressman. Claypop. The one whose niece was raped. By the way, remind me to put a commendation through for the MP officer who conducted that investigation. He did fine work. And I want that MP captain who ran into me and the MP on traffic duty who left his post disciplined! Severely!"

"Will do, Sir," Fogerty says. This is no time to explain the conflict unfortunately inherent in all that. "Well, jeezuzz, finally!"

The MPs are all aboard the trucks. "Let's roll!" Maj. Dickinson, jumping in his jeep, bawls, and his jeep and the Ford lead this convoy out onto North Flinders Street at a good clip. The MPs in the first deuce will peel off at intervals and halt any cross traffic and all the vehicles have their headlights on, signaling an urgent mission.

The convoy rips through Townsville at 40 mph, startling the military personnel and civilians up and about and very nearly hitting the Cummins sisters at the foot of Hill Street, on foot with their tandem bike laid up for repairs. It swings onto Garbutt Road by the Tivoli Cinema and the Barrier Arms, startling Louise, busy pulling tea-stained sheets off the Sergeant's bunkbed, then stops, halted by a long line of westbound traffic waiting to cross the new bridge.

"Oh shit!" Fogerty wails.

Maj. Dickinson leaps from his jeep, runs to the bridge, splashing through potholes, and grabs the MP directing traffic there. Considerable confusion ensues but the eastbound traffic is halted, a tanker backs off the bridge, very nearly toppling into the Ross River, over its banks now, and the convoy pulls out of line, bumps over the bridge, slows, picks up Dickinson and resumes speed, hitting 50 mph.

"Oh shit!" Fogerty wails. "There's a goddamn flyboy! Taking off! Looks like a goddamn Forty-Seven!" The 47, it is a 47, rising off the north end of the main Garbutt Field runway, makes a wide climbing turn to port. It's southbound. Fogerty heaves a great sigh of relief and the convoy sails through the Main Gate, ignoring the RAAF sentry, and slides to a halt. It's that or run over Wing Cmdr. Hewlitt-Packard and Sgt. Keeney.

"Damn!" Bargle says. "My plane was supposed to have priority! All right, let's find the ranking RAAF officer and get this search underway." He climbs from the Ford followed by Fogerty and promptly encounters the ranking RAAF officer.

"What the bloody hell is this!" Wing Cmdr. Hewlitt-Packard says. "Get those bloody lorries out of the way. They're blocking traffic. Who the bloody hell are you?"

"I, Sir," Bargle says, in his big general's voice. "Am Brigadier-General Sedgewick O. Bargle, deputy commander, United States Army Service Force, Southwest Pacific Area, and I have orders for the Royal Australian Air Force commander, Garbutt Field."

"I'm the bloody field commander," Wing Cmdr. Hewlitt-Packard says. "Move those bloody lorries! Park them somewhere. Now! You're holding up the bloody war."

"Sir!" Brig. Gen. Bargle says. "I have a GHQ Order, verbal but nonetheless binding as you well know, granting my command here authority to search the aircraft on this airfield. As you were informed, supposed to be informed, by Royal Australian Air Force Headquarters. I have good reason to believe there is a valuable shipment aboard one of the aircraft. A shipment that was pilfered."

"Bloody valuable plonk! What bloody I was informed? Show me your bloody verbal order!"

"Don't be an ass, Sir!"

"Arse my bloody arse! Get your bloody lorries off my airfield!"

A skinny RAAF clerk, Lance Jack Digby Binsley, pops out of the RAAF barracks waving a yellow teletype, races across the ramp dodging the puddles and settles this sticky Allied Relations Problem. The teletype's from RAAF HQ in Brisbane, confirming Brig. Gen Bargle's verbal order.

"Bloody well then," Wing Cmdr. Hewlett-Packard says with exceedingly bad grace, bloody Yanks run the bloody war these days. "Go look for your bloody plonk."

At which instant Col. Robert (Big Bob) Betrandus comes tumbling down the Control Tower stairs waving his arms, pointing in the general direction of Hawaii, trailed by Lt. Col. Gerber and Maj. Richall. "Fifty-Four's coming in!" Big Bob bawls. "First one Direct from The States!"

Ops also knows this. The word spreads like wildfire and, like The Spirit of Bataan's arrival, this historic event takes precedence over all else. U.S. officers and GIs, Flots, Jets, Pops and RAAF other ranks pour out of Ops, the Canteen, the hangars, the Air Freight sheds, the ATOP, the USAAC Transient Area and the RAAF barracks. The 301st MPs on the search detail jump from their trucks and so do the drivers. Squinting into the blazing sun in the northeastern sky, all watch the C54, a big fat silver bird with four engines, three hours out of Noumea, descend. It drifts across the north end of the field, flies its downwind leg away to the west, executes a wide 180-degree turn to port, drops its wheels, slides across Garbutt Road, touches down, Direct From The States via Honolulu etc., and rolls along the main runway. A ragged cheer greets its arrival.

Big Bob, Gerber and Richall pile into Big Bob's staff car parked outside Ops. Bargle and Fogerty jump in their Ford. Half a dozen jeeps fill with other curious. The C54 rolls by the Control Tower and along the main runway, slows, executes a 90-degree onto the parallel taxiway and rolls along the taxiway, then halts, confronted by the traffic racing up the taxiway in defiance of the field's 10 mph limit. It halts adjacent to the hardstands occupied by the Lucky Lil and Brig. Gen. Dumphy's C47, looming over Saljeski's truck. Its props wind down. Hewlitt-Packard and Sgt. Keeney are coming along too at 10 mph in their Afrika Korps command car and the 301st MP detail and other personnel are thundering up the taxiway on foot, at the double. Saljeski jumps from his truck: he's got a ringside seat. So have Lt. Hunker and his crew. Cpl. Johnson and Eddie scoot through the Lucky Lil's cargo compartment, Johnson pops the cabin door and along with the passengers aboard they peer from the open door at the first C54 Direct from The States. Billy Gote and Lt. Donald watch from the cockpit.

All these spectators are amply rewarded. A half-ton truck loaded with GIs and the portable stairway, dispatched by Ops, weaves through the other traffic and rolls up to the 54. The GIs push the stairway into place beneath the 54's cabin door. The door opens and out steps Linda Lewis, The Blonde Bombshell, star of stage screen and radio. Followed by her faithful secretary and longtime companion, a stocky woman in shapeless khakis struggling with three bulging valpaks and other miscellaneous baggage. Linda Lewis' khakis fit her ripe figure like the paint on an airplane. She has in her arms a small hairy little dog. Pausing, she treats all present to her famous smile then sways down the steps, a living promise of unimaginable carnal pleasures. A hundred shrill whistles and wolf howls, louder than the Mormon Tabernacle Choir in full voice, greet her.

"At ease, you men!" Brig. Gen. Bargle, emerging from his Ford, bawls (a voice crying in the wilderness for all the good that does) and heads for the foot of the stairway, trailed by Lt. Col. Fogerty.

But it's Col. Big Bob Betrandus gets there first. "Welcome to Swappa, Miss Lewis!" Big Bob says, beaming, extending a big hand. Linda Lewis grasps it and the hairy little dog, squirming, jumps or falls from her other arm, lands hard on the taxiway blacktop, squeals, bounces up and scoots through the crowd, grabbed at but missed by Moneybags Sheldon, into the hardstand with Brig. Gen. Dumphy's airplane.

"Mayer!" Linda Lewis squeals. She's under contract to MGM but doesn't much like L.B., he puts her in lousy films. Mayer (the dog) ignores her and trots right up to Attila, on guard beneath the cabin door on Brig. Gen. Dumphy's airplane. Attila observes this strange life form with interest. It smells edible and Attila, Saljeski forgot to feed him, is hungry. He pins Mayer with one forepaw, crunches Mayer's head and starts eating Mayer, hair and all. Linda Lewis screams, finds Lt. Col. Gerber close at hand and faints. Gerber catches her and, opportunity knocking, cops a feel, surprised to find her mighty bosom feels sort of rubbery, like sponge rubber, which it is, a secret known only to five-thousand people in Show Business including Siggie Ferk.

Big Bob, proving chivalry is not dead, leads the charge to the hardstand, grabbing en route and hauling along a search detail MP, Pvt. Vincent D. Poole, Leonard's little brother, another former Upper Darby cop. They enlisted together with the understanding they'd serve together and the Army for once kept its promise.

"Shoot that big dog, soldier!" Big Bob, pushing Pvt. V. Poole forward, bawls.

Pvt. V. Poole draws his Forty-Five, jacks a round into the chamber, then hesitates. He has a dog named Fred back home. "I can't, Sir," he says. "Shoot a dog."

"Shoot the goddamn dog!" Big Bob bawls. "That's an order, soldier!"

"I can't Sir," Pvt. V. Poole says.

"Gimme the goddamn gun then!" Big Bob, grabbing at Pvt. V. Poole's Forty-Five, bawls. "I'll shoot the goddamn dog!"

"No. Don't, Sir! Please, Sir!" Pvt. V. Poole, clinging tight to his Forty-Five, says. The MP cadre hammered it into him in training: never ever no matter what surrender your weapon.

"Give it me, goddamn it!" Big Bob snarls and they struggle for the Forty-Five. Big Bob's bigger but Pvt. V. Poole though small for an MP (5-11, 185 pounds) is wiry and younger, and the Forty-Five fires, its heavy roar followed instantly by Big Bob's piercing howl when the round rips through his right flight boot, shattering his big toe, ricochets, nicking Lt. Col. Fogerty's left ear and sails off into the wild blue yonder. Fogerty howls and grabs his ear.

Big Bob dances around on his left foot, howling he's wounded and wants that man's name, the man who shot him. Lt. Col. Gerber cops another spongy rubber feel, hands Linda Lewis to her faithful companion and rushes to Big Bob's aid. Pvt. V. Poole holsters his Forty-Five and melts into the MP detail. Attila, Mayer all gone, settles on his stomach, licking his fangs, honey-colored hair all over his muzzle.

Gerber and Richall bundle Big Bob into their staff car and rush him off, still howling, to the 12th Station Hospital. Between howls, Big Bob abruptly aborts their half-formed plan to seize the missing booze. "Screw the goddamn booze!" he says. "I'm wounded!"

Linda Lewis sobs and embraces her faithful companion. Brig.Gen. Bargle offers condolences and puts them in his Ford. "It ate Mayer!" Linda Lewis wails between sobs while surveying herself in her compact. "Ate him all up, Mattie! Oh shit, my mascara's a mess!"

Pfc. Steffanelli, at the wheel in the Ford, realizes he'll have something tell his kids, he ever he has any, they ask, What you do in the The War, Daddy? I saw a MP shoot a colonel in the foot and a dog eat a movie star's dog and she sit in my car, bawling!

All this excitement gradually subsides. Most of the vehicles parked on and along the taxiway depart. Most of the spectators slowly disperse, trading sundry versions of the recent events. A dozen officer replacements lugging valpaks who watched those events from the 54, they'll long remember their arrival in Swappa, disembark, load into a deuce-and-a half and depart for the 3rd Repple Depple. The portable stairway is removed. The C54 winds up its props and rolls down the taxiway to the apron: Brisbane and Sydney await its arrival. Lt. Hunker and his crew return to their standoff with Attila. Lt. Col. Fogerty, a bloody o.d. handkerchief clamped to his ear, and Maj. Dickinson round up the MP search detail and assemble it on the taxiway. Pvt. V. Poole remains in its midst keeping his head down, modestly accepting murmured congratulations, resigned to the fact he'll have to clean his Forty-Five. Brig. Gen. Bargle, Fogerty, Dickinson and the detail commander, Second Lt. Michael Sweeney, confer. Wing Cmdr. Hewlitt-Packard and Sgt. Keeney observe this conference from their Afrika Korps command car parked fifty yards up the taxiway now beside a RAAF Fiat in which Sgt. Keeney's six harmed men are discussing with some amazement the recent entertainment provided by the bloody Yanks.

A Second Air Depot half-ton arrives with a sergeant, Pvts. Frenchie LaCroix and Dade Brewer and a tire for Brig. Gen. Dumphy's airplane. But the sergeant refuses to mount the tire or even try "until somebody gets that goddamn big dog out of there." Lt. Hunker advances on Attila but halts when Attila growls and shows his fangs and the standoff with Attila continues. "No way, that goddamn dog's here," the sergeant says.

Capt. Fats Forney arrives, late as usual, in a '41 Studebaker staff car, finds Linda Lewis and her companion in Bargle's Ford, introduces himself, welcomes Miss Lewis to Swappa, says he has quarters for Miss Lewis and an "evening officers' reception" for her laid on at the George Hotel, also some visits to troops if Miss Lewis feels up to that, and wonders who the lady with Miss Lewis is?

"Mattie Fratt," Linda Lewis, busy restoring her mascara, says. "My secretary. The USO wanted to send an officer with me but I said no. Mattie's been on all my tours. She knows how to handle things. If you don't have quarters for her she can share mine."

Saljeski, this no place for him with Forney present, gets Billy Gote's attention up in the Lucky Lil's cockpit, points a finger at the MP detail, gives Billy a V for Victory sign and gets into his truck and departs. Forney helps Linda Lewis and Mattie Fratt out of Bargle's Ford and into his Studebaker, tells his driver, Cpl. Bruno Fazoli, "Put the ladies' baggage in the trunk," and gets into the Studebaker with them. Fazoli puts the ladies' baggage in the trunk, no 40-pound limits for them, they got enough they could stay the Duration, gets behind the wheel and away they go. And in his rearview mirror Fazoli watches Mattie Fratt hug Linda Lewis. "Please don't cry, honey," Mattie says. "We'll get another little dog." Jeez, a couple lez! Fazoli's a man of the world, pretty sophisticated.

"Okay," Billy Gote, up in the Lucky Lil's cockpit, says. "Show's over. Go tell Johnson shut the damn door. Tell our passengers get settled. We're about ready to roll, I hope."

Lt. Donald does that and returns to his copilot's seat. Johnson pulls the cabin door shut and returns to his cubicle. Eddie Devlin slides into the flight engineer's cubicle. Harry Parker, Pvts. Benson and Jukes and David Dudley Hull settle on the hard plastic seats beside the tarped cargo, which David Dudley Hull, more or less terrified, judges to be a considerable amount of ammunition.

Billy Gote starts the Gert's engines. Both cough, sputter, belch blue smoke, then settle into a reassuring roar, though the port engine's running a little rough. Just a smidgen. Billy runs the engines up, throttles them back and converses with the Garbutt Field Contol Tower.

"Oh shit!" he says. "Tower says we're on hold. There's a A-Twenty with a goddamn general on it just landed and the courier's ahead of us, take off."

The conference on the taxiway concludes. Brig. Gen. Bargle, Lt. Col. Fogerty, Maj. Dickinson and Lt. Sweeney lead the MP detail into the hardstand ruled by Attila. Flopped down on his belly beneath the cabin door on Brig. Gen. Dumphy's airplane, spitting hair, Attila rises, growls and displays his fangs.

"Is the pilot who flies this aircraft present?" Brig. Gen. Bargle, his big general's voice booming in view of the noise produced by the Dirty Gert's engines, says.

"I'm the pilot, Sir," Lt. Hunker, stepping forward and briskly saluting, says.

"Step aside then," Brig. Gen. Bargle, returning the salute, says. "We are going to search your aircraft, Lieutenant. We have reason to believe there is stolen liquor aboard your aircraft and there is a GHQ Order, as you may know, prohibiting the transport of liquor to Forward Areas. Now get that dog away from the aircraft and open the cabin door."

"And if there's bloody plonk on it," Wing Cmdr. Hewlitt Packard, steaming into the hardstand with Sgt. Keeney and his six harmed men, says. "I shall implement appropriate action forthwith, per that bloody order, and confiscate the bloody plonk."

"Oh no you won't, Sir," Brig.Gen. Bargle, restraining Lt. Col. Fogerty, says. "The liquor will be returned to its rightful owner."

"Our booze!" Fogerty gargles.

"The bloody hell it will!" Hewlett-Packard says. "This is my airfield. I'm the bloody airfield commander."

"And I, Sir," Brig. Gen. Bargle says. "I am the ranking Allied Forces officer present!"

"General, Sir, Wing Commander," Lt. Hunker says. "All due respect. But this is Brigadier-General Humphrey Dumphy's personal aircraft. He's First Corps deputy commander and I swear, word of an officer, there's no liquor on this aircraft. General Dumphy doesn't drink."

"Humpty Dumpty Dumphy?" Bargle gargles. Lt. Hunker nods. "Oh shit!"

"Then what's the goddamn dog doing here, Lieutenant?" Fogerty says. "What's the goddamn dog guarding, it ain't booze?"

"I have absolutely no idea, Sir," Hunker says. "All I know is the dog was here when I came out this morning, check the aircraft. Which I haven't done yet. All I did was call the Air Depot, get a new tire. But we can't mount it. The dog won't let us near the aircraft. I'm afraid of dogs, Sir. Dogs like that one."

"Nonsense!" Fogerty says. "You a coward or something, Lieutenant? Get the goddamn dog out of there!" Another 47 is rolling off the apron onto the main runway, his ears hurt, especially the one the MP nicked with his Forty-Five, and his morning coffee laced with gin is curdling in his belly.

"How, Sir?" Lt. Hunker says.

"Hell then I'll do it!" Fogerty says, and advances on the aircraft. Attila gets to his feet, the hair on his back rises, he shows his fangs and emits a low growl and Fogerty halts, then retreats.

"We're not going to waste any more time!" Bargle says, turning on an MP, Pvt. Edgar Eveleigh, a large Las Vegas, Nevada, real estate salesman in civil life. "I don't care whose aircraft this is! Shoot that damn dog, soldier. Or by god I will!" Then remembers the disaster that befell Big Bob Betrandus. "No, you shoot it. That's an order, soldier!"

Pvt. Eveleigh, who owns no dog and never did, draws his Forty-Five, whacks a round into the chamber and takes aim at Attila. But a jeep sails into the hardstand, skids to a halt and a squat little man in crisp fatigues with brigadier's stars leaps from it.

"Lower that weapon!" Brig. Gen. Humphrey (Humpty-Dumpty) Dumphy bellows. He has a very loud penetrating voice for such a small man (5-7, 180 pounds) and he's a belligerent little fellow, a regular banty rooster. Pvt. Eveleigh lowers his weapon. "What the hell's going on here? What are all these troops doing here? We ready to roll, Lieutenant? Christ, you got a flat tire! Whose dog is that? Who are you, general? Oh jeezuzz! Stinky Bargle! You're Stinky Bargle! Christ, what happened to your nose?"

"Sir!" Brig. Gen. Bargle, wincing, says. "I was in an automoble accident. And I am, for your information, should you need this information, deputy Service Force commander, Southwest Pacific Area, and I have reason to believe there is stolen liquor aboard this aircraft in probable violation of GHQ Order Four-oh-Four-Forty-Four prohibiting the transport."

"Stinky Bargle! Well I'll be dammed!" Brig.Gen. Dumphy bellows. "Ought-fourteen, right? I used to haze the hell out of you. Last I heard you were passed over. Supposed to retire. And now by god you're a Brigadier! Took a war but you're a Brigadier! As of when?"

"Fifteen May, current year."

"Ha! Thirty-one March, current year! I got the time in grade. I'm the ranking brass around here. Now what the hell's all this about liquor? There's no liquor on my aircraft! I don't touch the stuff. What the hell's the dog doing here?"

"I don't know, Sir," Lt. Hunker says. "All I know is the dog was here when I came out to check the aircraft. It won't let anybody near the aircraft, Sir."

"Bullshit!" Brig. Gen. Dumphy says and marches across the hardstand. Attila bares his fangs and growls. "Down, boy! Down! Good dog!" Attila, sensing a master's voice, subsides, sits, then rolls over, paws in the air and wags his tail. Brig. Gen. Dumphy scratches Attila's belly. "Whose dog is he?" No one present knows. "Well by god then he's mine. Open the airplane, Lieutenant." Brig. Gen. Dumphy strides to the wheel strut, Attila obediently heeling, unties Attila, takes the rope off Attila's collar and coils it while Lt. Hunker, one eye on Attila, opens the cabin door. "In, boy! Jump!" Attila jumps in the airplane. "All right, you men! Get the lead out! Mount that goddamn tire you're fiddling with. As for you, Bargle. You're at attention, Stinky! Superior officer addressing you!" Brig. Gen. Bargle snaps to attention, tucking in his skinny buttocks. "This hallucination you got about liquor you take it somewhere else! And take these troops with you. Now! That's an order! Move 'em out! On the double!"

*"You're at attention, Sir!" Brig. Gen.
Dumphy braces Brig. Gen. Bargle*

"Sir!" Brig. Gen. Bargle says and leads his command in abject retreat out of the hardstand onto the taxiway outside the Lucky Lil's hardstand.

"You get that instrument fixed, Hunker?" Brig. Gen. Dumphy says. Lt. Hunker nods. "Okay! Let's get this show on the road then! Hey! Who the hell are you?"

"I, Sir," Wing Cmdr. Hewlitt-Packard says. "Am the airfield commander. And if in fact there is bloody plonk aboard this aircraft, I shall confiscate."

"Jeezuzz!" Brig. Gen. Dumphy bellows. "I thought we settle that! There's no liquor aboard this aircraft! And I rank you too. Get out of here! Take any these man are your's with you. Now! On the double! You men with the tire, speed it up!"

"Sir!" Wing Cmdr. Hewlitt-Packard, suddenly sick to death of all the bloody Yanks and their bloody plonk and this small belligerent bloody Yank, turns on his heel, dammed if he'll bloody salute, and stalks from the hardstand trailed by Sgt. Keeney and his six harmed men.

"General, Sir!" Lt. Col. Fogerty, aiming a finger at the Lucky Lil, he's not licked yet, grabbing Brig. Gen Bargle's elbow, says. "That might be the one! It's started up! Come on, Sir! We'll stop it and search it!"

Billy Gote, up in the Lucky Lil's cockpit, observes this threatening finger, a scowling brigadier general, other officers and a great many MPs, all staring at the Lucky Lil. "Hell we're on hold!" he says, releasing the brakes and pouring on the power and Brig. Gen. Bargle's command ducks and scatters, it's that or risk decapitation by whirling propellers as the Lil trundles out of the hardstand and rolls down the taxiway.

"Forget it!" Brig. Gen. Bargle snarls, freeing his elbow, abruptly relinquishing his command and climbing into his staff car, his general's cap with the gold braid blown off, upside down in an oily puddle. "Forget your goddamn booze! I'm going back to Sydney. Forthwith." Stinky! The little bastard braced him and called him Stinky! And everybody heard him. You can hear the little bastard a mile.

"But that might be the one!" Lt. Col. Fogerty wails. "The one with our booze!" And sets off at a clumsy run down the taxiway in hot pursuit of the Lucky Lil, grab it by the tail maybe. He steps in an oily puddle, his feet go flying and he lands on his ass in the puddle, wailing, sobbing, "Goddamn flyboys!"

The Lucky Lil rolls down the taxiway and across the apron, missing the first C54 Direct From The States by inches, onto the main runway. The runway's clear. Billy Gote runs the engines up, ignores babble from the Control Tower, he's not got the whole runway but enough, the Lil's lightly loaded, and shoves the throttles far forward. The Lil rolls down the runway, picks up speed, Lt. Col Fogerty shaking a fist at it, lifts from the steel matting with twenty yards to spare, skims the muddy water spread across the flat ground beyond the runway on both sides of the

Ross River and begins its climb, up up and away into the wild blue yonder, 650 miles to go to Seven-Mile Strip.

Pvts. LaCroix and Brewer, struggling with the tire on Brig.Gen. Dumphy's airplane, pause in their work and watch the Lucky Lil fly away and their vague dream of vast wealth fly away with it. "C'mon, you guys, get the lead out," their sergeant says. "I don't want that fuckin little bastard bitchin' at me."

The Control Tower lieutenant phones the Ops captain. "Sir, that Forty-Seven just took off did not contact us, it was on the runway! Might not had clearance, Sir."

"Of course it had clearance!" the Ops captain says. "You trying and get my ass in a sling or something? Now listen up. I got a Service Force general here I'm putting on that Forty-Seven southbound is fourth in line. Move it up, next off. Goddamn general is breathing fire. Claims he had some kind a priority. I want the sonofabitch out of here."

* * *

An hour and ten minutes out of Townsville, sixty miles off the coast in bright sunshine at 7200 feet above the Coral Sea, droning through the sky at 140 miles an hour, the coast a low dark smudge on the western horizon, the Lucky Lil's starboard Pratt & Whitney coughs, sputters, belches blue smoke and quits, this promptly depriving the Lil of 1200 horsepower.

"What the hell!" Billy Gote says and does several things very quickly: disengages George the automatic pilot, feathers the starboard propeller, corrects the Lucky Lil's sudden yaw and shallow dive, hears but ignores several cries of alarm behind him and scans all his instruments. They tell him nothing he doesn't know and he tries three times to restart the starboard engine. Nothing doing. It's deader than the well known doornail. Lt. Donald, pale beneath his sunburn, grabs his yoke, helps control the yaw and retrims the Lil, more or less. The altimeter reads 6600 feet and seems to be holding steady. Back in the cargo compartment David Dudley Hull's squealing, "We're going to die!"

"Eddie!" Billy Gote shouts. Eddie's pale pinched face appears at his shoulder. "Go tell that asshole shut up! Tell Harry and his pals, don't worry." Eddie's pale pinched face disappears and Billy Gote makes a number of rapid calculations.

Hour-ten out of Townsville. He could turn back, be about ninety minutes flying time on one engine. Like hell! Not with the booze aboard and MPs crawling all over Garbutt Field. Be his ass. And a C47 will fly all day on one engine. Do it all the time. Well, when they must. But they're a long way from Seven-Mile Strip, 500 miles say, four hours on one engine. All of it over water. Tropical sea full of sharks, poisonous sea snakes, deadly sea wasps. Set course for the coast then, hug the coast all the way to Cape Melville, the tip of Australia, then set course for Seven-Mile? Be 350 miles over water that way. Fuel's no problem. But five hours flying time, almost three over water. On one engine. With options though, much of the way. The airstrips at Woorammoolla and Cooktown, the old fighter strip outside Woory. There are MPs in Woory and Cooktown but the uproar set off by the Great Booze Heist may have subsided. Landing with one engine is a little bit tricky but nothing to worry about. And Porky Wallace, ace mechanic, might get the starboard engine going. But Porky's in the 12th Station Hospital with blisters all over his private parts.

It's decision time. Temporary decision anyway. The port engine's still running a little bit rough. But a C47 never loses both engines. Well, almost never. And there's $59,776 worth of booze (at Nadzab prices) aboard, along with all their dreams.

"Let's take her in," Billy Gote says. "Few miles off the coast. Land if we have to. Woory or that an old fighter strip or Cooktown. We'll see."

They bank the Lucky Lil gently to port. The altimeter's steady at 6300 feet, the airspeed's holding at 130 mph. They'll be just off the coast in less than thirty minutes. Back in the cargo cabin,

Hull's subsided: he may be praying. Eddie Devlin, back in the flight engineer's cubicle, is praying. "Please, God, help us!"

The port engine coughs, sputters, belches black smoke. It's running more than a smidgen rough, rattling and banging. The Lil's at 6000 feet and the airseed's dropped to 120 mph.

"We're in deep shit!" Lt. Donald gurgles.

"You may be right!" Billy Gote says. "Eddie!" Eddie's pale pinched face pops up at Billy's shoulder. "Get Johnson and go back the cabin. Tell Johnson pop the door then get on his radio. We better mayday. Throw some stuff out the airplane. Baggage, whatever. Not the raft." If there is a raft. There's supposed to be a six-man self-inflating liferaft equipped with a radio homing beacon, flashlights, water, emergency rations, shark repellent, but Billy's not seen it lately.

Johnson, pale and obedient, leads the way, Eddie at his heels. They climb over the booze stacked well forward in the cargo compartment. Johnson whacks the latches on the cabin door and gives it a little push. The airstream catches it and bang it against the fuselage. Johnson scoots back to his radio and Eddie, Harry, Benson, Jukes and David Dudley Hull instinctively recoil, staring out at the void, air, nothing, at 6,000 feet over the Coral Sea. The airstream whistles by the open door. Hull whimpers, propels himself backward along the bench seat and plants his fat rear end against the forward bulkhead.

"Pilot," Eddie shouts. "Says throw some stuff out!"

Harry, since he can't throw with his bum shoulder, sits on the cargo compartment's ribbed floor, his big feet close to the open door. Benson, a firm anchor at 230 pounds, sits behind him, gripping Harry's torso. They start with Hull's baggage, ignoring his feeble protests: his portable typewriter, two musette bags, two bulging valpaks. Jukes and Eddie, working on their hands and knees, place these items at Harry's feet and Harry kicks them out the open door. They vanish instantly. The port engine coughs and sputters. Black smoke whips by the open door. The MPs' musette bags go next. Eddie crawls back to the cockpit and collects the baggage there. Out it goes, the Lil's lightly loaded but every little bit helps, and Harry, Jukes and Benson crawl back to the bench seats beside the booze.

Eddie crawls back to his cubicle and resumes his prayers, promising the Lord he'll lead a good clean life from this day forward, breaking no Commandments, kind to children, animals and the elderly. If only he's alive to do so. The port engine coughs, sputters, belches black smoke and rattles on. But it's losing oil. Black streaks are creeping along its nacelle.

"Hope to christ we make Woory!" Billy Gote says. "Fifteen minutes maybe. You better buckle up."

Lt. Donald, gripping his yoke with one fist, drenched with sweat, likewise praying, struggles into his harness. So does Billy Gote. They're at 5400 feet, the airspeed dropped to 110 mph and the Lil's getting hard to fly, yawing and losing a little altitude each time the port engine sputters. The coast is a thick dark smudge on the horizon, the low hills behind it just visible. The port engine coughs, sputters and belches black smoke and the Lucky Lil drops, a sickening drop, to 4800 feet.

"No use!" Billy Gote says. "Got to do it! Eddie, go dump some the boo—The ammo!"

Nobody argues or protests. Harry cuts the ropes on the tarp and resumes his place on the floor anchored by Benson. Jukes and Eddie peel back the tarp and one by one, while the port engine coughs and sputters and the Lucky Lil, the open door banging the fuselage, dips and sways and sinks to 4400 feet then 4000, Harry kicks half the booze, case at a time, gin, brandy and scotch, out the cabin door.

"Jeezuzz!" Pvt. Jukes says. "This that booze was liberated!"

"No," Harry says, Billy Gote's ass may still be on the line. "This one them ham-and-egg flights."

"Like shit," Jukes says, but the port engine coughs and sputters, the Lil drops to 3700 feet and that's the end of that discussion. They can see through the open cabin door a swath of sea and the coast, closer but not close enough. The port engine sputters and rattles.

Johnson pops out of the cockpit. "Loo'tent says all it! All the amm'nition! But chrissake not the tarp!" The tarp might catch on the tail, wrecking the minimal manueverability the Lucky Lil has left.

They go back to work while the port engine sputters and the Lil drops to 3000 feet, 2000, 1000. The rest of the booze but for one case of Gilbey's gin and Jukes' and Benson's tommy-guns and the one Eddie had when posing as an MP go out the open door and down down down into the Coral Sea. Along with three dreams of great wealth. But what good's a dream if you're dead? Jukes, wrestling with the last case of gin, casts a speculative eye on David Dudley Hull: another 200 pounds, about. Hull shrivels up in his corner and whimpers. The Lucky Lil banks awkwardly to starboard and Jukes loses his grip on the gin.

The Lil levels off at 300 feet. Dark green mangrove swamp, trees with roots like spider legs sunk in the mud a quarter-mile away, and a gray-green mudflat flash by the open door. The port engine sputters, coughs and dies and in the sudden near silence, the only sound the airstream whistling by the open door, they hear Johnson squealing. "Mayday! Mayday! Mayday! We're going in!" The port engine comes back from its near death experience, sputters, belches black smoke and revives the hydraulics.

"Full flaps!" Billy Gote, hauling on his yoke, he'll stall the Lil in if he can, says. "I never done this before but here goes!" And, though seldom a praying man, prays. "Please, Lord, no stumps!"

"Flaps full and locked," Lt. Donald squeaks, then hauls at the lever on the cockpit floor that drops the wheels. "Wheels down and."

"No!" Billy Gote smashes Donald's nose with a swinging forearm (where's Porky Wallace with his Stillson when you really need him) but hears the "thunk" the Lil's wheels make, dropping from their wells. Billy hauls on his yoke. The port engine dies. Billy chops the ignition and the Lucky Lil goes into the mudflat wheels down at 68 mph with a great noisy splash, mud and muddy water flung high. Both wheels promptly sink into the mud, tipping the Lil nose down. Billy heaves on his yoke. The open door bangs the fuselage and vanishes, torn from it hinges. The port wheel hits a stump, so much for prayer, and snaps off. The nose comes up, the tail drops, the Lil swings broadside and slides through the mudflat in a welter of mud and muddy water, whacking another stump along the way, the starboard wheel snapping off, for 700 feet. Then slowly settles into the mudflat.

In the sudden comparative silence, all aboard take stock. Billy Gote, strapped in, is intact though badly shaken and drenched with sweat. "You asshole!" he says, meaning Lt. Donald, but it's too late now to go into all that about wheels-up crash-landings in mudflats. They can thank their lucky stars (and his forearm smash) the asshole did not have time to lock the wheels. The Lucky Lil most likely flipped right over then and killed them all. Right away or, trapped inside the airplane, slowly. Lt. Donald whimpers. Likewise strapped in, he escaped serious injury but his nose feels broken. It's bleeding buckets at any rate, tears are rolling down his fat pale cheeks and he's shaking like a leaf in a Force 10 gale. Cpl. Johnson, also strapped in, likewise intact though buried in comicbooks flung from the Flares Only rack, is still babbling, "Mayday!"

But aft in the cargo compartment, muddy water sloshing through the open cabin door, Eddie Devlin, Harry Parker, Pvts. Benson and Jukes and David Dudley Hull, not strapped in, were tossed every which way by the violent landing, a jolt when the port wheel hit the stump, the subsequent quarter-spin, another jolt when the starboard wheel detached, and splattered with gray-green mud splashed through the open door. Eddie, Harry and Benson are sprawled in a heap on the tarp in the muddy water and wreckage (broken glass, gin and kindling) left when the last case of Gilbey's (but for a single bottle), likewise tossed around, smashed. They disentangle themselves and sit up. They have numerous bruises and miscellaneous lacerations and Eddie has a deep gash on his forehead and, he thinks, some cracked ribs. Harry has a broken right thumb and thinks his bum shoulder is dislocated. Benson lost three front teeth snapped off at the gum and thinks he has a broken wrist: it hurts like hell anyway and so does his mouth. Pvt. Jukes, who wound up dumped on top of David Dudley Hull on the starboard bench seat, has sundry bruises, skinned knees and a bloody nose but that's still functioning.

"Jeezuzz, what the hell stinks?" Jukes, disentangling himself, says. Then discovers what. "Be dammed! This guy shit in his pants!"

David Dudley Hull, essentially intact though bruised and deeply ashamed, whimpers. His bowels betrayed him. His pants are full of it. Scrunched up against the forward bulkhead, he wishes he were, well, not dead as he fully expected to be, but somewhere, anywhere, else. Back in Milwaukee on the copydesk even, taking his chances with the draft.

Billy Gote emerges from the cockpit, roughly half his usual ebullient self, and picks up the single surviving bottle of gin. "Well," he says. "We got her down. One way or another. All present and accounted for? Oh shit! There's a snake!"

The snake, six feet long, black as sin, no doubt a poisonous sea snake, is nosing around in the muddy water inside the open cabin door. Benson and Jukes whip out their Forty-Fives and, before Billy Gote can stop them, there may be high octane fumes lurking about ready to explode, blast away. They miss, the slugs ricochet through the open door and away in the general direction of the mangrove swamp and the snake slithers out the door. There weren't any fumes or not enough anyway to set off an explosion.

But there's another problem. "The water's gettin' deeper!" Eddie says, and so it is. It's a foot deep in the cargo compartment and rising.

"Oh shit!" Billy Gote says. "Tide's coming in. There'll be more goddamn snakes!"

"We'll drown!" David Dudley Hull wails. "Trapped like rats."

"Oh for chrissake shut up!" Billy Gote says. "We ain't gonna drowned. We're gonna climb out the exit in the cockpit and get on top the airplane."

It takes all Juke's 230 pounds and considerable strength spurred on by his fear of snakes and consequent burst of adrenalin to push open the emergency exit in the cockpit ceiling, sprung by the violent landing. He pushes it open though and they climb up through it, one by one, a tight squeeze for the MPs. Eddie, Harry and Benson, hampered by their injuries, go first, then Jukes. David Dudley Hull goes next though he tried to go first and his fat rear end, his khakis stained a rich brown, gets stuck in the exit. Billy Gote whacks it with the ten-inch Stillson and Hull, squealing, pops out of the Lil. Johnson and Lt. Donald follow him. Billy Gote goes last as befits the aircraft commander, captain of the ship, the gin that survived the crash stuffed in his shirt, the muddy water by then two feet deep in the cockpit.

All out, they sit in a row on the Lucky Lil's battered mud-splattered fuselage, rather like crows on a fence, squinting into the sun, very hot now, the Coral Sea stretching away to the horizon in front of them, the mangrove swamp a hundred yards away across a shrinking strip of gray-green mudflat behind them. There's a blunt point black with mangrove a quarter-mile away to the north and the tide's still coming in, splashing over the Gert's battered wings and broken flaps, creeping across the mudflat.

"What are we going to do?" Lt. Donald, dabbing at his bloody broken nose with his shirttail, says.

"Wait," Billy Gote says. "You get any response your mayday, Johnson?" Johnson shakes his head. "Somebody might heard it though. There prolly be a boat along. Sooner later. So we sit here and wait. There ain't anything else we can do."

"Wade to shore," Harry says. "Ain't that far. Water ain't that deep."

"No way," Billy Gote says. "You be up to your ass in mud. Guy from the Squadron tried it. Dint get three feet from his airplane. And there's snakes." The rising tide laps at the Lucky Lil's cabin windows and a long black snake slithers through the water over the starboard wing.

"We'll drown! We'll die!" David Dudley Hall, scrunched up near the Lucky Lil's tail, made to sit there because he smells bad, wails.

"Oh shut the fuck up!" Billy Gote says. "We won't drown! Tide here ain't but two three feet."

They wait, soon bathed in sweat, the sun beating down, bouncing off the shimmering Coral Sea, the Lil's muddy aluminum skin too hot to touch. This mud and the mud splattered on those in the cargo compartment dries and cracks. The injured look to their injuries. Pvt. Jukes opens the first-aid kit on his pistol belt and ties a bandage around Eddie's head, the gash Eddie suffered still oozing blood: his ribs hurt too. Lt. Donald dabs at his nose with his shirttail. Harry cradles his broken thumb in his other hand. Benson stuffs his left wrist, the one he thinks broken, in his shirt, sucks his bloody gums and stoically endures his pain.

They could be where they are, Eddie thinks, marooned atop the Lucky Lil, for hours. Days even if they don't die of thirst or starvation or fry first or slip off into the water and a snake gets them. And there'll be no Packard convertible or a house for his parents After The War. But those dreams are of no consequence now. He's alive! That's the main thing. There were long still frightening minutes while the Lil sank through the sky over the Coral Sea when he was almost sure he was going to die. An idea so shocking he scarcely could grasp it but doubt's he'll ever forget. Harry Parker thinks the same about the lobster boat he planned to buy and proving to his old man's satisfaction he's a worthy son.

Neither dream matters now. Billy Gote thinks he may After The War if there is for him an After The War just march into the First State Bank of Onamee, Kansas, punch old Jeremiah Grabb the president in the mouth and let it go at that.

"A boat!" Cpl. Johnson squeals. "There's a boat comin'!"

The boat is rounding the blunt point off to the north, headed for the Lucky Lil. It's a small craft chugging along with foam under its bow, an LCVP with several people aboard they soon determine. They stand, careful to maintain their balance, wave and cheer, and the LCVP closes on the Lil.

"This calls for a drink!" Billy Gote says. He pulls the bottle of gin from his shirt. The LCVP, slowing, circles in the deeper water off the Lil's starboard wing then bumps gently against the fuselage and a big man in fatigues with a red meaty face standing inboard high on the bow ramp thrusts out a big meaty hand.

"Major Clarence Borgan," he says. "I'm the XO, Jungle Training Center up around the point there. We seen you smoking, going down, we jump right in our landing craft. One my men say it look like you throwin' stuff out your airplane."

"Yeah, we were," Billy Gote says. "Bunch ammo. Mixed cargo. We never get this far, we dint."

"Okay," Borgan says. "Let's get you all aboard here. Easy now, there's prolly a bunch a snakes in the water. Hey! That liquor you got there?"

"Roger," Billy Gote, gripping Borgan's big meaty hand, says. "We just about were gonna have a drink. Celebrate we're all alive and pretty good shape. But I'm gonna give it you, Major. Fair enough, huh? You come right out and rescue us." Billy hands Borgan the gin. The last bottle of Gilbey's. So much for the Great Booze Heist. Borgan grabs it and his red meaty face lights up like a lighthouse on a rocky coast.

6

**21 JANUARY 1944
GENERAL HEADQUARTERS, SOUTHWEST PACIFIC AREA
DAILY COMMUNIQUE**

Allied Ground Forces under Gen. Douglas MacArthur's command operating from Arawe and Cape Gloucester on New Britain linked up with long-range patrols, securing the western portion of the island, and are continuing their pursuit of scattered enemy forces. Allied Ground Forces under Gen. MacArthur's command operating from Finschafen and Saidor in New Guinea are nearing link-up on the Huon Peninsula and inflicting heavy casualties on fleeing enemy forces. Allied Air Forces under Gen. MacArthur's command flew 85 sorties inflicting heavy damage to enemy positions and personnel at Wewak and Madang. Light Naval Forces under Gen. MacArthur's command sank three enemy barges in coastal waters off New Britain.

* * *

The War goes on. And on. And on 26 December, Christmas Day Back in the States, the First Marine Division (pretty well shattered when pulled off Guadalcanal a year ago but rejuvenated, rehabbed, up to strength, the chronic sick transferred out and replacements absorbed during a year in bivouac outside Melbourne, on loan to Swappa) makes an assault landing at Cape Gloucester on the northwestern tip of New Britain, overcomes scattered enemy resistance, establishes a perimeter, captures the beat-up Jap airstrip and launches long-range patrols for a linkup with the 112th RCT mopping-up at Arawe while Sea Bees (a Navy Construction Battalion) repair and improve the airstrip, operational as of 12 January.

On 2 January a task force organized by the 32nd Infantry Division (likewise pretty much shattered when pulled out of Buna Government Station ten months earlier but since rejuvenated, up to strength, replacements absorbed, all its Limited Service personnel transferred elsewhere, with a new commanding general, a tough little West Pointer) makes an assault landing at Saidor Village on the north New Guinea coast 150 miles west of Cape Gloucester across the Huon Strait, overcomes scattered enemy resistance, captures the beat-up Jap airstrip, establishes a perimeter and launches long-range patrols for a linkup with the Australian troops mopping-up at Finschafen while Air Engineers repair and improve the airstrip, soon to be operational.

* * *

None of which concerns Sgt. Arnold Saljeski, just promoted, busy at 0800 hours updating his movie records in the Townsville Base Section Special Services Office. Col. James Schwartz, the new Base Section Commander, runs a tight ship, everybody at work, even Capt. Fats Forney, at 0730 hours. Outside, slow rain is falling. The Bloody Wet's still going strong. It's rained steadily since Christmas but for two brief breaks and most likely will rain another bloody month, the Australians say. Saljeski's resigned to that. He doesn't have to sleep in it anyway and he finally got a print of Casablanca, said to be a hell of a movie (starring Humphrey Bogart and Ingrid Bergman) in a review he read in an ancient Newsweek at the Flinders Street EM Club. He's laid on a private preview for the 301st MP Co. come evening, always smart to do the MPs little favors, and Sgt. Harry Parker, his broken thumb in a light cast but his dislocated shoulder good as new, is at hand with Saljeski's recompense, a pint of Australian whiskey.

"All I could get, Sal," Harry, apologizing, says. "Colonel Schwartz, what I hear, give Burns-Phelps hell on account of the booze we liberate. He don't give a durn they're Allies. I still got kind of a connection there but it ain't worth much. Our chickens come home to roost, I guess, saying goes. Speaking which, I hear you ain't gittin' any chicken-and-dumplings any more."

Saljeski shrugs. "Yeah, fuckin' Fogerty ace me out. Fuckin light colonel, what can I do? But I don't begrudge Mickey nuthin'. Mickey's okay. And her girlfriend Sally works the QM, she's pretty fuckin dumb but she's okay in the sack."

"Good on you," Harry says. "Sal, I know you know we only throw the goldurn booze out the airplane because we had to. It was it or us, Sal. Durn near was us anyway." They've discussed this before but Harry still feels bad about it, all their dreams shattered. Feels worse about it now safe back in Townsville than at the time.

"Sure, I know. What the fuck, Harry. Booze dint cost us nuthin'. We got a few drinks out it and fuck the fuckin O Club! I hear they gonna open it again."

"Yeah, t'night. They finally gittin' some booze, Cummins and Campbell. Under heavy guard. You ever worried, Sal, Mickey, now she's shackin' up with Fogerty, gonna tell him it was her run off them extra req and p.o. and so on for that booze and give it you?"

"Fuck no. Like I said, Mickey's okay. She'll keep that fuckin little secret. Anyway, she don't know for sure it was them papers we liberate the fuckin booze with. I never tell her and it be her ass too prolly, that all come out. I ain't fuckin worried. I got the booze we promise Booney for his dog out a her place and give it him before fuckin Fogerty move in."

"Okay. You aint worried I ain't, I guess. I wish Jukes and Benson quit shootin' off their goldurn mouths about we throw a million bucks worth booze in the Coral Sea. Well, not Benson so much. They made him partial plate, the 12th Station, but he talks, it falls out. I told both them keep their goldurn mouths shut but they ain't. I guess it don't matter though. I think I convince the Provost we was on a ham-and-egg flight and he convince Fogerty that. Nobody connect that booze with us anyway. And there's a rumor. First Platoon the 301st be shippin' out to Oro Bay pretty soon. Jukes and Benson be long gone, that happens."

"I heard a rumor," Saljeski says. "Today's the day, them coons did Boots. You really think, I know you voice some doubts, them the ones did her?"

"Wish I knew, Sal. Ones we bring back from Oro Bay swear they dint, but I expect that. They admit they miss Retreat that night but claim they just stayed the Goose and Feathers, drinking, then went back their outfit and ship out. Aussie runs the Goose and Feathers dint corroborate that though when we question him. But he said he dint know any blackfellows by name and they all look alike to him. And the one we pick up here confess. I ain't so sure about that though. I know Raskovic plant Boots' prints on that deuce-and-a-half you liberate. But there ain't anything anybody can do about that now, they all court-martialed and everthing. Rumor you heard is right, my information." The tricky business with Boots Davis' fingerprints still bothers Harry's seamy conscience some but not a whole lot. "I got to shove, Sal. I still breakin' in our new clerks and somebody liberate a staff car off the docks and that pig farmer's the CID chief now is hot we recover it."

Harry departs and Saljeski resumes his updating. He's largely resigned to the fact he won't be rich, not right away anyway, and has come to the conclusion running a bar, running Fazio's, would have been a lot of work, a lot of headaches. Stock to buy and inventory, trouble with help and the tenants in the upstairs apartments, drunks to contend with, customers who write bad checks, you have to cash checks in a neighborhood bar. And his old job with the Vacuum Cleaner Co. will be waiting for him After The war, that's the law, along with an occasional lonely West Philadelphia homemaker ready for a demonstration.

* * *

Lt. Col. Parnell (Cob) Fogerty, the Base Section chief-of-staff, fortified with coffee surreptitiously laced with medicinal gin, is humming a little tune and zipping through some paperwork in his Base Section HQ office at 0830 hours while outside slow rain falls. Not a lot of paperwork. Col. James Schwartz does his share. More than Allen, that goddamn Weekend Warrior, ever did anyway. Goddamn Weekend Warrior was not court-martialed either, though he tried to choke Brig. Gen. Bargle. Lt. Col. Pulaski at Service Force HQ came through with that disgusting information a week ago. Pulaski's story, GHQ got cold feet, something to do with politics Back in the States, hushed the whole thing up, yanked Allen out of the Nut Ward at the 5th General Hospital in Brisbane and shipped him somewhere. Nobody seems to know where. Somewhere unpleasant, Fogerty hopes, but doesn't really care. Allen after all was just another among the many assholes encountered in the course of Cob Fogerty's long Army career.

Pulaski had other grim news as well. Oro Bay will soon be Swappa's major supply base. A goddamn engineer outfit blasted a passage through the coral reefs there and Service Force HQ is giving serious thought to sharply reducing the Townsville Base Section over the next ninety days, shipping numerous TBS units to Oro. "You all be in the islands pretty soon," Pulaski said and, safe in Sydney where Service Force HQ no doubt is entrenched for the duration, laughed his irritating laugh. He did promise though to look for a slot somewhere on the Australian Mainland for a light colonel with Lt. Col. Fogerty's qualifications. He also said, needlessly, "Schwartz is a hardnose."

Col. Schwartz arrived 1 January, up from Service Force HQ, just in time for the court-martial, relieving the Acting Base Commander, but that's all right. Lt. Col. Fogerty really didn't want the C.O. job, too damn much responsibility. Schwartz as advertised is a hardnose. Regular Army, a permanent captain. A goddamn stickler. Everybody at work on time. No drinking on duty. Some mornings are pretty tough. But there's a jug of Gilbey's in a safe place known only to Sgt. Costello and Schwartz is pretty busy, out every day jacking up the Townsville Base Section. That no doubt will wear him down in short order. Drive him to drink maybe.

And the O Club is reopening. Tonight. Under new management, Second Lt. Earl Lambert. Young fellow plucked from the 3rd Repple Depple, another lucky Infantry replacement, a Cornell School of Hotel Management student Before The War. Properly thankful too, happy with the usual arrangement. Won't, good bet anyway, peddle any booze either. Promised, word of an officer, when told of the vengeance wreaked on Lt. Bernie Witters. The Club was closed for a month, a real horror of war, the holiday season a dismal time, not much real stuff left after the watered stock was identified and removed and no way to get more until the January req was approved, goddamn War Authority meanwhile adamant. Lucky thing Flapp the QM, still making amends for the QM's presumed dereliction in the matter of the booze the goddamn flyboys liberated, came up with some vanilla extract and a rare case of after shave.

Goddamn flyboys got away with the booze too, though he, carrying on despite his wounded ear, did his level best to prevent that. Ran the MP detail all over Garbutt Field, searched three C47s but found them empty and goddamn 47s were taking off the whole time, no aid naturally forthcoming from the goddamn flyboys who run the Ops Office and the Control Tower. Then, immediately following Brig. Gen. Bargle's foul-tempered depature for Sydney, that RAAF asshole, Hewitt-Packer, pulled his rank and ran them off the field, GHQ Order 404:44 notwithstanding.

Claimed they were slowing the speedy prosecution of The War, that superseding.

Bullshit! That defeat at the hands of the RAAF still rankles Cob Fogerty. He ceases his humming and, a habit now, fingers his left ear. The tip is missing. No Purple Heart either. Wound not inflicted by the enemy, way the Army sees it. Both his ears are still red and tender. He may be allergic to wasp venom, the dumb sawbones at the 12th Station thinks. That's a diagnosis, no treatment offered.

There is of course a juicy rumor the C47 with the booze aboard crashed or crash-landed somewhere near Woorammoolla on its way to New Guinea after jettisoning its cargo, though all aboard unfortunately survived, the three MPs who picked up the three rapists in Oro Bay among them. That's the Provost Marshal's story anyway. He wants commendations, Bronze Stars, for the MPs, who carried on with their mission though injured. Not likely. The Provost and his MPs did not get the booze back. The three MPs when queried, this also the Provost's story, said they were on a ham-and-egg flight and gave wildly varying estimates as to the amount of booze jettisoned. There's been no official confirmation though, just the three MPs' report, that C47 did crash or crash-land, goddamn flyboys mum as stumps on the subject of aircraft disasters. Claim word of same gives aid and comfort to the enemy.

More bullshit! But Lt. Col. Fogerty decides he'll believe that C47 was the one with the booze and it did crash or crash-land, all the booze in the Coral Sea now, making fish happy. This makes him feel better. He won't pursue the matter further. Besides, if that was the 47 with the booze, it got away in violation of GHQ Order 404:44 while he was the Acting Base Section commander who failed to implement appropriate action forthwith. Or so GHQ no doubt would view it. Best let sleeping dogs and crashed or crash-landed C47s lie.

The booze situation at any rate is back to normal, sixty assorted cases awaiting pick-up under heavy guard later today at Cummins & Campbell Island Traders Pty. Ltd. And after the Club reopens and closes tonight he'll have chicken-and-dumplings with Mrs. Dwight (Mickey) Rooney. One smart thing he did anyway was go talk to Mrs. Rooney about her chickens. They discussed White Leghorns, way they always get out. The 118th Engineer Co. subsequently built a new fence for Mrs. Rooney's Leghorns and he paid her out of his own pocket for the four she claims that asshole Witters killed. Money well spent. She had at the time, she confessed, a Yank boyfriend, a Lance Jack, but he talked her out of that nonsense pretty quick and into bed. Pulled rank but what the hell's rank for? Mrs. Rooney makes a mean dumpling and she's quite a dumpling herself. A big woman. Short but big. Rolling around under him in her double-bed she feels like a big soft pillow covered with skin. Sometimes, afterwards, down in the dumplings, she cries a little, says she feels bad about cheating on Dwight, missing at Singapore. Cob Fogerty though bored consoles her, says Dwight if alive would want her to be happy, blames it all on The War.

Outside, rain's pounding down. Lt. Col. Fogerty, skimming Revised Instructions for the Salvaging of 55-Gallon Oil Drums, resumes his humming, paraphrasing an old song, "I got me a new insatchable babbee." And wonders is it raining at Saidor? He hopes it is. Last he heard, Lt. Bernie Witters was a platoon leader in the task force chasing Japs in the jungle outside Saidor Village.

* * *

It is raining, a steady drizzle, in the dismal jungle three miles south of Saidor Village at 0900 hours, but Second Lt. Bernard C. Witters no longer knows that. He was killed instantly at 0859 hours, shot through his left eye by a sniper in a tree while trying, his helmet tipped back, to orient a sketchy map, he had it upside down, on a narrow trail Fox Co.s' First Platoon is supposed to be clearing of enemy forces.

Everybody left in First Platoon (31 men, booby-traps, occasional enemy fire, the usual fevers and scrub typhus having taken their toll) cheer the sniper before shooting him out of his tree. They've had some Platoon Leaders, Ninety-Day Wonders, who were doozies, but none as bad as Witters. Asshole still wore his gold bars, bright and shiny, binoculars around his neck and a holstered Forty-Five and demanded salutes, all stupidities guaranteed to draw sniper fire. Asked for it and got it, drilled through one eye and his tiny brain.

Cpl. Robert Douglas, the ranking non-com, promoted late in the Buna Government Station campaign, one of the twenty-odd BGS veterans left in First Platoon, assumes command. He orders the late Lt. Witters' body wrapped in Witters' poncho and rolled off the track. The Task Force GRU will collect it and that of a draftee killed during a brief dawn firefight with Second Platoon on an adjacent trail, each platoon thinking the other Japs until loud Americam oaths were heard. Cpl. Douglas also appropriates Witters' Forty-Five and binoculars, useless though they be in the jungle. He stuffs them in his pack, posts perimeter guards and sends a runner, the sound-power phone as usual defunct, back to Fox HQ with word of Witter's demise. The little Mexican, Sgt. Pablo Diaz, tripped on a trip-wire day before yesterday, he should have known better, and died in the Battalion Aid Station. May have wished to, all his manhood blown to shreds.

"Take ten," Cpl. Douglas says. First Platoon settles down along the trail, Task Force HQ no doubt will send them another Ninety-Day Wonder presently, and breaks out damp smokes and cold Cs, sharing Witters'. They'll let The War take care of itself for awhile, no sense pushing it.

* * *

Three miles away at Task Force HQ amid the smashed thatched huts that were Saidor Village before the pre-landing bombardment leveled most of them, David Dudley Hull, wearing his only clothes, baggy ill-fitting sweat-soaked fatigues he's been wearing for a month, sits bent over an old L.C. Smith typewriter balanced on a empty 50-calibre ammo box like the one he's sitting on in a leaky stinking damaged native hut, staring at a blank sheet of soggy Japanese rice paper rolled in the typewriter. Task

Force HQ has but two typewriters and he only gets to use one when nobody else wants it. It's like writing on deadline, which he never did like or did well, and his muse as the saying goes has deserted him.

David Dudley Hull is the only war correspondent left at Saidor. A Life Magazine photographer and five other correspondents (AP, UP, INS, Lou Sebring of the New York Herald Tribune and Bluey Mahaffey, pretty fast company) made the landing, going in with the early assault waves, but left three days later on the first LST evaccing wounded. The area by then was officially secured and the Task Force troops were officially mopping-up. So David Dudley Hull has an "exclusive" now but he's not filed anything for three days. No doubt Jake Jasper, the Milwaukee Herald executive editor, is livid. And the stories he did file, approved by the GHQ censor with the Task Force so long as all the GIs quoted sounded cheerful and gung-ho and the GIs in David Dudley Hull's stories always do, may be anywhere. They went out with the Official Priority Mail on the LST evaccing wounded and another LST evaccing more wounded, both bound for Oro Bay, but that's no guarantee. David Dudley Hull got those stories from lightly wounded GIs in the 28th Portable Surgical Hospital accompanying the Task Force, but it wasn't easy. The wounded, he's learned to his dismay, are often inarticulate. Or surly. Several told him, "Fuck off, asshole!" He's seen dead GIs too, bundled in ponchos. They look awfully, well, dead. Those with some of their parts missing or their insides falling out make him sick.

David Dudley Hull's also learned to his surprise and dismay that, though he's practically Up at The Front in a great big war, there's not all that much to write about. The GIs' stories have a certain sameness. "Fuckin Jap pop out his fuckin hole, pop my buddy inna belly and I blowed the little fucker's fuckin head off." David Dudley Hall embellishes these reports with patriotic quotes but he's running out of quotes. And steam.

He's not actually been up to The Front since making the landing with the sixth and last wave on 3 January. The Front is mostly patrols now, pushing through the jungle, looking for trouble, though there's a perimeter around the old Jap airstrip the Engineer outfit is rebuilding. He's not had a look at the perimeter either, which has twice in the middle of the night repulsed Jap banzai attacks. And Wisconsin GIs are getting hard to find. The Task Force musters many replacements, Draftees from all over. And the food is awful! Warmed up C-rations. And he's not had any sleep! There are Jap aircraft overhead almost every night. Well, usually one aircraft, the one the GIs with a warped sense of humor call Washing-Machine Charlie. It circles somewhere overhead in the darkness for two hours, eliminating sleep, then drops a bomb! And twice there were several aircraft dropping several bombs! One of those bombs killed two Task Force GIs a scant 400 yards from the wet hole behind the leaky hut in which David Dudley Hull lay curled, praying with all his might.

And his finger hurts. He is in a manner of speaking wounded. He somehow while falling into the landing craft bobbing off the lowered ramp on the LST he was aboard tore half the nail off his right forefinger. That was extremely painful and once ashore he went immediately to the 28th Portable Surgical Hospital, set up in another smashed hut. But the surgeon he saw there, a physician markedly lacking in bedside manner, did not deign to even look at this injury (wound). He merely said he had an amputation waiting and tossed David Dudley Hull a roll of bandage. That's wrapped around David Dudley Hull's finger now and pretty grubby. Should gangrene set in and the 28th PSH have to amputate his finger. Well, that surgeon will be sorry.

David Dudley Hull would gladly give his manhood to be back in Woorammoolla, an awful dump he thought when there but it looks like Heaven now. It had a hotel anyway, the King Something, with a bar and halfway decent food and a bathroom in which he could clean himself up. Again. He cleaned himself up once in a primitive shower at the Jungle Training Center, where they went ashore following their rescue, but once was not enough. He also got the fatigues he's still wearing at the JTC, trading a GI from Green Bay a promised big story for them. Then the officer who saved their lives (who was from Indiana, unfortunately) took them to Woorammoolla. They were in Woorammoolla four days, rain pounding down the whole time, waiting for a break in the weather, those injured when they crashed patched up by the battalion surgeon at a parachute outfit.

David Dudley Hull was of course thankful to be alive, briefly euphoric in fact, but that evaporated instantly when on a rare clear day a C47 out of Townsville picked them up and flew them, the true meaning of "a wing and prayer" learned en route, to Seven-Mile Strip. Where he finally found Fifth Air Force HQ and the PIO there, the asshole who mother-hens the war correspondents in New Guinea, a St. Louis Post-Dispatch editorial writer in civil life. An asshole who, turned censor, killed the first-person story about that terrible experience in the air over the Coral Sea that David Dudley Hull wrote on a borrowed typewriter at the King Something Hotel. A hell of a story called "Death in the Sky" that did not include any mention of the trouble with his bowels. Aircraft disasters not reportable, the PIO asshole said, give aid and comfort to the enemmy. Bullshit! Anyway, the asshole also said, "You're not dead." Asshole no doubt envied the crisp colorful prose in "Death in the Sky." Then the asshole put David Dudley Hull on a C47 (a notably unreliable aircraft) to the Trobriand Islands off the northeast New Guinea coast, where the Saidor Task Force was staging, then loading. On Christmas Day!

A mosquito lands on David Dudley Hull's still pudgy though shrinking sunburned right forearm. The Task Force has no scales but he guesses he's lost twenty pounds. The mosquito is a welcome anopheles by the look of it, tail in the air. David Dudley Hull's not taking the Atabrine tablets laid out in the all-ranks Task Force mess. If he catches malaria, the Task Force will have to evac him to Australia or at least Port Moresby. Jake Jasper can't bitch about that. But the anopheles if it is an anopheles lifts off and flies away without perhaps infecting him. Shit!

The future looks bleak. The rumor is the Task Force units will never see Australia again. Instead, David Dudley Hull though no strategist supposes, they'll just push on along the north New Guinea coast, 1200 miles of swamp and jungle and tropical diseases, and he with them. Unless, that is, he resigns his position and somehow wangles transport back to Milwaukee. But they're drafting people to age thirty-eight now. He might wind up in New Guinea again, an Enlisted Man. An Infantry replacement even!

David D. Hull. If he catches malaria the Task Force will have to evac him

It's nearly 1000 hours. Somebody will want the damn typewriter and he's got to file something. Chewing his fat lower lip, David Dudley Hull types, slowly, his bandaged finger a real nuisance:

> Special to the Herald. By David Dudley Hull.
> Somewhere in the Southwest Pacific—The Japs are bad enough. But the GIs fighting on this jungle Front, which suffered another heavy enemy air attack only last night, also must do battle with deadly swarming mosquitoes . . .

* * *

In Townsville at 1000 hours in the 14th K-9 Detachment HQ tent, a sagging pyramidal in the infield at the Charters Downs horse track, Sgt. Daniel Boone and First Lt. Arlen Carlson, the Detachment commander, are discussing personnel.

"I guess Attila just gone, Lieutenant," Sgt. Boone says. "Gone for good. Been more'n a month now. He done it before once, you remember? Run off when he smell a bitch in heat. But he come back. Somebody prolly got him this time. Put him down AWOL, I guess. Doggone, I miss him! He's a good dog, Attila."

"Month gone," Lt. Carlson says. "He's a goddamn deserter. Okay, I'll take him off the roster. Second time this happen, you got no dog, you're not a handler any more, Boone. I'll find something else you can do. Dismissed."

"Sir!" Sgt. Boone says and goes back to his pyramidal to await word of his new duties. He does miss Attila but he'd trade him again in a minute for five cases of booze, that Saljeski a man of his word. He still has four cases, bottle here, bottle there, buried in the scrub behind the Fuel Dump, a precious map locating same tucked in his campaign hat. He could sell that booze, twenty quid a jug easy. But what would he do with the dough? Buy more booze most likely. Next jug he opens he'll toast Attila.

* * *

"Get off the bed, Stinky!" Brig. Gen. Humphrey Dumphy, First Corps deputy commander, says. "Lie down! Roll over!" Just back from Arawe, where he chewed some ass and got long-range patrols launched in the general direction of the big Jap strong hold at Rabual, Brig. Gen. Dumphy's taking a little break at 1030 hours in his quarters, a plywood hut at First Corps Advance HQ beside the Dobodura airstrip.

Stinky, formerly known as Attila, flops off his new master's bedroll, lies down, rolls over and Brig. Gen. Dumphy scratches his belly. "You're a good dog, Stinky."

Stinky wags his tail. He'll be back on the bedroll the minute his new master leaves. This is no dog's life. He's finished the way it looks with all that "Stay! Guard! Attack!" nonsense and he's developed a taste for C rations, especially the beans-and-franks. He spends long hours on the bedroll, dreaming dreams featuring Lassie, an Alsatian he knew intimately in Shaker Heights, where his name was Chief, before he nipped the smelly kid who delivered the Cleveland Plain Dealer and his master, an orthodontist fearing litigation, enlisted him in the Army's new K-9 Corps.

In the ready tent beside the Dobodura strip the Ops officer hands Lt. Archie Hunker, on standby with his crew, Dumphy's going to Saidor, ETD 1100, to chew some ass, an official looking envelope, some kind of crown on it, addressed to Leftenant A. Hunker c/o U.S. Army First Corps. Lt. Hunker leaves off pitching shillings with his crew and opens the envelope. "Chrissake!" he says. "This a summons! I got a goddamn summons. For a parking ticket! From the Keystone Cops in Tville!" He blithely tears the summons to bits. "They got to catch me first!"

Thirty minutes out of Dobodura en route to Nadzab in the flight engineer's cubicle aboard a C47 called the Sizzlin' Sally, Sgt. Porky Wallace gingerly fingers his private parts. The damn thing still hurts when he's got a hard-on and he's got one on now. No wonder. He's been, what's the word, celebrate, since Thanksgiving, when they RON Tville three days on that ham-and-egg flight. The blisters are gone, punctured and drained by a goddamn medic at the 12th Station Hospital who seemed to think the agony accompanying that procedure a big joke. But his dingus was pretty badly burned and may always have, the 12th Station sawbones who briefly examined it said, "Some scar tissue. Give some girls a big treat somewhere down the road. But I wouldn't rush that, Sergeant."

"Fat fuckin chance," Porky said. "I'm back in New Guinea!"

"You might run a couple off by hand first," the sawbones

also said. "Be sure everything's hunky-dory. Understand that's a popular indoor sport in Guinea."

"Indoor, outdoor," Porky said, and though reluctant he's considering that. But it still hurts!

Ten miserable days he was in the 12th Station, burns slow to heal, before they booted him out to make room for casualties from Cape Gloucester and a place called Saidor. He returned to the Barrier Arms, three quid and four condoms in his wallet, found all his stuff gone, and was told by big Biff Smith, no sign of Louise, he no longer was "bloody welcome" at the Arms.

Ten more miserable days then he lived, existed, in the USAAC Transient Area, rain pounding down, everything socked in, losing his three quid at poker, bumming cigarettes, his kakis growing riper by the day, before the weather broke, briefly, and he hitched a ride on a Squadron 47 to Seven-Mile, almost glad to get there. Took awhile, convince the goddamn First Sergeant his absence was authorized, but he had his discharge from the 12th Station, finally convinced the First. Billy Gote was in Nadzab with the Lucky Lil II and a new flight engineer so Squadron assigned him to the Sizzlin' Sally, it's flight engineer in the 7th Station with FOU. The well-known Wallace luck, Porky thinks, if you don't count getting laid. Or not laid.

* * *

In Woorammoolla at 1100 hours, where a slow steady drizzle is soaking everything already soaked, Maj. Clarence Borgan, the JTC XO, stands dumbstruck in Col. Jefferson Davis Ives' room at the King Edward Hotel, staring at Col. Jefferson Davis Ives' large dead body, naked but for cavalry boots, spurs attached, sprawled on Col. Jefferson Davis Ives' torn-up double bed.

"What do you think?" Mr. Arthur Swan, the King Edward's resident manager, somewhat less dumbstruck, says. "A heart attack?"

"Oh, gosh!" Maj. Borgan says. "I don't know. He, he's dead!

Jeepers! What'll we do? I don't know what to do! What are we supposed to do?"

"I'll phone Mister Ranfranz the undertaker," Mr. Swan says. "He'll handle the uh initial procedures. That's what we usually do, these cases. And you'll want to call your people."

"Yeah, my people. Golly! I'm the Acting JTC commander! I mean I guess I am. Cripes! He was okay. Looked okay. Last time I saw him. Tuesday."

"His driver phoned," Mr. Swan says. "Mrs. Forbes-Fowler. She wondered why he'd not phoned her, pick him up. Then you phoned. Said you wanted to talk to him, something about an inspection. I came up and knocked on his door. Several times. No response. So I opened the door with my master key. These things happen, you know. You learn, running a bloody hotel. Then I phoned you."

"Gosh! He died with his boots on!" Borgan says. "Way he would of wanted to, I guess. What's that?" That's a pearl earring nestled close to the late Col. Ives' large naked buttock. Borgan hesitates then picks it up. "Oh gosh! He might died in the saddle! That's a saying. Way he would of."

"I know the saying," Mr. Swan says, primly. The King Edward's a respectable hotel: or was until the bloody Yanks turned it into a whorehouse. "Shall I call Mister Ranfranz?"

"Yeah. I mean. Well, yeah, I guess so. But then what? I mean what are we supposed to do with the uh well uh the. His remains?"

"Mister Ranfranz will take care of all that for now. While you work it out with your people. A final resting place, I mean. No point, I should think, to involving the Constabulary. I see no evidence of uh foul play. Autopsy, anything like that, be up to your people. Best we cover him now? You won't be wanting the uh jewelry, will you?"

"Golly, no!"

Mr. Swan takes the earring. They cover the late Colonel Ives with a sheet tangled at the foot of his bed and depart, locking the door. Mr. Swan phones Ranfranz the undertaker and drops the earring down the nearest loo, the King Edward's a respectable hotel or was, and Maj. Borgan speeds back to the JTC in his jeep, beset by command decisions.

He'll have to phone Base Section HQ in Townsville, report Colonel Ives' sudden demise. Service Force HQ in Sydney to, if he can, though phoning Sydney is a bitch. Seek instructions, what to do with the late Col. Ives' remains. GHQ too? No, GHQ scares him. Lower the JTC flag to half-mast maybe, sign of respect? Phone the MP Detachment in Woorammoolla, cover his ass. Phone the late Colonel Ives' WENL driver, that good-looking redhead, tell her she's no longer employed. But that can wait. Have to get her number from Swan. He seems to know her. Decisions, decisions. They come with command. And on top of all this, a warning from Lt. Col. Fogerty in Townsville, Col. Schwartz, the new Base Section C.O., reputed to be a hardnose, will be up to inspect the JTC two days hence.

What he needs, Maj. Borgan concludes, is a drink, if he had anything to drink. The gin the flyboys gave him, pretty small recompense considering he saved their lives, which he had to share because everybody on the LCVP knew he had it, lasted but a day.

The late Col. Ives' WENL driver, Mrs. Patricia Forbes-Fowler, sipping gin with a dash of tonic at 11:30 a.m. in the master loo in the Forbes-Fowlers' old family home in Woorammoolla, drops a pearl earring down the commode and notes with dismay, she's a big girl, her hands are still shaking.

Well, no wonder. Good God Almighty, she doesn't ever want to go through anything like that again! A big naked male body heaving around under her, playing "bucking bronco" he called it, his damn spurs a menace, suddenly going rigid, gasping for air, eyes rolling up, face turning purple behind his mighty mustache, what he called his "saddle horn" collapsing.

A massive fatal coronary or equally massive equally fatal

stroke was her diagnosis. She was a nursing sister, Patsy McGarrity, at Brisbane General when she met AIF Capt. Lewnes Forbes-Fowler, then in traction, tossed by his steed at the 1937 Queensland Horse Fair, heir to the Forbes-Fowler's sugar cane holdings, missing at Singapore. Her canefields if ever Lewnes is declared dead, though both his uppity sisters no doubt will contest that, move to have her found unfit, unfaithful.

But no one saw her, she's pretty sure, slipping half-dressed down the King Edward's backstairs at 2 a.m. and driving away in the late Col. Ives' Packard. Minus a damn earring, she discovered later. But those earrings, fake pearls, are a dime a dozen. Could be anybody's. And if anybody did see her and talk starts, that ass Swan will shut it off. He won't tangle with a Forbes-Fowler, likes to think he runs a respectable hotel. She can picture Swan bowing and scraping when she phoned to inquire about Col. Ives, pretending confusion because he'd not phoned her. A smart move. Proves, indicates anyway, she had no contact with the old reprobate during the night.

Mrs. Forbes-Fowler sips her gin and shudders. Terrible experience though. She won't soon forget it. And she'll be a good girl now, canefields to think about. Or find somebody young and healthy. Stocky little Yank captain who parachutes perhaps, a regular in the King Edward's public room. He looks healthy.

* * *

Some 600 miles southwest of Woorammoolla as the crow or a C47 flies, Capt. Dominic Raskovic stands at parade rest in a swarm of tiny black flies at the edge of the dusty parade ground at the Flat Mountain Stockade outside Cloncurry. His khakis are soaked with sweat. He's squinting in the blazing sunlight, the sun a white smear in the northern sky. With him are Sgt. William Young, the Stockade's current top kick, and, sagging in the heat, batting at the flies, a fat major from the GHQ Adjutant-General's office and a thin Medical Corps captain from the 5th General

Hospital. The low men on the totem poles in their respective units, Raskovic surmises. They and a pale Army chaplain, a first john, flew in from Brisbane at 1030 hours in a shiny little C60. The major is present to "officially observe the sentences of the court carried out." The captain will pronounce them officially dead. The chaplain will mumble a few final words and they'll all fly back to Brisbane, Raskovic also surmises, immediately thereafter.

The gallows a sullen inmate detail spent four days building casts an ugly shadow across the parade grounds. It's an eight-by-eight-foot platform with a trapdoor at its center, set on twelve-foot posts, steps leading up to it, the space beneath it hidden behind canvas. There's a big wooden lever that springs the trapdoor at its rear edge and a rope with a noose and hangman's knot dangling from its overhead arm.

It's 1145 hours, almost time. The Navy chief who flew in with the lumber in a C47 and supervised the construction, a big man stripped to the waist who claims to have spent many years on the cadre at the Portsmouth, N.H., Navy Brig, is testing the lever that springs the trapdoor. The detail also built three plain coffins, one extra large for former sergeant Washington. They're stacked beneath the gallows. Another detail dug three graves in the Stockade cemetery, where four former inmates rest: an acute appendicitis case the Stockade medic failed to diagnose, a suicide who slashed his wrists with barbwire, a rare escapee who didn't get far and a Latino queer beaten to death by two upright heterosexuals.

The chaplain, a pale skinny fellow, some Protestant denomination, is offering former sergeants Franklin and Jefferson religious solace in their pup tent. Former sergeant Washington declined such solace.

The temperature is 116 F. in the sun and climbing. It topped out at 119 F. yesterday, a typical mid-summer day in Cloncurry except a sprinkle of rain, about two minute's worth, fell late in the afternoon. The Bloody Wet pretty much peters out well east of Cloncurry. At intervals of three seconds or so, Raskovic, Sgt.

Young, the official observer and the Medical Corps captain wipe spread fingers across their faces, dislodging a few tiny crawling flies, a gesture the Stockade inmates and MP complement call the Cloncurry Salute.

"Christ," the official observer says. "These flies! How do you stand them?"

"You get used to them," Raskovic, lying, says, and silently, often the case these days, curses his luck or lack thereof. Banging into a staff car with a goddamn vindictive brigadier general aboard and a lousy incompetent GI driver at the wheel! Raskovic does not remember the collision. Normal retrograde amnesia, they told him at the 12th Station Hospital. But he's heard enough about it. The lousy incompetent GI driver was one Pfc. Giuseppe Stefanelli on the accident report. But Brig. Gen. S.O. Bargle, that sonofabitch, blamed him, Capt. Dominic Raskovic! And nobody of course had the guts to argue with a brigadier general. Capt. Raskovic would like to see Pfc. Giuseppe NMI Stefanelli in the Flat Mountain Stockade some day. It's a little dream he has.

Oh, sure, Fogerty and the Provost were sympathetic when they called him in immediately following the court-martial and told him he was the new permanent until further notice Flat Mountain Stockade commander. Brig. Gen. Bargle's recommendation, they said, recommendation meaning flat out order. Pretended to be sympathetic anyway, probably bullshit. Said Bargle's first recommendation was a fast transfer to some Infantry outfit. Claimed they sidetracked that, no Infantry training in Raskovic's 201. They also said he'd done a fine job, wrapping up the rape case in record time. Mentioned a Bronze Star, Legion of Merit perhaps. But hands tied, they said, Brig. Gen. Bargle scotched that idea. More bullshit.

The court-martial. That went well at any rate. Well enough. Sgt. Parker and his detail brought the perps back in shackles from Oro Bay, along with a long boring story about the airplane crash they survived and the booze they dumped in the Coral

Sea, the booze the goddamn flyboys liberated, Capt. Raskovic surmises, but that no longer interests him. Maj. Cain, the A.G., then moved swiftly. Perps all swore they were innocent of course. Perps always do. But Cain had a strong case. Strong enough anyway. Thanks in large part to good police work. Capt. Dominic Raskovic's good police work. The girl, Davis, was pretty shaky. Told her story, way she was grabbed, abducted and so on, but could only say she thought the skinny one, Pvt. Douglas MacArthur, the one she was told confessed, might have been the driver, and the big one, Sgt. Washington, might have been the one grabbed her first and raped her first. MacArthur throughout the two days the proceedings lasted was seated well apart from the other three in the prisoner's box, Pvt. Benson with three missing teeth beside him, Pvt. Jukes and six more MPs close at hand Perps didn't testify, didn't have to, and Cain thought MacArthur, a possible prosecution witness, dubious and unreliable.

MacArthur's confession, composed by Cpl. Finneman, was introduced, however, read into the record. Likewise the incriminating trip-ticket produced by Lt. Stanley Bannon placing MacArthur and Washington in the deuce with Davis' fingerprints on the dashboard. Bannon, a fairly good witness, laid the foundation for the trip-ticket. He also testified that MacArthur missed Retreat on the night in question. But it was Davis' fingerprints in the deuce, matched with hers taken later at the Constabulary, along with some partials said to be MacArthur's and Washington's, all that testified to at interminable length by Constable Jack Crowe, that clinched the case. Got a conviction. That and the fact perhaps that the perps' counsel, a captain versed in real estate law selected by Service Force HQ and shipped up from Sydney, was no great shakes at trial work. No match for Cain anyway. He told Cain later at the usual legal post-mortem the one thing he remembered from Trial 101 was never to put criminal suspects on the witness stand, thus exposing them to cross-examination. He did tell the court Sgt. Washington was a college man or former college man, once a Big Ten All-Conference fullback, an educated man unlikely to commit rape. But the court apparently was not impressed by that.

The court (Col. Schwartz presiding, Lt. Col. Flapp, Majs. Boldt and Nitpicker, Capt. Forney) was out but ten minutes, time to smoke a cigarette, before returning with its verdicts: guilty as charged. Col. Schwartz asked those convicted if they wished to make statements. Sgt. Franklin and former sergeant Jefferson stood and babbled they didn't do it. Pvt. MacArthur shook his head. Sgt. Washington stood, his attitude clearly one of indifference and colossal distaste, and said, "I don't know why we waste two days on this farce. You might just as well stuck it to us a week ago, saved your honky asses some time."

The court did not react and Col. Schwartz promptly handed down sentences prescribed by the ARs and the Code of Military Justice. Washington, Franklin and Jefferson: dishonorable discharges, forfeiture of all pay and allowances, Washington and Franklin first reduced to privates, hang by the neck until dead. Pvt. MacArthur was granted leniency on grounds he'd assisted in the investigation: dishonorable discharge, forfeiture, forty-to-life in a Federal Prison, eligible for parole after eighteen. Lt. Gen. Richard Sutherland, the GHQ chief-of-staff, was so advised minutes late (he'd asked to be) and, though a man seldom given to praise, congratulated the court on its good work.

Washington, Franklin and Jefferson were shipped off to the Flat Mountain Stockade the following day, shackled hand and foot in a deuce-and-a-half in a supply convoy, four MPs with tommy-guns in a jeep behind the deuce. Capt. Raskovic was a passenger in the lead jeep in that convoy, twelve miserable hours on a beat-up gravel road through pounding rain, a slow drizzle and blazing sunshine.

Capt. Raskovic sighs, scrapes a few flies from his face and surveys his new domain. He can see all there is to see from the top of Flat Mountain, actually a low hill, but there's not much to see. A vast bowl of blue sky, no sign of a cloud, a lot of brown parched ground slashed by gullies, dust devils dancing in the distance, a few windmills and corrugated tin roofs glittering in the sun in Cloncurry. He checks his watch and tells Sgt. Young, "Routh them outh." He has a partial denture, four front teeth manufactured by the blacksmith masquerading as a dentist at the 12th Station Hospital. It feels like a goddamn bicycle in his mouth and turns everything he says into a thick lisp.

"Sir!" Sgt. Young says and goes off to blow his whistle, roust the Stockade's hundred or so inmates from their pup tents, those on KP from the mess hall, and round up the off-duty MPs. The Stockade normally is dormant during the blazing mid-day heat but this is a special occasion. The MPs posted to the Stockade are mainly there to keep peace between the inmates, of whom more than half are Colored. Unlike the rest of the U.S. Army, the Flat Mountain Stockade is more or less integrated but the races don't mix much except to fight. Escape is not a big problem. A barbwire fence twelve-feet high surrounds the Stockade, there's nowhere to escape to, and there have been only two escapes. One was a Colored homosexual recaptured the same day in Cloncurry's only pub, where he was entertaining local pensioners and two sheepherders with his feminine antics. The other one was white, a deserter. His bones, picked clean by ants and rodents, were found a week later in a gully a mile away.

The inmates, rousted out, wearing baggy blue denims with a large white P on the jackets, form four ragged ranks on the parade grounds, facing the gallows, the Colored in the rear ranks. "I want the coons up in front," Capt. Raskovic says, and the ranks, First Sgt. Young bawling orders, reshuffle. The MPs form up behind the inmates with tommy-guns at port arms. They have orders, "Fire over their heads," if there's any trouble. The Navy chief, the hangman, is getting into his uniform coat.

Capt. Raskovic, standing well apart from the inmates with the official observer and the Medical Corp captain, wipes sweat from his forehead and scrapes a few flies from his face. He's bone-tired, can't sleep in this heat, has prickly heat raging in his crotch and armpits and is more than a little nervous. Stomach's a little queasy too. Naturally. He's never witnessed a hanging and he's not exactly looking forward to these. Bastards have it coming though. Raped a white girl. True, Pvt. MacArthur's confession, some might say, was induced. Encouraged anyway. And the fingerprint business was a little tricky. But that was his job. Colonel Allen's orders. Solve the case, make some arrests. "Get it off the board," they used to say in the LAPD. And the four were convicted. Fair trial and all and their sentences for once were not commuted. Not by the real MacArthur at GHQ or the commander-in-chief in the White House. There is a rumor, rumors cross the Pacific faster than a speeding bullet, Davis' uncle, that fat Congressman, had a hand in that. But that's not Capt. Raskovic's business. His conscience is clear or clear enough. He believes in capital punishment and it'll do the inmates good, especially the Colored, to watch the hangings. Teach them a valuable lesson perhaps.

Capt. Raskovic wishes this business was over with though and wonders what he'll do with the gallows when it is? Tear it down? There are half a dozen other inmates once sentenced to hang but their sentences were commuted to life. Whatever, what to do with the gallows can wait. Good thing probably the Stockade is having a rare entertainment tonight. Sad little civvie with an accordion, asleep in the MP barracks, who flew in with the official party. Flat Mountain, he said, the last goddamn stop on his goddamn USO Tour. Little bugger doesn't know it yet but he'll spend ten days at Flat Mountain waiting for a supply convoy and transport back to civilization.

The Navy hangman mounts the gallows. Former sergeants George L. Washington, Benjamin W. Franklin and Thomas NMI Jefferson (civvies now technically, Capt. Raskovic supposes, though subject still to military discipline) emerge handcuffed from the Stockade's high-security enclosure, two pup tents inside a hurricane fence topped with barbwire. They're accompanied by the chaplain, four MPs and First Lt. Bayard Mulberry, the Stockade's second-in-command. Mulberry, Raskovic notes, a young man employed by a Community Chest in civil life, how he wound up an MP a mystery, looks pretty shaky, and so does the chaplain. Will somebody, the perps' former C.O. probably, have to write "I regret to inform you" letters? Whoever, what the hell will he write? But that's not Capt. Raskovic's problem.

The perps were supposed to draw straws or something, who'd hang first. Capt. Raskovic wonders who won. Or lost. Looks like Washington. He's going up the gallows steps anyway with the chaplain and two MPs, case he proves recalcitrant.

"Tell the prithners," Capt. Raskovic says. "Tathe their hath off."

"Remove hats!" Sgt. Young bellows. The inmates remove their baggy blue denim hats. Capt. Raskovic's prickly heat flares. Be dammed if he'll claw at his crotch though. Not with all the inmates watching him with unfocussed hatred. He won't give them that satisfaction.

"You must feed your prisoners pretty good, Captain," the official observer, observing, swallowing air, says. "Those three look fat."

"No," Capt. Raskovic says. "It's they're wearing diapers."

"Diapers?" the official observer, perplexed, a law school instructor who led a sheltered life Back in the States Before The War, says.

Capt. Raskovic shrugs. "Hangman said they should."

"They may void," the Medical Corps captain, a trained physician, says. "Sphincter's sometimes an involuntary muscle. Often so at instant of death. Bladder too."

"Oh," the official observer, sorry he brought this up, says.

"Guess they're ready for me," the physician says. He takes a stethoscope from his pocket, hangs it around his neck, walks to the gallows and disappears beneath it.

Former sergeant Jefferson, waiting with Franklin at the foot of the gallows steps, abruptly bends forward and vomits and Lt. Mulberry look as if he might. An MP grabs Jefferson's denim jacket and pulls him upright. The MPs have orders. They'll carry Jefferson and Franklin up the gallows steps if they have to, hold them upright until they drop into the hereafter.

There's a problem on the gallows. Former sergeant Washington, his broad dark face hard as stone, does not want the traditional black hood dropped over his head. The hangman, holding the hood, seems to be explaining this tradition and the chaplain's hovering around, looking useless. Leave it to a goddamn coon, Capt. Raskovic thinks, screw things up! And wonders should he go up there and do something? He's the officer-in-charge, supposed to be in charge, of all this. But it looks like Washington is bowing to tradition. The hangman drops the hood over Washington's head, drapes the noose around his neck, adjusts the hangman's knot beneath his left ear and, stepping back, grasps the big wooden lever.

What, Capt. Raskovic wonders, is former sergeant Washington thinking at this moment? But the criminal mind is hard to fathom. He is not at any rate making any more trouble. Capt. Raskovic, though their acquaintance is slight, silently thanks his Eastern Orthodox God. The hangman heaves on the lever. Former sergeant Washington drops from sight. Done. Finished. The official observer gurgles. Capt. Raskovic grunts. One down. Two to go.

A mile away in the POW Camp at the foot of Flat Mountain's western slope (a half-acre surrounded by barbwire in which there are pup tents and, outside the wire, six pyramidals for the MP complement), Pvts. Elrod Finneman, Herb Steussie and the Poole brothers are taking a little smoke break in the camp kitchen before starting on the pots and pans.

The thirty POWs (two more were taken at Arawe, both wounded) and the MPs were fed at noon: spam, dehy spuds and lemonade. The Japs as usual complained, their leader, a sergeant with one arm who speaks a little English citing the Geneva Convention, claiming they're entitled to rice, but who gives a shit. The camp complement (a captain, a second john and twenty MPs) also complained too, sick of spam, dehys and the lemonade they call "battery acid." But things are tough all over.

"What you gonna tell your kids, Finneman," Steussie says. "You ever have any, they ask What you do in The War, Daddy? I help feed Japs and wash pots and pans?"

"Oh shut up!" Finneman says. Steussie's been on him ever since to their surprise and dismay they were suddenly relieved of their clerk duties in the CID Detachment on 27 December, Finneman broken to private for unspecified causes, and shipped off the next day with a supply convoy to the POW Camp. Where the camp commander put them on permanent KP. Orders from on high, he said.

That asshole Cain's orders, Steussie figures, but it was Finneman's fault. Another asshole. It was Finneman barged into Maj. Cain's HQ office, Cain up to his ass in preparations for the court-martial, and told Cain that Pvt. MacArthur's confession was "extorted." The axe fell an hour later.

Pvt. L. Poole at least, though they're sick of his tale of woe, is babysitting POWs for a good reason. He deserted his post, incurring the wrath of a brigadier general and almost wound up in an infantry outfit. His stint on KP, it's not permanent, is pretty light punishment, considering. His brother Pvt. V. Poole is a camp guard. He's only in the kitchen to share a letter from home with L. Poole. The 301st MP Co., like police departments everywere, takes care of its own. Both Pooles were shipped off to Cloncurry for their own good, get them out of the line of fire until the uproars they triggered blow over. They'll go back to Tville with the next supply convoy.

And Finneman, the asshole, minute they reached the POW camp, said he was going to write the GHQ Inspector General, tell him Pvt. MacArthur's confession was extorted. Steussie talked him out of that foolishness. "Chrissake!" he told Finneman. "That coon, his pals, they just coons! You write the I.G., we are gonna wind up in a fuckin Infantry outfit!"

Pvt. V. Poole departs and Pvt. L. Poole looks at his watch. "Twelve-hunnert-thirty," he says. "Guess it's all over, them three coons. Don't take very long, does it, hang people? We better get started the pots and pans." Mess Sgt. Martin Touhy's taking a little siesta but he'll soon be up.

* * *

USAAC Col. Big Bob Betrandus, his right foot heavily bandaged, is finishing lunch with his subordinates in the Air Depot Officers' Mess at 1300 hours. Lunch was spam and strange vegetables, the fishermen under contract to SAD dry-docked during the Bloody Wet, and little conversation accompanied its consumption. Big Bob's in a foul mood. He's wearing bedroom slippers, his right big toe though missing still hurts like hell and its absence may spoil his tennis game After The War. Orthopedist named Brooks at the 12th Station Hospital said it might, big toes contributing to balance, quick starts in pursuit of opponents' sneaky little drop shots. Outside, rain's pounding down, churning up the mud that used to be the putting green.

"Goddamn it, Gerber," Big Bob, waxing loquacious, says. "You get a line on that goddamn MP shot me yet? ID him? Any confirmation what happened to that booze?" He's been asking these questions for two weeks, since discharged from the 12th Station.

"No luck yet, Sir," Lt. Col. Gerber ruefully confesses. "Provost Marshal claims he didn't see the uh shot fired or who fired it. He knows but he won't tell us. The booze. Well, there was a crash, Sir. Or crash-landing. Near Woorammoolla. We know that. Fact, Engineering here was up there with some men yesterday, evaluate any possibility salvage the aircraft."

"So?"

"We checked the aircraft, Sir," Maj. Richall says. "There's a

Service Force training facility there with a landing craft we borrowed and went out in at high tide. The aircraft is empty. Not a damn thing in it. Well, some snakes. Jeezuzz, I saw about a dozen! Goddamn sea snakes. Can't say it was the aircraft with the booze or not, Sir. Or that rumor the flyboys had to jettison the booze, their 47 lost both engines, might be true. It's not a salvageable aircraft. It's pretty beat-up and there's no way to get near it except the tide's in and like I said, it's full of snakes. Might get the engines. Mount a crane on a barge."

"Forget it," Big Bob, writing off a $300,000 aircraft but C47s are a dime a dozen, says. "Goddamn Provost is bullshitting you. Keep after him. Chrissake, Enlisted Man shoots a superior officer, he ought to be brought to justice! And we better lay on a sortie to Sydney, this goddamn weather ever breaks again. Or we're going to be rationing booze. Like the Base O Club was before they closed it. Heard it's opening again. You got a transfer going yet for that ballplayer, Reeves? What's his name, Rapke?"

"Radke, Sir. Uh no, Sir. Not yet, Sir. I talked to him twice but most our games been rained out. He was busted to private for awhile and he liked the idea then. A transfer. But then he made corporal. Now he says he thinks he's got it made where he is. The Base Section."

"Chrissake, tell him the Base Section's going to Guinea. But then I guess there won't be any ballgames anyway. Nobody left we play. The hell with it! I'm going to go get some sack time. My goddamn foot hurts."

With that this dismal lunch breaks up. There's a rumor the evening entre will be spam again. Gerber and Richall head for the PX to buy some candy bars, case that rumor is the straight goods.

RAAF Wing Cmdr. Haines Hewlitt-Packard, beset by the second thoughts that frequently plague him these days, is picking at a late lunch, a meat pie and tea brought up from the mess, at the desk in his barracks office at 1330 hours. A few northbound aircraft took off early in the day but Garbutt Field's shut down now, the weather socked in again, rain pounding down.

And he was a bloody ass, that business with the bloody Yank Red Cross girl. Good god, what if she is bloody pregnant! And names him! And he bloody well might have caught something, no bloody rubber, though that's less likely with each passing day. He'll bloody well deny everything of course. There must be others she could name, bloody Yanks, any number. Bloody mess though. Would wife, Hortense, believe him, bloody flat denial? She's never been one to ask hard questions, voice accusations. Bloody trouble though, even bloody rumors. He was a bloody ass and bloody hell, he misses Hortense! No great shakes in bed but he misses her all the same, misses married life, misses her indifferent cooking even. Damn The Bloody War! Misses daughter Sybil, too. Doing fine, her last letter, bloody Syzmonski's little bastard kicking in her belly.

The rain pounds down. He's getting bloody tired of the bloody rain, The Bloody Wet, the bloody Yanks, the bloody War. The bloody War goes on and on, no end in sight. He'll carry on of course, do his duty, no bloody choice. But there's no bloody War today, not in Townsville, rain pounding down. By god he'll write Hortense and Sybil. He doesn't understand Sybil, cheerfully prepared it appears to become a single mother two months hence. But he'll write her. First though he'll take a little nap in his barracks quarters and so informs Sgt. Keeney. Wing Cmdr. Hewlitt-Packard's not been sleeping well lately.

Lt. Col. Flapp the Base QM and Maj. Dickinson the Provost Marshal are dawdling over coffee in the George Hotel dining room at 1400 hours. They had lunch an hour ago with their new C.O., Col. Schwartz, who finally got around to them, chewed their respective asses some on general principles then charged off to chew somebody else's ass. Outside, rain's pounding down.

"What do you think," Dickinson says. "Our new C.O.?"

"Strictly by the book," Flapp says. "Way it should be, of course. Might wear off though, he fights The War here awhile. By the way, you ever hear what happened to our previous, Allen?"

"No. Not really. They sent him down the Fifth General. I know that. The Nut Ward. Second time, my information. But he wasn't there very long. GHQ got into it and shipped him somewhere else. Don't know where. I got all that from Fogerty, who got it from a light colonel he knows at Service Force HQ. He wasn't court-martialed. Allen, I mean. Won't be, way it sounds. I figured he would be, choking General Bargle. Superior officer, same as striking, I thought."

"They might went easy on him," Flapp says. "View his rank and all. Colonel, temporary colonel, National Guard officer. Allen might have some political connections Back in The States. Lots of those Guard officers do. Speaking politics, I understand our Allies' previous requests are bearing fruit. GHQ Order forthcoming, my information. No more colored troops on the Mainland. Good riddance, I say. Some of those (C) oufits aren't bad, but they're mostly trouble, my experience."

"Amen to that," Dickinson says. "Last oufit here is shipping out tonight. Rest of the Four-oh-Fourth QM Truck. Outfit those bastards raped that Red Cross girl were in. All over for them now. Raskovic phoned me, officially report that. Hung by their necks until dead. Noon, little after. Three of them. The other one's still in our Stockade. The one who confessed. I'm waiting for orders, put him on a ship Back to The States. Leavenworth Prison. Seems sort of funny, don't it? Guy commits a crime, he gets to go home. Well, not home exactly."

"No, not exactly." Flapp says. "Four-oh-Fourth's a crummy outfit. Too bad about Raskovic, stuck out there in Cloncurry. Shrivel right up in that heat. Way the ball bounces, I guess. Maybe we better shove. Schwartz might comes charging through here again, see who's taking a long lunch."

Lt. Col. Flapp and Maj. Dickinson climb into their raincoats and depart. Both have jeeps and drivers waiting. The rain's changed to a slow drizzle dripping through the droopy palm trees along North Flinders Street. There's an AMF sentry in a wet bush hat and poncho at his post beside the rolled barbwire protecting the George Hotel's private beach, on guard though the nearest operational Japs are 900 miles away. He's staring out at the gray Coral Sea, dreaming of sunny Perth.

"Gahdamn it, Lieutenant, get your men loaded!" Maj. Shiloh Bragg, the 404th QM Truck (C) C.O., prancing around in his raincoat in hard pounding rain at 1430 hours, bawls. He's prancing in the mud and trash the last 404th EM, Charlie Co. and Baker's Fourth Platoon, left when they struck their tents. "We're due the docks at fifteen-hundred! Crank it up!"

"Sir!" Lt. Stanley Bannon says. "You men! Mount up! Get in the goddamn trucks! But we're not supposed to board until midnight, Sir."

"I know that!" Maj. Bragg says. "But we got to load the veehicles. Then wait. Men got rations, right? They can eat on the dock. Maybe us officers can eat the George. One last good meal."

Slowly, reluctantly, Lt. Bannon's Fourth Platoon EM climb into three waiting deuce-and-a-halfs. These GIs, Maj. Bragg knows the signs, are mutinous. So are those in Charlie Co. Somehow, the goddamn grapevine, the EM learned two hours ago that former sergeants Washington, Franklin and Jefferson, once fairly popular figures in the 404th, were hung by their necks until dead at high noon in the Flat Mountain Stockade. The EM have been vaguely rebellious ever since, slow and sloppy to break camp. They were in no hurry anyway to embark for Oro Bay. They also know, everybody in the 404th (C) knows, that Lt. Stanley Bannon, never a popular figure, was a witness for the honkies at the courtmartial. Helped the honkies stick it to Washington, Franklin and Jefferson.

In fact, a party unknown put a 30-calibre round through Bannon's tent at 0200 hours, missing him high by three feet, the first and so far only shot fired in anger by the 404th (C). Bannon spent the rest of the night huddled on the floor in Maj. Bragg's tent, wide awake, a cocked Forty-Five in his fist. He's wearing his Forty-Five now, strapped around his raincoat, case there's another attempt on his life, and first thing this morning put in a for a transfer, some white outfit. But nothing will come of that. Maj. Bragg will scuttle that request. The 404th like every (C) outfit needs all the good old Southern boys it can get.

Charlie and Baker's Fourth Platoon get loaded finally. "Move 'em out!" Maj. Bragg bawls. "You take the lead jeep, Lieutenant." Maj. Bragg will trail the convoy in his jeep, make sure they don't lose any vee-hicles on their way to the docks. Safer there too should the driver in the lead deuce take a run at the lead jeep. The convoy, twenty GMCs jammed with troops and gear, starts engines, bumps and splashes out the muddy track, over the Q&NR tracks, down Charters Road to the busy intersection, all traffic there halted, and out along Dock Street. The rain's slowed to a steady drizzle.

Gimpy Callahan, slouched in the rear door at the Goose & Feathers, watches the 404th (C) roll by, not without regret. Some of the GIs in the trucks wave. Gimpy responds with a half-hearted salute. They were good trade, the blackfellows, but the big question now is will his former trade, mostly AMF, return to the Goose & Feathers? Have to wait and see, Gimpy decides. Hope for the best. Set up a few rounds for the lads, restore good will. If there are any lads.

In the Smith family's private quarters behind the public room in the Barrier Arms (few "Afters" or "Befores" now, all the bloody Yanks on duty, afraid their new C.O. will catch them pissing off) Biff Smith is having another heart-to-heart in the kitchen with his daughter Louise. Mrs. Smith is taking a little nap and outside rain's pounding down.

"Hi hasks yer this before," Biff says. "Yer sigh No. But Hi wants the bloody truth, gurl! That sar'ent, the marnin' yer spill 'is bloody tay. Did 'e bloody do hennything to yer, gurl? Touch yer or hennythin? Hi wants the bloody truth, gurl!"

Louise, she's getting pretty tired of these inquisitions, decides she'll tell the bloody truth. "No, Da, 'e dint touch me or hennythin. But 'e kick 'is sheet hoff and 'e dint 'ave no clothes on. Not nuffin' and 'is Thing. Like a big banger hit was! Hit scire me, Da."

"Bloody hell!" Biff says. "Bloody Yank perwert sets foot 'ere again, I'll tear 'is bloody Thing hoff!"

Half a mile down Charters Road in the 12th Station Hospital, Capt. Leon Sussman, still in his scrubs, just out of surgery, a tricky uretha repair on a double amputee, and Second Lt. Susan Peters, who assisted, still in her scrubs, are having coffee and a cigarette in the Officers' Mess. Outside, rain's pounding down.

"What are you doing tonight, Captain?" Lt. Peters, whose shape even in scrubs Capt. Sussman notes is voluptuous, says.

"Get some sleep, I expect," Capt. Sussman says. "Make rounds. Write a letter. As of now, I've no surgery tomorrow."

"Why don't we have a drink then?" Lt. Peters says. "Write your letter tomorrow. My roomies's on leave and I've got some Johnnie Walker."

"Johnnie Walker! How?"

"Friend in Air Transport Command," Lt. Peters says with a smile Capt. Sussman finds both mischievous and inviting. "Just a friend but he's C54 pilot. He brought it from The States."

"What about Captain Brooks, the world famous orthopedist?"

"Captain Brooks," Lt. Peters says, her full red lips a delicious pout. "No longer is in the picture, Sir. I've had it with the world famous orthopedist. Him and his damn wife in Minneapolis! We broke up last night. Drink would do you good, Captain. Coin a phrase, just what the doctor ordered."

Capt. Sussman considers this. Dollop or two of Johnnie Walker with sultry Lt. Peters might in fact be just what the doctor ordered. His letter can wait. What the hell do you write anyway in response to one of those famous Dear John letters? Well, Dear Leon in his case. Rachel Grossman is awfully really truly sorry but he's been gone such a long long time and she sometimes thinks The War will never be over and Lester Salkow, with whom she couldn't help it she's fallen deeply in love with, is exempt from the Draft, considered essential, managing his father's firm, which manufactures those messkit things for the Army, and Rachel and Leon can always be friends.

"By golly, I think you're right, Lieutenant. Drink will do me good. Your quarters then? Say twenty-one-hundred? After I make rounds." He'll take precautions of course in view of Lt. Peters' lurid sexual history, but what the hell. The way it looks The War may never be over.

"It might be the MacNabs'," Mrs. Dermond (Lefty) Kelly, a skinny little woman in her middle thirties adding spuds in their skins to the mutton stew bubbling on the bottle-gas stove in the kitchen, also the dining room, in the Kelly's modest home next door to Mrs. Rooney's on North Flinders Street, says. It's 4 p.m., the Kellys don't truck with military time, and outside rain's pounding down.

"Be daft, woman!" Lefty, a big man in his socks, pants and a dirty undershirt, a longshoreman by trade, thumbing through a fistful of quid notes at the table, says. "Youse can bet ould Mac took ever bloody farthin' wit 'im, they went Melbourne. Thirty years on the docks wit 'im, Hi knows the ould skinflint. Youse tells me again, lads, the bloody truth now, where youse find this."

"Hit was Whiffy find hit, Da," Lefty's son Sean, ten, says, and his son Brendan, nine, nods. Whiffy, a small white dog of uncertain ancestry half sleep by the stove, hearing his name, thumps his tail. "We seen Whiffy diggin' by a jasmine hin the yard the Yank local be and went over there and 'e dig hit up awready. Tin hit was hin. So we bring hit 'ome. We dint know there was quid in hit, Da. Not'll we opens hit."

"Blimey!" Lefty, done with his thumbing, says. "There's near nine-hunnert bloody quid 'ere!"

"It must belong some Yank," Mrs. Kelly says. "Maybe we should tell somebody over their local."

"Be daft, woman!" Lefty says. "Bloody Yanks got more quid'n we'll hever 'ave. Some bloody Yank bury hit, hit was somethin' 'e was 'idin'. Stole maybe. And like Hi toll youse, things be slowin' down, the docks. Last bloody Yank blackfellows shippin' out t'night. Some bloody Yank wessels dischargin' Horo Bay awready. Hi soon be workin' short dies, Hi expect. This come in mighty 'andy, dies ahead. Finders keepers, Hi allas say. Wotta youse say, lads?"

"Good on youse, Da!" Sean and Brendan, their beady little eyes fixed on the late Lt. Bernie Witters' illicit stash, say. Mrs. Kelly shrugs. Lefty's the boss, makes the decisions, runs the Kelly household, runs a tight ship.

"'Ere, lads," Lefty says. "Youse done a good thing." He gives Sean and Brendan a ten-quid note: they were hoping for more. "Youse too, Sadie." Generous to a fault, Left drops a ten-quid note on the table. "Git yersell a new bonnet. Hi'll put the rest this hin a sife plice." That'll be under his underwear in his bottom dresser drawer: touch it and your dead. "Then we'll 'ave us a cel'bration! Me and yer Ma'll 'ave shandies. Youse lads can 'ave ginger beers."

* * *

In Sydney in the Service Force HQ Officers Club (the former Acropolis Restaurant on York Street, leased to the U.S. Army by its proprietor, George Pappadapalous, when the Bloody Austerity just about put him out of business), Brig.Gen. S.O. Bargle is having a drink at 1630 hours with Linda Lewis The Blonde Bombshell and Mattie Fratt. His nose, it was broken, is still swollen but his shiner's dwindled to a faint bruise.

Linda Lewis and Mattie were at the bar when Brig. Gen. Bargle arrived direct from his Service Force HQ office, drinking with a dozen drooling junior officers, celebrating the conclusion of Miss Lewis' USO Tour, which took her (and Mattie) after they left Townsville to the USAAC beachside R&R facility in Mackay and sundry Base Section installations in Rockhampton, Newcastle, Brisbane and Sydney. Brig. Gen. Bargle promptly pulled rank, sent the junior officers packing, moved the two ladies to a table, sent the GI waiter for drinks, scotch-and-water all around, and turned on the charm. He's heard how "absolutely thu-rilling" it was for Miss Lewis (and Mattie) to meet so many Boys in the Service, the Good Old USA's Fighting Men, bring them a touch of home, etc. Though Miss Lewis is a little bit miffed. The Army wouldn't let them go to New Guinea, which they heard so much about at the R&R place.

"Oh, no no," Brig. Gen. Bargle, displaying his dentures, says. "Army can't take any chances, Miss Lewis, lovely lady like yourself. Lovely ladies, I mean. Up there where bombs are dropping. Say, are you ladies free tonight? At loose ends, I mean. Maybe you'd like to see some of the night life here in Sydney? Best Liberty Port in the world, the Navy says. I'm sure I can find a date, uh escort, for Miss Fratt here." He'll dragoon some lesser rank for that unpleasant mission.

Mattie Fratt giggles and, out of Bargle's line of sight, sticks out her tongue and makes a face. Linda Lewis thanks the general for his kind offer. But, barring bad weather and the sun is shining in Sydney, they'll be leaving Swappa at 0600 hours tomorrow on a C54 Direct to The States. Somebody's supposed to pick them up at the Australia Hotel at 0400 and they still have to pack and get some rest, it's been a long busy month.

Brig. Gen. Bargle let's his idea slide. Fact is, he's heard some strange stories about Linda Lewis and Mattie Fratt. Hard to believe, way Lewis is built, but you never know, people in Show Business often perverted. Besides, his back still hurts. Damn collision. Damn MP captain, wild man in a jeep. Got him shipped off to Cloncurry though. Brig. Gen. Bargle's not been to Cloncurry but he's heard reports, weather there will fry the captain's genitalia. Too bad temporary Col. Webster R. Allen is not there too. Or somewhere doing time. Goddamn Weekend Warrior tried to choke him. Obviously insane but should have been court-martialed all the same. As subsequently recommended by the Service Force A.G., egged on by Brig. Gen. Bargle. But GHQ squelched that. Subjecting a ranking officer to court-martial said to be bad for morale, likely to raise questions regarding leadership etc.

Bullshit! The real story, apparently, is Allen has powerful political connections Back in The States. GHQ got cold feet, backed off, pulled him out of the Nut Ward at the 5th General and shipped him somewhere. Brig. Gen. Bargle's been unable to discover where. You'd think it was a Military Secret. In fact, it is a Military Secret. Brig. Gen. Bargle fears temporary Col. Allen has a soft job somewhere. While Brig. Gen. Bargle soldiers on, doing his duty, beset by many responsibilities, and good scotch is getting hard to find in Sydney, confounded War Authority's cut production again. In addition to which there's an ugly rumor Service Force HQ, six months down the road, will be establishing a Forward HQ somewhere in New Guinea! A logical spot for its deputy commander.

Brig. Gen. Bargle swallows his scotch, wishes Linda Lewis and Mattie Fratt a safe trip home, says he must be on his way, duty calls. He has a little party waiting, on standby so to speak, a pert civilian typist in the PX Section, and time may be running out. Six months will go by like a flash.

* * *

Back in Townsville in the Base Section Officers Club at 1700 hours, rain pounding down outside, Second Lt. Earl Lambert, the new manager, and Pfc. Vinnie Dugan are busy preparing for the Club's Grand Reopening. The bar's stocked, all the glasses washed and Dugan's wearing a white ward boy's coat this Lambert got for him at the 12th Station. A barman's jacket, this Lambert calls it, and he's talking about getting BSOC embroidered on the pocket. This Lambert also wants tableclothes on the tables: he's put in a requisition. All the tables have candles Dugan had to melt, burning his fingers, and mount in shot glasses. They remind him of the votive candles he used to light at St. Malachy's on West 48th Street when he was ten and praying for a bike, before he swiped one a dumb kid going to confession left parked at the church door.

"We're going to run this place like a Club instead of a saloon," this Lambert says. He says this about every five minutes. This Lambert could turn out to be a real asshole, Dugan fears. Hell, he is a real asshole. There's a goddamn clipboard behind the bar now on which, this Lambert says, Dugan is supposed to write down, keep a record for chrissake, of every bottle removed from inventory and every bottle emptied, time and date. There'll be no more pilfering, this Lambert says, or drinking while on duty either. He'd fucking quit, Dugan thinks, except his tips, though seldom large, increase by half the $54 a month the Army pays him.

"Bartender!" this Lambert, popping out of the storeroom, he was taking another inventory, says. "There was a dog digging under a bush out in the yard. He scattered dirty all over. Clean it up. Then wash your hands and make sure the candles are all in the center of the tables."

"Sir!" Dugan says. What an asshole.

* * *

Pfc. Edward T. Devlin is working overtime at 1730 hours, typing at the field desk in the 4th AHD's sagging pyramidal a quarter-mile off the seaward end of Seven-Mile Strip outside Port Moresby, in which he also sleeps, roused daily at first light in good weather when aircraft start warming up and taking off. The weather now is hot and steamy, a light drizzle fell earlier, but the ceiling, thin gray clouds, is at 2000 feet and the day's last incoming aircraft from elsewhere in New Guinea, New Britain and the Trobriand Islands are roaring in low over his head at intervals, slapping the pyramidal with their prop wash. A few 47s from the Australian Mainland came in earlier before the Mainland weather closed in again. The 4th AHD jeep is parked outside between the pyramidal and Capt. Clapham Panmander's officer's tent.

Eddie Devlin's working overtime, typing Panmander's Initial Notes on the Arawe Campaign, staying late to, well, make amends. Prove he's a dedicated soldier. He beat Panmander back to Seven-Mile by a day but did have three cracked ribs sustained when the Lucky Lil went banging into the mudflat. The battalion surgeon at the parachute outfit outside Woorammoolla, a sadist in a white coat, poked them for awhile then taped them up and put four stitches in and a fresh bandage on the gash on his forehead. Panmander, naturally, he's a sympathetic old coot, minute he saw Eddie, said, "What happened to your head?"

Eddie told the truth, more or less. The Lucky Lil's crash-landing still was the subject of a lot of talk around Seven-Mile and he figured Panmander might hear he was aboard at the time, one of the survivors. "I got a chance to go to Townsville, Sir, on a ham-and-egg flight. Just down and right back. I was bringing you back a ham, Sir. But that was the Forty-Seven had to crash-land in the mudflat. We had to throw the ham out, Sir." He didn't mention his forged travel orders.

"The Forty-Seven with all that liquor aboard?" Panmander said. "I heard about that. You went without my permission then?"

"Well uh, yes, Sir," Eddie, appearing contrite, said. "But it was just down and right back, Sir. And you weren't here, Sir."

"Don't do it again," Panmander said.

"Oh, I won't, Sir," Eddie said. "I won't ever fly again, Sir. Not if I can help it." And that was and is the God's truth.

Panmander grunted and let it go at that. He was, still is, pretty happy. He went out with a patrol at Arawe armed with one of the new light 30-calibre carbines. The patrol flushed four starving Japs out of a hole and killed them and Panmander's pretty sure he killed one of them. Helped kill him anway. He's cut a notch in the stock on his carbine and is booked on the first C47 to Saidor once the airstrip there is operational, another day or so is the current sitrep, but first wants to read his Arawe Report after Eddie types it. He aims to kill more Japs at Saidor. He's a bloodthirsty old coot and Eddie's prayers will go with him. He'd hate to lose the old coot.

Eddie bends to his typing. The old coot's notes are clear enough but some got wet and are smeared. "28-29 Dec. The Arawe perimeter was extended an additional 400 yds against weakening enemy resistance, placing the landing beaches beyond enemy mortar range, and plans made to launch long-range patrols for a link-up with the US Marines at Cape Gloucester." Working overtime, Eddie will miss supper at the 34th Troop Carrier mess. He won't miss the spam and dehys but the last 47 up from the Mainland was a ham-and-egg flight with a cargo that included fresh milk. He'll miss the milk. That 47 subsequently took off again and is circling at 7000 feet out over the ocean to keep the milk cold. He won't see Billy Gote at the officers' end of the mess tent either, but so it goes. Eddie's supper will be a PX candy bar he never heard of Before The War, peanuts in something pink and gooey.

Eddie's leading the clean life he promised the Deity he would while the Lucky Lil sank through the sky over the Coral Sea. There are of course no major opportunities to do otherwise in his present circumstances. But he did go twice to the Sunday outdoor Mass at Twelve-Mile Strip, though missing last Sunday. He's still thankful he's simply alive, content with life without a Packard convertible, happy in fact to clean Panmander's carbine, a chore he detests. Alive and breathing: that's the main thing. They were in Woory four days, rain pounding down the whole time, waiting for a break in The Bloody Wet and space aboard an aircraft bound for Seven-Mile, living, existing, in the Transient Area, six leaky pyramidals at the end of the Woory Strip, scrounging lousy meals at the Woory MP Detachment, nursing their injuries, nothing else to do after Billy Gote got a message through on the ACS reporting their whereabouts. Four wonderful euphoric days all the same, as Eddie remembers them. Because he was alive! Harry meanwhile had a little talk with Pvts. Benson and Jukes. Convinced them, he was pretty sure, that the booze they threw from the Lucky Lil was just a super ham-and-egg flight cargo. Or even if it wasn't, they better not talk about it. Lt. Col. Fogerty, Harry said, he ever found out they helped throw all that booze into the Coral Sea just to save their own necks, he'd skin them alive. Then a 34th Squadron 47 picked them up for a white-knuckle flight over water to Seven-Mile.

The 34th Squadron GI who, riding a bicycle, delivers the mail, sticks his head in the pyramidal. "Mail for you, Devlin," he says, and tosses Eddie a bundle. Eddie sorts it, sets the Official and a V-mail for Panmander aside. There's a V for him too and two letters. One is from Ann Silvers. The Arawe Campaign can wait. Eddie wrote Ann a steamy letter in Woory and another two weeks ago but this is her first reply. He opens it, finds flowing cursive, brief and to the point:

> Dear Eddie. I enjoyed your letters but please do not write me any more. I am engaged (to be married) to Major Abel Cain, the Base Section Adjutant-General, as soon as he gets official permission, and I do not think he would enjoy them. Keep safe, Ann

The V-mail is from Miss Merrilee Pretzell in Winatchee Falls. Her writing is very small (said to indicate intelligence) and neat:

> Dear Edward: I am writing to tell you that I am going to be married on March the 10th. My husband to-be is Captain George W. Orthby. He is a Princeton graduate with a degree in anthropology and, presently, the head of a section in Medical Administration at an Army Headquarters in Chicago. We met a month ago when I was in

Chicago visiting Arlene Wapshot, one of my best friends from Wedgewood. George is from Grosse Point, Michigan. His father is with General Motors. We will be living in Chicago. Or elsewhere perhaps should George be transferred, but he does not think that likely. I trust this finds you safe and well. Merrilee.

Jeezuzz! Two Dear John (well, Dear Eddie) letters in a single mail call! Is that some kind of record? The score at any rate clearly is Cupid 2, Devlin 0.

But these are not exactly Dear John letters. He scarcely knows Ann Silvers but for one quick one-night stand which was more like a quick twenty-minute stand. Merrilee is in another category but it's not like they were engaged or anything. Eddie dated Merrilee in high school and, also, when he was a Winatchee Falls Junior College student and Merrilee, shipped off to The Wedgewood School, a fancy Philadelphia girls school, was home summers. But Merrilee's father is Dr. Wayne Pretzell, the principal founder and big chief at Winatchee Falls' world-renowned Pretzell Chiropratic Clinic, and it was always clear to Eddie anyway that Dr. Wayne and his wife Vera did not consider Eddie a suitable long-term (or even short-term) companion for their beloved daughter. Nevertheless, he loved Merrilee, or thought he did, and frequently wrote her when first in the service. Merrilee's replies however were brief and infrequent and Eddie met other girls, most recently Ann Silvers, and this correspondence lapsed. He may write Merrilee, wish her well and Capt. George too. Or then again he may not. Whatever, he is if Merrilee really cares safe and well. He's alive! In one piece! That's the main thing.

The other letter is from his mother, who distrusts V-mail. Not much new in Winatchee Falls, everybody still praying The War will soon be over though it doesn't look like it will be, Dad's worried about the tires (on the Devlins' '35 Ford) but it's hard to get new ones. Enclosed is a clipping from the Bugle Call, Winatchee Falls' daily-except-Sunday newspaper:

SERVING THEIR COUNTRY

Compiled by Pearl Mulch, Bugle Call Society Editor & Military Reporter

Pvt. Warren Olson, son of Mr. and Mrs. Olav Olson, 412 7th Ave. SE, who is attending the Army Cooks & Bakers School at Fort Leonard Wood in Missouri, recently placed second in cake decorating in a competition at the school.

Sgt. John P. Rahilly, son of Mr. and Mrs. John P. Rahilly of rural Salem Township, has been promoted to First Sergeant in his Army unit in Italy.

Pvt. Marjorie Bremer, daughter of Mr. and Mrs. Werner Bremer of Stiles, has completed her Basic Training in the Women's Army Corps at Fort Oglethorpe in Georgia and is awaiting an assignment.

Word has been received from the International Red Cross that Air Force Lt. Chester Bennett, son of Mrs. Pauline Bennett, 210 11th Ave. SE, is a Prisoner-of-War in Germany. Lt. Bennett, a P47 Fighter plane pilot in the Air Force in England, was shot down in Germany in December. Other pilots reported seeing Lt. Bennett parachute from his stricken airplane, but what had happened to him thereafter had not been previously known.

That last one is a shocker. Chesty Bennett was, most of time for almost ten years, Eddie's best friend in Winatchee Falls. And now he's a POW. The Krauts got him. But Chesty, Eddie is pretty sure, will survive if anybody does. As to the others. Well, Stub Olson was always thought to be a little bit swishy. Whip Rahilly, a distant cousin who enlisted right after The War started in Europe, is a natural-born Top Kick. Margie Bremer was Eddie's first sexual encounter, they were nine at the time, and now she's a WAC! But Chesty, Stub, Whip and Margie, like Merrilee Pretzell, belong to that distant life Before the War. None of the five, Eddie surmises, could find New Guinea on a map. Swappa, both a place and a state of mind, is where Eddie is now. And he's alive!

Eddie says a little prayer now and then, thanking his Lord for his life and adding a reasonable request. Please, Lord, when the 4th AHD moves forward (as no doubt it eventually will) please let it be on a ship. He'll take his chances with Jap submarines. And he has an appointment tomorrow at the 7th Station Hospital at the other end of Seven-Mile Strip (where a medic removed the stitches in his forehead two weeks ago, no scar worth a war story left) to get the tape off his ribs and some salve or something, he hopes, for the prickly heat raging under the tape. Which he can't even scratch. He'll try and find Rose Pearl Stevens too, he heard she's quartered at the 7th Station. Be a chance if he does to talk about the good old days in Tville, the few there were, and Billy Gote.

Munching his candy bar, Eddie returns to his typing while the daylight lasts. Panmander's a prolific old coot. The Japs seldom bother the Moresby area with more than a single bomber now and that infrequently but the blackout's still in effect.

*   *   *

Half-a-mile off the other end of Seven-Mile Strip at 1830 hours, Rose Pearl Stevens and Boots Davis are sharing the last of a quart of Australian whiskey cut with GI grapefruit juice in the 7th Station Hospital pyramidal they share. They're wearing baggy khaki slacks and shirts with ARC shoulder patches, the sleeves rolled down. Bare skin excites the mosquitoes. Native Papuans with tanks strapped on their naked backs roam around every day spraying all the stagnant puddles they find with oil, but the mosquitoes apparently thrive on this oil. Outside the clouds have lifted, the sun is setting and the western sky's an abstract painting, a blaze of red and pink and orange. The local sunsets, enhanced by the dust kicked up by aircraft and the everlasting military traffic, are stupendous.

Boots and Rose Pearl ate an hour ago in the 7th Station Officers' Mess (spam, dehys, greasy canned carrots, bitter lemonade, Atabrine and salt tablets) and have an hour to kill before jeeping to the Red Cross EM Club in a quonset in Port Moresby and a busy evening fending off the usual propositions. If the Club opens and it probably will. The Club is closed if air raids are thought likely, but there have been no actual air raids since 31 December, New Year's Eve, just a few Yellow Alerts soon followed by All Clears.

Port Moresby (mainly native huts, Australian-Papuan government buildings, a ramshackle hotel, a trading post and a few bungalows for the government officials, population 2,000, when the Pacific War began, most of those evacuated) was pretty much smashed flat along with its docks by heavy Jap air raids in early months of 1942, but the rubble's been cleaned up, some of the docks rebuilt and some of the government buildings replaced with quonsets. Gen. Douglas MacArthur's Advance HQ, rumored to be air-conditioned, is in a villa on a low hill outside the city, previously occupied by the Papuan Territory's chief officer, where the breeze, if there is a breeze, disperses the mosquitoes.

Boots arrived a week ago during a brief break in The Bloody Wet, bringing the whiskey, with a clean bill of health thanks to 20-million units of penicillin for a mild gonorrhoeal infection, the grand news she wasn't pregnant and a vaguely uneasy conscience stemming from the court-martial, though she's pretty well hammered that into submission. It may indeed have been those four nigras or two of them raped her and somebody by god was going to pay for that! The big one looked the type. A huge man, handsome in a brutal sort of way, with a face like carved dark stone, impassive throughout the proceedings, who then belittled the court in a brief statement. The other two, she judged them to be field nigras, also looked like rapists. It never was clear as to which of the two raped her, but no matter. She did feel almost sorry sometimes for the skinny one said to have been the truck driver the way the other three glared at him the whole time, murder in their hearts if she was any judge. But he was the one who confessed. His signed confession, surprisingly articulate, was read into the record. And he got off, in a manner of speaking. Wasn't sentenced to hang anyway. Whatever, it's all water under the bridge or over the dam now, whatever that saying is. Except she'll have to live with it, raped by two nigras, infected by one or both of them, all the rest of her life.

"I wonder who they'll send?" Rose Pearl says. There are two empty cots in their pyramidal tent and two more staff assistants are supposed to arrive from Townsville, next break in The Bloody Wet. They were supposed to arrive yesterday but the Army units relieving the First Marine Division on Cape Gloucester had first call on the available aircraft.

"Ann Silvers, I hope," Boots says. "Betty Lou. Anybody but Score and Tucker. I'd hate to share a tent with that cat fight. Ann would rather stay in Tville though. I told you she's engaged. Major Cain, the Base Section A.G. They got acquainted when I had to go and see him before the court-martial. Go over my testimony. Ann came with me. I think he's a jerk but Ann fell for him." Boots shrugs.

"Mmmm," Rose Pearl, studying her whiskey and juice, says. "Boots, something I have to tell you. Have to tell somebody! I think I'm pregnant."

"Oh no! Who? I mean if you."

"That damn RAAF Wing Commander. The one kept taking me to the Australia Club. He wouldn't use a rubber and, naturally, I was in mid-stream. It's my own damn fault! I should have made him use one. But we'd had I don't how many drinks and two bottles of wine. Good wine. And he was so damn persistent. I missed my period."

"Go to Townsville, Rose Pearl. The 12th Station Hospital. We'll think of a reason. There's a captain there, Captain Sussmann. He'll do a d-and-c, no questions asked. Tell him it was my idea. Hell, I'll give you a note. Or the 5th General in Brisbane. They do early abortions there, Sussmann told me. Harder to think of a reason though, go to Brisbane. Or there might be a doctor here at the 7th Station."

"Oh God! I don't know, Boots. An abortion. That's against my religion. I'm Catholic, you know. Supposed to be. Abortion's like murder, they tell us. Worse than rape. Oh, Boots, I'm sorry!"

"Oh no it's not!" Boots says. "But that's all right. Forget it. I know you didn't mean. I was just making a suggestion."

"I know. I appreciate it. I really do. Boots, it's none of my business. But have you? I mean since, you know. The night Billy Gote was here and I went for a walk?"

"No. We did not. I didn't feel like it. I don't feel like it. I hope that wears off before I'm forty! But I'm sorry now, we didn't. You know, Billy proposed to me that night. Well, he didn't exactly propose. But he said he was thinking he might like to marry me some day. After The War and he was divorced. I didn't know he was married. After The War! Yes, I'm sorry now, what happened, we didn't. I guess that's why I was crying this afternoon. You know, I read somewhere once, Rose Pearl. We don't regret the things we do, whatever they are, half as much as we regret the things we might have done. But didn't."

"I'll keep that in mind," Rose Pearl says. "And wait a while, my little problem. See what happens. Or doesn't happen. Might be a false alarm. Oh, hell! Let's finish this damn whiskey!"

What happened was the Lucky Lil II and all aboard (Billy Gote, Lt. Donald, Cpl. Johnson and Sgt. Darrell Hendershot, Porky Wallace's replacement) disappeared, vanished, a week ago, somewhere over the Coral Sea en route to Noumea on New

Caledonia, 1400 miles over water with extra fuel tanks in the cargo compartment. There was a report the French in Noumea would sell booze to flyboys at reasonable prices and New Cal's in the Central Pacific Area, ignorant of and not bound by GHQ SWPA Order 404:44 prohibiting the transport, etc. The Lucky Lil II (the superstition is aircraft replacing lost aircraft should have the same name) was selected for this mission because Billy Gote was thought to be good at bargaining for booze and still owed his Squadron C.O., Lt. Col. Brandon Hampstead, three cases of scotch.

Boots got the whole story such as it is yesterday, they'd only heard the Lucky Lil II was "missing," when she ran into Hampstead at the main PX at Five-Mile Strip and asked him, Was the Lucky Lil II still missing?

"Missing presumed gone," Lt. Col. Hampstead said. "Terminally kaput, I'm afraid. Our best guess is the aircraft exploded. There wasn't any mayday anybody heard. No time for that, most likely, no warning. Just a big bang. There probably were fumes in the cabin. Damn extra tanks are always prone to leak a little. Doesn't take much then. Errant spark, somebody drops a wrench, lights a cigarette. Doubt they were smoking though. Lieutenant Gote knew better. He was one of my best pilots. Anyway, we heard there was a cruiser, think it was the Little Rock, had a bogey on its radar screen, time and place about right. Then, bang! The bogey went off the screen. Navy mounted a search, they got our Missing Report. Didn't find anything. There wouldn't been anything to find, really. Little oil slick maybe. I hate to send boys up, extra tanks in the cargo compartment. But it's fourteen-hundred miles to Noumea and we weren't sure about the refueling situation there. Damn it all! I'll miss Lieutenant Gote. Kind of a wild kid. Hard on airplanes. Lost my old one. Got it down in one piece though. No fatalities. Mudflat near Woorammoolla. Guess you heard about that. He was one of my best pilots."

* * *

In the 301st MP Co. Orderly Tent in Townsville at 1900 hours, rain pounding down, hammering the taut canvas, Lt. Michael Sweeney, a self-employed Yosemite National Park guide in civil life, who in addition to his other duties is the Company censor, is peering hard at a damp V-mail form, deciphering with great difficulty the illiterate scrawl produced by one of the prisoners in the Company Stockade.

> Mrs. Martha M'Arthur c/o Doheny's Sawmill, Greenboro Florda Deer Mama I is in bad trubble white mans say I do a bad thin to a white gurl I din do it Mama but white mans hurts me awfull bad I say I do it but I din do it they senning me to prizzin back home prizzin call Leven Wurth long long time 40 yeers if you can come see me Mama I din do it Mama honess they hurts me reel bad I say I do it & 3 my buddes do it & they hangs them but I din do it Mama I luv you Mama Yur Lucky 13. Pvt. D. MacArthur.

Be dammed! It's the skinny little coon confessed his buddies raped that Red Cross girl! And his scrawl though illiterate has a ring of truth. Lt. Sweeney chews his grease pencil and wonders. Should he do anything? Tell somebody something? Who? What? Those coons were court-martialed, convicted following a fair trial, three sentenced to hang by their necks until dead and, the report is, those three, hung by their necks until dead at high noon in the Flat Mountain Stockade. There's nothing he can do about them. And Pvt. MacArthur was granted leniency. Wasn't hung anyway.

It's not his problem, Lt. Sweeney decides. But there'll be no references to white mans hurting Pvt. MacArthur bad. That'd shake up morale among the coons on the Home Front and it's prejudicial to military discipline. Lt. Sweeney blacks out those references with his grease pencil, stamps the V-form "Passed by

Censor" and initials the stamp. There's no more mail to censor, the O Club is reopening in less than thirty minutes and Lt. Sweeney aims to be on hand for that. The talk is the new Club manager has really spruced the place up.

* * *

In a sagging pyramidal tent in the 404th QM Truck (C) camp outside Oro Bay, where the tropical night is falling swiftly at 1930 hours, the great fiery red ball that was the sun long gone behind the misty dark green mass of the Owen Stanley Range, Sgt. Leroy Brown, last seen lifting a few beers with three pals at the Goose & Feathers the day the 404th (C) began its move to Oro Bay, and his pals are having a serious discussion.

The other GIs quartered in the pyramidal, there are two, told by Sgt. Brown, "Take a walk," are taking a walk. All six spent the day, twelve long hours with a brief lunch break, unloading ammunition from an LST up from Townsville. LSTs from Townsville and Direct from The States creep through the channel the Engineer outfit blasted in the coral reefs and beach at Oro Bay now. So the four are tired but there's this matter they must discuss. Or so Pvt. Clinton (Lips) Silvester, seems to think.

"Honkies gonna hangs them!" Pvt. Silvester says. "Sar'ent Washington and them. Hangs them till they daid. Might be they is daid. Cook on that LST we unload tell me everbody in Tville sayin' it t'day the honkies hangs them. Hangs them till they daid for some'pin us done! That don' seem like it right, sar'ent."

"Better them then us," Sgt. Brown, a realist, says. "So what you got it in your head to do, Lips? Confess? You was gonna confess you better done it when them MPs come and tooks them. Honkies court-martials them awready. Hangs them till they daid maybe. Honkies ain't gonna pay you no never mind now. But I might, you opens your big fat mouth."

Sgt. Brown's reputation is he's meaner than a junkyard dog and skilled as a surgeon with a straight razor. And he goes about

6-2 and 230 pounds. Pvt. Silvester, prey to second thoughts, vows no word will pass his lips. He'll live with a bad conscience, given the choices presented, though mumbling, "Don' seem right, honkies hangs them for some'pin us done."

"It ain't right," Sgt. Brown says, then offers a little philosophy. "But that be life, Lips, honkies runnin' The War. I guess this discussion close then?"

Not quite. "That muthafuck Loo'tent Bannon, Baker Company," Pvt. Houston Scales says. "Cook that LST say Loo'tent Bannon, he testify it prolly Wash and Ben and Kayo done it, fuck that cunt, when them honkies court-martials them."

"Never you mine that muthafuck," Sgt. Brown says. "Loo'tent Bannon be up here pretty soon. We throw a snake in his tent some night. Or a grenade, we get one. We fix that muthafuck. C'mon, less go the movie. Honky run the projector tell me it The Second Front wi' that Linder Lewis in it. The one wi' the big boobies."

There's an outdoor movie every night, rain or shine, at Oro Bay, the screen behind homeplate on the softball field, though the film's sometimes delayed or interrupted by Yellow Alerts. Everybody brings their own seat, empty packing crates or ammo boxes, and ponchos or raincoats, case it rains. The Colored sit in the rear.

* * *

There's also an outdoor movie, rain or shine, at Happy Valley, the Base Section EM Camp in Townsville, and at 2000 hours several hundred GIs in ponchos and raincoats, sitting on various things in a light drizzle, are awaiting its start. It will start when the officers who sit in front on the permanent benches arrive and get settled.

The movie tonight is Me and My Gal starring Judy Garland and Gene Kelly and many in the audience have seen it before, several times. But there's this great scene in it. Judy and Gene are a song-and-dance team just booked, it's 1918, to play the Palace. Every hoofer's dream. Then Kelly gets his World War I Draft Notice. He thinks of something though. He opens their wardrobe trunk, lays his left hand on its edge and prepares to smash his fingers with the lid, thus Dodging the Draft, then hesitates. That's going to hurt! At which point all the GIs, they've been waiting for this and know whereof they speak, will shout, "Do it, you asshole!"

"Y'know," Pvt. Ray Dashman, a Buna Government Station veteran with chronic malaria, a Limited Service cook trainee at the 12th Station Hospital, says. "I wisht we had grenades like the fuckin movies got we was in Guinea. You see that movie last week, The Second Front, wi' Tyrone Power and that Linda Lewis we heard was here but we never see her in it?"

"Mmmm," Cpl. Gordie Peterson, a second cook, Pvt. Dashman's mentor, busy lighting a wet Fleetwood, says. "The one with the big boobs."

"Yeah. Y'know, I think when I see that movie. Fuckin grenades we had in Guinea, some dint even go off. They did, you was lucky they kill a fuckin Jap in his hole. They never even make a dent in a fuckin Jap bunker. But jeez! Tyrone, he thrun a grenade in that Kraut bunker, steel doors come flyin' off, bodies come flyin' out, few fuckin Krauts still kickin' surrender! Army oughta find out where the fuckin movies gets them grenades."

Cpl. Bruno Fazoli, he's seen it, skips Me and My Gal. At 2030 hours he pulls on his raincoat in the pyramidal he shares in Happy Valley and plods through the rain, Col. Schwartz scuttled his previous arrangement with the staff car, to the Base Section NCO Club in a decrepit bungalow behind the horse track, where he finds as he figured he would the Motor Pool's new first sergeant, the former acting Top Kick, at the makeshift bar with a Foster's in his fist. It's a slow night at the club, everybody just about broke with ten days to go to pay day.

"Yo, Top," Fazoli says. "Buy you a Foster's?"

First Sgt. Wallace Shields, a dumb tough husky Midwestern farmer who got carried away and enlisted (Fazoli's heard) the day after Pearl Harbor, surveys Fazoli with surprise and suspicion. "Yeah, sure. Whatta ya want?"

"Well I heard a rumor," Fazoli, while the GI bartender sets up two Foster's, says. "Base Section gonna ship some units, personnel, up Oro Bay pretty soon. For a Advance Echelon. That a real rumor, Top?"

"I guess," First Sgt. Shields says. "Motor Pool C.O. told me make up a list anyway. Fuckups we wanna get rid of. They prolly ship out next week. Why?"

"I like and be on that list, Top."

"You mean you like volunteer! You wanna go Oro Bay? You must be nuts, Fazool!"

"Well, I'm kind a tired a Townsville, Top. I know Guinea, Oro Bay, they're a bitch. But we all be up there sooner later prolly. So what the hell. You put me on the list, Top?"

"Sure. That's you want. I don't care you're crazy." They seal this bargain with two more Foster's Fazoli buys and he goes out into the rain and back to Happy Valley.

Crazy like a fox. Little Susie Buncom thinks she's pregnant. That's a mystery: he always took precautions. He suspects little Susie has other boyfriends who have her. But he's the one she's picked, she's threatening to tell her parents and her big brother, a goddamn AIF lance jack about the size of a Sherman tank, Fazoli's seen his photo, done with liberating villages in the Markham Valley, will be home on leave two weeks hence. But Bruno Fazoli, whose mother did not raise a fool, will be long gone by then. Safe. Somewhere in New Guinea.

What, Fazoli wonders, is little Josefina Scalzi doing these days? He left little Josefina in a similar alleged situation in Hoboken when, propelled by her alleged situation and his draft notice, he quit his part-time job driving a Yellow Cab and enlisted. Josefina's situation, later reports from Hoboken disclosed, was a false alarm, but Fazoli by then was awaiting embarkation with an unattached Motor Pool Detachment bound for Swappa.

* * *

At Manic Manor at 2100 hours, a thin drizzle falling outside, the usual party is working up a head of steam, thirteen states and Puerto Rico represented, bugs banging the light bulb over the kitchen table, etc. Billy Eckstine is silent. He gave out two weeks ago, his final words, "It's gawnnn and gawnnn and gawnnn and," until somebody took the record off. The music tonight is Glen Miller's "Tuxedo Junction," rapidly wearing out. The drinks, unfortunately, are Australian whiskey and 12th Station Hospital medical alcohol cut with GI grapefruit juice, nothing else available. The goddamn War Authority's cut production again and Burns-Phelps and Cummins & Campbell, the island traders, are reluctant to sell to Yanks in view of GHQ Order 404:44 and Col. James Schwartz's hardnosed reign. Pop's not mixing Swagmans, there's no brandy, though he's offered, finding no takers, to lace the whiskey with his secret ingredient, now thought to be sheep dip.

Sgts. Harry Parker and Arnold Saljeski arrived ten minutes ago with rave reviews for a bonzer movie, Casablanca, parroting some of its best lines, and Saljeski's promised the Manor residents he'll let them know, they won't want to miss it, which outdoor movie it will be playing tomorrow night.

"I see the usual suspects been rounded up," Harry, quoting further from Casablanca, says. "Too bad about Billy Gote, huh?"

A 34th Troop Carrier pilot northbound from Brisbane who landed in Townsville yesterday and RON and is making a move doomed to failure on Betty Lou Fricker's knickers brought word of Billy Gote's presumed death and 34th Troop's conclusion regarding it, "Aircraft prolly just blew up," to last night's party. But this is Harry's first opportunity, he missed that party while running a blackjack game, heard it from Saljeski, to express his sympathy. And it is too bad about Billy Gote and for a brief moment, touched by the dirty breath of war, the party falls silent. They all miss ebullient Billy Gote, and his gin.

But life goes on. The discussion turns to the Women's Army Corps. There was a story in YANK Magazine. WACs are replacing GIs in soft Stateside jobs, freeing those GIs for service overseas, and there are WACs in the ETO, replacing GIs with soft jobs there for service nearer The Front.

"Couple guys the fuckin Rep Dep I talk to," Saljeski says. "Sorry, Agnes. Claim they was replaced by f—Wacks. I wunner the fuckin Army, sorry, gonna send some over here? Relieve the shortage women."

The consensus is that's not likely, the ETO gets all the goodies, and the 12th Station Hospital supply sergeant revives a discussion launched earlier. How much longer will The War last? Estimates vary, ranging between four and eight years, but the supply sergeant belittles those rosy projections.

"I figure it out," he says. "I look at a map. Starting from where the Japs petered out there thirty-two miles from Port Moresby year ago last September, that's sixteen months, and measure where this Saidor is. Allied Forces advance around two-hundred-fifty miles, the crow flys. In sixteen months. That's two-hundred miles a year like. You know how far it is, this Saidor to Tokyo? Twenty-six-hundred miles, the crow flys! More, you go island island. War's gonna last thirteen more years, easy."

"Jeezuzz!" Harry says. "I be forty-two years old! I prolly be out a the goldurn Army before it's over!"

Others also hoot at this projection, but the supply sergeant sticks to his guns. "Look history," he says. "There was a Thirty-Year War and a Hundred-Year War." But no one present wishes to contemplate a Thirteen-Year War.

"Oh, it won't last that long," Agnes Moore, who in thirteen years will be fifty-eight, she just had a birthday, says. "You girls all packed?" The 34th Troop pilot said earlier a brief break in The Bloody Wet is expected tomorrow.

"I am," Betty Lou Fricker says. "Except for some laundry. I'll pack that wet if I have to."

"I can't find one of my skirts," Ima Score says. "That damn Tucker probably swiped it. Otherwise, I'm packed. Ready to go. I'm ready for another drink too. Juice and."

"I thought it was Silvers was goin' to fuckin Guinea," Saljeski says. "Where is she anyway?" Damn it, watch your mouth, Agnes says. Sorry, Saljeski says.

"No, we drew straws," Betty Lou says. "And I won. Or lost. Depends on your point of view. Ann would rather stay here. Now she's found true love."

"That where she is?" Saljeski says. "With Cain? All I ever heard, he's a fu—royal jerk. Where's Flots and Jets? And Tucker? She found a new boyfriend with lots a rank yet?"

"Flots has a date," Betty Lou says. "Major at the Air Depot. Jets is up in their room sulking. Tucker's in bed. Red Lined. Her period always knocks her out."

* * *

Up in her cot in the Manor bedroom she shares with Ima Score, though not much longer, Jill Tucker, damn period always lays her low, wearing her pad and harness and the silk pajamas she hauled all the way from Boston, the shaky floorlamp she shares with Score on, is rereading her father's V-mail, wild script on the microfilm, some of it blurred. Pa no doubt was bawling.

Brother Ralph (no bombardier, just an Eighth Air Force bomb jockey) is dead. Run down by a lease lend deuce-and-half in the blackout in an English Midlands village. Drunk, she surmises, looked the wrong way for on-coming traffic. But Pa no doubt thinks Ralph a patriot who gave his life for his country. Not Jill. Ralph was five, a spoiled only brat when she came along and wrecked his world, and mean. Ralph pulled her hair, pinched her, broke her dolls, hit her, bit her, Ralph liked to inflict pain, then lied, whining denials when she howled accusations. Never punished either. Just told he should be nice to his little sister. Pa'd already put Tucker & Son on the tin fence around the scrapyard and Ma, the former Mary Malarkey, by then was deep into the drink.

More memories, unbidden and largely unwelcome, assail Jill Tucker, while outside the everlasting rain pounds down, drumming on the Manor's roof.
"Jillene," Mrs. Mahoney the eighth grade teacher said. "Is a very imaginative child. She has a vivid imagination." Mrs. Mahoney, fifteen years in the Saugus public schools hammering knowledge into stubborn little minds, was prone to redundancy.
"That's nice," Ma, breathing Bushmills single-malt Irish whiskey from the world's first distillery (est. 1608) on Mrs. Mahoney, said. "We're very proud of Jill."
A year later, Pa divorced Ma, rather a stigma at the time, but Ma'd been to treatment three times then failed her finals, which was why Pa got custody and their house in Saugus. They'd met at a summer dance on a Boston pier, wed before the first snow fell. Ma, Jill suspects, pregnant with Ralph. Ma also, she surmises, though a tub of lard after taking to the drink, was at the time attractive: petite, busty, with good legs: the body Jill inherited. They were married by a judge and that was the end of Ma with the Malarkeys, a large loud quarrelsome South Boston family Catholic as the Pope. Pa worships the almighty dollar. He somehow kept the scrapyard going through The Great Depression while a series of housekeepers, middle-aged women who needed the money, came in by the day to cook and clean and do the laundry. A series because they all sooner or later, usually sooner, had had it with Ralph, a miserable kid become a miserable adolescent, a foul-mouthed whiner who thought he was lord of the manor. Between housekeepers, Jill did the cooking and cleaning and they sent the laundry out. Ralph when home, he was a freshman twice at Northeastern, living in a dorm, criticized her cooking and otherwise made her life miserable. Ralph was big like Pa,

230 pounds, no athlete, still liked to inflict pain. She was not domestically inclined but put up with this, had no choice really. She missed Ma though they met now and then at a coffee shop near Foley Square and had what Ma called "nice talks." Ma said she was "living with a friend in a nice apartment" in Southie, her home turf, and gave Jill her address. They also talked on the phone but by mid-afternoon Ma's conversation was slurred and rambling.

She was often home alone. Japan was buying scrap by the boatload and Pa was busy at the yard or out with his flavor of the month, picked up in a bar. She was not always home alone though. It was then, Jill recollects, she suddenly developed firm 34Cs and an abiding interest in boys. Sex. Though that was not a word nice girls used then. There were boys who came to the house and she necked with them. She would not "go all the way" but often thought about that. "Making love." It was then too she put her vivid imagination to work. Pa became a stockbroker who looked like Clark Gable. Ma lost 60 pounds and looked like Carol Lombard. Ralph died in an auto crash. She was accepted at Radcliffe.

This better imaginary life often sustained her and she began to embellish it. In fact, home alone, washing the breakfast dishes on a warm spring night when a senior, she was embellishing it with a romance involving Mr. Mahoney the gym teacher when Ralph, a junior on probation at Northeastern, came banging into the house with a pal, a grubby-looking kid with pimples he called Rollie. Both were half-drunk, on their way to a party, and Ralph got busy picking the lock on Pa's dining room liquor cabinet.

"You shouldn't do that," Jill clearly remembers saying while drying the cast iron skillet in which Pa liked his eggs fried. "Pa finds out he'll have a fit."

"Fuck him," Ralph, coming into the kitchen with a fifth of Four Roses in his fist, said. "Hey, Sis, whyn't you give Rollie a treat. Show him your tits."

"Don't be stupid," Jill clearly remembers saying. Aw c'mon,

Ralph said, grabbing her blouse with his free hand. "Leave me alone!"

But that was a plea Ralph had ignored for seventeen years. He tore her blouse, popping two buttons, and like the women who came in by the day though later rather than sooner, she finally had had it with Ralph. She hit him with the skillet, a looping two-handed forehand, possibly the first of those, smashing his left ear. Ralph's eyes rolled up, he sank to his knees, dropped the Four Roses and she hit him again, another two-hander, as if he were a post she was driving through the kitchen floor. Ralph toppled over and lay still. Rollie said, "Jesus!" and fled.

She was sure Ralph was dead, knew Pa would have a fit about that, grabbed from the window sill the dollar for the kid who delivered the Globe, ran from the house matching Rollie's exit speed, caught a bus into Boston and a bus to South Boston and found Ma's "nice apartment," a third-floor walk-up over an Irish bar called Blarney's in an old brick building near the gas works. Ma was asleep, drunk, but roused finally when Jill pounded on the door. The apartment was a mess, dimly lit, smelly, the sparse furniture ratty. No matter. Jill told her tale, poured her heart out. She'd killed Ralph but he had it coming. Ma sobered some when she understood there'd been a death in the family, but didn't know what to do except hold Jill and cry. They both were crying, huddled on the ratty couch, when Ma's friend came home in high spirits following a good $200 day at Suffolk Downs.

His name was Corny Shanahan. He knew Ma, he said, "from years back at Holy Angels." His high spirits subsided when he heard Jill's story. They might, he muttered, be "harboring a fugitive," in which case he foresaw "trouble with the cops." But he guessed Jill could stay the night and, a practical man, said, "Are you sure the guy was dead?" A ray of hope but how to find out? They left that for morning. Corny bundled Ma into bed and found a smelly blanket for Jill. She slept on the ratty couch and in the morning it turned out Ralph was not dead. She cranked up her nerve and phoned Pa at the scrapyard and after he had a fit he said he'd come home and found Ralph on the kitchen floor, conscious but disoriented.

"Ralph says you hit him! With a frying pan! He's in Mass General with a concussion and you, young lady, where ever you are, you better get your butt back here!" Jill said she'd think about that but not to worry, she was in good hands, and hung up before Pa had another fit.

She spent ten days with Ma and Corny, skipping school. Corny had another good day at the track the first day, came home in high spirits and suggested they all have a drink, though Ma'd had her quota. They had in fact several drinks, Bushmills and Coke, and when Ma fell asleep (or passed out) on the ratty couch, Corny took Jill into the bedroom and introduced her to the joy of sex. They "made love." It hurt a little but not much. Corny, a wiry Southie in his forties with a long history of steamy romantic entanglements, knew what he was doing and, granted she was drunk, she enjoyed this major milestone in her life. Immensely. So apparently did Corny, who said before falling asleep, "Holy christ! A vurgun! You're one in a million, kid! Though I ain't quite had a million."

In the morning and on subsequent mornings Corny went off to the track and Ma started on her quota. She tried to talk to Ma, learn something of Ma's childhood and the Malarkeys, but Ma was reluctant to review her life, said, "That's all water over the bridge, Baby." Ma's present life was Blarney's, where men bought her drinks, meals she picked up (when she remembered) at a Chinese place and the Bushmills Corny provided when flush or some bar brand when his steeds proved slow of foot. Giving up on Ma's oral history, Jill spent the days downtown and, after Ma passed out, the nights in bed with Corny. If Ma knew that, she gave no sign. Corny gave her "walking around money" and she bought a skirt and underwear at Filene's. She wondered what

Corny saw in Ma, then guessed it was Ma's alimony, $75 a month, which Pa always paid though screaming he was destitute.

Then Corny had several bad days at the track. When he said he had friends who'd pay $10 for fifteen minutes in bed with Jill and she could keep $5, she said goodbye to Ma and took two buses back to Saugus. She didn't have anywhere else to go.

She tried to tell Pa why she hit Ralph but Pa said Ralph would never do that and "grounded" her for a week, big deal, but wrote an excuse, touch of flu, for the school she'd missed. She went back to Saugus High. She still had the diaphragm Corny had her buy and in due course introduced several classmates to the joy of sex but found them disappointing in the backseats of cars. Mr. Mahoney the gym teacher was older, better at it and had a friend at the John Hancock Insurance Co. whose apartment they used. But Mr. Mahoney was terribly afraid his wife, the Eighth Grade teacher, or the school authorities would "find out." She dumped Mr. Mahoney for his friend and in due course other gentleman, married and single, at John Hancock and elsewhere. She was petite, attractive, busty and acrobatic and all these gentlemen were grateful. Most seemed impressed when told her father was "in investments" and that she was "at Radcliffe." Several gave her presents: she wouldn't take money. Two who were younger, thinking her twenty, the age she gave if asked, proposed marriage. She turned them down, said she first wished to finish at Radcliffe.

She lived at home with Pa but saw little of him. The scrap boom and flavors of the month kept him busy. Of Ralph she saw little and that was fine with her. He dropped out of Northeastern and went into the business, Tucker & Son a fact, and had his own apartment before she enrolled at Northeastern and moved into a dorm with a half-ride bestowed when she graduated third in her class. She saw Corny but once again at Ma's funeral and burial in ground not hallowed, Pa and Ralph passed those up, Ma killed when she jumped (or fell or was pushed) from a window in the walkup, denied the solace of The Church, her death ruled a suicide. Corny, one of a handful of mourners from Blarneys, the Malarkeys unforgiving, said he "wouldn't mind getting together again." But Corny looked seedy, older, down on his luck. She told him he should be ashamed, a graveside proposition.

Corny. No doubt, Jill Tucker thinks, she'll always remember Corny. Her first. Followed by a several classmates whose names she no longer remembers. Mr. Mahoney. Various gentlemen at John Hancock. Some jocks at Northeastern. The Marketing prof there who took her to half the short-time motels on Route 128 and gave her As. The head counselor at the rich kids' camp in Vermont where she worked summers. The rich kid's dad with a job for her in his New York public relations firm. The rich kid's dad with a "position" for her (position indeed!) in his firm, something to do with pipelines. The Filene's recruiter recruiting management trainees. The old but lively gentleman who ran the Trainee Program.

Until, The War on-going, in a burst of patriotism on St. Patrick's Day, she gave notice at Filene's and joined the American Red Cross. Ralph by then, Pa's efforts to have him declared "essential" failing, enlisting before he was drafted, choosing the Air Corps, was on his way to England. The Red Cross honcho in D.C. with peculiar tastes who made assignments sent her at her request to Australia, by train to San Francisco and across the Pacific in a convoy with Ann Silvers, Score and three more staff assistants in a peacetime cabin for two, celibate all the way, to Sydney, where at a Service Force HQ Officers Club welcome she met Brig. Gen. Sedgewick O. Bargle.

Bargle. A pompous old fart who huffed and puffed and grunted in bed. But he always had good scotch, tables at Sydney's best restaurants and sent his staff car to pick her up the Red Cross EM Club. She was faithful to Bargle but for one little treat she gave his driver, Dallas Something, a simple-minded farm boy from Valley City, N.D., where ever the hell that is, who thought it a big treat, and one fling with the dirty little USO performer with the accordion. And Bargle like others before him, no doubt impressed by a father "in investments" and a Radcliffe degree, presently drifted into fantasy land. He began to talk about retiring After The War "to a little place on the Maine coast, your part of the country, I bet you'd like that." Mrs. Bargle, he'd let slip there was a Mrs. Bargle, meanwhile apparently conveniently disappearing. Then the Red Cross despite Bargle's objections dispatched her to Townsville and she met Col. Web Allen.

A B-plus in bed with a little training. She really rather liked Web Allen, a good man whatever that means and there aren't a whole lot of those, married, plagued by a guilty conscience, she knows the signs. A good man who also had the bad luck to fall in love with her. Think he was madly in love with her anyway and she with him, though she never said that, never does. But West Cork, Wisconsin! Web Allen, fantasizing, spoke highly of the good life there and she somehow suppressed her immediate reaction, which was to laugh. She'd last about a week in West Cork, she surmises. Still, they had six pretty good weeks together. Long enough as these things go. A nice affair. Then Allen tried to choke Brig. Gen. Bargle and vanished.

Jill Tucker wonders, briefly, why Web Allen tried to choke Bargle. The garbled letter Allen wrote her (posted from Brisbane via the Royal Mail, contrary to regulations) did not go into that. It mostly just vouchsafed his undying love, said he was awaiting assignment and included an office address in West Cork should their paths not cross again for a time and she wish to keep in touch. Web Allen clearly wishes to keep in touch, see her again, but that's unlikely. The Army though prone to surprising assignments won't send him back to Townsville. She's not answered his letter and won't. Old love affairs, she's had some experience, are best laid quietly to rest.

Jill Tucker yawns. Damn period's easing. Day or two she'll be fine. There's been no word from Bargle or ARC HQ about the transfer she suggested Bargle engineer. Might as well forget that. No doubt the old goat's still sulking, nursing his sore back. So what's she got going in Townsville? Or who? The new Base Section C.O. is said to be hardnose. Col. Betrandus at the Air Depot is another pompus ass. The RAAF wing-commander? Rose Pearl spoke highly of the Australia Club. If you like brussels sprouts. The fact is, she's tired of Townsville. So, what? Volunteer again? For New Guinea? Put up with more Score even for a change of scenery? There's a rumor two more staff assistants will soon be going to New Guinea.

Whatever, brother Ralph is dead. She'll write Pa, express sympathy but not much. Pa no doubt is planning a hero's last rites. Military funeral, flag, firing squad, etc. The War Department, this the latest sitrep, will return After The War the remains of U.S. Servicemen (and women) killed or who died in foreign lands if so requested by next of kin.

* * *

In West Cork, Wisconsin, a village on a low bluff overlooking the Mississippi River at 44 Degrees North Latitude, six inches of new snow fell in the night and at 8 a.m. Webster R. Allen, still a temporary colonel so far as he knows, is out shoveling his sidewalk, wondering why he ever bought a house on a corner lot with 200 feet of sidewalk. Mel Whipper's house at the time, but Mel, the Chevy dealer, facing bankruptcy three years into the Great Depression, was selling cheap and Mert liked the house. Mel's gone now. His son Ed's running the dealership, which survived.

Web Allen is in civvies: longjohns, two pair of pants, a flannel shirt, two sweaters, a hip-length woolen jacket, overshoes, a lumberjack cap with the earflaps down and leather chopper mittens, but after years in the Deep South, the tropics and sub-tropics finds 18 degrees F. bitterly cold. The shoveling is warming him up though. He's finished the long side and half the short side and his prickly heat, be thankful for small blessings, has disappeared. Or is in remission. It doesn't itch any more anyway. His genitan violet's faded and he's growing new pubic hair. Otherwise, his life as he sees it is a mess. On hold and a mess. His wife Mert did not find his blue balls hilarious.

Warren Hoffstad, next door neighbor, a heavyset man in his mid-fifties with a fat red face and two grown children, otherwise Hoffstad Realty, his '38 Buick parked at the curb covered with new snow, comes out of his house wearing overshoes, a cashmere overcoat and earmuffs and pauses to pass the time of day.

"Criminy, Web," Warren says. "You look like a damn Eskee-mo, way you're all bundled up."

"Still feel the cold," Web Allen says. "I—"

"Miss them tropic islands, I guess," Warren, a born salesman quick to ignore others' comments, says. "All them gals with their bare boobies hanging out. I seen pitchers. There's times I envy you boys Over There. Was Over There. I tell you my Scrap Drive, Boy Scout Scrap Drive I run, collect a hunnert-and fifty pounds last month? We're doin' our part, y'know, Web, here the Home Front. Well, I got to go tangle with the goddamn Ration Board. See I can get some new tires. Damn recaps prolly. Tires're a sonofabitch, Web. Army, damn Roosians get alla new ones. Some on the blackmarket, I guess. But poor real estate man can't afford them. Tell me, Web, just between us boys, you ever get a whack at any them gals with their bare boobies hangin' out?"

Web Allen, suddenly, clearly remembers the rare native women they saw in New Guinea, their scaly skin and their bare scabrous breasts hanging down to their navels. "You fucking civilian!" he says, and throws the snow on his shovel at Warren.

"What the hell!" Warren, recoiling, snow all over his cashmere overcoat, squawks, then steps on an icy spot and falls on his butt. "Jeezuzz, Web! Are you crazy or something? What I say!" Web Allen grunts, throws the shovel in his yard and goes into his house and Warren lumbers to his feet, brushing snow from his overcoat, yapping. "Jeezuzz, Web! You're crazy!"

"My god!" Mert, who watched all this from their bay window,

says. "You threw snow on Warren!" Mert watches him a lot these days in view of his "condition" without knowing just what his "condition" is.

"Yes, I did," Web Allen says. "I threw snow on Warren and called him a fucking civilian and I might do it again. I'm going for a walk."

"You'll have to apologize," Mert, blanching at the seven-letter word, says. "But, well. Not right now, I guess. Yes, go for a walk. It'll do you good, dear. Calm you down."

Web Allen, bundled up like an Es-kee-mo, goes for a walk. He's gone for a lot of walks in the three weeks he's been home though avoiding Main Street, too many people there who want to yap, welcome him home, talk about The War. He sticks to a few blocks in his neighborhood, all residential: Oak, Elm, Fourth and Fifth. Streets he traversed a thousand times when a child, in his youth and later, Before The War. They hold many memories but most of his memories now are of a more recent vintage. Some of the sidewalks are shoveled, some not. These streets are lined with frame houses, mostly white, big yards, houses he knows or knew once. His boyhood home: somebody else lives there now, Dad dead, Mother with his sister in Chippewa Falls. His law partner's, but Wiley Endicott's got a personal injury suit, farmer on a tractor hit by a semi, at trial in Eau Claire and is staying there, the sixty-mile drive over slippery roads too much for him and gas rationed. They'll get together when Wiley gets back. The Hills. Old Charlie, long retired, was the high school principal for thirty years. The Wellers. Young Ben's still Missing at Anzio, no further word from U.S. Forces, Italy. Melanie Svensen's, when he had a terrible crush on her and she had a terminal crush on Barney Clark Sr. Melanie's mother, up in her seventies, still lives there.

Melanie. God, he's got to go see her! Tomorrow maybe. Can't put if off any longer. Others too. The next-of-kin of a dozen Fox Co. GIs killed or fatally wounded at Buna Government Station.

Three or four former Fox GIs, home now, struggling with prosthetics. He should visit them. It's the least he can do. He'll tell the next-of-kin lies of course, everybody killed instantly, still in one piece, feeling no pain or at any rate very little. Everybody in West Cork knows he's home. Albert Albrecht, the octogenarian editor and publisher of the weekly West Cork Endeavor, put an item in last week's Endeavor. "Col. Webster Allen, our former West Cork National Guard commander, is enjoying a month's leave with his wife Mirt and daughters following odorous service in the Pacific Area." Albrecht, who has trouble with names and spelling, presumably meant arduous and wants to interview him, but Web Allen's staving that off.

He'll tell Melanie a big lie, again. Barney Sr. most likely won't be home. He's working long shifts at the Arsenal. Barney Jr's. mutilated ghost nags briefly at Web Allen but it's mostly been replaced by Jill Tucker's far livelier manifestation.

Jill. Mert's never asked about other women. Never will, he's sure. And he'll never say anything. Rip his tongue out first. Just live with his secret, no longer sinful. He went to Confession yesterday, urged on by Mert, who worries a lot about his immortal converted soul. Previously an indifferent Episcopalian, Web Allen converted to Catholicism before he wed Mert, a condition set by Mert, the former Mertha Mueller. The two liturgies are not all that different but he's not wild about private Confession. Admitting your sins out loud. But he went to Confession, pleasing Mert, and admitted to breaking the Seventh Commandment. "I confess to you, Father, and to Almighty God. I committed adultery."

The Rev. Leo Connolly, thirty years the St. Bridget's pastor, another octogenarian but used to the dim light in the confessional, no doubt recognized him, Web Allen thinks, but gave no sign he did, maintaining the secrecy of the confessional, and seemed to take this admission in stride. He'd heard it before no doubt, thirty years worth of West Cork Catholics' transgressions in his memory.

The Rev. Connolly did ask, "How many times? With a number of women?" No, just one, Web Allen said, uh several times (several sounding better than about forty). "And are you truly sorry?" Oh yes, Father, Web Allen said, and he truly was (and is) sorry, some ways. The Rev. Connolly went easy on the penance, a Rosary. Web Allen mumbled that before leaving the church and did feel better afterwards, a man making a clean start, for about an hour. Then vivid memories of Jill Tucker, naked, came roaring back.

He did tell Mert one lie. Said he had to go to Fort Snelling and "check with the Army." He took their '37 Chrysler, used precious gas coupons, drove instead the sixty-odd miles to St. Paul and found in the Reference Room at the St. Paul Library a Boston phone directory. He did not find Tucker Investments in the Yellow Pages but did find Tucker & Son Salvage. So Jill lied to him, a little, and Bargle was telling the truth. Web Allen wonders why? The salvage business is not a criminal endeavor. Not that it matters, a little white lie. He's living with a big one. He'd choke Bargle again, given the chance.

Web Allen's come slowly to the unhappy conclusion that, though one never knows, it's unlikely he'll ever see Jill Tucker again. Wartime liaisons seldom survive. Or so he's heard. Jill's not answered the letter he posted from the 5th General. Not yet anyway. Dumb thing to do maybe, give her his office address. What if she writes and Mert finds out? But that's unlikely. He's been to the office and instructed his and Wiley's legal secretary, Clara Sommerfest. "Just hold any mail I get from Australia, Clara. I'll pick it up. Be from a soldier I gave some legal advice." Clara's a faithful old bird, she'd die before revealing office business.

Be best all around of course if he somehow forgets Jill Tucker. Easier said then done though. Oddly, and Web Allen finds this somewhat disturbing, he no longer remembers much about the many serious and interesting discussions they had regarding Life and What It All Means. But Jill, naked, and their sexual shenanigans are vivid memories. Eighty years old if he sees eighty and doddering to boot, Web Allen suspects, this also somewhat disturbing, he'll remember Jill Tucker naked and the brief steamy weeks they had together. In Townsville, Australia, of all places. Townsville. And the wet holes in the jungle and kunia grass outside Buna Government Station. Those smallish locations on the face of the Earth mostly seem a million miles away now in another time long ago. But sometimes they seem as close as yesterday and his house a block up Fourth Street and at these times Web Allen misses (yes, misses!) Townsville. Townsville more than Buna Government Station, Brisbane very little, Sydney not all. Townsville, his last command, and its sullen GIs and thieving flyboys and his incompetent subordinates. Lt. Col. Fogerty, Flapp, Dickinson, Cain, Abott and Costello, Fats Forney, Fazoli with hair over his ears, the CID captain, Rasputin, some name like that. What are they all doing now, this very minute, pushing midnight in Townsville as near as he can figure the time difference? What's Jill Tucker doing? They're still in The War and he's not and for a few brief moments Web Allen is overcome, overwhelmed, by a strange deep sadness and a terrible loneliness.

He circles the block again. Old Charlie Hill, eighty-plus but spry as a squirrel, out shoveling his walk, nods a greeting. Charlie never did recognize his students but assumes most middle-aged West Cork residents were once his students. "Got to get her cleaned up," he says. "Weatherman says more snow coming."

"Wouldn't surprise me," Web Allen says, the weather a favorite subject in West Cork, all over the Middle West, for a hundred years, and walks on, old Charlie's simple problem, more snow coming, somehow comforting.

Look at the bright side. He's not in an officers' brig somewhere and that was touch and go for awhile. "A propensity for violence is a dangerous tendency," the shrink at the 5th General said at their first session. A thin bald shrink in his late thirties prone to long silences this time. "Can't have that, you know, Sir."

Long silence. "Though I understand you did not actually uh strike a superior officer."

"No," Web Allen, leaving the shrink with a problem, said. "I tried to choke the sonofabitch. When he said I couldn't wear my Combat Infantry Badge."

"I see," the shrink, not seeing at all, said. Long silence. "We'll have to work on that, Sir. This uh tendency to resort to violence." Long silence. "Assuming I see you again." Another long silence. "There's a possibility, you know, you'll be court-martialed."

But then somebody at GHQ got it into their head again that Col. Webster R Allen was a "close friend" of the Honorable Ernest Rapwell, Governor of the Great State of Wisconsin, and just about the only thing the shrink said at their next last brief session, was, "I understand, Colonel." Long silence. "You're a close friend of the Governor in Wisconsin?"

"Yes, I know the Governor," Web Allen said. He'd met the old pol at fund-raisers and once with muted enthusiasm when Rapwell was a state senator chaired his re-election campaign in Pierce County. "My brother's a deputy commissioner in the state Revenue Department."

The GHQ Order came late the same day, the Army acting with blinding speed as it can when it wants to. Indefinite Medical Leave and a 5A Travel Priority for Immediate Return to the Continental United States and, therein, Chicago, via FAMOCA, further rail transport authorized.

Web Allen was aboard the weekly ATC C54 departing Brisbane at 0700 hours the following morning, still in his Sad Sack khakis, Combat Infantry badge attached, and an officer's cap and jacket with captain's bars, both too small, he found and swiped on his way out of the hospital. He replaced the bars with his colonel's eagles. He also had thirteen Australian quid and thirty Atabrine tablets a ward boy gave him as he was climbing into the GI bus bound for the airfield.

He spent New Year's Eve and New Year's, Swappa time, somewhere over the endless empty miles of the southwest Pacific. The

54, lightly loaded with a four jubilant war correspondents bound for the ETO, a few badly wounded attended by two Air Evac nurses and some brass with whom he did not converse much, their presence aboard as mysterious as his, crossed the International Date Line into the day before, made three brief stops for fuel and landed at 0900 hours Pacific Time at the Fairfield-Suisun Air Base outside San Jose, California, where a Medical Corps captain, eyeing him askance, said he'd been "advised regarding the colonel's arrival" and put Web Allen on a B24 converted to passenger use bound for Chicago. He'll not forget 1944, Web Allen often thinks, the year he spent parts of two New Year's high in the sky.

The 24 made stops at Air Bases in Cheyenne, Wyo., and Rapid City, S.D., and landed at Chicago's Midway Airport late in the afternoon. He phoned Mert from the terminal, a surprise that left her crying with joy, and caught a GI bus to Union Station, where he spent the night, hungry and exhausted, his Australian quid not legal tender and the USO Canteen closed, shivering in his baggy khakis, the temperature outside 15 below zero F. and the heat in the station turned down in aid of the War Effort.

The Canteen opened at 0600. He had a complimentary USO doughnut and coffee, found the RTO (Rail Transport Office), presented his travel orders and caught the westbound Empire Builder. Mert and the girls met him in Red Wing, Minnesota, at 4 p.m. and after everybody was done hugging and laughing and crying, Mert drove them home between snow-covered fields at 30 mph, the tires just about shot, she said.

They've made love (Mert's term) twice in the usual fashion. The earth did not shake and Web Allen was careful not to introduce any of the variations Jill Tucker taught him, reminded both times of the Army joke. Guy comes home from The War in one piece after four long years, sits down to a big family dinner celebrating his safe return, a grandmother and three maiden aunts present, and the first thing he says is, "Pass the fuckin butter."

As to his sudden Indefinite Leave, he's only said he was "under a lot of stress," and Mert's only said, "I'm sure you were, dear. You lost a lot of weight. I'll have to fatten you up."

They've not had any friends over though Mert thinks they should. They will when he feels better, Web Allen says. Mert's plying him with food he's not used to, pot roasts purchased with the coupons she saved, beef stew, chicken-and-dumplings. He eats as much as he can. Mert's a good woman, good wife, good mother. He loves her too and sometimes wishes there never was, or he'd never met, a Jill Tucker.

Web Allen circles the block again, finds old Charlie Hill refueling his bird feeder. "Not so bad today," Charlie says. "Weatherman says colder tonight though."

"No, not bad," Web Allen, though freezing, says, and circles the block again, exchanging at intervals other comments regarding the weather with property owners out shoveling their sidewalks. There's a Village Ordinance. Property owners are supposed to shovel their sidewalks or have them shoveled within twelve hours following snowfalls exceeding two inches. Neighbors shovel the shut-in's sidewalks. Not old Joe McCoy's though. Old Joe's an ill-tempered old widower, once the Volunteer Fire Department chief, living alone, who doesn't want anybody on his property. Old Joe's cited four or five times each winter for "failure to shovel sidewalk." Web Allen used to cite him when assistant county prosecutor doubling as village attorney. Old Joe always pled not guilty, forced the village to trial, resurrected his "rights guaranteed by the Constitution," paid a $10 fine and costs when found guilty of said misdemeanor and waited for spring to clear his sidewalk.

Web Allen picks his way through the narrow path carved by other's footsteps in the snow on old Joe's sidewalk. Japs would make short work of old Joe. Nazis too. No doubt old Joe's perceived rights are one of the things the boys Over There, or Down There given Swappa's location, are fighting for.

Strange War Aim, Web Allen thinks, and wonders: will he be "fighting" for it again? A Medical Review Board at Fifth Army HQ in Chicago is considering his case, perusing his medical records, deciding his future. He has a form letter to that effect from a Capt. George Orthby. He may get a discharge, he supposes. Honorable, he hopes. Good of the Service maybe. Or Medical. The Atabrine's keeping his malaria at bay, but he's had one mild reoccurrence and has only six tablets left. He wrote this Orthby, requesting more, but Orthby's not reponded. Or the Army may find for him a Stateside job pushing paper. At some out of the way post, he hopes, if that the case, where he can get by with two uniforms. He'll have to buy uniforms if back on active duty.

Whatever, the girls, at any rate, his beloved daughters, seem to be okay, though they often seem to him to be strangers. And he to them, no doubt. Busy with school, they've not asked him much of anything about The War, which is fine with him. The Glider Ground School shut down on 30 December, the young man Barbara still has a terrible crush on gone with it. He's written her once from Ft. Campbell, Ky., where he's now a proud member of the 82nd Airborne Division, and Barbara's mooning around as the saying goes. Web Allen can empathize with her. But she'll get over the glider pilot: she's only seventeen. She'll get over her lost love sooner than he will. Betsy's just fine, far as he can judge. Bit plump, Mert all over again. Kind like Mert too. Betsy's favorite subject is Home Ec. She bakes pies for the village shut-ins, practices her flute without being told. Betsy like Mert will make some man a wonderful wife some day. Barbara too of course though in a different way.

Web Allen slows his walk at his corner lot. He is, seems always to be, very tired. Exhausted. He could check his office again, see if there's a letter from Australia, but Clara Sommerfest's trustworthy as a Swiss banker. And he should tell Warren Hoffstad he's sorry he threw snow on him. Offer some explanation if he can think of one. But Warren's Buick is gone. Warren's tangling with Ration Board. He'll leave his apology for another time. And try of course to suppress his newfound propensity for violence. Warren called him "crazy." So did Bargle. Might they be right? No, Web Allen decides. He was, is, under a lot of stress. And they're both idiots.

Mert's at the door to their glassed-in front porch, the glass a sign of wealth in West Cork. She opens the door. "My, that was a lot of walking, dear," she says. "Why don't you come in. Have some coffee. I made some fresh. You don't want to catch cold."

Web Allen goes into his house, he might as well get used to this, life goes on, and unbundles down to one pair of pants and a sweater and sits at the kitchen table, the one they bought in Milwaukee the year they were married. It was their dining room table then. He was just out of law school, the new boy in the Legal Department at the Milwaukee St. Paul & Pacific Railroad Co., riding the MSP&P system with his pass, settling claims for alleged prize bulls, champion cows, blue-ribbon swine and thoroughbred horses struck and killed (or so badly damaged they had to be destroyed) by MSP&P trains. Settling out of court because juries composed of retired farmers still harboring grudges having to do with freight rates liked to stick it to the railroads. It wasn't the worst job a green young lawyer might hold, except for the travel. He logged thousands of miles on the MSP&P system. But he did not like Milwaukee and neither did Mert. They were small town kids and Mert missed her family, her parents and two brothers, the brothers run a big dairy farm now, 400 acres, 300 head of Holstein. When in 1932 he was offered the assistant Pierce County prosecutor's job, he took it and they returned to West Cork and bought Mel Whipper's house. Web Allen thinks his late father, a District Judge at the time, had something to do with that but he's not sure. Four more years and County Attorney Wiley Endicott, not re-elected in a close race, went into private practice and Web Allen with him. Barbara was six, Betsy two, and he was thinking about joining the West Cork National Guard unit, Fox Co's. First Platoon. Mert, then not so plump, didn't like that idea, but he joined anyway. He'd had ROTC in college, River Falls State, spent three months at Camp Grant in the Other Big War and found he rather liked Army life. He also felt vaguely patriotic and did not, of course, know there was another war coming. Adolf Hitler at the time, mentioned now and then in the newspapers and Time Magazine, was an obscure German politician recently jailed.

And here he sits now, Web Allen thinks, at this table they've had for nearly twenty years, a full if temporary bird colonel in deep disgrace. A temporary bird colonel with a broken wing, or so he sees it, and memories and a secret he'll have to live with. Well, he's not the only member of the U.S. Armed Forces with that kind of secret. There are, or will be, Web Allen surmises, some thousands of others. But he's the only one with his secret.

Mert pours his coffee. "Put a little whiskey in it, dear. I know you like your Irish coffee. It will warm you up." Mert's trying, really trying, she doesn't hold with drinking before sundown, but the Jim Beam is on the table and damn it, he does love her. "It's so good to have you home for awhile." She's said this about eight-hundred times. "Here's the newspaper. See how The War is going."

The newspaper is the Milwaukee Herald's outstate morning edition. It reaches West Cork aboard the MSP&Ps' westbound Omaha Flyer, two bundles dropped at the depot. Oakley Weller, thirteen, missing Ben's reliable little brother, delivers it. He always puts it inside the porch, which is more than Ben ever did when he had the paper route.

Web Allen doesn't much care how The War is going but, lacing his coffee with Jim Beam, he skims the front page. There's a story by David Dudley Hull, Herald War Correspondent, something to do with heavy Jap air raids Somewhere in the Southwest Pacific, which Web Allen skips. A thousand British bombers hammered the Ruhr again. Krauts still hold Mount Cassino, blocking the road to Rome. Allied aircraft under Gen. Douglas MacArthur's command inflicted heavy damage to enemy positions and personnel at Wewak and Madang. And the War Department is thinking about a $10-a-month bonus for combat Infantry. Web Allen pursues that story, the jump is on Page 11, and there finds a brief Associated Press story.

3 U.S. Soldiers Executed

Washington (AP)—The Army High Command today said three U.S. Negro enlisted men, two sergeants and a former sergeant, court-martialed and convicted of raping an American woman serving with the American Red Cross in Australia and sentenced to death, were executed by hanging today at an Army Stockade in Australia.

An Army spokesman at the Pentagon said a motion to commute the death sentences to life in prison was filed by the officer appointed to defend the three servicemen. He said that is customary when death sentences have been imposed. He said the motion was considered at "the highest level" but denied.

The three servicemen were not identified by name but were said to have been members of a Quartermast Corps truck unit serving in Australia at the time.

No matter. Web Allen can identify them. The three Colored who raped the Red Cross girl, Davis. So they were court-martialed and convicted and their sentences, for once, were not commuted. Web Allen briefly wonders what happened to the fourth one and thinks. By god, that's one thing I did right! Leaned on that CID captain, Rasputin, gave him a direct order. Forget the damn booze the flyboys liberated, catch the bastards raped that girl. He also wonders, briefly, whatever happened to that booze and those flyboys, but surmises he'll never know and decides it doesn't matter. He's got his own miserable life to get on with. "I'll have some more coffee, Mert."

Plump Mert pours another cup. Web Allen puts a little whiskey in it and lifts his cup in a silent toast to Townsville, The War he no longer cares much about and Jill Tucker, where ever she may be. Mert frowns. "Not too much whiskey, dear. My goodness, it's only ten o'clock!"

So two more hours have passed in the rest of Web Allen's not altogether miserable life. He'll live with his secret. Mert will never know and always love him and take good care of him and he'll take good care of Mert too and love her as best he can while their daughters grow up, marry and most likely move away, few young folks remain in West Cork any more, and thereafter as well. For all the rest of his life. While the years roll by. Web Allen hoists his Irish coffee in another toast. "To you, Mert."

TO BE CONTINUED

NORMANDALE COMMUNITY COLLEGE
LIBRARY
9700 FRANCE AVENUE SOUTH
BLOOMINGTON, MN 55431-4399

Printed in the United States
35770LVS00002B